CW01240151

DEAD LUCKY

DEAD LUCKY

CONNOR HUTCHINSON

corsair

CORSAIR

First published in the United Kingdom in 2025 by Corsair

1 3 5 7 9 10 8 6 4 2

Copyright © Connor Hutchinson 2025

The moral right of the author has been asserted.

All characters and events in this publication, other than those clearly in the public domain, are fictitious and any resemblance to real persons, living or dead, is purely coincidental.

All rights reserved.
No part of this publication may be reproduced, stored in a retrieval system, or transmitted, in any form or by any means, without the prior permission in writing of the publisher, nor be otherwise circulated in any form of binding or cover other than that in which it is published and without a similar condition including this condition being imposed on the subsequent purchaser.

A CIP catalogue record for this book
is available from the British Library.

HB ISBN: 978-1-4721-5906-9

Typeset in Electra by M Rules
Printed and bound in Great Britain by Clays Ltd, Elcograf S.p.A.

Papers used by Corsair are from well-managed forests
and other responsible sources.

MIX
Paper | Supporting
responsible forestry
FSC® C104740

Corsair
An imprint of
Little, Brown Book Group
Carmelite House
50 Victoria Embankment
London EC4Y 0DZ

The authorised representative
in the EEA is
Hachette Ireland
8 Castlecourt Centre
Dublin 15, D15 XTP3, Ireland
(email: info@hbgi.ie)

An Hachette UK Company
www.hachette.co.uk

www.littlebrown.co.uk

For Alan, Jane & Simon

'What am I? I am zero—nothing. What shall I be tomorrow? I may be risen from the dead, and have begun life anew. For still, I may discover the man in myself, if only my manhood has not become utterly shattered.'

Fyodor Dostoyevsky, *The Gambler*

1

I slip off her wedding ring and add it to the rest of the jewellery on the tray. She's starkers on the bed with the white light beaming down on her. Body withered, sagging. The colour of egg-washed pastry. Her face is relaxed and peaceful, not constipated like most of 'em that get rolled in. It looks as if she's having a quick kip and'll hop up to make a brew any second. Shame she'll be a pile of ash in twenty-four hours. Crumbled and blended. Shovelled into an urn for the rest of her days.

I don't need to look at the name on her toe tag to know it's Paula. She's an eighty-year-old Pat Butcher type who used to be my dinner lady in high school. Purple eye shadow, chandelier earrings, the full whack. Lads from the boozer think it's weird that I see people I've known bollock-naked after they've snuffed it. It never crosses my mind. You even forget they're naked. At the end of the day, I provide a service. My task is to make 'em look presentable. I'm not rolling in it but it pays a decent wedge, covering the rent and a cheeky bet. The main thing is being there for people when they need it – when they're most vulnerable and think the world's caving in on 'em. Being paid is just a bonus.

It's serious shit. I'm responsible for that last image that'll stick in your noggin' for years. Believe me, I know – that's why I got into this bonkers job in the first place, but I'll get to that. The only weird thing is seeing how still they are. The silence proper freaks you out at first, until you get used to it. Everything about death seems quiet. The room I dress them in, the cemeteries, the mourners as the coffin's carried into the chapel, even that last breath is always a small whisper.

It's more apparent when someone comes in like Paula, a brutal force of a woman who would slap that cottage pie on your tray hard enough to break ya wrist. Those cold, waxy hands, peacefully crossed on her stomach. They used to switch from tray to tray with blurry speed. Sweat beading off her head, dripping into the food. A wipe of the nose with her arm here and there. She was a right cunt to be honest, but respect the dead and all that. When people die, that's all in the past. It's not for me to worry about what they did in their life, it's how I prepare them for what's next, wherever the fuck they go. It's an art, what I do. A dying art, you might say. A tough one as well.

Paula's clothes and jewellery are off now. I wash the body with a wet towel, digging into the nooks and crannies of her armpits, behind her knees. Cleaning them is an important part; you have to have a delicate touch about you. You can't go all rough like you're scrubbing the kitchen worktops 'cause you'll end up snapping a bone or summot. It's all about patience, finesse. Think of it as polishing your nan's favourite crystal swan, or whatever ornament's got leathery skin and sandbags for tits if you wanna be more realistic.

After drying her, it's all about arranging the features of the face. This is what family and friends remember the most. No one inspects the fuckin' ankles, do they? Or says, Aww, *didn't she have nice elbows?* I use these plastic eye-caps that slot in under the eyelids. They have small spikes that grip on to the lids to keep them shut. Your dead relative winking or staring the fuck out of you from the coffin isn't the one. Next, metallic wires are inserted inside the roof and bottom jaw of the mouth, then tied to keep the mouth shut. Without it, relaxed faces lie there catching flies. Glue's then used to seal the lips shut. The satisfaction of doing that if you knew they were a right mouthy fucker. I've thought about using it on Rebecca, my girlfriend, once or twice. She works at Selfridges and is actually way out of my league. Right mouth on her too at times.

Anyway, when you've got a lass on the counter like Paula – one that used to rant and spray spit in your face if you were caught chatting shit in the dinner line – you make sure to slap that glue on and seal those fuckers up for good.

After scrubbing any excess gunge from the ears and nose with a cotton bud, the face is pretty much set, ready to apply make-up to later. You try and arrange the features to a happy, content expression. I'm half-tempted to have her grinning like fuck for a laugh but Paula was never the one for smiling. I arch the corners of her mouth slightly upright. It's an expression that says, *It's okay. I'm ready. I'm at rest now.* That's all the family want to see. Getting the balance right is tough. The goal is to make them look 'natural', not 'life-like'. If they're lying there looking like they'll sit up any second, it'll scare you shitless.

While I crack on with all this, a mixed solution of formaldehyde, alcohol and water whirs away in a machine by the scalpels. It's a loud thing, swishing away, ruining the calmness of it all. This is the 'tissue builder' I pump into the body to plump it out and give it some colour if I think they need it. I use it ninety per cent of the time 'cause anyone who snuffs it round Openshaw is likely a skinny, jaundiced alky. I get some big fellas in now and again who don't need it. Like this fat fucker, Brian, last week, who took an hour to just wash. I was relieved I didn't have to fill him up with a shedload, like some lorry before a long trip. These chemicals ain't cheap.

Once the solution's ready – about two or three gallons of it – I do a small incision under the right collarbone and insert two tubes: one that goes into the carotid artery, and one into the jugular vein. The first pumps the solution towards the heart and replaces the blood, exiting the body through the second tube into a tray or directly into the sink. I dropped the tray once, sending blood splattering over the white tiles, covering the floor. Proper Bambi on ice situation. Took a fuckin' week to clean. You get used to the thick look of it, the amount that comes out. Worst is the sound. Paula's is coming out in tepid squirts, like when you're busting for a piss but it's just dribbling out into the urinal. I have to stick the radio on during this bit sometimes, block it out. No matter how many bodies you do, it's always rank.

While the transition of fluid happens, I massage her body. Not for pleasure; I'm not a creep. This is to make sure the solution's distributed evenly throughout her body. If you don't, you have one chunky pink arm and one yellow skinny one. Under my rubber gloves, her skin feels like rolling out floured dough. It ripples, moving as one. The more I massage, the more I see her cheeks filling out. Life returning to her expression, almost convincing enough that she could start serving dinners again. I rub her swollen ankles, up through her fleshy thighs. Her body gradually expands like an air bed. Wrinkles ironed out, bones vanishing. I only wretch twice, which I'm quite impressed with.

I remove the tubes then and chuck them in the sink to be washed. I stitch the hole up and powder it with make-up as if nothing was there. Next is the even more unpretty bit, the one no embalmer enjoys doing. We have a tool called a trocar – sort of a long, hollow needle – which we jab into the central cavities of the body and thrust around for a good twenty minutes. There's no nice way to explain it. It's to remove any build-up of gas, fluid or shite that's lurking around in there. I've had plenty of bodies let one rip while I'm working away. It's not even that the sound shit me up, the smell is fuckin' rancid. Like letting one go in a hot car after a Chinese.

The body jolts as you stab around the stomach, making sure to get every last bit of excess rubbish before filling the cavities back up with a higher-concentrate solution. Once they're all filled up, you block the hole with a tiny plastic screw as if bottling an oak-aged whisky.

Paula's nearly ready now to be put on display in the viewing room. I give her another wash, dry her off, then get to putting the finishing touches on. I apply heavy moisturiser to the face and prepare the make-up, dependent on the preferences of the relatives. Paula always wore this pink lippy, so it didn't surprise me her daughter opted for that. 'Plush Romantic', it's called. It makes me wretch again. Her mouth's like a cat's arse, but I manage to find the lips and wipe away the smudges, so it looks all neat and nice. Purple eyeshadow and a thick foundation to accompany it. Make-up for dead people isn't the same as the stuff you find in Boots. Those are made for warm skin, for cheeks with blood pumping through 'em. I have to order in special cosmetic ones. Dense, opaque pastes that bring a human look back into their faces. Paula's a bit like polishing a turd, I'm no fuckin' magician, but I know her daughter will be happy. It's how she remembers her, looking like this. The lippy, the eye shadow, that's her mam. That's how she wants to remember her and how she should be remembered. I'll go as far to say Paula looks beautiful.

I comb her hair, positioning her fringe to the side. The fringe I saw dripping with sweat, pasted to her forehead over hot stoves. Here it was, wiry but clean, a sweep of grey like a plume of smoke. The last touch is the clothes her daughter kindly presented on a hanger. Black pin-striped suit with padded shoulders and a white silk blouse to match the cushioned interior of the coffin. I use a hand-held steamer to iron out the creases before dressing her slowly. Pulling black stockings over the thin legs of a dead eighty-year-old woman never gets easier.

The annoying thing is that my fine work will be up in flames in twenty-four hours. Name another job where your work consistently gets destroyed in a 900-degree oven. Paula will be in a casket made of pine, lighting up in no time. Think of lighter fluid on a barbecue. Poof. The flames'll engulf the fucker before my finger even comes off the button. Hundred times better than those posh, lacquered finished caskets made out of walnut or hickory. Like throwing your chicken in a slow cooker them ones. Best to get it burnt, get it in the urn and crack on with your life. No point dragging the thing out. Some mourners I've had though, fuck me, they'd get in the casket with 'em if they could. They really struggle with that bit, which is understandable I guess. Never think of the hours it took me to prepare the bastard though. Sometimes, I'm more gutted than they are!

At least Paula will be in the display room so family and friends can go to visit and admire my work. I hope they appreciate the application of the eye shadow, the way her hands are placed delicately so the wedding ring's the focal point. That's the problem when you're dealing with mourners: they're never in the right headspace to appreciate all the work that's gone into it. Especially when you've got a Paula. Details matter. Details you'd only pick up on years down the line. A stray hair. A make-up smudge. Visible stitching. It all matters, it all has to be perfect. The death industry doesn't do second chances.

Paula's all done now. She's ready for the viewing room. I ping off my rubber gloves into the bin and remove my white coat and face mask. The stench of the solution still lingers in the air, mixing with make-up powder and the indescribable scent of death.

Paula lies still in the middle of the room. All I hear is the buzz of the lights and the fluid machine whirring into sleep.

'Night, Paula.' I say, before turning off the lights and leaving her at peace.

**

Before I head to the boozer, I say bye to Janice in the casket room, who's arranging the new coffin arrivals. Janice is the funeral director who hired me years ago. A chubby, tiny woman with a brunette perm – not too much younger than Paula. Think of Danny DeVito in a wig, with heavy foundation, thick-rimmed glasses, and wears nothing but black suits. Animated jowls and a mole on her chin you could land a helicopter on.

'All right love, all okay?' she says, rolling a glossy pink coffin into the corner of the room.

'The fuck is that?'

Half of it is open, showing a baby-blue silk lining. It looks like something Barbie would be buried in.

'Mingin' innit? The old ladies love it though. We've had three sales in the last week already.'

'Are you one of 'em?'

'Cheeky twat. Got plenty left in me yet.'

Around us the walls are cracked. Beige wallpaper patched and peeled. Each casket illuminated by a golden light, a recent addition after Janice won a few quid on the Irish Lotto last year. The far wall by the window is dedicated to our selection of urns. Teetering shelves full of wooden boxes and metal containers, even velvet drawstring bags if that was preferred. It never stops amazing me the way people fuss over how to contain something that doesn't exist any more.

'You okay?' Janice asks. 'You look rough as a bear's arse.'

I rub my eye and blink until my vision's back.

'Yeh, sound. Just tired.'

'Rebecca all right? Not kicking off at home, is it?'

'Nah nah, nowt like that. Just need some kip, that's all.'

Janice gives me a look. Me and Becca bicker more often than not, but it wasn't that.

Janice is like a second mum to me. She's a belting woman, always keeping an eye out. We run the Openshaw Funeral Home, just the two of us, with me doing all the body prep and Janice doing more of the sales and admin side. Coffins, urns, funeral packages, official paperwork, flowers – she takes care of all that. There's shitloads that goes into a funeral and the organisation of it. The average one costs over four grand apparently, so I assume the business doesn't do too bad. But we're a small area on the outskirts of Manchester, we always have to work hard to keep things ticking over. Luckily, Janice is an expert. Everyone comes to her in Openshaw if they need help.

'She all ready in there then?' asks Janice, changing the subject and lighting up a fag in the middle of the casket room. She could have us both cremated in a sec, the material of some of these coffins. I learnt quickly that she does what she likes.

'Yeh, should be all set for tomorrow, what time they comin'?'

'Fuck knows,' she says. 'Daughter will be here all day, I think. In absolute bits when I went through the paperwork with her.'

'What, 'cause you wiggled a gold-plated urn out of her? I'd cry at that price.'

'Pays your fuckin' bills dunt it?' she sniggers, inhaling a deep drag.

I laugh and give her a kiss on the cheek.

'Anyway,' I say, 'will see you Monday. Give us a ring if you need anything, yeh?'

'Ah piss off, I'll be fine.'

I walk through a cloud of smoke out of the room and through the exit. The smell of fresh air gives me a kick up the arse. I realise how much I'm gagging for a pint.

2

The first dead body I seen was me old fella's. Ray Fletcher. Booze finally caught up to him at fifty-three. Liver damage, fed through a tube for two weeks. I watched him melt into a pile of bones in the hospital bed, being kept alive for the sake of it until Mam decided to turn the machines off. There was no point; he drank himself into oblivion and, if he could speak, would probably tell us he's quite happy with the innings he had. He was young, he knew that. He should have died years before. It never made the reality any easier to take. Especially walking into that chapel of rest, it hits you like Mike Tyson's right hook. I was only eighteen.

His body was a paint by numbers: lips purple, hands blue, face yellow. Not to mention the brown holes left from all the tubes and injections. He wasn't embalmed for whatever reason, and you couldn't half tell. Maybe Mam couldn't afford it. His temples sunk deep into his skull. Eye sockets dark and hollow like snooker pockets. Sounds obvious but he looked dead, like proper dead. I stood there thinkin', *Who the fuck was this geezer? Where's me old man? This surely can't be him?*

Of course, Mam's in bits, clutching his bony fingers, nearly taking the bastards off. Head on his chest, getting make-up all over the navy suit that fit him perfectly a couple of years ago. He was a reasonably porky fella, me dad. In that coffin, he looked absolutely tiny. Later on, Mam said he looked like those little action figures in the boxes you used to see on the shelf at Woolworths. He was never an action figure or superhero. He was a dick. A man with problems bigger than his son. Booze came before anything. Towards the end, I only ever seen him if he popped by the house pissed-up, haggling Mam for a spare tenner. She couldn't stand him either, but she still loved him. They were both lonely people, and the loneliest people cling to whoever's closest. They couldn't live without each other.

I honestly thought I'd be okay seeing him dead when Mam asked me if I wanted to see him. Yeh, why not? Nice to see him silent and not slurring his words for once. I thought I'd regret it if I said no. You can never prepare yourself for walking into that room, no matter what your relationship. It's eerie, man. The atmosphere's fuckin' weird. Nothing matches it.

I didn't cry. I felt I should, it just didn't arrive. Looking at him, it fascinated me more than anything. I was amazed that was my dad there in that coffin. *That man made me. He's why I'm here. Now he's gone. Nothing but a static waxwork in a small matchbox coffin. A sack of muscle and bone.*

Even at the crematorium service, seeing him disappear behind a closing red curtain, I had no expression or feeling whatsoever. Through the whole process I felt guilty not showing anything, especially with Mam in hysterics next to me, blowing into a raggedy tissue, explosion of mascara on her chops. I think it was like a week after when it sunk in. I went to sleep every night and couldn't get the image of his face in that coffin out of my head. I tried to remember the happier memories: him taking me to football on Sundays, getting his car all muddy from my boots, or when he used to take me to Gran's on Saturday mornings for a bacon butty, while he put his bets on for that day's racing. I spent that first weekend under the covers, looking through grainy photos of him on my phone, trying to remember what he looked like.

Weeks, months went by, and I couldn't stop thinking of that image. It was in my dreams, my nightmares, every thought when I was awake. It was tarnishing my entire memory of him. I was remembering my dad as this waxwork, nothing else. I tried to look at more photos of him from our holiday in Blackpool when I was a kid. Smiling, having an ice cream on the beach. It made no difference. The man in the picture was a stranger now, the man in the coffin was my dad.

Weirdly enough, that's what pushed me into doing embalming. I left school with okay GCSEs but I was stuck as to what I wanted to do with my life. Sixteen and nowhere to go. Seeing Dad like that, I wanted to do embalming so other kids, other relatives didn't have to have their memories twisted like that. So, I thought, fuck it. On my breaks from cleaning up soup-burst cans or mopping baby sick on the aisles of big Tesco, I googled how to get into it. Turns out I could do a two-year apprenticeship in embalming at the same time as working in that shithole. Spending my nights and the odd weekday studying and learning about the body. How to clean a corpse, how to apply make-up, how to use the tissue builder. All while cashing in a bit of John Doe.

It's so fucked though. Even though the nice funeral director geezer warned me it might be a bit of a shock, I didn't think Dad would look that horrible. It has a bigger impact than you think. I thought, if I can be responsible for preparing the dead as best as I can, I can prevent any other kid going through what I went through. Maybe it was a coping mechanism, I don't know, but my apprenticeship at this college in town got me to grips with the process, understanding that the dead don't have to look like that, that I can play a part in how people are remembered.

Mam thought I'd lost me marbles, that I was broken for life. My fascination with it got her worried. She'd slip university leaflets under my door, ask lads in the club if they were taking on any trainees on the building sites. She didn't understand. The nutjob thought I'd end up killing people and start dissecting their bodies in my room. Using the freezer to store a foot beside the turkey dinosaurs. Mam got better with time, soon understanding it wasn't a reactionary thing and was something I actually wanted to do with my life. She realised me having a goal, a career path, was rare as unicorn shit compared to most of the kids round Openshaw. Anything to keep me off the streets, robbing off-licences and smashing up bus stops.

Seeing more dead bodies did help. After my apprenticeship, Mam, now actively helping, asked Janice, a friend of hers, if I could pop my head in to learn a few things. They were reasonably close, playing bingo twice a week together on Tuesdays and Thursdays at the club. Janice said yes straight away and took me under her wing. She was surprised to find an eighteen-year-old so keen and eager to learn about something so taboo, plus the recent passing of her hubby Ian meant she could do with some extra hands around the directory.

When I arrived outside the funeral home on my first day, I thought I'd got the wrong address. It looked so basic, like a dentist's or an estate agent's or summot. Two storeys, faded red brick, and a disabled ramp with a flaky white banister. One frosted glass door and windows made up with beige blinds. I rang the bell. Even that sounded tinny and dying.

Janice led me in and gave me a quick tour. To the left of the reception desk was the waiting room, where Janice discussed paperwork with relatives, or where mourners hung around waiting to pick up a bag of their nana. The room was minimal and bland. The walls an off-white. A sofa and two armchairs in the centre, separated by some big leafy plants to try and give some life. Framed pictures of fruit bowls or vases hung wonkily on the walls. Janice looked at me as if for a verdict.

'Nice,' I said. 'Very cosy.'

Next was the casket room. I was shocked to find out how many varieties you could choose from. And the prices, fuck me. I nearly keeled over and landed in one of 'em. All shapes, sizes, finishes, carvings, handles, weights, decorations. What a load of fuckin' faff. I could tell from Janice's face she was impressed with this room.

She clearly worked hard for it. You could also tell this was where she made her living. Her charm was ignited in this room. This was where the real money was.

'Try it out if you want?'

It wasn't really a question, and I wanted this job. An hour into my first day, I found myself lying in a mahogany coffin, my head on a white silk cushion.

'Nice. Comfy,' I said.

'Now, what a way to be buried ay?'

She looked down at me as if it was my wake. I gave a thumbs up, thinking what the fuck am I doing in here at my age. Can't lie though, I'd get a decent kip in there. Well plushy.

Before the embalming room, Janice dipped her head into the cremation room to check if the fires were going, the way you dip your head into the oven to check your pizza and get a waft of warm air slapping you in the chops. She looked excited and led me in.

Taking up the entire room were two huge metal machines. The sound they made was deafening, the heat from them making beads of sweat form on my forehead as soon as I stepped in. Janice shouted over the noise, explaining this is where the bodies were burnt. They need to keep being checked on apparently, shifted about among the flames like a kebab to make sure all sides were cooked. She talked me through all the colourful buttons on the side. Something about airflow, regulating the temperature. It was basically a giant fuckin' microwave. And bodies were in there right now, burning to a crisp.

Janice opened one of the ovens and used a long rod to poke around. I could see a skull flashing red with heat. Dust bellowed out and clung to the back of my throat.

'Nearly done,' said Janice, like this geezer was a fuckin' lamb shank. Unbelievable.

She informed me that once the burning was done, all the bones and ash were raked out and separated in a metal tray. Then the bones were ground down for a short time using a machine called a cremulator. It sounded like summot from *Transformers*. I tell you what, that sound isn't pretty. At least when they're making a Frappuccino in Starbucks, you know whatever they're blending is gonna be creamy and delicious. When you hear someone's fibula and hip rattling about in there, it's hard not to throw up.

I was relieved to get out of the cremation room and continue our journey down the pale corridor. We passed through strips of plastic curtains that separated the passage, keeping the cold air in, on the way to the embalming room and where they kept the freezers. I imagined the lifeless toes and strands of hair that had brushed those strips as I shimmied through them, the plastic feeling dirty as it touched my face.

'There's not many kids brave enough to try this, ya know?' said Janice, guiding me into the embalming room, where a freelance guy from Longsight was preparing a body.

'What's there to be scared of?' I said. 'It'll happen to everyone eventually.'

'Ee yarr then,' said the guy, handing me a plastic razor. 'Give this fella a shave for us.'

The embalmer's name was Graham. Wire-rimmed specs balanced on the edge of a bulbous nose. He had a full salt-and-pepper beard and a belly that bulged under his white coat.

'Go on, he doesn't bite,' he said. 'Not that I know of anyway.'

Graham said things with no expression. A man you could tell works with the dead every single day.

Janice laughed and patted me on the back before leaving the room. Graham followed, placing the razor in my hand.

Alone, I stood looking over the body for about ten minutes before doing anything. A can of shaving foam and bowl of warm water were waiting for me on the trolley. I inspected the toe tag. Samuel, aged sixty-three, from Gorton, date of death was two days ago.

The first body you work on feels like your first shag or summot.

You never forget it. Probably as one-sided as well if we're talking about mine. But it's one of those landmarks in your life you can't bring up as much at parties. I'd hardly even started shaving myself yet, and here I was stood over a sixty-three-year-old dead fella, trusted to get him looking spick and span for his viewing.

I squirted foam onto my palms and started to apply it to his cold, sunken cheeks. The skin felt tough and leathery. Taking my time, I slowly shaved away the grey stubble sprouting out, trying my best not to nick him and leave any scars. The scratching sound of the razor took over the room. It was me and Samuel, no one else. It's such an intimate act, shaving someone else, especially when it's someone you don't know. His eyelids hadn't been capped yet so he was looking straight at me, judging me. He looked paralysed, unable to scream and let me know what a shite job I was doing.

I took my time, talking and apologising to him now and again whenever I thought I'd nicked his chin. The more time that passed, the more relaxed I felt. Our relationship was growing; we'd shared something together. No longer strangers. I'd issued the final swipe and cleaned him up with the towel when Graham walked in with a clipboard.

'Good job,' he said, looking over my shoulder and inspecting my work. 'Not a nick in sight. You're a natural.'

And that was it: my first interaction with a dead body since my dad. I started to enjoy coming into work. The more I watched bodies being prepared – making notes and focusing – the more the memory of my dad was reappearing and sharpening. The normalisation of death made me think beyond that shell in the coffin. All I needed was to learn about death, hit it head on, and understand the practicalities of it. I started to shave myself better too – my mates were proper impressed at how smooth my cheeks were and that I didn't have red blotches all over my neck like they did. Little did they know how much practice I'd had, and that's only from the furry legs some of these old biddies come in with.

I got used to having ash in my nostrils, the thrum of the cremation machines. I raked bones with the calmness of a gardener in the autumn, collecting the red embers like fallen leaves. I learnt about coffins, about wood, about prices, about salesmanship. Janice always said: *What's more important than death? Life!* And fuck me, she rinsed the most out of life as much as she could. She was a cracking mentor. Her sternness and ability not to take shit made me get on with it. I continued to work and learn as if none of it phased me. And it doesn't. Death is now a part of my life. And nothing's more important than life.

Don't get me wrong, I know not everyone's an oddball like me. No one *wants* to speak about death. But it should never be avoided as much as it is. I shrivelled at the sight of my dad out of shock. I wasn't ready for it. Only through embalming, making it my everyday job, have I learnt to accept and welcome it. I've made many people happy, or at least relaxed and at peace, because of my work. That's the reward. That's why I go to work every day. The fact I can remember the good things about Dad now is just a bonus.

I'll be on that table one day, getting pumped to fuck, getting the farts jabbed out of me, getting shaved by some gormless ginger twat. At least I'll be dead knowing I've done a good thing, knowing I've done something meaningful for people. Burn me and toss me in the bin for all I care, I'll be happy.

3

I leave the directory after prepping Paula, the taste of Guinness on my lips. Thursday night meant snooker and a few scoops down at Stanley Street Working Men's Club with Trick. I run from the car park pissed wet through, sopping from head to toe. It's been lashing buckets all week. I have to cower under the entrance arch to finish off my cig before throwing it onto the shiny cobbles.

'Time you call this then?'

Trick's shouting from the smoky back room, already chalking up his cue with a pint ready for me. His belly bulges over the table. Blue Umbro polo speckled with white paint. Even in the darkest corner of the club, light manages to find his bald head and ping off it.

'Sorry mate,' I say, walking past the bar and giving Linda a nod. 'Caught up at work.'

Trick looks like Barney the Dinosaur – face purple from high blood pressure and always a big smile on his mush, exposing his gold tooth. He's tall as he is wide, and waddles around hunched, as if ducking from a ball that's been launched at his head. If he wasn't a sound fella and didn't have the arm tattoos that made him look hard, he wouldn't half get the piss taken out of him.

Tommy Murphy is in too, as always. Sat near the broken juke-box, mulling over the racing lists for the next day. I can imagine him ending up on my table in the next year. Looks like a corpse already. Rotted teeth and golf balls for cheekbones.

'Who was in today then?' says Trick, passing me a cue to chalk up.

'Paula McGrath. Lived off Denver Street.'

'The dinner lady?'

'Yeh that's the one.'

'Fuck me, I thought she died years ago.'

Trick's already racked up. Bent over until his cue's eye-level and sliding up and down the bottom of his second chin. His flushed cheeks say he's already about five pints in. There's not much decorating work to be done round here at the moment so he's had all week to booze and practise. Whereas people are dying all the fuckin' time. No time for me to practise.

Other than Tommy Murphy, the only ones in are a couple of elderly birds on the bar stools and Coley, the local nutcase who wears a leather jacket no matter what the weather. The women are probably Linda's friends. Chatting about the new fruit stalls opening up on Ashton Old Road, how it's hard to find a bloody pound shop any more. Cloudy pint glasses glint above their heads, stacks of soggy coasters, sagging elbows on the counter. Coley grips his pint and stares at the floorboards, big goofy grin on his mush. Proper greasy mullet on him and a big whopper of a nose that can smell a Sunday dinner on a Thursday.

Trick's cue ball softly nicks the corner of the red triangle, making the route of a diamond, then returning behind the safety line, hugging the cushion.

'When's the funeral?' says Trick, supping on his Guinness.

'Next Wednesday, I think. Picked fuckin' "Dancing Queen" as her funeral song.'

'Christ alive. Never danced in her life that miserable sod.'

'I know,' I say. 'What song would yours be, Trick?'

'"Stayin' Alive", the Bee Gees ... or, or "Another One Bites the Dust", that'd be a belter that.'

'Not the Barney theme song?'

'Piss off.'

I chuckle and chalk up; puffs of blue dust vanish into the musty air.

The club smells stale, an air of piss about it. It always does but I love it. Doesn't help that the table's near the bogs, furthest you can get from the door or any fresh air. The smell of memories in this place, good times with the boys in my teens, sinking pint after pint, hurting from laughter. Pre-drinks before flights to Magaluf. Crying at the TV over England in the World Cup. Quiz nights, bingo nights, tribute nights with Sniff Richard or Take Shat. Even getting to know Becca in the early stages, chatting over there by the jukebox. Plenty of good times.

The rain starts to dry on my face from the hot table light. I take a swig of Guinness before cracking on, the cue slipping nicely along my bridge hand.

'Work been busy then?' asks Trick, taking a seat. He must notice the bags under my eyes.

'Yeh, been mad this week,' I say. 'Crem's booked up until next Friday.'

I go for a long pot. A red that's broken from the pack. It pings off the nearest cushion and pisses off to the other end of the table.

'Good business though,' says Trick. 'At least you've urned it.'

Drink sprays out my mouth onto the floor.

'Fuck's sake.'

He's been waiting to tell me that one all day.

Trick stands up on the second try and lets out a rumbling fart. I lean on the wall, next to picture frames of celebrity visits to the club. Cantona, Hatton, Gallagher.

Trick eyes up his angles and starts telling me about his few days off. How his wife's driving him up the wall, giving him tasks to do around the house to keep him busy and away from the boozer. Rachel's lovely, known her for years, but fuck me they don't half bicker. Proper at each other's throats. And it's me that gets the brunt of it every Thursday night. The blood rising to form vessels on his cheeks as he reels off stories about her deleting his Tiger Woods documentary off the Sky planner, or shaving her foof with his Gillette razor.

'Aw, mate, she's doing my nut in. Look what she's had me doing.' Trick points to his paint-smeared top. 'Had me doing up the bathroom, living room, you name it. I'm meant to be off for fuck's sake. You're lucky I'm even here tonight, thought she'd have me pullin' up the bastard weeds next.'

He shakes his head then flukes a red into the middle pocket.

'Worst thing is. She's sat on her arse watching *This Morning* and *Loose Women* while I'm busting me bollocks on ladders. Can ya believe that? Lazy cow. Just like her fuckin' mam she is.'

'Can't ya make up an excuse?' I say. 'You worked your arse off over Christmas, haven't had time off in ages.'

'Tell me about it. How ya think I'm here now? She thinks me mam's had a fall. Had to rush out.'

'Slimy bugger.'

Trick pots a blue into the same pocket and spins back to set up an easy red.

'Not the brightest spark, mate,' he says. 'Plus, she has that book club on Thursdays.'

'Book club?'

I can't help but laugh into my pint, foam spitting out again.

'Don't ask. Wouldn't surprise me if she's out on the lash herself.'

Trick's frustration makes him miss the easy red. I start getting into the swing of it then, making the cue ball dance across the felt. The table has bumps and rips in the green everywhere, but I know it like the back of my hand. Trick has an empty glass, waiting for me to get 'em in with foam creeping towards the bottom. I'm on fire. I'm not going anywhere. I'm thinking about the next shot before I pot one, lining up beauties Steve Davis style. Red, colour, red, colour. Trick knows whenever I get into these rhythms. He sits there chewing his nails, breathing like a dog from years of Bensons and kebabs. Twenty-eight he is, black lungs and cholesterol higher than Ant McPartlin's forehead.

I chuck him a tenner and shout to Linda for refills. He waddles off like a penguin to the bar, leaving me and the table to crack on.

For a minute, I forget I'm in the club. The week's hard graft doesn't take long to come back and make my limbs go limp. Hands cramping from drilling the trocar into cavities for hours on end. Tired arms from massaging fluid around Paula. On my feet all day, cleaning equipment, taking the chemicals delivery, raking the cremation machines, making Janice fifty brews. Thank fuck for Trick though, these Thursday nights. It's nice to rest my eyes on the colours, knocking balls around and zoning out for a bit. He's a gooden, Trick, heart of fuckin' gold. Wouldn't have been doing this for years if he wasn't a proper mate.

He returns with the goods, glancing down at the small number of balls left, then back at me as if to say, *Don't be taking the piss.*

'Don't be taking the piss,' he says.

'What? Ya know what I'm like when I get going.'

'Yeh, I do. And it gets on my tits. Now piss off, my shot. Ya ginger twat.'

Trick uses his anger to pot a few balls, enjoying the sound of them rolling into the nets. They clunk along the rails underneath. It doesn't matter that he's on good form, he knows he has no chance. The last time he beat me I had a full head of hair and a thin waistline. Now I'm a fat cunt and my hairline's so far back it could be in a history book.

'How's your Rebecca then?' Trick asks, a more conversational tone about him now he's potted a couple.

'Ahh ya know. Usual shite. On to me about saving for a house lately.'

'Woah, serious shit then. How long you been with her now?'

'Coming up nine years.'

'Fuck me. Was gonna come eventually then. Rach was walking slowly past ring shops and estate agents after nine *weeks*.'

'Suppose it was coming, yeh. She's in proper saving mode though. Asking me to get overtime in at the directory, maybe help Janice with the admin side now she's getting on a bit. Thought, the cheeky cow, I'm fucked enough as it is. Once she gets summot in her head though, she won't let it go. It's house, house, house lately. And she starts getting suspicious then, thinking summot's going on just 'cause I don't want a joint bank account yet.'

'And you're not keen?'

'It's not that. Just don't see the rush. The flat's not too bad and it's not as if we're rolling in cash.'

'Mate, you're twenty-five and live above a kebab shop. Get fuckin' saving and out of that shithole. I mean, look at ya. Yeh you've got Daniel Craig's eyes, straight teeth and all right clobber, but you've got a receding ginger barnet, your stubble's patchy, and you feel up corpses every day. Count yourself lucky you've got a gem like her!'

I let out a fat sigh and drink my sorrows. Trick's married, settled with a mortgage, and a lot uglier than me. He's already taken the plunge.

'She's got a jar and everything,' I say. 'A saving jar with "House Fund" written on it.'

Trick laughs, making him miss his colour and leave an easy pot for me near the middle pocket.

'Sounds like you're fucked then,' he says.

Trick's right. I'm not getting away from this one. Rebecca can be stubborn when she wants something. And it's not as if I'm complaining; it's nice she wants a future with a lump like me. Bonkers really. If only I wasn't on my arse. Like, well and truly skint. More skint than she can ever know. Even Trick doesn't know – he thinks my line of work must be getting me somewhere. They have no idea. The struggle of it. If I'm being crystal, I probably even kid myself most the time, telling myself everything's hunky-dory, lying so I don't feel guilty about blowing money rather than taking Becca out or saving for that house. I convince myself debt's temporary, that there's always a way out, and if no one else knows about it, well then that's for me to deal with. No one knows more than me how hard it is to earn the money and how easy it is to let it go.

'Sup, mate?' says Trick. 'Looking a bit glum there.'

'Nah, I'm good, just going for a wizzer.'

I lean the cue against the wall and walk into the gents. With piss lashing off the urinal cakes, I try to think of the best outcome. How long it'd even take for us to save that much money to move. What it'd mean for me and Becca. The love's there but this is different gravy. Yeh, we have the odd petty row now and again, who doesn't? I know how lucky I am to have her. What an even worse state I'd be in if she wasn't in my life. Commitment and finances are just not my thing. I'm a plodder, a wing-it sorta fella. Take each day as it comes without bothering to plan. To plan is to set up for failure. When you're already a failure, well, there's no point in planning, is there?

I shake, zip up and watch the yellow stream down the gullet towards the plug. I shouldn't be thinking about this shit. I just want a game of snooker, a pint and a laugh.

'All right?' asks Trick as I walk out. He knows summot's up, he's known me long enough now. 'Did I touch a nerve there?'

'Ahh, did you fuck. Just a bit skint lately is all.'

'Should have said, ya daft bastard. I could have got the rounds in.' He flags to Linda with two Cumberland fingers. She nods back.

'You need a few quid to tide you over?' he asks, holding both hands on his cue like a microphone stand. His eyes fall on me with sympathy, genuinely wanting to help.

'I should be fine, mate. Thanks though.'

It's the worst. Every man's a grafter round here, they'll do anything they can to earn their crust. Builders, painters, joiners.

I know fellas who've been elbow-deep in turds for seven days, or worked on building sites night after night to feed their kids. It's part of life. It's what you have to do to get by. Admitting you're on your arse though, with people knowing you have a cushy wage in comparison – it ain't half embarrassing. Having the money and blowing it is another thing. Especially when your best mate's the one struggling for work and offering *you* money.

'Fair enough, mate.' Trick offers a wink that says he's there if I need him.

'Suppose you'll have to keep Becca happy in other ways if you're steering her away from saving.'

It's my shot. There's nothing on so I hammer the cue ball into a cluster of reds, making them explode across the table.

'Having a laugh, aren't ya?' I say. 'Been getting home from work at all hours. You think I'm up for a bit of hanky-panky after a day of graft, smelling of some dead geezer's shite?'

'Just saying, mate. If you're not cutting the mustard in the bedroom either ... you're asking for it. I do it all the time whenever Rachel wants summot. Give her a good night under the sheets and Bob's ya uncle. The amount of times I've got out of paying to get her hair or nails done.'

'Ahh, behave. I'm not eighteen any more. Not got the stamina to go at it like rabbits like you two.'

'Ay ay, steady on. Everyone's gotta have fun once in a while. Besides, maybe you need to spice shit up. Throw her off the scent. Make her feel lucky to have ya.'

I outstretch my arms as if to say *you're having a laugh aren't ya? Look at me!* From the form he's on, Trick goes for a long pot into the bottom right and sinks it. I gulp a few mouthfuls, thinking for the first time in a while that I could get beat here if I don't shape myself. After he misses his colour, I up the tempo and clear up a few. Bish, bash, bosh.

Coley shuffles past then on the way to the bogs, smelling of fags and that cheap cider he always drinks. I can't shoot with him creeping past so we both watch him slither like a slug into the gents.

'Anyway, what you mean *spice shit up?*' I ask.

'Yeh, ya know, summot different. Surprise her. Go home in that daft apron and mask you wear. Bet she'd love that.'

'Hilarious. What you mean though, like whips and shit?'

'Nooo, none of that creepy dungeon malark. Just a few little toys, like a feather, or those dirty card games. Rachel brought some oil home from Superdrug once. Worked a—'

'Woah, woah, mate. None of that.'

'What? Was great! Sliding about like Roy Keane.'

'Hahaha! You dirty bastard.'

I wipe my cue clean again, dust the tip, and eye up my shot. I slot in two reds and two colours before missing a banker on purpose.

'Fuckin' 'ell,' I mutter, tucking into a fresh pint that Linda's brought over.

Trick's eyes light up then, and not 'cause Coley emerges from the gent's half hanging out. By the time he gets to his seat, he notices, zips up, and returns to staring at the floor. Trick has a chance and he knows it, whether he knows I let it happen doesn't matter. I can tell he's gonna fluff it from the sweat on his fod. Up and down he is, eyeing up his shot like a pigeon eating bread. He chalks his cue about twenty times. Arm tense, strangling the grip. He wants it too much.

'How about we up the stakes?' I say, planting a crisp twenty on the table's outer rim. The last twenty I have in my pocket until payday next week.

Trick looks at it, then at me, then back at the money. He knows I'm a daft bastard flinging money about like that if what I'm saying about being on my arse is true. But this is Trick. A man that never turns down a challenge or a chance to beat another man, no matter what it is.

'Sure, mate. Twenty it is.' Trick layers it with his own twenty, Queen Liz's head more wrinkled than in real life.

We both know deep down I'm gonna win. I always do. But the way the game has panned out makes him think otherwise. More pressure's on the shot now. I've never felt more confident in my whole life. Trick arches his bridge hand, saws the cue along the groove and strikes the cue ball with enough force to send it hopping on the table. It clatters into the red on the wrong side, sending the balls walkabout on the table and completely opening up the play for me. He's bottled it. Lost the game in one, rash swipe.

'Ahh, mate. Hard luck,' I say.

I'm kind. I don't let the mistake linger in the air along with Coley's piss. I clean up the table, slotting in the rest with ease before offering a handshake.

'Same again?' I ask.

Trick shakes my hand and sniggers.

'Shove it up your arse.'

Being the winner, I get another round in and ask Linda about the family and that at the bar. How her kids are doing at school, whether she still goes to them Zumba classes ... the usual bollocks. Linda's fella, John, went in for heart surgery last week so she fills me in on that, getting on to hospitals and how the smell stays with you after you've visited someone week after week. I have a feeling I'll be catching up with John very soon, if you know what I mean.

'Was there nearly every day before my old fella passed,' I say, keeping one of the stools warm while the ladies are out for a fag. 'Depressing as fuck it was.'

'Aw, shame that. We miss Ray. You must get sick of it, with your job and all?' Linda fills up the pints with one hand, the other on her hip. 'You were a right wreck when he passed. God bless his soul.'

I spin a coaster between my fingers, silent. Linda wipes a

damp cloth over the sticky bar, planting two pints down on the wounded wood.

'Six eighty, love.'

'One for yourself as well, Linda.'

'Cheers, flower.'

She throws the money into a till that survived the eighties. Them ones that open so fast they could kill ya if they catch you on the bonce. I spot the rows of notes, stacked up nicely. Trays of coins full to the brim. If only. If only I could stick my hand in and pocket whatever's there.

'Don't thank me, Linda,' I say out loud to get Trick's attention. I give her a wink and make way for the table. 'These ones are on Trick.'

Trick looks up from his phone, muttering insults to himself and sticking me the Vs. Either side of a round table, we drink in the dark, enjoying the dusty light fall in through the back windows and onto the floorboards. Soft squares of orange. Tommy Murphy's half asleep, nursing a warm lager with his head nearly touching the newspaper. The ladies are in the corner now underneath a TV showing a darts match, whispering and raising eyebrows over that week's gossip. Coley's tapping the jukebox, forgetting it hasn't worked for ten years. I crack my neck and feel the knots in my shoulders, scrubbing at my eyelids to keep my body awake.

'You look fucked, mate,' says Trick.

'I feel it.'

'Maybe it's you that needs a week off.'

I turn my glass on the table. Once. Twice.

'Can't afford that.'

'Yeh, I get ya.' Trick nods his head. 'Honestly though mate, if you're struggling. I don't mind.'

He leans back in his chair and gives a sincere look to say he isn't having a laugh this time.

'Appreciate that, Trick.'

The glare from the windows soon dulls into a reflection of the inside. Night has kicked in. A few more punters come and go for after-work pints. Linda squeaks glasses spotless and returns them to the top rack. Tommy Murphy wakes up then falls back asleep again. The jukebox stays silent.

'Fancy another game?' asks Trick. 'Can't be fucked going back to that house, mate.'

I check my phone for the time: 8.17 p.m. It'll still be open. Jim Ramsbottom's. My home from home. Where dreams and nightmares coexist.

'Actually mate, I've gotta shoot. Sorry.'

Trick returns the cues to the stand before coming over to me. He feeds fifty quid into my front pocket.

'Don't mention it, lad,' he says. 'You get the first round in next week, yeh?'

He's a good man. He wouldn't let me give it back; there's no point kicking up a fuss.

'Cheers, Trick, really appreciate that. See ya next week, yeh? Have a gooden.'

We shake hands like we always do. As I leave, I hear his hoarse voice pop up from the back room.

'Oi, Fletch. Why was the graveyard so noisy?'

Great, another one.

'Because of all the coffin!'

His laugh booms through the club. I laugh too, returning him the Vs and walking out into the rain.

4

I park at the big Tesco in Openshaw and walk round the corner towards the bookies. The sky's chalkboard black. The road loud with wet tyres and the buzz of street lamps, twitching and blinking from dodgy electrics. Jim Ramsbottom's on Ashton Old Road is my local betting shop. The one next to the pound shop with mop buckets and laundry baskets spilling onto the pavement. Opposite the pet shop that sells sad fish for a fiver, wiggling about in brown water in the window. It's a bookies where dreams have been made, where souls have been crushed. Fuck knows what it holds for me tonight. And what's more exciting than that?

Before I get there – smoking happily on my fag knowing a few crisp tenners are nestled nicely in my pocket – I experience the usual dose of Openshaw raucous. A huddle of trackied teens smoking up a couple of bifters on the corner by the old butcher's shop. A blaring speaker, bass rippling through the alleyways. A homeless man asks me for a cig, so I give him three. His face lights up like Christmas. A drunk girl with one working heel, swaying from side to side shovelling a Big Mac into her gob. There's sauce on her dress, a stray bit of lettuce. She sits at a shattered bus stop and gives me the finger for staring. Distracted, I nearly go arse over tit slipping on a balloon cannister. She chuckles with a bit of bread in her teeth, as if I'm the embarrassing one.

I finally get to Jim Ramsbottom's and finish my ciggy with one deep drag before flicking it into the night. I get a rush. That feeling. That hope before you step in the bookies and place a bet.

'Ayy up.'

Jacky's in and waves at me from behind the plastic screen. Raw gums and tarred teeth, grinning like the Cheshire Cat scranned a brownie.

'Jacky. All right love?'

'Oh aye. Just back from seeing Trick?'

Jacky leans back in her swivel chair, saggy breasts resting on her waistline. Her hair's tied back into a ponytail. Her novelty glasses making her look like Ronnie Corbett.

'Yeh, easy win tonight,' I say. 'Fancied a dabble so thought I'd see which meetings are on.'

'You know full well which meetings are on, Fletch. Ya don't fool me.'

I smirk, picking a blue pen from the dispenser on the counter.

'I'd love one,' I say, nodding to the kettle in the brew room behind her.

'What did your last one die of, cheeky bugger.'

I have a scan of the newspaper listings on the back wall, pinned to the cork with drawing pins. Chepstow. Lingfield. A couple of decent races on the flat in France. There's a dog running called 'Hat Trick' in the 9.15. Why not? It'll be a giggle telling Trick next Thursday if it brought in a few quid. It's his money after all.

'E arrr.'

Jacky's Primark flats squeak closer, a steaming mug in her mitts.

'Ahh, cheers love. Kids all right then?'

She leans on the counter, ready to delve into some fuck-long spiel about how her fella's not coughing up for child support or how her little Molly shat up the wall again. I'm too busy lost in analysing form to listen.

'Ooo don't get me started, Fletch,' she begins. 'So I'm there, having a fag in the garden scrolling through Facebook, and I hear this "MUMMMMM ... MUMMMM" from upstairs. So, like ya do, I'm shitting myself thinking what the fuck's she done now. Stuck Barbie's foot into her eye or summot. So I fling ma cig, sprint upstairs . . .'

It takes everything not to laugh. *Sprint*.

'. . . barge into her bedroom and she's there crying her mince pies out. I'm talking proper bawling, face like a baboon's arse. I don't have a clue what's going on, so I'm patting her back asking *What? What?* Looking her up and down for injuries and that. Then she goes: "THERE'S RUMOURS HARRY STYLES IS GOING SOLO, THERE'S NO HOPE LEFT ANY MORE!"'

I look and Jacky has her mouth gaped open, shaking her head from side to side.

'Can ya believe that?' she says, 'I nearly had a bloody heart attack and she's there still winging about the end of fuckin' One Direction. I could have slapped her into next week.'

'Kids for ya,' I say, trying to decide which jockey's had the better run of winners lately. I don't have kids. Thank fuck. And that's why. No doubt that'll be Becca's next mission after the house is tied up. Can't even take care of myself for fuck's sake.

'Anyway,' she says, knocking on the counter before shuffling back to the brew room, 'I wouldn't mind giving that Harry Styles a go, so suppose I get where she's coming from. I tell ya, there's only one direction he'll be—'

'Thanks again for the brew, Jacky.'

Christ.

I place my bets and sit on the furthest side of the bookies near the roulette machines, so I don't get roped into any more of her twaddle. My brew tastes soapy. It's the same shade as the make-up line on Jacky's collar. I hear her fingers over the TV commentary, hammering a furious Facebook status on her phone. Some fake, soppy shite about being your best self or talking about how her late friend Tamara is looking over her from the heavens, even though she got hit by a bus and secretly called Jacky a gossiping cow whenever she wasn't around. I can't be arsed, I just want a bet. I finally manage to zone out and get lost in the magic.

Lines of TV screens show all different sports from around the world. Footy, horses, dogs, even golf. I watch the horses trot leisurely into the traps. Jockeys in vibrant silks, bobbing on their saddles. The milky sweat dripping off their backsides. Mine – Little Dream – is a grey horse with a line of knotted plaits down its neck and a fluffy white noseband. Its ears are pricked, always a good sign. A couple are unsettled, flinging their muscular necks about and hopping up and down like rodeo bulls. Not mine: 16/1, calm as a cucumber. Let's see if Trick's dosh can nab me a £320 winner.

And they're off...

My pits are damp already. Edge of the seat stuff. The beautiful thud of hooves tearing up the turf, flicking mud in their tracks. The jolt of the cameraman keeping up with the speed. The jockey's chequers blowing in the wind. What a gorgeous fuckin' sport it is.

Little Dream is gliding steady in third place, nosing up the arse of second, ready to pounce in the final furlong. The one in front's blowing out his backside already, chugging out more gas than my rusty Transit. He's gaining. Little Dream's fuckin' gaining. Coming into the final mile, he's neck and neck with second and then *BAM*. He turns on the accelerator big style, using those gammon shoulders to thrust into a long stride, leaving the rest of the pack for dust. The sheer class of it. With each gallop, she seems to get further and further in front. I leap from the chair and punch the air, sending my brew spilling over the lip.

'GO ON YA LITTLE DREAMER! GO ON!!'

The jockey doesn't even need to hit the bastard. It's like Forrest Gump with four legs. Tanking away. The easiest win I've had all year.

And it's Little Dream who cruises home to an easy victory. Another stellar win for Mullins this week...

'Get in, ya beautiful twat!'

If that plastic screen wasn't there, I would have been tempted to run up to Jacky and snog the chops off her. Thank god it is. On my arse and days away from getting paid, now I'm quid's in. Trick, you absolute gem! On the TV, they're chucking buckets of water on the horse. Steam rising off its grey coat. It looks like it could go again. Unbelievable stuff.

'Cash that for us will ya, Jacky.'

I slam the slip on the counter and enjoy Jacky counting the money. There's chocolate on her fingers from wolfing a pack of Jaffa Cakes but I couldn't give two shits if she wiped her arse with it. It's £320 in the bank.

My balls tingle with the weight of the notes in my pocket. I like running my fingers in and out like a pack of cards, counting it in my head. The last time the Queen's head was this smooth was her coronation.

I check my watch and it's 9.30 p.m. Rebecca would be wondering where I am. I probably should have been home a half hour ago, but on this form ...

I don't know. Surely, it'd be stupid of me to do a runner. There's times as a punter where you just feel it. That luck courses through your veins like nowt else. The adrenalin floods every sensible thought. You want that buzz again, you never wanna leave. And why should you when you call a blinding 16/1 shot like that? It only takes one night of hot form to get you out the shit. To not have to worry about how much your weekly shop is, to book that all-inclusive holiday you've been dying to go on, to put that deposit on a house to keep ya missus happy. All it takes is a good streak. And I'm already on a great one.

I return to my seat and scan the newspapers.

Wait. You're fuckin' joking me. Am I reading that right? *Camelot*. Fuckin' Camelot in the 21.50? Running with that lot? Jesus lord. Camelot's tipped for a stunning run at the National in a couple of months. A once-in-a-decade horse that has the potential to challenge any seasoned mare. Imagine Usain Bolt with a tail.

And it's running at Lingfield? Fuckin' *Lingfield*. That's like United playing on Debdale Park.

I run up to the counter, catching Jacky with a mouthful of Jaffa Cake, scrolling through Tinder.

'Whack it all on Camelot, love.'

Jacky finishes chewing, then swallows as if it was a watermelon. I follow its journey down her throat.

'Fletch. Come on.'

'I'm serious Jacky. It's a banker.'

'Fletch. That's a decent bit of dosh that.'

'You're right. It is. Imagine trebling it.'

She gives me a look through those magnified lenses. She looks like me mam when she found out I wanted to work with corpses for a living. The disappointment, borderline disgust. The look of wanting to help someone and knowing you have no chance.

'Honest, Jacky. Trust me. I'll even get you a drink in the club next time you're in.'

I've never seen a bet placed so fast.

'Cheers, love,' I say. 'Any luck on there?'

I point to her phone. Fuckin' Tinder. What's the world come to?

'Oh aye. Meeting up with a fella after my shift. No Harry Styles but he's worth one. Should see what I've got on under this uniform.'

I throw up a bit in my mouth and sit back down.

This is it. There she is. Her shiny brown coat and white blinkers. The blue and pink hoops of the jockey. Stevie Baron. The best in the game. I feel like jumping through the TV and kissing him already. Run me a cracker, Stevie boy.

Before the race, the commentator sings Camelot's praises. Reeling off victories and awards. The eye-watering track record. The potential as a landmark name in horse-racing history, alongside the greats. As soon as the traps open and the jockey arches forward with reins in hand, I know. I fuckin' know. Something doesn't look right. Not right at all.

Camelot always darts out of the traps. Always leads the pack most of the way then engines home. His ears aren't pricked. His neck is lagging. Panting, struggling, with only half the race run. An injury maybe? Surely not. I should scrunch up my betting slip and chuck it in the bin right now. It's running like it has the shits. I can't believe it. I must have glossed over something in the *Racing Post*, a random column somewhere urging punters not to back it this time around. Fitness, bad ground, ill jockey, there must have been something.

The race isn't finished but I already have my head in my hands. Tommy Murphy probably knew not to back it. Of course he did. Why didn't I ask him for a few tips in the club? Ahh fuck. Fuckin' fuck fuck. I watch Camelot jog, saunter, die. Not literally. His legs go limp and send him to the back of the pack as if he's on a treadmill. I throw my betting slip at the screen and storm out. Jacky mutters something behind me but I'm not in a state to hear it. I just lost £320 and now have to go home to a fuming girlfriend. It's not looking good.

***

'You taking the piss?'

I waltz in just after midnight, bouncing up the walls of the stairs. I had a chat with Solomon who runs the kebab shop downstairs and charmed a few chicken wings out of him before heading up. We get on well. He's used to seeing me bladdered, struggling to get my key in the door next to the shop entrance. I apologised in advance for the ranting he's about to hear above. It was no bother to him. We bumped greasy fists. He wished me luck.

When I manage to get the key in and open the fucker, Rebecca's stood in the middle of the living room with a glass of water.

'B-Babe, I know,' I slur. 'I'm sorry. I know. It's late.'

'Late? Fuckin' *late*? I've been worried sick, Jamie.'

'Y'know I'm out with T-Trick on Thisdays. Iss s-snooker night.'

I do a drunken motion of a pool cue that makes me look like I'm tossing off a ghost.

'Yeh. I fuckin' get that. But don't come swanning in here at this time pissed out ya brains without even a single text.'

'I'mnotpisst.'

The glass is down, her arms are folded. Who am I kidding? I'm fuckin' steaming.

'Babe, I'm so sorry. I know. I know.'

I've not even shut the door yet. I'm trying to get my shoes off, resting my head on the wall above the shoe rack. The space is like getting undressed in a phone box.

'Here, let me do it.'

She yanks my shoes off, nearly my feet with 'em, then launches them somewhere too far to see. I try to focus but see three shoes and give up.

'Babe. Comehere.'

I try to go in for a hug. She shrugs me off like I'm a creepy old man in a nightclub. I know exactly how I look. I've seen it too many times with Dad. Becca's seen it too many times with me. Too many times I've been beaten by the urge to walk into a bookies and try my chances. The decisions I've made. The money I've spent which could have been totting up nicely in that House Fund jar on the mantelpiece. A few dirty coins and limp notes sit in the bottom, that's all. Money that Rebecca probably would like to use for a delicious lunch or branded shampoo but resists. Owning a house means more to her than that. And here I am, eyes all bloodshot and swollen with guilt. Pockets bare and empty. Nothing to offer.

'I'll speak to you in the morning,' she says, nudging past me upstairs to our shoddy box room.

'No, wait.'

She turns on the stairs, waiting for whatever excuse I'm about to vomit up.

'Me and Trick got shatting and I l-lost track ofthetime. Thas all. Sorry, I know I shoulda text or summot.'

'I'm not arsed if you go out with Trick but just don't take the piss, all right? I'm sat here on ma tod expecting you home and you don't even let me know. Makes me feel like a mug, Jamie.'

'I know. I know.' I look down at the carpet all glum. Place could do with a hoover.

'It's fine, honest. Just get some water down ya for fuck's sake. Not having you chundering on me in the night.'

She leaves me with the buzz of the fridge and a flickering kitchen bulb. If I close my eyes, it sounds like the embalming room. I gulp some water, try to wash away all that guilt settled in my stomach. I close my eyes and see TV screens, odds, pints. I felt I had no other choice but to try and drink away the decision I'd just made. No one loses £320 and then goes home with a smile on his face to watch *Game of Thrones* with his bird. The reality of having that money, possibly more, and losing it all in a matter of minutes hit hard. It's the life of a gambler. There needs to be some medicine, some consolation for shit like that. And for me, that's booze and more bets. Drink yourself senseless, bet into oblivion to forget how stupid you've just been.

Rebecca doesn't know I gamble, not a clue. Having separate accounts helps keep it that way. She knows I like a drink too, but who doesn't in Openshaw? I'll give her the same old excuses tomorrow. Stress with work. Snowed under with death. It's horrible. Having the desperation to make Becca happy, to give her a house, but not having the resources to. She can never know the real reason. I mean, *never* know. That'll be a disaster. Chaos. I'll lose her. The one good thing going for me in my life. No, she'll never know. If I'm gonna carry on this way, I'll need to do better at hiding it. I've got to stop coming home in this state all the time. The answer is simple.

I have to win.

5

The first body on a Monday is always the worst. I'm either still hungover or reeling from the weekend's lost bets. Sally isn't doing me any favours either. The hospital sent her in this morning after having stroke while hiking through the Woodhead Pass in Glossop. Thump, right on top of a hill, barrelling down through thickets of thorns, bashing her skull off every rock on the way down.

On the bed, half of her head is caved in, and her eyes are ballooned purple. Patches of bruising run down the length of her body. A dislocated shoulder, an arm pointing the wrong way as if I asked her where the bathroom is.

I take a breath and button up my white coat before organising the sanitation products ready to clean her wounds.

Right, Sal, looks like we'll be here a while, so we might as well get to know each other.

Sally's mouth is wide open. Cracked teeth, bleeding gums. A moment captured mid-stroke. Frozen in time. I wheel my chair in close and start to clean the open wounds on her stomach and arms. Thick lacerations, splintered with wood.

Not necessarily the extremity of the injuries, but the shock they leave in my gut, brings me to think of Dad. How, if he was still here, supping ale, pissed off his rocker down the road, I wouldn't be here picking wood out of this random lass. I almost feel obligated to tell Sally why I'm doing this to her, like a policeman showing his credentials before he arrests someone.

The reflections start to stir. The history I've buried begins to creep to the surface, splinter by splinter. I suddenly get the urge to pour out to Sally as a mark of respect, of validation, that I'm the right man honoured to have this job.

So, Sal ... tell you what, I'll keep it light, seeing as you've had a bad day. Speaking of trips, let me tell you about my first holiday. Blackpool, around 2001. I sat in the passenger footwell by Mam's crusty bunions poking out of her flipflops. My cousins, Lucy, Anna and Daniel, bagsied the back seats so it was me left in the pit the whole journey, holding in my piss until we hit a Maccie D's or service station. Mam kept pushing my head down if she saw a cop car or some evil witch in the next car looking like she'd call child services. Dad tapped the steering wheel to his Oasis CD and ruffled my hair between switching lanes. The car smelt of mints and sun cream. Rays pounded down on Dad's bogey-green Renault, windows fully down and the wind twirling Mam's hair like a tornado. Big smile on her mush, beaming she was. Mam loved the seaside. She couldn't wait for me to see it.

When we got to the caravan site, I got out to stretch my legs and feared they were too numb to walk again. I was a big drama queen. Daniel gave me a dead leg for good measure. 'See,' he said. 'You can feel it fine.' I made a mental note to hide his CD player later and send his holiday into a frenzy. That or fart in his mouth when he's asleep. I hadn't decided yet.

I use tweezers to carefully remove shards of wood from Sally's body. I place them down on a cloth where they gather like a tiny firepit. Each gash is like a pick 'n' mix. I find stones, thorns, bundles of soil. Painstakingly hunched over every scratch to make sure I get it all. The earthy contents gathered on the tray take me back to the patch outside our caravan.

Turned out it wasn't a caravan site at all, Sal. It was a shoddy, wonky-doored caravan on someone's gravelled driveway. Dad knocked on the front door of the house, exchanged keys and money *with an old, tanned geezer with shorts and varicose veins, then walked back to us rattling them in his hands like they were for a new Mercedes. The structure rocked as we all boarded it and threw in our bags. I made sure to bagsy the couch, or 'cushioned bench' more like. The thing was fuckin' tiny. Mam and Dad had to hunch to stop knocking their heads on the roof. Mam unpacked those small cereal boxes and five tins of hot dogs, still with that same grin on her face. Dad tested the plumbing taking a shite, while Lucy, Anna and Daniel chased each other in circles around the caravan outside. I looked around, thinking there was more space in the bastard footwell and that I might kip there for the night. I was excited though, I'd never experienced anything other than Openshaw. Anywhere would have been magical. And this was.*

I soon realised parents are different when they're on holiday. They're as excited as the kids. Dad didn't hesitate getting his Bermuda shorts on, with fluorescent palm trees and wave-riding surfers. Horrific they were: couldn't be more contrasting to his pasty chicken legs. His bald forehead was burnt from having the car windows open and his aviator shades were already making tan marks. Mam – a woman with 'gifted' breasts, as Dad would say – had her bikini on and shawl over the top as if it was thirty-odd degrees. It was probably hotter back in Manchester. We were by the sea, though. I soon learnt it was a must for a British tourist, no matter the weather, to dress and act like they're in the Caribbean if they're ever by the sea in summertime.

Fuck me, this is killing my back. I give it a stretch, doing one lap around the bed. During my rest, I get my phone out and load up the betting apps. I scroll, scan, weighing up the prices. Austrian basketball and Saudi Arabian golf – the options are shite at this time of day. Still, I keep calm and lump on. You don't bet, you don't win. I press odds and bet without thinking. I have no knowledge, no context on what's more likely to win. But just like the lottery, you gotta be in it to win it.

I pocket my phone and give my back one last stretch before getting back to it.

Sorry Sal, not as young as I used to be. Anyway, I had a Spider-Man T-shirt on with a matching pair of webbed flippers I carried under my arm. I was eager to test them in the brown ocean, regardless of the johnnies and plastic bottles floating about. Like Dad, my pale legs were on show, scraped and marked from endless days of footy over half-term. We weren't in the caravan for long, no faffing and all that. We were out and on our way to the seafront in a matter of minutes, ready to drink in the sights as well as a fuck-load of Slush Puppies.

Nearly there, Sal. A quick check of the phone. Everything still in play.

Thinking back, this trip was probably my first introduction to gambling. I dragged Mam and Dad into the endless strip of arcades along the front. Magical portals, dancing tunes that spilled out onto the tramlines. Candyfloss hanging in the outer doorways, claw-grabbing machines lined up on the pavement, a cocky teen punching the boxing machine and nearly breaking his wrist. It was a wonderland, a world I never wanted to leave. I begged Dad for a small pot of 2ps that all the kids were carrying around. He rolled his eyes, obliging, probably proud to see his young son so drawn to the lights. Who was he to know they would flash throughout my adult years, blinding my every decision?

Now the wounds are clean, I start to lace up the skin with thin stitching. The skin pops as I feed in the needle. Back and forth, back and forth, shutting the mouth of each wound tight. I'm reminded how Becca can sew. How for years she's stitched up the hole in my crotch whenever my jeans have split cause I'm too tight (or skint) to buy a new pair. The way she can watch telly, weaving the needle in and out, without even looking at it. Could Sally sew? Did she have her kid's uniforms to fix? Did her fella have holes in his crotch? Who would deal with all that now?

The thought of holes reminds me of golf. I go to check my phone, lift it halfway out my pocket before letting it drop and carrying on.

Before I knew it, I had a small bucket in my hands, hammering 2p after 2p into the slits at the top of the machine, watching them roll down onto the sliding platform. I remember aiming for a red Ferrari key ring. It was teetering on the edge, nudging slightly with each coin. I watched one boy give up on it before me. I knew it was close to dropping. My 2ps were rapidly vanishing. The Ferrari must have had its fuckin' handbrake on 'cause it was refusing to drop. I dropped my last 2p on top of a pile on the platform and felt like crying. It was a key ring, for Christ's sake. It might as well have been a hundred grand waiting to drop, the way I felt. While I was busy sticking out my bottom lip, an arm came over my shoulder and thudded into the Perspex glass. The key ring rolled over the edge and clunked to the bottom, ready for me to collect.

'You gotta play dirty sometimes, son.'

Dad got the shiny red key ring out from the flap, placed it in my palm, and ruffled my hair like he did the whole journey here. I felt loved. A happiness that only shines in your youth. I attached the key ring onto the loop of my shorts and kept it there, swinging for the whole holiday. The kids on the beach looked at me a bit funny but I didn't care. I'd won something.

The fun didn't stop there. I smothered my new United shirt with sick after a session on the waltzers. A seagull flew off with Daniel's ice cream before he could give it a lick. Dad had to swim full-on Michael Phelps when Mam started floating out into the Atlantic on an inflatable crocodile. Lucy and Anna – younger, prettier, but considerably more stupid – even offered to play badminton on the beach with me. Running around swinging at the salty air, feet getting shredded up by cracked shells. Toes tangled in seaweed.

After that, we went to Madame Tussauds. Ya know, them sweaty waxworks of famous people? I recognised Michael Jackson and the

Queen, that's about it. Mam got a picture with Doctor Who when she's never even fuckin' seen it. Dad got told off by a steward for doing rude gestures, like picking a wedgie out of John Travolta's arse or fondling James Bond's pistol. Mam got some decent pictures on her disposable camera though, chuckling away as she peeked through the lens, winding the wheel with her cracked thumb. It's the most I seen her laugh with him.

I'm onto washing Sally's body now, being careful to dab over the scars with the towel so I don't open them up again. There's a hint of Frankenstein's monster about how her now, covered in streams of stitches. The wet cotton glides until it reaches a bruise or scar, where I have to slow down like a car on a speed bump.

I use the drop in pace to check my phone with my other hand. Loss. Loss. Minor win. Loss. I spread all my winnings over new bets and return to Sal.

That night, we sneaked onto the local caravan park to have a gander at the entertainment. When we got there, it smelt of retirement homes and Pepsi. A parrot was flying over the round tables in front of the stage. Some magician was on, one that could hardly do any magic. He made this parrot get him a beer from the bar and then tell him to fuck off, that was about it. The kids were busy in front of the stage, playing tig or wrestling or some shit. Seemed a bit rough for me, so I sat by Mam's chair as she and Dad hammered back colourful shots and pints of lager. Lucy and Anna hid under the table playing Kerplunk while Daniel picked his nose and ate whatever he could dig out. It was boring at first. I wanted the magician to do what it says on the tin and make himself vanish or summot.

He finally went off to two claps and a 'you were shite' from a bloke at the back. After that we had a clown folding balloons into animals, a game of bingo cut short by a pissed-up granny, and a run of karaoke songs that threatened to make my ears bleed. Mam and Dad were in their element. Clearly steaming. Throughout all this I was watching this one girl a couple of tables away, sat with her mam and dad looking as bored as I was. She had blonde pigtails and a pair of hazel eyes that glimmered from the disco ball. She caught my eye through 'Come on Eileen' and smirked, sipping on her Vimto. I found her dimples cute and was a fan of her Wonder Woman T-shirt. Proper into my superheroes at that age. In swimming pools, I'd go underwater and crawl along the side of the pool as if I was Spider-Man. Any sign of an actual spider, though, and it was getting a boot to the head. Like tryna be a non-gambler really, I had a habit of trying to be someone I couldn't be.

Now the ugly bit. I grit my teeth as I stand and push Sally's shoulder back into the socket. I lift her broken arm to wash the armpit and feel the bone moving about in there. I hold it up away from me with two fingers like someone does with a leaky bin bag. I try not to look at it. Bobbing about with a mind of its own.

I stretch my back again, only because I want to put more bets on. I look for greyhound names with 'Sally' in and find one called 'Funtime Sally' running in France. I lump fifty dabs on, watching the full race on my phone and watching it tumble after the second bend. I throw another fifty on the same number in the next race. It comes third. I swear at the overhead lights then remember my manners.

Sorry, Sal, where was I? ... Oh yeh, so this sunburnt heifer named Barry waddled on to the stage to sing 'Love Me Tender', which sent the whole audience yawning. When this cute girl caught my attention, I nodded to the vending machine at the back of the room and held up a pound coin as if it was the key to her heart. The dimples appeared again. She asked her dad to go to the toilet or summot and started walking to the back of the room. Her Mam and Dad didn't even know she'd left. They were as trollied as the rest of them. Pints sinking faster than the Titanic.

I nudged Mam, saying I'm going for a walk, a stroll, a mooch.

'All right son,' she said, eyes on Barry. 'Don't get in anyone's car.' She burst out laughing as I walked off, Barry shaking his legs and

unbuttoning his shirt to tease some chest hair. 'Suspicious Minds' boomed from the speakers now. The girl was looking into the rows of chocolate bars and crisps when I reached her.

Now the make-up, thank fuck. Powdering up each bruise to match the pigmentation of her skin. Sally's pale so I pick a colour from the drawer labelled 'Linen'. Always makes me chuckle how these powders have names like you're picking which Dulux paint to slap on your chimney breast.

'Hiya,' I said.

'Hello,' she said.

'My name's Jamie.'

'Nice to meet you, Jamie.'

Her eyes were even more beautiful close up. I thought of how I liked the word 'hazel'. I thought maybe that was her name.

'You not gonna tell me yours?' I said.

'Well, depends if you're gonna buy me something.'

Her voice wasn't like mine. It was like someone took a nail file to it, evened up the edges and made it shinier. I had a scan, fancying a Mars bar, but I knew she was gonna have to pick if I was gonna have any chance of tonsil tennis.

'What would you like?' I asked.

'Hmmm ... that one.'

She pointed to the Mars bar. My kind of girl. I rolled in the coin and punched in the digits. It clunked like the drop of my heart. We both reached down to the flap and touched hands by mistake. Mine were clammy, sticky from my ice cream earlier. Hers were soft like puppy ears, smooth as an ice rink.

'Urgh, fuck, shit, sorry,' I stuttered.

She claimed the Mars bar, smiling, and broke it in half before unwrapping it. We both looked at each other, chomping loudly, caramel clogging up our teeth.

Barry'd finally left the stage in a sweat, returning to his table on the brink of a 999 call. His wife patted his forehead with a napkin, a face on her that showed she was used to him grasping these moments in the spotlight. The kind of couple that have tolerated each other for thirty, forty years, show no sign of love, but couldn't live without each other. They didn't need to show love. That's what love was to me as well. Fuckin' invisible.

'Is that your mum and dad over there?' she said, chewing politely.
'Yeh.'
'They seem nice.'
'Do they? Pissed as a fart they are.'
'So are mine. So much for a family holiday.'
'Where you from anyway?' I asked.
'Yorkshire. Little town called Skipton.'
'Skipped in?'
'Skipton.'
'Skipton? Where's that?'
'Yorkshire,' she said.

Sally's cheeks and forehead are lifted somehow. Her eyes are less purple. Some form of life is brought back to them. I start to apply her mascara with soft sweeps. Watching them grow and curl outward as if they're blooming. Now she doesn't look so much like she's fell down a hill and cracked her head on every rock.

I stupidly check my phone from habit after hearing it ping and see I've lost more bets. I start to apply the make-up more aggressively and have to tell myself to calm down. Who am I to bring my problems in here? Sally will only have this moment once. I've got all night and all week to bet. I need to focus, keep talking.

I swallowed the last of my Mars bar. She had chocolate on her lip that I couldn't resist wanting to kiss off. Even at that age I knew I shouldn't look at girls like that. I just couldn't get over how stunning she was.

'You still not gonna tell me ya name then?' I asked.
'Not decided yet.'
'Tough nut to crack you, aren't ya?'

I leant my forearm on the vending machine like those guys in leather jackets do in Grease. *Probably 'cause of seeing John Travolta at Madame Tussauds. All I needed was a toothpick and a bucket full of hair gel.*

'I don't know you, do I?' she said, sheepishly.

'I told you. I'm Jamie and I just bought you a fuckin' Mars bar when I could have had a full one to myself.'

The girl faced the stage and chewed on her nail. Her silhouette showed an upturned nose and eyelashes that could rake garden leaves. If you had a garden.

'I like your T-shirt,' *I said, trying to rewind my rudeness. She looked down at Wonder Woman lassoing her whip and nodded.* 'She's cool.'

'Yeh, she's my favourite.'

'I have Spider-Man flippers that my dad bought me for the sea tomorrow.'

I immediately regretted it and realised how uncool I sounded. I stopped leaning on the vending machine and faced the stage with her.

'Cool,' *she said.*

If this was my first experience of love, it was shit. Love was overrated. Boring. Does nothing but reveal what a sad little prick you are.

'I like your key ring by the way,' *she said.* 'Where did you get it?'

She pointed at the Ferrari swinging from my belt loop.

'Oh, this? I won it today in the arcade.'

'Can I see it?'

She held out her soft palms and had me unclasping it in seconds.

'Yeh sure, here.'

Looking at the car, I wanted to be in the palm of her hand with it. She fiddled with the key ring and rotated the glossy sheen in the light.

'How much do you want it?' *she asked.*

I try to brush Sally's hair over the parts of her head that are caved in the most, untangling the clumps and knots as much as possible.

I have to cut chunks out because they're so mangled, using long strands to conceal the patches.

Looking up through her eyelashes, a glint appeared. Not cute. Summot darker. I couldn't read this girl, Sal, she was a puzzle.

'Huh?'

'How much do you want the key ring? Like, if I stepped on it and smashed it right now, what would you do?'

'Why would you do that?' I asked.

'Or maybe, what would you do to get it back?'

I'm not one for games. I was starting to get annoyed. I'd only had that key ring a few hours but it had more sentimentality than most of my pointless possessions at home. My foam Hulk hands, my Space Jam *DVD, my football sticker swapsies pile: they meant nothing. Dad had won this for me. It was a marker of my joy of being on holiday, of having fun, of winning something for the first time in my life.*

'Can I have it back, please?'

She swung it from her finger like a pendulum.

'Come on, please?' I said.

'What are you willing to do?'

'Whatever, I don't care. I just want it back.'

Before I could process what a bitch she was being, the girl darted off through some double doors and into a room on the right. I sprinted after her, nudging through limbs and making people spill pints on the way back from the bar. I barged into the room and shut the door. Pitch darkness. Like, if I waved in front of my face, Sal, there was fuck all there. My heart pounded. I thought of the worst, like I had walked into a stranger's car like Mam told me not to.

Now the lipstick. 'Sangria Summer'. More hopeful, and calmer, I whack on more bets that I feel confident about. It helps me apply the lipstick with gentle care.

Shitting me up even more, a light flickered on to reveal a tiny broom closet and the girl standing right in front of me with a big smile on her face. It was the first time I'd seen her teeth. They were perfect. Of course they were.

'The fuck you playing at?' I said.

'Calm down. I'm only messing. Now how about I give you this back?'

She swung the key ring again and snatched it away as soon as I went to grab it. I felt like punching those little white teeth out of her beautiful fuckin' face.

'How about a kiss first?' she asked.

A kiss. All this for a bastard kiss? I was willing to snog her face off five minutes ago. Never mind, running around like fuckin' Road Runner for a farty key ring. Something relaxed in her flushed cheeks. Those hazel eyes beamed back, fluttering like butterflies again. The dimples rose into a smile. I looked at her lips, the red tint, how they were pouted for action.

Before I could answer, her face was a centimetre from mine. I slapped one on her before I could talk myself out of it. One of them that's just an instant lunge of tongue and spit. She tasted like cherries and bits of caramel. Her skin smelt like coconuts. Our mouths sounded like mixing tuna and mayonnaise with a fork. I don't think we came up for breath for like five minutes. My lips were raw by the end of it. My front teeth sensitive from the clashing.

When we finished, she kissed my cheek as if she felt sorry for me, as if she did this all the time and could tell this was my first time. Truth be told, I couldn't give a fuck if she grabbed that screwdriver from the shelf and jabbed me in the neck. I'd be happy to say adios there and then.

'I'm Anabelle, by the way.'

She offered her hand, which I held awkwardly. Inside her palm was the key ring.

'Nice to meet you, Anabelle,' I said.

Sally's body is clean, made up and cracked back into its original sockets. I've tried my best to make her look as presentable as possible. To convince whichever family member is coming to see her this afternoon that her death wasn't as violent as it was.

Final touches now, Sal.

I do one last inspection of the body to make sure I've not missed anything.

So, on the way back to the caravan, Mam and Dad relied on each other's weight to stagger along the promenade to our driveway. The tanned man we were renting it off was still up in his living room, reading a book with a glass of whisky for company through the window. I hardly slept a wink that night. Not 'cause I was on a rock-hard couch, or 'cause Mam and Dad were shaking the caravan going at it hammer and tongs. I just couldn't get Anabelle out of my head.

I wondered if girls would always be that difficult to win over, whether they'd always be a puzzle I'd need to bend arse over tit to solve. If it meant getting this buzz by the end of it though, I was willing to buy a ton of Mars bars and not even take a nibble.

I played with my key ring, making vroom vroom noises and driving it over the back of the sofa. The red paint job was already fading from being handled. I swear it had a scent of cherries just like her. I made it my mission to go back to the arcades tomorrow and try and win her a teddy from the claw machine. I vowed never to return home until I did it. I even dug round the back of the sofa and found two pound coins coated in a film of fluff. I'd present the teddy to her tomorrow night by the vending machine while Barry's banging out another hit. I'd kiss her cheek delicately like she did to me.

I always hear about love in films and those cheesy pop songs. It's all they seem to go on about, ay Sal? I lay there, staring at the rain trickling through the cracked roof, assuming this is what love was. I spent pretty much the whole holiday in that arcade. I must have won about four teddies and never seen Anabelle again. I wasn't too fussed, though. I didn't know it then, but I know now my new-found love wasn't for her. It was for gambling. How about that, ay?

I wheel back the stool and take a look. I think she's done. It's the best I can do. An impressive job to be fair, especially for the first body on a Monday. I look down on her, thinking how unfortunate it is to be on a nice stroll in the Northern countryside, feeling the wind in your hair, looking out at the green hills, then suddenly being hit with the end of your life. Is there such thing as a good way to go? I dunno. I just hope she didn't feel anything on the way down. She looks like a nice enough woman, and she's a cracking listener.

I agree, Sal, you look stunning.

As much as I want to be compassionate and take a moment for each body that comes in here, I simply don't have the time. It's more important not to get connected. Emotional distance is a must. You need a hard stomach and a cold view towards it all, otherwise it's the wrong job for you. That's why, looking down at Sally, I'm heartless enough to still be thinking of myself, my problems, my gambling.

I check my phone and I've lost hundreds more. I growl out loud, frustrated.

Speaking to Sally made me realise how it might have started, but it didn't solve any of my issues. If I learnt one thing, it's what Dad said was right: sometimes you have to play dirty. So, unfortunately, that's what I'm going to have to do.

6

The next morning, I pick Umar up from the local Baptist church. Hauling him into the back of my Transit in the car park. Even dead, he has an intimidating aura about him, covering the entire width of the bed with his bulky shoulders. He's fresh, he doesn't need filling up. Heart attack yesterday morning. Cheeks still puffed, eyelids bulging. I almost expect him to feel warm as I wire his jaw and glue his lips.

I'm distracted, not fully concentrating. I'm rough taking his rings off, his gold Rolex, his heavy encrusted necklace. The tray moves as I clatter them down. I get annoyed sifting through the drawers because I can't find the right make-up to match his skin tone. There's dozens of options, and the wrong shade just doesn't sit right with me. I have to take breathers, make a brew, nip out for cigs. You can't be agitated doing this job. Every body should be treated with the same care and precision. All problems need to be left outside the embalming room. Let them linger in the bookies, the boozer, at home – as long as they're not in here.

As it worked with Sally, I think about talking to relax and get things off my chest. How many conversations can you have where you won't be judged or talked back to? I fill a tub of warm water and soak a towel before wringing out the excess moisture. I roll my swivel stool in close. Bathing Umar's shoulders and furry chest up close, he reminds me of Mike Tyson and the boxers of old that Dad used to watch on the telly, supping on his Carling.

Dad's head would weave with them. He'd jab the air of the

living room. I'd enjoy watching him, the anticipation and anxiety on his face, knowing now he probably had a few quid on a third-round knockout. Years later, I'd end up doing the same while Becca laughed at me tiptoeing round the coffee table as if it was me on the canvas. One bet was triple the amount it cost for the pay-per-view to watch the fuckin' thing. And it wasn't cheap. She thought I loved boxing, grew up with watching Hatton, Pacquiao, Mayweather. Just another hobby inherited from my family. I did love it, if I had money on it. I couldn't give a fuck if I didn't.

As I grew older, like with the horse racing, Dad would start letting me in on his bets. Again, that subconscious desperation to form the family's next-generation gambler. He'd allow me to have a quid on which round the stoppage would be in. *A bit of fun*, he said. A harmless bet. Something we could watch together, bond over, oblivious to the larger impact of it all.

Even after Mum fucked him off, you'd think he would steer me away from gambling with it being the reason why his marriage collapsed. It was the opposite. It only cemented how invisible addiction can seem, even to the person suffering from it. He'd use gambling as our main way to reconnect, to continue our bond. I'd watch horse racing with him on Saturdays, followed by the football, followed by whatever boxing was on. Nearly twenty-four hours of bets, week after week. Still, it was always only just *a bit of fun*.

To this day, I still bet on Dad's favourite horses, the jockey colours he liked, any names with Ray in. Would he like me doing that? Was that what he wanted? Or did he realise what I inherited might be damaging? It's all ifs and buts really. I realise I'm getting distracted from Umar.

I question whether he was ever a boxer. A security guard maybe? Had to give up the ring due to a weak knuckle which kept dislocating. A friendly giant. A man dedicated to his family. Good morals. Tried his best to give his family a head-start in life. Taught them about the world, what troubles they might come across when they're older. Walked them to primary school every day. Drove them to and from house parties in high school. Cried at their graduation. Welcomed them round for dinner every Sunday when they settled with their family elsewhere.

I imagine Umar's funeral will be packed. People will travel high and low from all over the country to say goodbye. His teachers, church-goers, school friends he hasn't spoken to for decades. Unlike Dad, he's left a legacy to be proud of. One of respect and joy. They will smile and sing at his funeral, not shake their heads at what could have been. And afterwards, they'll share memories of what he meant to them.

All this reminiscing gets me talking to him about how it all started. Trying to understand how, after Blackpool, gambling slowly took over my life and led me on a path so dissimilar to Umar's.

Right Umar, we might as well have a chinwag while I get you washed. I'll let you into a little story. It must have been about 2005, I think, when it all properly started. I was meant to be in maths class when I placed my first bet.

'Come on, don't be a pussy. Let's go for it.'

That was Reece – cock of the school, shit-hot footy player and, whether it was my choice or not, my closest mate. He was leaning against a brick wall at break time. Tie halfway down his shirt, blazer sleeves rolled up like he's fuckin' James Dean.

'Yeh, come on, Fletch. Don't shit out on us,' said Pinky. *He was our favourite chubster and made up the trio. He got the name from being kecked in PE once and having his tiny little todger flashed. Proper button mushroom. His fleshy face always bright as the colour of a pig's arse as well, so Pinky it is.*

'I'm not shitting it, man. Just if me mam finds out, I'm fucked.'

The little shits of our year were running around giving each other dead arms or gossiping about the latest nude picture going round. One of Paige playing with a can of Lynx.

I dip the towel, wring it, and start on his legs. They're covered in a sea of black hairs. They all move as one, as a flock of birds would, whichever way I rub the towel. I imagine them dancing around a boxing ring, shiny blue shorts baggy above the knees.

Me, Reece and Pinky were in the far corner near the concrete footy pitch. Had a view from all angles there. The teachers on duty never wandered that far; they preferred to patrol near the entrance of the building to stop us floating in and out. Mr Griffiths, who had an elbow-patched blazer and peroxide hair, stood by the door like a hawk. He's the one you had to look out for. Ran the isolation room. Got caught with dildos in his desk drawer once but was still allowed back the following summer. That's how powerful he was, Umar – the big cheese.

'She's not gonna find out, is she?' said Reece. He had this habit of running his fingers through his spikes. 'We'll be like a half hour, if that. Easy. We'll just jump the gates when they call us in. It's only maths we've got as well. That gormless cow wouldn't even notice if the classroom was empty.'

'I dunno, man,' I said.

I remember me mam had been on to me recently. I'd been caught a few times for pestering a few kids. Nothing too dodgy – I wasn't like Reece, who smashed beaks off lockers and slapped the arse of every lass that walked past. Nah, I only dished out a few verbals. A dead arm or two. Was just unlucky to pick on a couple of criers, the ones that run to Head of Year acting like they've had a gun pulled on 'em. Anyway, Mam heard of my warning from school through one of the other mums in the club and went apeshit. Called me a waste of space and said that if I didn't get my act together, I'd be out the fuckin' door.

'You're coming, man. Whether you like it or not.'

Reece gave me a look that wasn't menacing. It didn't need to be. It was almost a smirk. He knew I loved the crack and that I was a shithouse with these sorts of things. All I needed was a nudge, 'cause what's the worst that can happen? That was Reece. He was *a bellend, but he could read people better than some dipshits could read their own name.*

'Fuck's sake ... Right, what's the plan?' I said.

Reece and Pinky looked at each other all buzzing and that before ruffling my hair. Annoying – I'd just gelled the fucker in the bogs.

Soon as the bell rang and a swarm of students darted towards the building entrance, we pegged it the other way while Griffiths wasn't looking, our bulky Kickers hammering along the concrete. Pinky was lagging behind, but I had a fistful of his blazer. He had no choice but to keep up. He was a big lad like you – it didn't half take some doing.

We mounted the loaded dustbins around the corner and out of sight of the teachers. Bin bags full of mouldy fruit and hard milk spilled out all over the floor. Me and Reece each pushing on Pinky's arse cheeks to launch him over the fence. He fell over the other side with the grace of a wrecking ball. Reece was up and over like he's fuckin' Spider-Man, even doing a pirouette on the way down, the flashy bastard. I couldn't help but keep looking behind me, thinking Griffiths was gonna snatch my collar at the last second like they do in the films. All clear though. They probably wouldn't give a fuck anyway. It was more hassle having us in class.

I wheel around to Umar's other leg and do the same. Making patterns out of his leg hairs to keep myself amused. I'm tempted to check my phone on the side. It's pinged a couple of times. A distinctive sound only belonging to the betting apps. Bets finishing. Winning. Losing. Am I richer than I was half an hour ago, or poorer? Just in the time it takes washing one leg, I could have won or lost hundreds of pounds. Today I'm more nervous because, after yesterday, I'm thousands of pounds in the red now. I need to start clawing it back sooner or later. Any further is a long way back to recover from.

I resist, delaying the truth, and carry on.

Once we're over the mesh fence, we darted it through the grass.

Heads low in the weeds like we're Special Forces or some shit. It wasn't long until we were home and dry, lost in a maze of trees. Rows of thick bark and hefty bushes you couldn't even spot Pinky in. That's why all the couples came for a fiddle round there after school. Going full pelt at it up against a rough trunk. No chance you'd get spotted. It became that much of a popular spot, you could come for a gander for the shits and giggles and not get caught. Reece came every Wednesday to see who's romping, hiding in a bush having a little peak. Even brought popcorn one time, the fuckin' loon.

I bet you've had a fiddle in them woods once or twice, haven't you Umar? Throwing a jab or two.

. . .

Thought so.

Anyway, we only stopped running when we reached Ashton Old Road. I was blowing out my arse but not as much as Pinky, sweating like a— Well, a fat-arse that's just sprinted through the woods. Not a bead of sweat on Reece's freckled head. Looked like he just got out the shower, the bastard. Always does.

Speaking of showers, I start cleaning the base of Umar's feet and between the toes. His nails are yellowed, with sock fluff stuffed in the crevices. I stop cleaning to give the nails a clip because they were just staring me in the face. One nail flies off the big toe and lands in my brew on the trolley. I ignore it. It was cold anyway.

Back to cleaning.

'Right dickheads, I know where we can head,' said Reece.

I didn't know there was a plan. That we were actually gonna use our time. I thought the buzz was fooling the teachers, the fact we were out and about and they didn't know anything about it. I was expecting to saunter about by the offy, maybe scran a pack of Space Raiders, kicking stones about. Even Pinky had an expression that said he hadn't thought this far. Worrying shit when you're with an oddjob like Reece.

'What you thinkin'?' I asked, not really prepared for the answer. He was right. I was a full-on shithouse.

'Me dad took me in the bookies last week,' said Reece. 'Mate, it was fuckin' mint. The lady knows me in there. We'll be sweet.'

'Bookies?' said Pinky. 'Like where all them smelly geezers go to blow their wages?'

'Ya know what a fuckin' bookies is, Pinky, Jesus man. But yeh, it'll be fun. I've got a few coins on me from shaking this Year Seven upside down this morning. We could be rolling in it in a few minutes.'

'I dunno, man,' I said.

'Pull ya fuckin' thong out, ya nonce. Only a few quid on the roulette machine. Not tanning ya mam's mortgage or owt like that.'

I travel down to Umar's arms. I lift one to get under the pits, his wrist resting limp on my shoulder. A bush emerges from underneath. I imagine a whole different species, a whole different life-form living in there. I'm tempted to sift through, see what I can find, but crack on with scrubbing it instead.

My phone pings again. Another bet finishing. I half stand to go over and check, letting Umar's arm drop. An instinct I only know I've followed when I'm stood up, looking over Umar with the towel in my hand. I sit back down, trying to focus. I carry on scrubbing.

Mam could barely pay rent, Umar, never mind dream of a mortgage. Just showed how disconnected Reece was. How not everyone was in the same boat as him. He lived in Beswick, one of the flashy houses outside of Openshaw. Plasma, dishwasher, the full monty. Got dropped off to school in a fuckin' taxi.

'Fuck it, I'm up for it,' said Pinky, like he'd just signed up for seven heavy nights in Benidorm.

'Let's get it over with,' I said.

Reece guided the way, punching lamp posts as he walked past them for no reason at all, only to appear hard. Truth is, Reece never swung a punch in his life, Umar. Not in school anyway. He had the confidence to scare people off. Simple as that.

The streets were pretty dead at 2 p.m. No crowds outside the pub like there usually was. Only the odd wino swaying in the doorway, puffing on a fag that's been burnt down to the filter. We passed charity shops, kebab houses and about a billion corner shops that weren't on a corner at all. You know how it is round here. Pretty much all of them had a window caved in. Big faded lottery posters on the doors and luminous star-shaped stickers offering discount booze. We booted a few stray plastic bags and empty takeaway boxes before we realised we were outside the bookies.

It was the first time I came across Jim Ramsbottom's. I didn't have a clue who this geezer was. If he lived round here. I thought Mam probably knew him. She'd probably nailed him. Fuck knows. I used to hear a different fucker every night through those paper walls. I'm probably his son. Anyway, Jimmy's, we'll call it, sat between a bakery called Westwell's and me mam's favourite pub, the Rag. Westwell's offered a steak pie that'd have you drooling more than a British bulldog. The Rag, which you've probably been in yourself at least once, was a staple of Openshaw, a guaranteed belter of a night out and home of my first ever pint. A fuckin' chapel of the community, wasn't it? Walk in there sober, crawl out wankered, and you've only spent a tenner.

'Here we are, boys.'

Reece had the coins out in his palm already. He sauntered into Jimmy's like he was gonna buy the place.

I move round to the other arm, where the forest is just as dense. The phone is just there. It would literally take a second to check. No. There's more important things to do.

So, Reece said: 'Don't worry, Izzy love. They're with me.'

The lass behind the plastic screen didn't even bother to look up. She was blowing a bubble of chewing gum. It was 2 p.m., for fuck's sake. Do what you fuckin' want in a bookies.

'Right, lads,' said Reece, prancing over to the roulette machines. 'Give us a number.'

Me and Pinky looked at each other. I instantly thought of two, cause that's how many chins I was looking at.

'Two,' I said.

'Two it is,' said Reece, licking his lips and clunking a pound coin into the slot.

'What do you do then?' I asked.

The lights and sounds were mesmerising. It was like a couple of years back, the first time Dad brought home a decent TV before Mam fucked him off for fiddling and gambling. Even the telly was won on the gee-gees, he told me in secret. Big juicy colours on the screen. It was like the pictures. But in our FUCKIN' HOUSE. Mad it was. I watched it for hours on end. Mam had to peel me away for a bath. I'd watch fuckin' anything. Top of the Pops. Catchphrase. Deal or No Deal. *I couldn't give a toss. I was in dreamland.*

Honest though, this was better. Reece pounded on the screen, lumping the money on two. He slotted in a couple of more coins and loaded on some back-ups. Twenty-four. Eighteen. An excitement tingled my limbs like the first time Annabelle laid one on me in Blackpool. I thought I could walk out a millionaire. I'd never felt a buzz like it.

'Do the honours, Fletch.'

Reece pointed to a button that I pounded with the hope of a virgin at prom. The roulette span. Pure magic. Where would the ball land? It whirled around, my eyes flicking between the numbers, trying to predict where it could end up. And guess what? Go on. Guess? Honest, go on. What did it land on? Yeh. You fuckin' guessed it.

Two, baby.

The screen screamed with light. The sound of money tingled through my bones, and I'm not talking pennies here, Umar, I'm talkin' real fuckin' money. Soon-to-be physical cash. It was the first time I noticed I was richer than I was five minutes ago.

I smelt the sweat and clammy skin of Pinky and Reece as we hugged and jumped in circles. School ties dancing up and down and over our shoulders. The old geezers snorted at us from across the bookies, fumin' some little dweebs were interrupting their studying. We didn't give a toss. We were quids-in on the first try. Beginner's luck. Grooving about like we'd won the lottery. It felt fuckin' amazing. God knows how much Reece slotted in, but we were up a hundred dabs. Unheard of for some spotty teens who should be finding out what Pythagoras means. It was the biggest thing I'd ever won in my life.

Now, onto the neck, stroking his protruding Adam's apple gently with the towel. It's huge, like his neck's pregnant.

The phone pings again. A win. Did that sound like a win?

'Cash out. Cash out,' Pinky said. 'Let's go try and get some pints in at the Rag.'

'We could get a snazzy pair of kicks each for this,' said Reece, rubbing his hands together.

Our imaginations were barmy with possibilities.

'Fuck that. Let's keep it rolling,' I said.

They both looked at me like I'd shat in their shoe. Yeh, just like that, Umar.

Umar's staring up at the ceiling in disbelief, waiting for his eye caps to be put in.

'What?' I said.

'You mad?' said Reece. 'We've won.'

'Yeh, but imagine if it was double. You could get two pairs of shoes.'

Reece and Pinky looked at each other. Reece loved his kicks, I knew his sweet spot as much as he knew mine. Not in a lovey-dovey way or owt. Truth is, them two had already spent the money. In my head, we hadn't even won it yet.

'You're joking, aren't ya? That's some decent bread,' said Pinky. He'd already spent his at Abra Kebabra down the road.

'Who's the pussy now?' I said.

This was way better than maths. Mate, this was maths. But when do you ever have the chance to win some serious coin listening to some shite about algebra and angles?

'We doing it or what?' I asked. 'We came in with fuck all, didn't we?'

'You did,' said Reece. 'I've just spent tomorrow's dinner money and got a shedload back.'

'Mate, you could be on Maccies every day for two months,' I said.

I couldn't tell ya what came over me, Umar. I couldn't. I was grateful to get two Yorkshire puddings on my plate rather than one. That was a win for me. But money? It was never an object for us. Even when my dad was around. It was never there, and even now, looking at this screen with the total we won, it wasn't in my hand in physical form, so it didn't exist. Even if we did double it, it still wouldn't matter. We could double that.

While Reece and Pinky were looking at each other worried, dithering, I threw in an extra pound coin and pressed the 'Bet' button to send the roulette scrolling. I lost it all in a matter of seconds. That's probably when my addiction solidified into who I would become.

One minute, Umar.

I place the towel back in the bowl, where black hairs begin to float. I sit upright to rest my back for a second. Thirty seconds pass where I listen to the formaldehyde rotate in the machine. My eyes stare at the phone, burning from the fluorescent lights. Sweat begins to soak through onto my white coat.

I think if I've lost every bet I've put on today, I don't know if I'll have any left to bet again with. What do I do then? Where's my way out? The answer is there, waiting on my phone. The bets are over, but I'm too scared to look.

I twist the towel and continue, burying the thought deeper than any body that's come through this room.

Where was I? Oh yeh. So, although I placed my first bet at Jim Ramsbottom's on that mingin' day that saw me get suspended for three days (Mam found out, mate, of course she did), it wasn't my first introduction to gambling. 'Proper' gambling, not the kiddie arcades, ran through our family like blood through a vein. It was our bread and butter. You were raised around it. Taught from an early age what it was, what it meant and the possibilities that came with it. It wasn't really a gold mine waiting to be won in our family; none of us could have really given a toss about the money. It was all about the enjoyment, the camaraderie, those nearly moments in family history, like when Uncle Mark was one off a placepot to win him thirty grand. We were all gutted, of course we were, but the laughs we've had with the story since have lasted way longer than the money would have. Betting just made us feel alive (no offence).

From as long as I can remember, horse racing was religion in my gran's house. It was where I spent every Saturday. We'd all congregate there early in the morning – 'we' being Dad, Uncle Mark, Uncle Lee, me, Grandad and Gran (but she stayed out the way, making us bacon butties) – and got ready for a day on the gee-gees. Being exposed to it from an early age made me excited to grow up, to walk into a bookies and experience the highs and lows my dad and uncles were having. Betting slips would be scrunched and chucked at the flaky walls. Bins were kicked over. Mantelpieces were slammed to the point of cracking. Along with that, fists were punched with joy. Pure fuckin' limbs of triumph when the horse they backed won on the line by a nostril. I had grown men kissing me on the forehead. I'd never seen so many emotions in one day, or seen men brought to the point of tears just over some horses and a tiny Irishman on the back. Every one of us loved it and competed with each other throughout the day. Who was quids in and who was going home skint rather than out to Stanley Street Club at the end of the night? None of them knew how the day was gonna end. And to sit there and watch it, mesmerised by the sweat on their foreheads, was incredible. Fuckin' incredible, pal.

The biggest event of the year in our family wasn't Christmas. Oh, god no, Christmas was overrated. Our Christmas came in March because of the best meeting in the horse-racing calendar – Cheltenham Festival. Uncle Mark would save his Christmas bonus from the lightbulb factory just for this momentous occasion. Bright idea. And Dad would book it off work as soon as he could – the full week – so he had time to study form, or have a recovery period after he'd tanned all his dosh. By the end of the festival, a crater would be in Grandad's seat as if a fuckin' meteorite had hit it. He wouldn't move for the whole week. Head in a newspaper, scanning the listings with his little blue pen, marking out the horses he fancied. Food was brought to him on a plate from Gran. She even brought him a flannel one year so he could clean his pits, bit like I just did with you then, so he didn't have to get up for a bath. You catch my drift, though: it was serious shit. I was brought up to understand this. What meant the most was just being a part of it. I was one of the lads in the family. I wasn't only part of the club, I was born into it.

To say I instantly fell in love with horse-racing gambling would be telling fibs, Umar. I'll be honest, I didn't get it at first. I couldn't understand why Dad was chucking his money on Black Beauty and not buying me a toy race car instead. Why did I have to stay in and listen to a bunch of confusing Irishmen babble on about trainers, paddocks, and odds, when I could be outside practising my David Beckham technique? It took a few years. It was an education I didn't know I was having. Dad made me watch it, drink in the colours, the atmosphere. I thought he was a twat because of it, making me watch it. I thought it was a form of punishment I didn't understand. Really, it was how much it meant to him for me to grow up and carry on the tradition that ran through generations of our family. Even when he and Mum were on the rocks, he would never acknowledge gambling as the road to their downfall. He would blame that on himself. His lack of employment, his lack of wages, his lack of masculine pride to provide for his wife and son. Never the fact that gambling contributed to all of those. Like the horses he was backing, he was blinkered. He wanted to guide me blindly into the darkness he couldn't escape from. And I followed willingly, believing it to be where families were made, not broken up.

There was a line, though. Dad didn't let me place a full bet until I was old enough. Why? Fuck knows. I think it was him making himself feel better by placing rules on the situation, as if an aspect of it was controlled. He knew what a Lucky 15 was when he come out the womb; maybe deep down he knew the risk of it all. He let me pick the odd horse though, an each-way single that meant fuck all in the grand scheme of things. If I picked it based off the name, I'd get an earful: 'That's not what you do. You study son, study. Look here, these numbers under the trainer's name. That's called form, son. Form. Where the horses were placed in its previous races. And this here is the odds of the horse winning. The shorter the number the more chance it has of winning. Comprende?'

He might as well have been speaking Swahili. Who was I to know I'd become fluent one day. That I would understand what all this was about. That I wouldn't give a flying shit about Christmas any more. The one in December anyway.

I look down at Umar and even he looks bored to fuck. He's washed and dried now. I powder his face in silence to give his ears a rest, puffs of dark powder sprinkling towards the overhead light. I wipe the residue caught in his beard and give it a comb. A dab of oil to finish. He's ready to be dressed in the boubou chosen by his wife – a formal, wide-sleeved robe. Umar's is a royal blue with gold details around the neckline, just how I imagined his boxing shorts. Intricate stitching, the silk reflecting like sun on the ocean. He himself looks royal, important. Fitting for the afterworld, fitting for any world, fitting for a world champ.

Not able to wait any longer, I walk over to my phone and unlock it. I've lost every bet I've put on today. Horses pulled up, dogs getting caught in the traps, Korean football matches postponed for waterlogged pitches. It's a fuckin' terrible day at the office. A complete and total disaster.

I chuck my phone in frustration and go to the tray to reapply Umar's jewellery. I find myself stopping, looking down at the gold Rolex and encrusted necklace. Is that diamond? No. Can't be. Even the rings look expensive. One with a glint of blue when the light pings off it. Sapphire maybe? One is definitely solid gold. I juggle the weight of the ring in my palm like I'm Gollum.

I look back at Umar. The sleeves cover his wrists, his calloused hands. The family would never notice. Plus, he's getting cremated. All jewellery has to be removed before they get sizzled. I can say we melted it down and mixed it with the ashes. A token gift. Or that he never came in with them in the first place. Grief plays with the mind. How sure can they be that he definitely had his watch and necklace on? I've prepared him well, we had a good chat, they'll be grateful regardless. I'm the last person they would think of if anything seemed suspicious.

I'm back to thinking about that night in the bookies. Losing a hefty chunk that I couldn't afford to lose. The House Fund jar, collecting dust on the mantelpiece. The tiny threads preventing the truth coming out, the future of me and Rebecca on a knife edge. I can't lose that. I have to take risks to fix this. It's the only way.

I fold the white sheet up to Umar's bearded chin, covering him in all his glory until he's ready to be presented tomorrow. He smells sanitised, clean. I thank him for listening to me, for his time and patience. I thank him most for the gifts jangling in the pocket of my white coat as I leave the room. Clanging like the bell to end the round.

7

Down Ashton Old Road, about five minutes from the directory, there's a Cash Converters. Yellow sign bleached and faded. Rust creeping into the window frames. Chipped mobile phones and worn guitars with missing strings behind grubby panes of glass. It's a museum of discount shite, but a fuckin' godsend whenever you need some quick dosh.

I speed in, the bell clinking above the door as I enter. A bone-thin girl in her late teens is stood behind the counter chewing gum. Black pigtails, winged eyeliner. Too many piercings to count.

'Hiya love, just wondering what I could get for these?'

I place the watch, necklace and blue-glinted ring on the countertop. I make sure to turn my back to the camera in the top right corner of the room. Only the back of my ginger barnet in view.

Heidi, from her name badge, couldn't look more uninterested. She picks each item up to check the weight, fiddling with them, twiddling each underneath the light of a lamp on the counter. She chews like a hungry dog, getting her spearmint breath all over my valuables.

'Where you get 'em?' she asks.

'Inherited,' I say, almost too quickly. 'My grandad passed recently. Found them in his loft. Used to be a blingy fucker, apparently.'

I laugh, thinking she'd join in. She continues to chew and inspect, emotionless.

'I can give you three hundred for the three.'

Her eyes are half shut when she speaks to me. The *Buffy the*

Vampire Slayer T-shirt is off-putting. Am I really going to have to haggle with a bloody child?

'Come on, now,' I say. 'This is decent stuff. Have you felt the weight?'

'Could be lead for all I know.'

Unbelievable. If I wasn't desperate for cash, I would have told her to do one and walk back out with the goods.

'Six hundred,' I say. 'You know they're legit.'

She huffs, staring at the jewellery as if they're going to tell her the truth, whether they're real or not, how much they're actually worth. I can't imagine many people walking into a Cash Converters in Openshaw, dumping a gold Rolex on the counter. This deal she can't push too far. The ball's in my court.

'The Rolex is fake, for one,' she says. 'That much I do know.'

Surely she's having me on.

'First of all, the crown on the side of the wheel here. See how it's smooth. All Rolex's have a three-dimensional design to them, some sort of ridge or definition. A smooth crown is an immediate red flag. Second, here . . . ' She holds the watch up to my ear. 'What can you hear?'

I squint at her, focusing, trying to read her game.

'Just ticking. Why?'

'Exactly,' she says. 'The second hand on a Rolex is near enough silent. It should glide around the clock face without any pauses. It shouldn't stutter at all – this one's got fuckin' Tourette's.'

She places the watch back on the counter and folds her arms. Still chewing.

'Right. Fair enough. Five hundred then.' I say.

'Four hundred.'

'Four fifty.'

'Four hundred.'

'Fuck it, deal,' I say.

We don't shake hands; it's not that sort of transaction. She probably thinks I'm going to use it for drugs or prostitutes; she knows the deal round here. Heidi gets the cash out the till and counts it carefully on the counter. The sound of the notes makes my balls tingle. Note after note, flapping and layering into a nice pile. Four hundred smackers. Just like that. I sign some paperwork without reading it and get out of there quick-time.

 I go straight to Jim Ramsbottom's across the road. After two hours, I've blown the lot and come out with a tenner, and that's only 'cause I need a pint to drown my guilt.

8

On the corner of Stanley Street used to be a small butcher's shop that could only hold three people at a time. Queues would snake along the pavement on Saturday mornings, whispers of gossip bouncing between the old ladies down the line. Dave would wave and blow kisses at the women waiting through the window, the other hand holding a huge gammon joint or working the bacon slicer.

Dave the Butcher was trim, olive-skinned and had a Hollywood charm to him. His eyebrows were a bushy, chocolate brown and his teeth paper-white. He was never without his white mesh trilby and blue-striped apron. A charismatic, flirtatious fella. The type you wouldn't associate with such a gory job. He'd flash those teeth and ask you how the missus is while hacking the head off a chicken or smearing blood on his apron. His lack of concentration cost him a finger once. Apparently even then, he wrapped his squirting hand in a tea towel and chucked his finger in the freezer, all with a smirk on his face, asking whether it was six sausages or eight the customer wanted.

Openshaw loved Dave, and Dave loved Openshaw. I knew he was ill, but not near-the-edge kind of ill. When I park up by his home on Ryan Street in the Transit, he's tucked up in the bed the carers brought from upstairs into the front room. He had a form of cancer, not sure which one. It ate away at him, I can tell in his face as I look down at the bed in the deep gloom of his home. The attractive, glossy sheen all gone. His teeth have the black outline of a cartoon. He looks slaughtered himself. Dead meat, the fatty trimmings left over from a once gorgeous beast, roaming the streets of Openshaw doing whatever the fuck he wanted.

Dave died alone. No wife, no kids, parents already dead. The house is quieter than any cemetery I've walked through. It makes me sad that. That's no way to go. An examiner who came and confirmed the death handed me a cardboard box of his belongings to be burnt along with the body. This often happens. We burn everything we can as long as its combustible.

Inside the box is a wallet, his mesh trilby, CDs from his favourite bands, his mum's pearl necklace, a leather jacket and a signed Man United shirt from Bobby Charlton. I place the box on the passenger seat and strap it in with the seatbelt before getting the gurney out the back. This rickety fucking stretcher with a dodgy wheel and loose straps will have you thinking the body's gonna fall out, splat, head first on a kerb while the family are watching.

It's hard moving a body on your own. Thank Jesus the carer helped me lift him on and wrap him in a white sheet. She's only young, the woman, around early twenties. Fresh from college. Blonde fringe and innocent glint in her eye. I could tell it was one of her first. She keeps looking at him lying there and is too cautious about touching him or strapping him to the stretcher tightly. I dangle his arm in her face as a joke, trying to break the ice, but I don't think it was appreciated.

I drive back with Dave bumping about in the back of the van, nearly sending his head through the roof as I go over speedbumps. I put one of his Stone Roses CDs on from the cardboard box. Singing him the lyrics, tapping on the steering wheel.

It's a weird one, having Dave here in the embalming room. The best thing I liked about him was he never minced his words, pardon the pun. He told it how it is. If you were too pissed, causing havoc at Stanley Street the night before, he'd fuckin' tell ya and charge you full whack for that week's bacon. He had a little book that kept tabs on what everyone owed him, 'cause not everyone can afford their pork chops when their pension or wages are two weeks away. He was kind like that, always helping out where he could.

As I prep my equipment, the same tools I use every day, just like Dave's cleaver, his mincer, I'm transported back to that small butcher's. How he even sold discount booze, fags, condoms and Viagra from a small room behind a magnetic fly screen. Soon enough, lads were joining the queue on Saturday mornings when they had a full fridge of meat at home. Everyone in Openshaw had a reason to visit him, he knew everyone as if they were family. People would queue just for a chat. A wicked sense of humour on him as well. He'd tell every fucker who wasn't getting a shag, who preferred flavoured johnnies, and who went for the extra small ones. He even paid me and the lads from school to release a box of rats through the window of his rival butcher shop one night. Poor fella woke up to no meat and a group of bloated rats smoking cigars on the floor.

I make sure to spend my time with Dave. I tell Janice I can't take any more bodies for the rest of the afternoon. She understands. Janice loved her meat too. When I undress him, I thought he'd left a bratwurst in his pants as one last joke. How wrong I am. Fuck me, is he hung. No wonder that queue of hunnies were stretching back into last week. Packing large is Dave. I have to lift it with metal tongs to wash his thigh. Maybe he wasn't lonely after all.

I know Dave loved a bit of jazz, so I stick the radio on. He always had it bellowing from the back room in the butcher's, shouting conversations over it. The hoot of Miles Davis's trumpet fills the embalming room, washing over us like a cool breeze. I sit on the chair and stroke his hair. It's fair, receded. I comb it from one temple to the other. Give those famous, bristly eyebrows a tidy while I'm at it.

He defo needs the tissue builder. I make the collarbone incision and wire up the tubes. The fluid washes through him and releases blood into the tray, a sight he's so used to seeing. Embalming is like butchery in a way. Caring for the dead, the tenderness and finesse needed to do it properly. Blood, muscle, sinew. Death as a business. The handling of bodies. Seeing his temples rise, his cheeks colour, his chest inflate – it's a Hollywood star reborn. Openshaw's finest.

I massage along with the riffs of the trumpet. I feel the form of the bones under his flesh, his flaccid muscles, mushy and weak. Cracking tan on him still though, and that wasn't the fluid. His skin, hairless and reflective, glows like a candle in a dark room.

I tell him the best stories I heard about him from people round Openshaw. When he chased Brian Scollins down the street with a cleaver for nicking a leg of lamb. When he poisoned half the club by serving dodgy meat at Big Kev's wake. And the best one, when Dave went on holiday and one of the gossipy old ladies started a rumour that he'd been locked up for being a child molester. Apparently, it was some guy called Dave Butcher they read about in the *Manchester Evening News*. Took a few weeks to get his sales back up to full whack but it was funny in the end. I get to his legs and have to stop for laughing. What a man. What a life.

When no relatives or family members are around to decide or pay for what happens to someone, the decision is left up to us. Sometimes if someone from the community I respect arrives on my table, I opt to embalm them anyway for free, preserving them in the hope a distant relative will pop up to decide their future. Selfishly, I tend to give them more hope than random strangers, because I feel it's what they deserve. Their lives are worth more than any embalming service.

Janice is happy for me to make the decision on Dave, seeing as I knew him for longer. What a decision to make though. Is he best buried, alone in the ground for eternity, with no one visiting him above? Or should he be cremated, discarded to ash and chucked into the wind to end up in someone's eye? There's an option Janice isn't aware of. An option I only discovered myself recently after seeing an article online. She wouldn't approve. Not many people would.

The article said how medical schools have a shortage of bodies and tissue for students to experiment on during their courses. Families often donate the bodies of loved ones for medical and practitioner purposes, for the benefit of science or their own bank accounts. Funerals and cremations can be costly, I don't blame them one bit.

I looked deeper into it, into the dark bowels of the web. The sites that have pop-up ads every five seconds and random phone numbers flashing in neon lights. Dodgy as fuck, but what an eye opener. This one medical school spent £70k on tissue imported from America last year. Seventy bastard K! Unrestricted laws in the US allow for the business of what they call 'body brokers' – people who sell body parts and organs to tissue banking companies. The donors give permission to dismember the body and trade the parts for profit. In return, the families won't have to pay the burial costs that don't half strain the purse strings. It makes sense. Pretty controversial though, as you can imagine. eBay for body parts? Who would have thought.

I kept looking. £500 for a frozen head. £200 for a foot. £1,500 for a torso. £300 for a knee. £150 for a hand. Selling one fuckin' body could generate £3,000–£4,000, and that's without the organs, which companies would cough even more up for. If this directory was in America, we'd be sat on a goldmine.

Louis Armstrong's buttery voice leaks from the radio. Dave lies still – washed, dried, embalmed. I try imagining him in sections. The butcher, butchered. Sending limbs to different addresses. Brain, special delivery. Knee, first class.

I could be out of the shit with one body.

***

I realise I'm going slightly mad and shelve Dave in the freezer before I think any more twisted thoughts. I'll leave him there until I decide what to do with him. He's sandwiched vertically between Mabel and Ethan. Cosy and intimate, like bunk beds at a youth hostel.

Outside the front entrance, I join Janice for a fag. The sky's a sheet of acid-wash denim. Big clouds plume from her mouth and spiral towards the ones above.

'Skiving again are ya?' she says.

'Spare shelf in that freezer with your name on it if ya carry on.'

Janice cackles and elbows me in the ribs.

'All all right?' Janice asks.

'Me? Oh yeah, sound. Plodding on, ya know.'

'I meant with Dave, but go on. What's up?'

She turns to face me, ash trickling from her cig onto her black blazer. The wind whips up and sends the trees dancing across the road. A woman walks by with a puppy on the pavement. I watch it piss up a bollard, a yellow stream weaving into the road.

'Nothing. Honest.'

'Bollocks. Is it Rebecca?'

I take a deep drag of smoke.

'It is, isn't it,' says Janice. 'What've you done now?'

'Woah, how do you know it's me?'

'So it's Rebecca. And cause you're a cunt sometimes, that's why. You're a man. It's always the man's fault.'

Janice bats ash off her breast, stomps out her cig, and lights another one.

'It's nowt big. Just a bit skint is all.'

'Don't I pay you enough?' Janice laughs sarcastically, looking me dead on.

'Oh, shit, yeh, it's not that at all. Don't be thinking it's that. It's just, she wants to save and all that, and I'm, I dunno, I just ... it's hard.'

Janice adjusts the glasses on her nose and takes a few seconds to smoke and think. Her nails are a vibrant pink. A bit rogue for her but she can be partial to a pop of colour now and again. Mainly if there's a fella she's met at the bingo, or a priest she wants to flirt with when going over an order of service. Her nails scissor the fag, strangling the butt.

'How long you been fiddling with her now?' she asks.

'Nearly nine years now, I think.'

'I think? Don't sound too interested, Fletch, fuck me. I know it's been a long time, but sounds like you got commitment issues.'

'Aye? Why?'

'Obvious. It's the next big step. Get a house, dog, or whatever you pretentious young fuckwits do nowadays to start a life. She wants to settle down, and who can blame her after nine fuckin' years. It's scaring the fuck out of you.'

'It's money though. I'm not arsed about that. We just don't have the money.'

'Why? You have a decent job, she works at that posh fashion shop still, doesn't she? H&M is it?'

'Selfridges.'

'Well, whatever. Where's the money going?'

I stomp out my cig and blow the last smoke from my nostrils. A spot of rain hits my forehead, the sound gradually picking up as it bounces off the windscreens of cars parked across the road. I stare ahead, looking up at the sky like people do when rain's expected. A cop-out to try and change the subject because they have nothing better to speak about.

'Jamie, don't be fuckin' with me. Where's the money going?'

I look at Janice and her gaze hasn't moved. My eyes are being burrowed into. I feel like that cigarette, strangled in her grasp and getting the life sucked out of me until I tell her the truth.

'I owe some money, that's all. To a guy called Jim Ramsbottom.'

'What you mean? The bookies down the road?'

I nod, my head going fuzzy from saying the truth for once.

'I bet on you finding a new fella,' I say. 'Lost the fuckin' lot.'

'Don't joke your way out of this, Jamie. It's serious.'

I snigger at the gravel, sending her a look telling her not to worry. If I can manage a smile, I'm okay.

'I've got a lot of bodies to prep,' I say. 'I'll catch you later.'

I dart off, leaving Janice in the rain. I enter the freezer again to get my next body. I can't get past seeing Dave there, in limbo, nowhere to go. He's been alone for too long now. It's time to put him out of his misery.

I fetch a bed and haul him down from the shelf. I wheel him into the cremation room, hoping to get this done swift so it isn't on my mind any more. The cremation room is already hot from the bodies that day. We start the day with the people who have more body fat, the bloated-belly lard-arses done in from the booze or too many takeaways. The end of the day is reserved for the old ladies or people stick-thin, like Dave. They don't take long at all, around two hours compared to the four-hour heifers.

I shimmy Dave into the oven like a frozen pizza. He goes in head first, lighting like a gooden. With time to kill, I sit down and get the betting apps up on my phone. I place random bets on Bangladeshi cricket, the World Cup of Pool, semi-pro basketball. Fuck all meaningful is happening in the sporting world at this time of the afternoon. Still, there's always something to bet on, money to be won. By the time Dave's a pile of ash and brittle bones, I'm even further in debt. It crosses my mind to get in there with him, roast my problems into a grey heap. The fire going for hours from the betting slips in my pockets.

I open the machine's gaping mouth to check on him, heat from the roaring flames sending my hair walkabout. I shut the door and sit there for a bit longer while he finishes off, listening to the rumbling of the machine. I will never see Dave again, not in his full charming form anyway. He's gone for good. His body evaporating, melting, dismembering as I look on. I decide, later on, I'll rake up the ash and drive to the boarded-up butcher's shop. I'll sprinkle him outside on the pavement, leaving a trail all the way down the street where the queue would stretch on Saturday mornings.

I'll then drive to the Cash Converters at the opposite end of Manchester, rather than the Openshaw one. I'll show them the Bobby Charlton shirt and his mum's pearl necklace, getting whatever money I can to add to the £120 I've already nabbed from his wallet. I'll go to the bookies and try again. And I'll keep trying until I'm out of this mess. My luck can't keep going like this for ever. There'll be a turning point, there'll be a moment that changes everything. I just have to be patient. It'll come.

It's all Dave ever wanted. For his customers to be happy, for them to live a good life, to have fun. Well, imagine this as my thank you to Dave, fulfilling what he always wanted. If it would be anyone, it would be Dave to put the 'fun' in 'funeral'.

***

I get £320 for the shirt and pearls. I probably could have got more but I'll take what I can get. I spend an hour in the bookies, coming out even and heading back to the directory to check whether there were any latecomers Janice needed me to prep for tomorrow.

She's in her office. I knock before entering. Janice is sat behind a flimsy brown desk, spotlighted in the dark by her desk lamp. She's hunched over a spread of papers, signing death certificates probably. Stacks of cardboard boxes pile high against every wall. Records of everyone who's passed through here, documentation of death and unclaimed belongings from over the years.

'Thought you were done for the day?' she says, looking over thick-rimmed glasses.

'No newcomers then?'

'Another retirement home jobby. Man, late eighties. He can wait though. Will be days until he starts to stink.'

'You sure?'

'Yeh, no bother, he's in good nick. You look fucked anyway. Go get some rest.'

A couple of flies start to circle the lamp. Janice swats them away with her pink nails.

'I'll live,' I say.

'I'd give you a break if I could, it's just—'

'Don't worry, Jan, honest. We're snowed under at the minute. You can't do it on your tod.'

Janice smiles as much as is possible for her. It's as if, already, she's had her jaw wired and lips glued.

'I'm making a brew if you want one?' she says.

'I'm all right actually. Gonna head.'

'Not to the bookies I hope.'

'No, don't worry,' I say.

She stands from her creaky chair and waddles around the desk, patting me on the back on the way out.

Before following, I spot something on the paperwork splayed across her desk. I look behind me, hear Janice filling up the kettle, and quickly scuttle behind the desk to get a closer look. On the header of a couple of pages is the Eternal Funeralcare logo – our greatest enemy. Eternal monopolised the death industry, the masters of rinsing mourners for their money and the main reason why everything to do with death is so expensive in the UK nowadays. Independent funeral directors like ours have no choice but to follow suit in regards to expanding the services we offer and increasing our prices. Things like the quality of caskets, funeral packages with added extras, the speed and efficiency in which people can be cremated and returned to their families. We have to work our bollocks off to keep up. Why the fuck would Janice want anything to do with them?

I take a closer look, keeping an eye on the door. The sound of the kettle's in full roar. The tinker of a teaspoon against a mug. I read as quick as I can, scanning over Janice's name, information about our directory, a list of options and figures.

They're trying to buy us out. Of course they are. That's what Eternal do. They want full control over as many directories in as many cities as possible, even little run-down shacks like ours. Everything I hate about them I learnt from Janice. It's baffling to see this on her desk, a black biro lying against the paper where she hasn't signed yet.

I hear the shuffle of her shoes in the distance and rush to the doorway. I emerge from the dark office, nearly headbutting Janice on her way back in. Tea spills over the lip of her mug onto the laminate.

'Jesus fuckin' Christ.' She slaps me hard in the stomach. 'I thought you'd already left. Could have had me in a fuckin' urn you twat.'

'Sorry.' I chuckle. 'Just checking the paperwork on that fella that's just come in. Heading off now.'

'Go on. Get out. Leave me in peace.'

Janice vanishes into the abyss of her office and shuts the door. I hope by the time I return tomorrow, that contract still isn't signed and I still have a job. If not, I'll really be in the shit.

9

'They do me fuckin' nut in, honestly Fletch,' says Joan.

I'm at the club, where Linda's pouring Joan a bitter behind the bar. She's ranting through those teeth that could chomp through a breeze block.

'Oh aye, not enjoying the new job then Joan?' I ask.

'Hate it. The hours are all right and that. It's just the dickheads I have to serve. Always pissin' moaning.'

'That's no good, is it?'

'It's all right Fletch. If they get on my nerves, I tell 'em to fuck off. None of them like me so I cut the shit, do me work, then go home.'

'Right. That's three eighty, love,' says Linda.

The cream wobbles on the pint as Linda places it down. Joan hands over coins with quivering fingers and takes her dinner-lady apron off the bar to go and sit down by the jukebox.

It's a quiet night in Stanley Street. The usuals are in still. A night of nattering and putting the world to rights. Big Mike and Tony are by the back wall, supping stouts. Tony's on the phone to his wife, blagging that his car's broken down on the way home from work and he won't be home until late. The imaginary valve's gone apparently. Big Mike's looking at him like he's a jammy get. 'Anyway, darling,' I hear Tony say into the receiver, 'sorry I can't make it. Wish your mam a happy birthday from me will ya. All right. Yeh, will do. See ya later, love.' He hangs up and flags Linda down for two more pints.

Mavis and Doreen are in the far corner. Almost identical they are. Rollers leaving tight grey curls on their little heads. Huge circular glasses with fishbowl lenses balanced on their ruby noses. Mavis has a flowery number on that she always wears for bingo. Doreen's rocking a blue knitted cardy. They sip on their shandies and cackle between the gossip.

'Ayy our Jim's got a new floosy,' says Mavis. Jim's her son, serial casino gambler who can't keep a bird longer than he can keep in a piss.

'Ohh that's big news innit,' says Doreen.

'Don't get too excited. Right sarky bitch she is. Brought her round for a bacon butty on Sunday and she's there complimenting me wallpaper with a smirk on her gob. Apparently, she used to be married but he snuffed it. Fit as a fiddle he was, then one day, kaput. Found him dead in the front garden pulling weeds.'

'You're joking!' says Doreen, 'They had a front garden?!'

'Yeh. Left her a house up near Beswick.'

'How many bedrooms?'

'Three, our Jim says.'

'Blimey!'

I sit on a stool by the bar and check my phone to see if Becca has text me back (after a few cheeky bets on the apps of course). I've been in the doghouse for about a week now because of snooker night. The silent treatment. Cooking me own microwave teas. Watching *Corrie* in silence. No football. Lying in bed with our backs to each other, scared to even fart and break the tension. Believe me, I grovelled, apologised. I even pulled a few flowers from the rose bush in Openshaw Cemetery and left them in a vase in the middle of the coffee table. They're on the windowsill now, behind a stack of bills and takeaway menus.

I sent her a long message before coming on shift. Harping on about how sorry I am. That I'll try better to let her know when I'm coming home, that I won't even come home so late and steaming any more. I make a point of the alcohol to steer clear of anything that could link back to the gambling. Drink always seems a more common, more understandable, more Openshaw way of dealing with things. It's a much more simple explanation than gambling. I couldn't even explain it to myself if I tried, never mind Becca. She probably doesn't even care about the reason anyway. Becca likes to see me work for it, graft, win her back. It's what she deserves, I guess. Can't grumble with that. She knows I always come crawling back. She knows how much I need her.

My phone pings with a text after Tony comes over to collect his two Guinnesses from the bar.

Forgiven. Takeaway tonight? You're paying x

I gulp for my bank account, taking more hits than a shit boxer. The fact the air's cleared overshadows that by a mile though. The fuckin' relief, honestly.

'All right, Jamie lad!'

I hear the change rattling in his pocket before I see him. Shaky Derek appears from behind the optics while I'm polishing off my Guinness. Rarer than unicorn shit to see him down on a Wednesday. Shaky owns the club and lives upstairs, where he watches back-to-back episodes of *Only Fools* over cans of Boddingtons.

'Ayy up Derek. Everything all right?'

'Yeh good mate. Heard you were in. Just come to see how y'are.'

Shaky has fluffy black sideburns and arthritic knees, meaning he gets Elvis jokes from all angles. Hence the name, Shaky. Another top fella, the best of the best. Really took me under his wing as a youngen and lent me money here and there to tide me over with my gambling debts (or rent issues to him). He's old and big, body like a boulder with those trademark off-white shirts on the brink of popping buttons. I often imagine his wife, Mandy, helping him in the mornings, kneeling on him while she fastens the buttons like zipping up an overflowing suitcase. Tonight, he has his white shirt buttoned halfway, the flash of a soup-stained vest underneath.

'All sound with me, mate,' I say. 'Bit of trouble at home lately but happy to be getting a few pennies in at the funeral home still.'

'Can't believe you're still doing that shit.'

'It's not as bad as you think, honest. Could do with an extra pair of hands to rake up the bones if you fancy it?'

'You can fuck right off.' He laughs, knee rattling like fuck down by the crisp box. 'Anyway. What's up at home? Becca pissed off with ya again?'

'Oh aye.'

'Coming home pissed?'

'The fuck do you know?'

'Women talk mate. Mand told me to keep an eye on ya, heard from one of Becca's mates . . . Don't worry, I told her where to stick it. That you're not an eighteen-year-old lad any more.'

'Feels like I'm on the run whenever I have a pint at the minute.'

'She only loves ya, mate, that's all.'

'Suppose.'

'Believe me mate,' says Shaky, 'we've all been there. Just take it easy with her. She'll be fine.'

Shaky dishes out a few nods to the gang. Big Mike and Tony raise their foggy glasses. Mavis and Doreen blow a kiss. Joan flashes her teeth. Both knees start going for it, full on 'Jailhouse Rock'. He knocks his knuckle on the wood of the bar and stretches upright, running his thumbs around a waistband that could orbit the Earth.

'You're a lucky fella, Jay,' he continues, 'especially with that hairline. Keep her sweet for a while, maybe lay off the drink for a week.'

We both look at each other and laugh at how ridiculous that sounded.

'Anyway,' says Shaky, 'I need the bog, got a turtle's head. See you around, Fletch.'

'Later, Shaky.'

He shuffles back upstairs then. All hunched and slow.

I tell Linda I don't need another one pouring as I'm about to head home when who else but Trick walks through the door. He's half-pissed, singing 'This Charming Man'. Gold tooth emerging bright from his purple face.

'Hey heyyy! Was hoping you'd be in!'

Trick rests his tattooed arms on the bar and nods from Linda to the Guinness pump. Spots of rain sit on his bald head like bubble wrap. He has a black Adidas polo on and dark, baggy jeans.

'You off out?' I ask.

'It's me holidays. Damn fuckin' right I'm out. Been on it since three.'

'Shit that bad at home?'

'Ahh, mate. Mental she is. Got my coat and done a runner while she was in the bath before I chucked a fuckin' toaster in with her.'

He gulps half his pint in two mouthfuls before Linda can get her hand off it. I check the time on my phone and start putting on my coat.

'Oi,' he says through a creamed moustache, 'where you think you're going?'

'Off home me. I've got a bhuna with ma name on it.'

'Are ya bollocks off home. Why do ya think I'm in here?'

No chance.

'Can't tonight mate, sorry,' I say.

'Why not?'

'You know I'm skint. Plus, I've just won her over from last week.'

Trick squints his eyes at me above his glass. Brow burrowing into a billion lines.

'Why?' he asks. 'Didn't leave that late on snooker night, did we?'

I've lost all concept of time from last Thursday, I was *that* wankered. Too many lies to keep up with, all 'cause I didn't wanna say I had a couple of bets and lost a pocketful. I just hope Trick doesn't get the idea I tanned the money he lent me.

'Aw, ya know what Becca's like,' I say, 'any chance to have a pop at me. Was meant to be home earlier for a night on Zoopla looking up houses apparently, but I forgot. She wasn't happy, mate. Not happy at all.'

'She'll get over that pal, don't worry. What's she doing planning that when you're out with me on Thursdays anyway?'

'Fuck knows.'

All that's left of Trick's Guinness is clinging to the glass. He gives me a wink and slaps my cheek. I can tell he's plastered 'cause he's blinking slow, twitching his lips in a way that looks like he's snorted a bag of charlie. Luckily, he's not into any of that. Drink does enough. He just can't handle it.

'Anyway, that's a shite excuse,' he says. 'You're coming out with me, son.'

'Honestly Trick. I can't tonight.'

'One sec,' he says.

Trick jumps up and goes for a slash, giving me time to think about it. He knows I can talk myself into it easier than he can. I think of Becca. The minus digits on my bank account. I think about darting for the door, sprinting home before my brain can convince me into another heavy session.

Linda opens the till and gets chatting to someone on the other side of the bar before putting the money in. I look down at the shiny plastic notes peering back at me. Big Mike and Tony are deep in conversation about football behind me. Mavis and Doris have gone off to the bingo in the next room. Joan's left too, probably a dentist appointment. It feels out-of-body. As if I'm looking down on myself cramming twenty-pound notes from the till into my coat pocket. I'm quick, stealthy. I keep both eyes on the back of Linda's head while my hands do the work. Fuck knows how much

I've taken, how it could be explained if Shaky pulls Linda up on it. This could cost her job.

Linda turns, laughing, and closes the till with a clang. I smile at her, hands in pockets. She smiles back. I've gotten away with it, by a millisecond. Trick's back at my side, leaving Linda to take more orders.

'I'm meeting Spud and Si then heading into town,' says Trick, zipping up his fly and plonking on the stool next to me. 'It's Spud's birthday, it'll be a laugh.'

I twirl the crisp notes in my pocket, getting flashes of that Thursday night argument with Becca.

'Where you off?' I ask, curious.

Trick smiles. Flash of the tooth.

'Casino.'

10

I text Rebecca that I have to work late. I lie that there's an emergency suicide victim I have to pick up from the hospital and spend all night patching up for a viewing tomorrow. I send a million 'sorry's followed by a million kisses, then put my phone on silent. We have another quick scoop at the club before we all pile on the 201 bus to town. With me and Trick are two lads we know well. Spud, the birthday-boy plasterer who's worked with Trick for years and has ears like the FA Cup. And Bog-Eyed Si, a geezer who's always hopping from boozer to boozer and tagging on to nights out he's got nothing to do with. Si gets where water wouldn't and has an unfortunate pair of wonky eyes that has his wife thinking he's seeing someone else.

The seats on the top deck are damp. Crevices jammed with bits of crisps and dead skin. It stinks of paint stripper and unwashed pits. Spud sneaks on a set of tinnies in his backpack and starts snapping them off the plastic, handing one to each of us. The sun's setting outside. A wash of purple welcoming the night.

'Been here before then lads?' I ask.

'Oh aye,' says Trick. They wink between themselves, communicating untold secrets. It takes me back a bit, with Trick never really being a gambler. He's the guy to sweat whacking a quid on the lottery.

'Spent a few quid, I'll tell ya that,' says Spud, screwing his little finger into one of those whopping ears.

'Spent more nights in prison than you have in there you tight arse,' Si pipes up. 'You just stick round the bar. Scared to put your hand in your pocket.'

'At least I can see which drink I'm picking up, ya cross-eyed fucker.'

We all chuckle and take a glug.

'Ayy I once had a teacher like you Si,' says Trick.

'Oh yeah?'

'Yeh, nice fella, but couldn't control his pupils.'

The oldies at the front of the bus turn round to scowl at us laughing.

'Cunts,' says Si, smirking.

We're off to one of the biggest casinos in the city centre. I haven't been there before but I know of it. It's a hefty venue, built into an old warehouse building, with endless slots and games that'll have you digging around inside your arse for any extra coinage. There's probably a good reason why I haven't been yet. I usually avoid town. Pint prices that can make your eyes water and full of youngens off to the Gay Village or Factory, a four-floor club filled with ecstasy-eyed student wankers. I'm too old for that shit now, to travel in and blow dosh I don't have. I don't do anything different in Openshaw, but travelling somewhere to do it seems unnecessary.

Casinos are different gravy. Proper dangerous. I always try to avoid them. In a way, there's no surprise Trick is the one to steer me here. Whatever stories and antics we dish out in the boozer come from a mad night out together. I can see in Trick's beady eyes he's feeling wild. He knows I'm skint. Still, he doesn't give a fuck because he knows I'm down for a good night whenever. Think of being on your deathbed and thinking about all them nights where you said no, just 'cause you were a bit short on money. That's not how I want to live. Tonight could be the night that changes everything. You just never know.

We get merry on the bus like teenagers horny for the crack on a Friday night, slurping on our Carlings and bitching about our birds. My god, it's good to be out.

'Where you been at then, Fletch? Not seen you out-out in time,' says Spud, as we pass the O₂ Apollo, the home of many memorable concerts in my pock-cheeked youth.

'Just stick round Openshaw now lad, too old for the big time,' I say.

'Fuck off ya dick, ya twenty-five.'

'He's chatting out his hole,' says Trick, leaning back against the window, legs splayed on the seats. 'He's under the thumb, that's why.'

'Am I bollocks,' I say.

'Mate, you go for two pints and she's on ya back.'

'She's all right, could be worse.' I give Trick a look to remember what his missus is like. The type that'd poison your brew and leave you paralysed if you didn't do the washing up. The lads all look at him in confirmation that he has the worst of the lot.

'Fair enough,' he says, 'but you're still whipped.'

Even though our breath's already reeking of the wet stuff, the bouncer doesn't bat an eyelid at us. He can see we're stupid enough to blow a load and contribute to his Christmas bonus. We ascend the glittery steps, towards our holy church where all prayers are answered and all sins are forgiven. Stepping through the double-doors, I honestly think: *I've entered Vegas here.*

Through a maze of twinkling carpets and golden banisters, we reach a hall where I'd happily have my ashes sprinkled when it's time. It's fuckin' glorious. Jim Ramsbottom's times a hundred. Endless strips of slot machines. Blackjack tables. Roulette wheels spinning something mad. Punters in suits, in trackies, in dresses. Cocktail glasses. VIP booths. Waxed legs. Loose ties. The sound of fruit machines, poker chips, winning. Every one of my senses are being tickled and spanked. I have to take a moment to drink it all in, rolling the cash from the club till around in my pocket. It feels like my last night on earth. I'm determined not to waste it.

Trick's already at the bar ordering lagers and lines of tequila shots. His bald head gleams from the neon. This is his blow-out before works starts to pick up again. He's on one, desperate for a legless night that keeps him away from home for as long as possible. Gambling to me is like alcohol to Trick. Soon as he smells it, he's on it like a hound.

Looking round, Bog-eyed Si is as mesmerised and shocked at the possibilities as me. He has one eye on the roulette and one eye on the slots so fuck knows where he's gonna start. Spud's more reserved, on his phone at the bar, probably texting his bird to lay the groundwork before he gets going. He can be a soft one, Spud, more under the thumb than me. My god did he used to be a laugh on a piss-up, but soon as he tied the knot, he took the back bench. It would be a mission to get him on our level tonight, even on his birthday. We're here now though; it's worth a try.

'Pack it in will ya, she can live without you for a night,' I say.

'She thinks I'm at a funeral,' says Spud.

'Can we not talk about death? It's me night off. A funeral on your birthday though?'

'Yeh, few updates then she'll be happy.'

'Mate, I'll put you in a coffin if ya carry on. Put ya phone away and get some bets on. We're winning big tonight.'

Spud finishes off his text. I spot an emoji love heart. The big-eared ponce.

'Hey, Fletch, you'll like this one,' says Si. 'You hear about them glass coffins they're trialling?'

'The fuck you on about, Si?'

'Those glass coffins. They're trialling them, aren't they? Remains to be seen though.'

Si smacks the bar in hysterics, watching me shake my head.

'Come on, lads,' I say. 'Let's get punting.'

Walking off, I think of Becca for the first time, sitting at home scranning a takeaway by herself. Slippers on, under a blanket on the couch, searching house prices on Zoopla, crime ratings in the area, local pubs, and travel distances to work. The House Fund jar is sat there on the mantelpiece, staring at her, calling for her. She looks at it, desperate to get it filled, desperate to start building our life.

I have visions of me walking out of here in the early hours, stumbling home with spit down my chin but a wad of money in my pocket. I'll fall in through the front door, ready to take the brunt of Becca's abuse. Pacing in the living room, ready to burst. I won't even let her start. I'll tell her how much I've won, and slap a deposit on a house. Right there and then, on the laptop. No viewing or fuck all. I'll leave her speechless. My antics would all have been worth it. I'll be in her good books. For months. Years. It feels more like a premonition than a dream. I have to make it happen. I have to.

I start on the roulette, the metallic bobble of the ball pulling me in from across the room. A flushed geezer with grey hair and an open collar like Harry Hill has his eyes firmly set on the wheel, willing it to stop on his number. The croupier, a young woman with dark eyeliner and a beauty spot on her cheek, gives me a nod. I take a seat next to him.

'Bastard!' he yells.

'Black twenty-six,' she says, removing the ball and a stack of the guy's chips.

A screen hovers above her head, showing which numbers have come up on the previous ten spins. There's a steady run of blacks, most of them in the twenties.

'Two spins on twenty-eight please, love,' I say, flicking twenty pounds worth of chips across the green table.

'No luck so far then?' I ask the guy. His nose is a map of purple veins, like a child has gone to town with a felt tip.

'Terrible,' he says in a cockney drawl.

He looks up at the screen and throws a shedload of chips on twenty-four. Because it has come up a few times, he thinks there's more chance of it coming up again. Whereas I think if it's come up often, it's got less chance of coming up again. Truth is, we're both idiots for even looking up at that screen because none of it matters. The odds are exactly the same. It's used to steer your judgement, to fool you into thinking you have an edge and can beat the wheel.

The woman – who's called Angela from her gold-plated name tag – stands upright in her waistcoat and tie. She throws the ball onto the varnished wheel with flair. Red, manicured nails release it at the perfect time to send it shooting in blurry circles. The wheel spins like a car tyre, sending me and this random dude into a tense paralysis that seems to last an age. It's an out-of-body moment, everything seems to hang in the balance. You know you're seconds away from an outburst of emotion, but which one? Anger or joy? The thrill of the unknown.

'Mother ffff!' he shouts, punching the cushioned rest.

'Black, twenty-eight. Congratulations, sir.'

My heart pounds an extra beat. She ushers a pile of red chips in front of me, ones he had in his pile a few minutes ago. First bet and I'm stacking more chips than a Pringles tube. I'm too excited to even think how much is in front of me. It isn't even money. Not in my head anyway. I'm off to a flyer but I can't get carried away.

The angry fella's sweating mad. Forehead like a rainy window. He rolls up his white shirtsleeves to do something with his hands. He has no chips to fiddle with any more. I chuck a few his way and he looks at me for the first time. His dark eyes are tinted with guilt. Slightly yellowed from years of alcohol and regretful choices. Wispy grey eyebrows hang over them like half-drawn blinds.

'Go on, a spin on me, boss,' I say.

'I don't need your money, mate.'

From the look of him – the textured cotton shirt, the pleated suit pants and hefty watch on his wrist – I know money's the last thing he needs.

'I know. For the buzz. Go on.'

The guy checks his watch, a weird gesture in itself. Time doesn't exist in a casino. All windows are blacked out. No clocks hang from the walls. You're tricked into staying, as if this room's the only one that exists on the planet. If you even think about time, you're in trouble. It means you're contemplating the money you've spent and the lies you've told your partner on your whereabouts.

'Fack it,' he says. 'Get it on twenny-four again darlin'.'

Nods all round. A smile as guilty as his gaze. Riddled with dirty secrets.

'Go on, I'll double up,' I say. 'I've got confidence in this guy. Twenny-four please, love.'

Looks and chips are exchanged. The man shuffles in his chair, elbows resting and hands laced. The wheel hypnotises us once more. Angela gazes beyond us, probably thinking about what she's gonna have for her tea, or if she'll go out on the lash later with her mates from behind the bar. I tap one of my remaining chips on the table. Impatient. Immersed.

The wheel stops. I can hear the bloops of machines in the background. Hammered buttons, anxious bums. The ice inside a cocktail shaker. The ball settles in the number. There's a moment of collective silence, as if the world has stopped.

A meaty arm flies around my shoulders. The man slaps a wet kiss on my cheek and punches the air. The little metal ball sits nestled under twenty-four. Even Angela looks surprised.

'You fackin' beauty! Nice one son!'

I feel the knots in my shoulder when he grabs it.

'Let me get ya a drink, young fella,' he says, gathering his fresh pile of chips.

'Don't worry mate. You crack on. I'm off to the slots anyway. Enjoy ya winnings.'

'You sure I can't get you one?'

'I'm good, thanks though.'

'No worries, pal. Thanks again!'

The man stays nestled in his high chair as I walk away. He doesn't move for the next two hours. Winning and losing. Winning and losing. From the slot machine, I watch him ride the same emotions. Head-in-hands, hands in the air. I notice whenever he fiddles with his watch, he's in trouble. Whenever he's sipping his drink, he's winning. If I can read this geezer like a book I can only imagine how Angela and the fellas running the casino cameras have him in the palm of their hands. He's a puppet about to get his strings cut.

The cockney means nothing anyway. What matters are the chips I have on me. Rattling like the sound of coins, of house keys.

I go to the slot machine beside Trick, while Spud and Si go and get a round in.

'Cig?' I say to Trick.

He hammers the button of his machine in frustration. The tune drowns to a halt.

'Too right, I'm gasping.'

Outside in an alleyway, the ground is damp and piled with bin bags. It must have rained while we were in there. Rats and all sorts of critters are scurrying behind big dustbins. Chefs sit on the steps of back doors, sucking on fags and checking their phones. Steam chugs from overhead vents. Taxis pass full of back-seat pissheads.

Like a daft twat, I check my phone to get an update on the footy scores. Five missed calls from Becca. Texts as well.

Where are you? Better not be on the piss again. Jamie, I'm worried, call me.

It's already midnight. Fuckin midnight! I told you. In casinos, time is irrelevant.

'What's she saying now?' says Trick.

He opens the packet for me to take a fag and lights it for me.

'Usual bollocks,' I say.

'What was your excuse tonight then?'

'Working late.'

'Ya bellend,' says Trick. 'Need to work on your lies, you.'

If only he knew how good I was.

'Will deal with it in the morning. Anyway, you're the prick that dragged me out,' I say.

'You don't kid me, Fletch. More up for a night out than George Best, you.'

I chuckle smoke out my nostrils. The cherries of our cigs glow like stars in the dark alley. Smoke spiralling up over the buildings, fogging fire escapes and vanishing in the blackness.

'What about you? What's your expert lie for tonight?'

Trick coughs before spitting a gobful of phlegm against the brick.

'Genius mate,' he says. 'Work conference.'

I stare funnily at the silhouette of his bald bonce.

'A fuckin' work conference? That's what you said?'

'Yeh.'

'You mental? She's not gonna fall for that, is she? You're a painter-decorator for fuck's sake, why would you ever need to go to a conference?'

'Ya know, they have exhibitions to get new tools and meet contractors and all that.'

'What a bellend.'

'Well, it's better than "Aw Becca, I'm workin', sorry!" isn't it? She thinks I'm in London as well. Two days.'

I choke on the smoke.

'You slutchy bastard,' I manage. 'She's defo knobbing

someone off if she's agreed to that. Probably rustling the sheets as we speak.'

Trick takes a few quick drags on his fag. The bin bags move. A loud hen party passes on the street, some inflatable hunk under the bride's arm.

'I'm joking, mate,' I say. 'She's just a good wife and doesn't ask questions. She probably thinks you're the one fiddling if anything.'

'Ahh, I'm not arsed,' he says, stomping out the dimp with his toe. 'I'll treat her to a flash meal or summot when I win big tonight.'

'That's my lad!' I say.

We squelch down the alley towards the casino entrance, ready for round two. It's a different bouncer but he greets us with the same politeness. The glittery steps are back in sight, soft under my feet. Those heavenly doors welcoming me in.

'Ay Fletch,' says Trick as we reach the top. 'Thanks for coming tonight, mate. I know you're skint and all that.'

'Ahh, no worries man. Never miss a work conference, me.'

We get kicked out at 6 a.m. when the sun's rising. Si called one of the dealers a nonce so the bouncers got involved. I haven't looked at my bank account once. Spud and Si get a taxi home, both of them now bog-eyed from hammering tequilas all night. Trick gets the bus back to his mam's to get his head down on the couch and avoid bumping into Rachel until he's back from 'London'. For me, there's no way I'm swanning in pissed now, an hour before Becca gets up for work. I stay out, going for a coffee at a greasy spoon in the Northern Quarter to sweat over how I'm gonna play it with her. Tell the truth and blame Trick for dragging me out? Blag about deep cleaning the cremation machines? A work conference? Fuck knows.

I take a stroll down Market Street, watching workers open shop shutters and flood into the Arndale for another day of mindless work. I get to Piccadilly Gardens when I feel a punch on my arm. It's the grey-haired guy from the roulette table.

'All right, young fella.'

It's the first time I see him smile. He looks haggard in the morning light. The sight of his cig-tarred teeth says he must have won. That veiny, bulbous nose twitches with excitement like a rabbit being offered a carrot.

'All right? Managed to peel yourself away then, did we?'

'Aw, mate.' He's all jittery, stepping on the spot and licking his dry lips. Definitely a cokehead. 'Got kicked out, didn't I. Good thing to be fair. Didn't half tan that table after you left. Should have seen the run I was on.'

'Nice one.'

I carry on walking towards the bus stop opposite the big Spoons. He tags along like a playful dog.

''Bout you?' he says. 'Any luck?'

I can't be arsed extending this conversation any more than I need to. I'm done for the night. Properly done. This guy's already a memory. I wanna fuck him off quick. I look him up and down, debating whether to be kind or go in blunt. The guy's got the swish clobber on, yet still looks like he's been dragged through a bush. Buttons undone, scraggy Boris hair and one trouser leg riding up and stuck in his sock.

'Sorry pal, that's my bus there,' I say, pointing. 'Nice meeting you though, yeh?'

The 201 pulls around the corner, brimming with office minions about to offload. I start pacing towards it, feeling a sudden hand on my shoulder.

'Ay pal. Thanks again for tonight, fuck knows where I would have ended up if you didn't throw me them chips.' A serious, grateful look washes over his yellow eyes. 'Let me make it up to you.'

The bus chugs to a halt about a hundred metres away. He still has hold of my shoulder.

'Listen,' he says, 'I work as a VIP Manager, dunno if you know what that is. It's for the bookies, ya know, working with proper fellas like yourself. Rewarding loyal customers and making sure they're well looked after. I could sort you out if you fancy it? Free bets, top odds, even sort you out with match tickets or a day at the races if you're into all that?'

I analyse him again, trying to take his slurred words seriously.

'Especially the horses if that's your cup of tea. Ascot, the National, the Derby, Cheltenham … you'll be swimming in offers, mate. I'll even give you a cheeky few quid here and there to tide you over if you're on a bad run. Won't get owt like it anywhere else.'

He lets go of me and switches to business mode. The guy's like a Russian doll with a hundred unreadable personalities. I believe him too. He definitely wants to sort me out, repay the favour sorta thing. I can see it in him. I've heard about these VIPs as well, just never been arsed to look into it. A few of the lads from the club got snapped up by them. They're always getting free shit and the best offers around for the big horse-race meetings and weekend footy matches. Young Jimmy got sent to Dubai for the Formula 1 when he doesn't even watch it. He thought Formula 1 was a fuckin' haemorrhoid cream.

The bus driver's checking his mirrors, the last stragglers filtering off into the city.

'Anyway,' he says, 'you catch your bus, but here's me number. Give us a bell if you fancy it, yeh?'

He passes me a glossy card with his name and number on, Jim Ramsbottom's one of the many betting logos sitting below. Vince Hannigan. He looks like a fuckin' Vince.

'Cheers, mate. Will think about it.'

I sprint for the bus as it's slowly pulling away. The driver stops and allows me to get on in a sweat. From the top deck, Vince gives me a thumbs up from the pavement and strolls off with hands in his suit pockets, as if he's off to work himself. I look at the card, stroke the shiny surface. I read his name and number over and over again, enough times for me not to even need the card any more.

I return it to my pocket, along with the two grand I've won that night.

11

It's the evening after, and I'm outside the club having a fag. I'm scared to go home. My head's not there. My mask doesn't feel strong enough to lie to Becca again, talking some bullshit about where I was last night.

I'm blowing smoke into the road when I see a black silky bomber jacket coming down the street. A new addition from Selfridges. Passing headlights make her gold hoop earrings glint. They remind me of that night I met her at the party. As Becca gets closer, I notice the face on her. Eyebrows horizontal, lips scrunched, a glare that can cut through the thick air. I try to look guilty, opening my arms as she reaches me. I'm greeted with a solid slap across the face. The force of it turns my head towards the window where Coley and Tommy Murphy are laughing into their pints.

'I don't even wanna fuckin' hear it,' she says, calmly, standing there with her arms crossed.

'Hi babe.'

'The fuckin' cheek, honestly. I say I don't wanna hear it but I actually can't wait to know what shit you're gonna come up with this time.'

My cig's now lying sad on the floor next to a dog turd. I light another and offer Becca one. She snatches and sparks it so fast it doesn't even give me any thinking time.

'Look, I'm not gonna start with the excuses,' I say. 'I know I'm in the wrong. I should have let ya know again but—'

'But what, Jamie? The fuck's up with you lately? I'm tired of dealing with your shit.'

My sigh makes the loose strands of her hair quiver.

'I dunno, Becca. Honestly. I don't even fuckin' know.'

She makes a gesture through the window because Coley's whistling. Even Linda has a G&T in her hand, sucking on a straw like she's in the cinema.

'Come on,' says Becca, 'let's talk somewhere else.'

Becca starts off down the street in a huff. I jog down the pavement, weaving between wheelie bins before I catch up to her.

We pace along the high street, wordless for about ten minutes. It's like the parade of shame. We happen to pass the whole of fuckin' Openshaw at some point, including everyone I know from the club, the Rag, the Oddies, the bookies. They raise their eyebrows, pout their lips. They know I'm in for it. The look on Becca's face says it all. I follow her like a crying child, waiting for his punishment when he gets home.

Home is where I think we're heading, until Becca dog-legs into Sol's kebab shop. He's behind the counter in a red apron, tying up a white plastic bag brimming with chicken. The oven behind him displays racks of golden, crispy meat. A blinding menu above his head, probably visible from the moon.

'Ahh, Posh and Becks!' he says, passing the bag over to a grumpy teenager who hoops it over the handle of his bike. The boy looks us up and down before cycling off.

Becca's face seems to change at the sight of Sol. He's a permanently happy guy, always raising spirits and never has a bad word to say about anyone. He loves his chats with me as much as his chats with Becca. Known him for two years and don't think I've ever paid for chicken since the first time we met. Explains why I'm still a fat cunt.

'Solly!' says Becca. 'How's things?'

She tiptoes to lean over the counter and kiss both cheeks. We slap palms, exchange a wink.

'All right, Sol,' I say. He signals to Riz, his chef in the back, to start cooking up some spicy wings, nuggets and two portions of chips.

'I'm good, I'm good,' he says. 'We made up yet then?'

I stand behind Becca, making a cut-throat action, telling him to shut up.

'I-I mean what you been up to?' says Sol. 'Not seen you guys in time.'

Becca takes a seat in one of the red leather booths and drums her nails on the tin table.

'Work mainly,' she says. 'Unlike some, who are out on the lash all the time.'

I lean up against the drinks fridge, silent.

'Been a naughty boy, has he Becca?'

'A cunt. That's what he's been.'

She gives me a sarcastic smile.

'Anyway, how was the weekend?' I ask. 'Busy?'

'Yeh,' says Sol, 'only the two fights on Saturday. Someone decided to try chucking a bin through the window.'

Sol points to the glass front where one of the windows has cracked like a spider's web.

'Dickheads, aren't they?' I say.

'All right though. Cracked the bastard round the nose with my mop. Can still see the blood on the pavement. Have a look on your way out.'

'Nice one. Police involved and all that?' I ask.

'Nahh. Just Gorton lads causing shit. Ya know, all that territory bollocks. Openshaw boys turned up, bout twenty of them, and shooed them off before anything got too hairy. Nice lads though them, always in here chalking out for wings.'

'Isn't Spud's son in with all that lot?' Rebecca asks me.

'Yep,' I say. 'Think he is in with them lot.'

We fall silent then. There isn't much else to say. The sizzle of chicken, the buzz of the menu and drinks fridge. Becca looks at her nails as if what to say next is written on her varnish. Me and Sol share a glance, acknowledging the awkwardness and the hole I need to dig out of. He gives me a nod and taps the counter.

'Just check up on that chicken,' he says, disappearing to the back with Riz.

Outside, buses cough along the road and kids in school uniform skip past screaming. A leaf blows in through the open door onto the chequered lino.

'Is there anything I can say?' I ask, taking a seat in the booth opposite Becca. She doesn't look up from her nails.

'Becca?'

'What?'

'Is there anything I can say?'

'It's not as easy as that. I wanna know what's going on. Why you can't be arsed letting your own girlfriend know that you're out on a bender all night and – I mean, it's not even that. The fact you'd rather get shit-faced all the time than spend time with me is fuckin' shit, Jamie. It's shit.'

'That's not what this is.'

'Then what is it?'

I don't think I've ever come closer to telling her about my gambling. If only I could say how much money I've wasted. Pile the guilt onto myself about how we could probably have had a house by now, how we could've had more holidays, how we could've had a better, happier life if I'd banked all that cash instead of using it for lost bets. I want the weight lifted off my shoulders. I want to tell her, I really do. I know she loves me but surely, she can't love me that much to accept it and carry on. I can't take the risk. She can never know.

'I'm just stressed,' I say.

'Stressed?'

'Yeh.'

'Why?'

'I dunno. All this saving for a house, work being mad. I'm no good with it. It makes me panic.'

'What, building a life and committing to a relationship is making you panic? Am I scaring you off, is that it?'

'No, it's not that at all. It's just a lot, ya know. You can't ignore that it's a big step and it costs a lot of fuckin' money.'

'Which is why we're saving, Jamie, that's the whole point.'

'You know what I mean.'

We're both looking at our nails now. Mine swollen, nibbled to the quick from watching screens in the bookies. Becca's pristine with blue gloss. We're scared to look at each other, to face our problem and tackle it head on like adults. It's times like these that we're reminded of how young we still are, that we have a lot more learning to do. Not just about life, about each other. Relationships are difficult for everyone. When you struggle for money, live above a kebab house in a mouldy one-bed, and have a secret gambling problem eating away at each other's trust, shit can be a lot more difficult.

'So it's about the house,' says Becca.

I look past her. The smashed window glints, shapes changing within the broken shards as cars zoom by. I smell a deep-fried fear, a sadness equal to an odds-on favourite falling at the last fence.

'I'm not sure. Probably. I just feel a bit stressed generally at the minute.'

Becca doesn't have an answer. Why would she? She wants to help, of course she does. She just doesn't know how.

'As long as you know it's not you,' I say. 'And that doesn't excuse, ya know, getting in pissed and all that. Staying out to mad hours. I know that's wrong and I'm sorry. I'll never do it again.'

Tension loosens in her eyebrows. Her lips relax. Not quite a smile but she now looks like she might not kick my head in.

'You can talk to me ya know,' she says. 'Even if it is about the house, saving, or even work. I don't know anything about prepping a corpse but I know how to listen. Whatever it is, I'm here.'

'I know. I know. Thank you.'

A smile. Definitely a smile. Her eyes are alive again. I see the woman I fell in love with. That fell in love with me.

'One spicy wing box meal and one chicken nugget meal for the crazy couple. Here we are!'

Sol plonks a brimming plastic bag on top of the counter, flashing a toothy grin through an oiled beard. He sprinkles the bag with sauce sachets and tells us to help ourselves to a drink.

'Now get upstairs, but no making up, rattling the bed frame, you hear? It's my peak hour soon.'

'Can you actually hear us?' asks Becca, mortified.

'It's all right,' says Sol, winking at me. 'Doesn't last long.'

I snatch the bag of steaming chicken.

'Dickhead.' I laugh.

I leave with Becca under my arm. On the pavement outside, I see drops of blood leading into the road. It makes me feel peaceful. My situation could be much, much worse. I could be caught up in all that bollocks. I could be alone, without Becca, without someone to bring me back down to earth. Nothing's scarier than that. Nothing.

***

Tonight, we sit in and drink cheap red wine watching *Britain's Got Talent*. Everything's normal. Becca is snuggled up under my arm on the couch, slippers on, moaning about how shit the magician is like everything's fine now. I can't concentrate on the telly. I'm listening to echoes of Sol's laugh underneath the floorboards, the shuffle of the chip pan. Our living room smells like fried chicken, overpowering the greasy pizza boxes by our feet. The smell wafts up through our window, leaving a permanent lingering in the flat, clinging to the walls. I look around. At the ripped-up leather sofa we're lounging on. The plastered holes on the wall. The festering mould on the corner of the ceiling. The tiny kitchenette with pots spilling over the sink, cupboards filled with chipped mugs and out-of-date beans. Even the view outside is grim. Nosy bastards on double-decker buses peering into the living room. The endless cries of sirens. A preacher on the corner by the bank, screaming how Christ is coming to save us from the Tories.

The jar on the windowsill looks emptier than ever. The lid has a coat of dust. What if we did put our minds to it, save and get out of this shithole? Just to leave here then crack on with our lives. Start fresh. How long would it really take? A few months without a bet? Surely, I can do that much? For Becca. For both of us.

I can't get it out of my mind all night. I lie in bed while Becca sleeps peacefully next to me. The room is blue with the occasional streak of light flashing from passing cars. I lie there tapping my fingers on the duvet. I should be shattered, but I know it's going to be hours before I get any shut-eye.

I sit up quietly and get out my phone. Five or six betting apps stare back. Just the sight of them embroils something in me, forgetting who I was a minute ago. I enter a new gear, as if going from tipsy to outright pissed. My face glows in the dark as I flick through lists and lists of random live football games in Romania and the US. Teams I've never heard of. I do a brief search on the form and league tables before placing a couple of little bets. Things like number of corners or how many yellow cards in the game. Before I know it, I'm knee-deep in bets on greyhounds, French horse racing, Chinese second-tier basketball. If fuckin' tortoise racing was on there, I'd fancy a punt.

I have a reason to be up now. My excitement's back. I feel like the world is asleep and I'm the only one up enjoying myself. I'm experiencing something everyone else is missing out on. Eyes drying from the brightness, I fall further and further down. Losing, losing, yet somehow feeling like winning.

I lose two hundred pound in the space of thirty minutes,

while Becca is lying there next to me. I don't really give a shit. The money from the casino has helped. I decide I need a smoke though, something to pull me from my phone for a few minutes.

Creeping out of the covers and tiptoeing along the quieter floorboards, I grab my cagoule from the banister and step out the front door. It's just past 2 a.m., the roads still lively with drinking teens and beeping taxis. I light up a ciggy, trying to switch off my brain. I close my eyes, listening to the sounds. Tyres swoosh on the gravel. Throaty laughs in the dark. People munching on chips, floating in and out of Sol's.

Hands in pockets, I lean on the doorframe and pull out the card. I wonder what Vince is doing now, whether he's at that roulette table fiddling with his watch again. Was this geezer really just a con man ready to milk money out of addicts? That's what some of the lads from the boozer have warned me about after getting swindled for their money. Those are too stupid to see decent odds or a nailed-on bet if it slapped them on the arse though. Those that bet on the flat courses, or who's going to win fuckin' Eurovision. I can't see it myself. Vince looks too peachy, too grey and polished to be so sinister. Plus, he owes me. He said it himself.

I spin the card in my fingers, sucking on my fag, wondering. A moment arrives when there's nothing on the road. All I can hear is the buzz of the street lamps and a plastic bottle rolling off a kerb. The black sky closes in on top of me. The moon white, cratered like Tommy Murphy's cheeks.

The bets on my phone would be over now. The results would be in. Because the returns won't even make a dint in my overdraft, I don't even bother checking. Throwing my cig in the grid, I get my phone out ready to check anyway. Money is money. And the more I think about it, the more I imagine having actual money in my pockets to spend. Fingers hovering, I find myself dialling Vince's number and pressing ring. There are rare moments when you realise you're an addict. This is one of them. I'm too curious. The 'what if' mentality taking over again.

A voice answers within seconds.

'Ello ello, Vince speaking.'

'Hiya mate, it's Fletch. From the casino the other night? I gave you those chips.'

A long pause. I question whether to hang up. Whether I've made another wrong decision.

'Wahayy, Fletch! Thought I wouldn't be hearing from you for a while, mate. How can I help ya?'

'I need some money, man, desperately. Can you get me some decent odds?'

It's as if I felt him smile through the phone.

'Let me see what I can do. You might have to cough up some big stakes though, to make the bets worth it? I'll give you a couple of free bets to start off with though.'

From the street, I look up at the bedroom window where Becca's sleeping, dreaming about our house.

'Don't worry about that. I'll get the money,' I say, praying to god my credit card checks will go through.

12

Rosie is, or was, thirty-two. She got hit by a speeding car on Ashton Old Road last week. Tragic, but not uncommon. It's like a Formula 1 circuit that road. Blacked-out bangers weaving between cars, dodging red lights. Rosie was on the way back from getting her nails done. They still have a glossy sheen of red. I scrape the gravel from underneath them and give the red an extra coat. I think she would've liked that.

Blonde curls drape over her shoulders like fusilli pasta. Her lips are pink and plump. Other than a few scratches, she looks completely normal until you get down to her legs, where one is bent and wobbles like a branch in the wind if you touch it. I crack it back into position and cover it under the sheet to keep it in place. I've had much worse in here. Suicides and murder victims that really test the strength of your stomach. Gouged eyes, limbs connected by a single tendon. Half-exploded heads, burn victims. They're never pretty and take much more work. But it's work that needs to be done. They mean just as much as the next dead body stretchered in here.

There's an American series called *Six Feet Under* – about a family-run mortuary – which Becca sometimes has on the telly to understand better what I do. This one scene shows a dead woman lying on the bed, who happens to be a famous porn star the embalmer has watched before. Not to be crude, but the knockers on that woman were massive and Rosie's remind me of hers a bit. They don't move an inch. Not the first time she's been under the knife.

Reason why I mention it, if there's any sort of surgical implant, I have to cut it out. The silicone tits turn to a messy goo in the cremation machine which is a bugger to chisel off the bottom. No one has time for that when you've got a constant stream of bodies flying in, ready to be sparked and blended. I've cut out a few pacemakers in my time too, slicing a short line along the chest and yanking it out. If you send a body into the machine with one of them on, you're fucked. The lithium batteries explode from the heat, causing damage to the machines and any poor fucker stood on the outside of them – like me!

Removing Rosie's jugs is more for practicality than danger. I slice under the breasts and dig my fingers inside and around the silicone to pull them out. They look like two little jellyfish. Smooth and translucent, wobbling on the tray as I place them down.

I sit down on the swivel stool and take my time stitching her back up. She has a look of Rebecca about her. Not just the way she looks after herself, but the confidence and maturity she holds just lying there. Becca can walk into a room and look in control. She can overhaul a conversation with one word, but not in an arrogant dismissive way, just someone who chooses the right time to say words. Smiles in a way, turns her head in a way, that no matter who she meets, they love her and respect her. I always wish I had that, but feel I appreciate her more because I don't.

Set on the thought of Becca, I babble away at Rosie like I do at home to kill the time, starting off where I finished with Umar.

Ya know, Rosie, you've got the look of my missus. Becca, she's called. She's class, though we're going through a bit of a sticky period at the minute. I have me money troubles which she knows nothing about. I like a bet, ya see. The horses and that. It's mad really. Since that first day walking into a bookies, I knew something changed.

I'm sure it was around 2005, summot like that, when gambling changed me and led to how I am now. A light switching on. The buzz from that spinning roulette. Neon frames blinking away.

Colours, sounds, pressing that button as you place your bet. Paper wasn't for English homework any more; it was for betting slips and footy coupons. Pens were for writing out Lucky 15s and marking up the Racing Post, *not drawing boring trees in art class. TVs were for horse racing, greyhounds chasing mechanical rabbits, not* X Factor *or fuckin'* Friends *on repeat. I entered a new world. The world of betting. Where dinner money had the potential to make you rich, rather than fill your belly with a soggy sausage barm for a few hours.*

I cut under Rosie's collar bone and wiggle in the translucent tube, trying to find the carotid artery. I'm fiddling about in there, tongue out in concentration, when my phone goes. I've not placed any bets this morning. Becca's at work. Maybe Trick sending me another one of his shit jokes?

With my rubber gloves, I prod in the pin with my little finger because it's the only one without blood on. It's Vince.

> I've put some money in your account pal. Have a dabble today if you like. Some decent odds in the link below too ;)

You fuckin' beauty. A hundred quid in free bets, just like that. I ping off my rubber gloves and whack on all sorts. A kid in a candy shop. It's fifteen minutes before I remember Rosie chillin' there, a rubber tube hanging out of her collar. I pull fresh gloves from the dispenser and ping 'em on.

Shit, sorry Rosie.

I pocket my phone, feeling the weight of expectation in the lining, as if already weighed down by the amount of money I'm going to win. I could snog the chops of this Vince fella!

So yeh, I'd go in Jim Ramsbottom's nearly every day after school. On my own, not with the boys. Some days I couldn't go 'cause my dinner money wouldn't get me far enough on the slots, so I had to save a bit until the end of the week for a chunky session on the roulette. I'd dabble in the other games as well. I got more confident.

Hunting for gold coins in treasure troves, getting Leprechauns to cross the rainbow towards the jackpot. Quizzes, poker, random card games. I'd try them all, seeing what I was good at, what captivated me most and had me chucking coins into the slot like I don't know what.

Finally found the carotid. Now the tube for the jugular vein. Feeding it in, I can't help but catch her red nails again out of the corner of my eye. It reminds me of Becca, painting hers the exact same shade, hands splayed on a cushion as she watches *Married at First Sight*. It makes me stop for a second. Guilt boiling up as if I'm confessing everything to her, the one person I don't want to.

I got friendly with the lass behind the counter. She didn't care about my age. Fuck knows what her name was, it was that long ago, but I remember she made me a cracking brew every time I walked in. I didn't even like tea then. But I felt cosy, at home with it steaming there on the side of the machine. It'd be freezing cold by the time I left, the sky darkening over the terracotta terraces. The lads from school would be in their trackies, having a kick-about in the park or gobbling their tea so they could play Xbox by the time I was walking home in my uniform. Mam couldn't give a toss, taking the blag that I was at after-school dodgeball or another detention. She just liked having a free house so she could mince the butcher (not Dave, this was his rival). I had my own little secret, which added to the buzz. Back then, the word addiction wasn't thrown around. That was for drugs, sex and alcohol. For grown men like me dad. I was a kid for fuck's sake. It was fun, and that's what kids had. What was wrong with that, ay Rosie?

If I was skint or Mam's benefits didn't come through for dinner money, I'd occupy myself by making up my own games at home. I was a pretty lonely kid after school and on the weekends, so would lock myself in my tiny bedroom and design ways to keep myself occupied. On the back of my door, I had a dartboard haloed by a scattering of holes that looked like Al Pacino had gone full-on Scarface at it. You seen that film? Cracking movie that. Anyway, I made a game sorta like the darts world cup, where I would be a certain country for each round and play against myself until there was a winner. I had a leader board and path-to-the-final poster and everything. Each nationality had their own distinctive throw. Belgium held the dart almost horizontal. Netherlands was quick-fire, rapid. Australia had a measured, narrow stance. England ended up winning the most world cups as the slow, Phil Taylor-style technique was what worked best for me. I spent hours, days doing it until my arm cramped up. It was fuckin' mint.

Both tubes are in now. I turn on the machine, hearing the tissue builder flow into Rosie's body and the blood pour out into the tray. I start massaging to distribute it evenly. Becca sometimes asks me for massages after work, so this is extra fuckin' weird. Stocking rails and hauling boxes of coat hangers wrecks the back apparently. Try bending over corpses all day, running your hands over every stretch of skin. But I oblige, I still do it, even though I've been massaging all day. She's always liked my generosity, my desperation to please her. If it wasn't creepy, I'd try closing my eyes and thinking it's Becca. Convincing myself, as always, that everything I do is for her.

My phone pings in my pocket, and I should feel guilty that it's not a text from Becca I'm excited about, but a change in my fortune. I check and my horse has won the first race by two lengths. I pull up Rosie's arm and high five her, even do a little jig around the scalpel trolley. What a fuckin' start.

I punch the air for good measure and carry on massaging.

Ignore me Rosie, getting carried away . . . so I'd bet on each darting nation, not with money, but with random shite like bottles of shampoo or me mam's grotty slipper. Whatever would win I'd keep as a token, a little memory of my success. I even had an empty Lynx shower gel as a trophy, where I'd write the country and year that they won on the back. At the end of Year Ten, I brought a bird home and, after sending the bed frame rattling, she spotted the shower gel on top of the wardrobe and read the back.

'Wouldn't have you down for a traveller,' she said. 'Been everywhere you, haven't ya?'

She thought they were the countries I'd been to on holiday. Dozy cow. Course I didn't tell her the truth. I had to blag about swimming with turtles in Australia, eating chocolate in Belgium. Like I said, I was a lonely sod. I didn't need a lass spreading round the school that I played darts with myself. I'd do anything to keep the friends I had, even if they were twats like Reece and Pinky.

Even before them two, I'd go to crazy lengths to make a friend or keep the one friend I had, just so I didn't look like the weird, lonely kid no one gave a shit about. Like in primary school, I was in the playground once with Snotty Ryan when he shat himself in the middle of a game of tig. He always tugged the berries off the bush that peeked through the gates and ate them. I could see the dread in his eyes, the moisture in his undies visible in his expression. He was basically my best mate, so to save him some embarrassment, I forced myself to shit my pants too. Squeezed my fists and pushed right there on the spot. My boxers went warm. A silent splatter. I got the brunt of the abuse, with me being the ginger, chubby, pale dumpling, and Snotty Ryan got let off the hook. I didn't get a thank you but we stayed friends. Probs for my endless supply of tissues, the big bogey bastard. Either way, we both got what we wanted out of it.

Massaging and massaging, feeling the fluid bubble beneath her skin. Wondering what Rosie was like in school. Whether boys chased after her blonde curls across the playground. If she started painting her nails then because all her friends started doing it. Whether she did any embarrassing shit like I did, just to please people and make them think she's someone that she wasn't.

Mam used to try and pair me up with her mate's sons. Toothless old hags she'd bitch with while they watched a shoddy tribute band in the club. Her favourites were Noasis and Blobbie Williams. She'd stumble in, lager down her chin, peanut-dusted fingers, telling me I'm going round to a random lad's house on Wednesday. I told her to fuck off and not interrupt my darts. Could have had her fuckin' eye out, the pissed-up moose.

I used to chew the sleeves of my hoodie, sucking on them until they were sopping wet. This lad called Jake – had a moley face and a camp walk like he was tryna hold in a fart – liked to chew on his zip, so Mam thought we were the perfect match. We'd sit in my room on each end of the bed, swapping our jumpers now and again, chewing in silence like a pair of loons. Cocky cunt had the cheek to call me weird one day so I had to throw a dart into his ankle on purpose so he wouldn't come round again.

I was a proper oddball. Girls were rarer than rocking horse shit until about Year Ten, when I started hanging around with Reece and Pinky. Once people think you're hard or you act a bit of a knob, the girls get interested no matter how you look. Even shagged this emo bird in the bogs near science. Asked me to slam her head off the toilet bowl. Proper wild one, her. She ended up stabbing a teacher with a pencil before howling like a werewolf. Few screws loose but I'd take anything I could get with the look of me. And Emily. Ahh, Emily. Nice set of Pamela Andersons on her, bit like yourself. Blonde plait, had a little brother in Year Eight who squatted and curled a Mr Whippy into the staff kettle. We had it out in Debdale Park once, rolling around in a bush getting that beautiful plait knotted with leaves. Nearly screamed the trees down she did. Flocks of birds flying off mid-orgasm. I knew she was faking it but no complaints here. I was used to birds trying to get away from me.

It's clear I was getting a bit better on the social front by the end of school. Once the betting started though, I couldn't give a toss if Emily walked past me stark naked in the playground. My mind was elsewhere, boggled with odds, with the form of footy teams, with which race meetings were coming up that weekend. It was all I could think about. I even suggested to Reece and Pinky about wagging school a few more times for another go on the slots. They were having none of it. Not so much the getting caught bit but I knew they seen something in me. Pressing that button. Draining the dosh down the swanny. That stupid impulse that gamblers have. That dangerous tic to carry on no matter what. They'd seen it. They were young but they'd seen enough round Openshaw to notice it. They didn't want anything to do with it. They wanted the respect of their dads, uncles, grandads ... not to be them. We've all seen how it ends up with the fellas round here. We never made a run for it again. I had to go solo.

Rosie's body is now pink and plump. I remove the tubes and lace up the incision, ready to wash her again. She looks radiant now, like Becca always does when she walks into a room. The way her cheeks flush when I tell a shit joke. How the sun blushes the skin on her chest when she sits out in it too long. Did Rosie have a man or woman who appreciated her in this way? Who knew her every freckle and could sense her every mood?

So that's exactly what I did.

'What you having in the 12.30 at Kempton?' I asked Dad one Saturday at Gran's, determined to start getting in on the action rather than being a spectator.

'Gallows Reach, I think. Why?'

He was on the sofa, leather creaking under his fake Levi's from Gorton Market. Slurping on his brew as if it was a billion degrees.

'You sure?' I said. 'Hennessey's not won one in a while. Plus, that jockey couldn't ride a roller coaster.'

Dad frowned at me. Blank. Blue pen behind his ear. Race listings splayed out on the coffee table in front of him. He checked the form again, trying to remember Hennessey's recent runners while Grandad fingered his belly-button.

'The fuck ya know all that?' said Dad.

I smiled. I knew my shit now.

'Sunshine Sally,' I said. 'It's a banker, trust me. Been cruising *over the jumps and is the only one Jarvis has out today. Would bet me life on it.'*

Come 12.35, Sunshine Sally bolted it home by four lengths and left Dad's jaw brushing the carpet. He chucked his betting slip in the bin, refusing to look at my smug face on the couch in the corner. Grandad had listened to me and scrubbed my ginger head with his knuckle.

'Well in Jamie son, great shout!'

Dad let me put a bet on every weekend after that. After a few weeks of grovelling, he ended up asking me for tips. Discreetly though. He would never concede to know less than me. He would disguise it in a way like: 'Lemon Pippa's got no chance in the 2.30, has it?' or 'I'm stuck between three in the 3.15, what would you have each-way?' I got him a few winners which he didn't bat an eyelid at as they trotted over the line, jockey wobbling his whip in the air. He claimed they were lucky punts even though he was throwing the money at them. He'd only ask me when he really didn't have a clue. Which was rare to be honest; he was a clever fella, been doing it for years. I was still a rookie. I wasn't getting on my own high horse just yet. The notes in my pocket felt nice, though, when a few trebles and the odd outside single came in. I had money to buy new trainers, new tracksuits, unlimited chicken wings, regular haircuts, actual branded aftershave and not the cheap shit from B&M. It never came to that though. The money never lasted long enough for me to walk out of a bookies into another shop. You know where it went? Back on to win more.

Sorry if I'm boring you Rosie, don't know if you even— It just helps to say it out loud, ya know? Helps me understand.

I imagine Rosie being a therapist or a care nurse. Someone unselfish, always offering an ear. Hauling everyone's problems onto her shoulders so they wouldn't have to carry them. Doing shopping for elderly neighbours. Painting the nails of her younger cousins, being the fun aunt. Bottling her stress and saving her crying for the shower, so those closest to her aren't burdened with worry.

I look down on her, trying to remember how I even started going on about this. I suppose it all came down to Becca. Trying to understand why I am like I am, why I may never be good enough for her. Why, like Rosie, she doesn't deserve any of this.

So, I figured if there was any hope I could get out of whatever this was, my first real experience of Cheltenham threw it out the window. I could put as many bets on as I wanted. I studied, cross-analysed between papers, listened to every pundit and ex-jockey I could find in the weeks leading up to it. A. P. McCoy. Ruby Walsh. Mick Fitzgerald. I listened to them all like gospel. I felt like I was signing my life away as I handed my scribbled slips and money over the counter. My pockets were wadded with all sorts of bets. Long shots, favourites, likely combinations, unlikely combinations.

I watched every trot at Gran's with the usual suspects: Dad, Grandad, Uncle Mark, Uncle Lee. The commentator rattling off names was music to my ears. Roars of the crowd, flinging their flat caps about. I rode each one of my horses right there in the living room, sweating like Pinky after the bleep test. It felt exactly like what it was: the Fletchers' Christmas Day.

I raked in a grand. A whole grand. One thousand English pounds. That amount of money was unheard of. I watched my final horse jog over the line in amazement. Dad and Uncle Mark had it as well, so were too busy jumping around to see the shocked expression on my face. I had to go to the outside loo in the garden to celebrate. Punching the air, jumping on the spot. Screaming, cheering into my T-shirt so no one in the house could hear me. I would be paying their bets for a month if they did. I was used to hiding my losses from everyone, never mind my wins.

I cashed it in at Jim Ramsbottom's as soon as they opened the next day. Not 'cause I was eager to splash the cash, but they have staff on that most of the regulars don't know. Less chance of word spreading round Openshaw that young Fletch won big. The spotty lad with a curtain fringe checked the bet three times 'cause he thought it was a fake. I leant on the counter like Billy Big Bollocks with a smirk wider than Pinky's waistline, imagining the wad he was about to hand over. After he realised I wasn't a blagger, he counted the notes out in front of me, pissed-off snarl on his gob. The notes felt gorgeous; there isn't owt like it. I'd won a grand. I did well to walk out with half.

I soak the towel with more warm water and carry on washing. I'm tempted to check my other bets but want to ride the wave of winning for a bit longer. The joy of free bets is that even if you lose, you don't really feel like you've lost. But that feeling of losing forces you on until you finally win. Now I have Vince, it's a safety net. He's my Santa Claus, ready to deliver gifts in my time of need. For the first time in my life, I feel it's kinda impossible to lose.

Funny actually – it was just before this period of paradise that I met Rebecca. It was a Friday night party around Christmas time. The December Christmas that is. Every window on the streets were glittering with multi-coloured lights. Sparkling silhouettes of trees behind mesh curtains. Mariah Carey whining through the speakers at Tesco. Rebecca was a year ahead so had already left school by then. She was working at Martins Bakery on Ashton Old Road, dishing out pies and loaves to miserable old hags like me mam. She had a faint smell of steak and kidney as she leant back on the kitchen worktop with a WKD in her hand. Her hair was tied up into a ponytail to reveal two gold hoop earrings. Blue eyeshadow and a lip gloss that left residue on the rim of her bottle. Everything about her was stunning.

'So you used to go our school as well then?' I asked, sweating through my Voi Jeans polo.

'Yeh, left last year. You in Year Eleven?'

'Yeh, can't wait to get out. Exams and all that are so fuckin' long.'

'You not clever then?'

'Do I look clever?'

'Fair enough.'

Her blue sequin dress hovered above the knees, and she kept pulling it down awkwardly with her spare hand. The kitchen was full of randomers stinking of hairspray. The back door in the kitchen was open for the smokers to float in and out. A game of beer pong set up on the concrete slabs which already had one lass trollied enough to fall into a bush and flash her knick knacks. Me and Becca watched from the kitchen window, chuckling and oohing if a ball clinked off the rim.

I stick the radio on for a bit of background music and refill the bowl with warm water now it's gone cold. I place my phone beside the sink, resisting the urge to check it.

'You not taken then?' I asked.

Getting back to washing.

Becca played with an earring and took a sip, staring straight through the window.

'Bit forward, aren't ya?' she said.

'Well, you gotta ask these things. No point beating round the bush.'

As if on cue, the drunk girl started to look for her lost heel, literally beating around the bush she'd dolphin-dived into. I got a refill from the fridge and nodded to some of the lads I knew from my form. This lad we call Kenco 'cause of the coffee-stain birthmark on his head and his bezzy mate Frodo, a stumpy little fella who had tacky rings on every finger.

The sink was cluttered with plastic cups and melting cubes of ice. A group of girls stampeded through the kitchen to outside, sucking on balloons.

'What was I saying?' I said.

'You think I'm taken.'

'Ahh yeh, that's right.'

'What if I was taken?' she said.

'Then I'd ask why you're flirting with me so much.'

'Flirting?' Her eyeshadow shimmered even brighter when she looked at me dead on.

'Isn't that what this is?'

She didn't comment, switching her attention to the beer pong again.

'Well,' I said, 'I'm definitely flirting so I must be wank if you haven't got the hint yet.'

'Oh don't worry. Hint received.'

I couldn't read her and it was annoying me, Rosie. She seemed a lost cause and I was in the mood to get absolutely shnizzled. I started to walk away from the sink and leave her to it.

'What's your name?' she asked. I had one foot in the garden. Wobbling.

'Fletch.'

'Nice to meet you, Fletch.'

The next time we saw each other was two hours later at the top of the landing, waiting for the bathroom. Somehow, I managed to get to the top, clinging onto the banisters like I was on a roller coaster at Alton Towers.

'Fassy seeing youhere,' I slurred, eyes half shut.

'Wow. Someone's had a few.'

'Canyatell?'

Her lip gloss shone like the moon as she laughed at the ceiling. All my weight was on one shoulder against the wall. My polo was messed with all sorts of fluids I didn't wanna question. I started to slide down the wall when she caught me and stood me up straight.

'Woah there, stay with me,' she said.

'You're bangin you, ya know.'

'Haha, thanks ... Fletch?'

I laughed and saw her wince at my breath.

'WAHAY, you remembered ... Nahh, honestly though like, you're a proper stunner. Like super sexy.'

Three lads came out the toilet then rubbing their nostrils. Becca ushered me in, clocking I was in a state to piss on the carpet right there and then. I sat and rocked on the toilet seat, rocketing piss into the bowl while Becca reapplied her make-up in the mirror.

'You not like me then?' I managed. It was so fuckin' bright in there. Felt like I'd walked into Simon Cowell's mouth.

'What you mean?'

'Like, am I not sexy too?'

I had spit on my chin. My jeans were round my ankles. My head lolled up and down like a bobblehead. I couldn't help but laugh at how stupid I looked.

'You looked sexier before.' She laughed.

'I'll take that.'

And then a rumbling in my stomach. I stood up, turned around, collapsed onto my knees and spewed into the bowl. I'm sure piss ricocheted back onto my face. It sounded like porridge dropped from a decent height. I felt a hand on my back but was too focused on emptying my guts into the bowl. There were laughs behind the door. My throat was on fire.

I use a fresh towel to start drying Rosie off. Weirdly embarrassed as if she was the one watching me chunder all them years ago. What was she doing while my head was in that bowl? Snogging lads in a club after too many porn-star Martinis? Jimjams in bed, shovelling Ben & Jerry's into her gob 'cause she'd just been dumped?

After five long minutes, I felt more sober and capable of standing up. I even had the senses to feel embarrassed. I picked up a random flannel and cleaned my face. Rebecca handed me a toothbrush, fuck knows whose, and a bottle of Listerine to rinse with. She could see I was coming around.

'How come you're being so nice? I'm bladdered,' I said, brushing me pegs.

'I'm not. I'm just making your breath smell like mint rather than sick.'

'Why?'

'Surely I deserve something for looking after ya?'

'What?'

'You want me to fuckin' spell it out with toothpaste for ya?'

It clicked then. I rinsed my mouth quickly and slapped one on her. This girl was different. She didn't hold back with the thought I still might have chunks of Mam's roast tatties in me teeth. Not at all. She had me up against the sink, tongue like a washing machine. Her lip gloss tasted of Haribos. Her waist thin, slotting perfectly into my palms. When we stopped, she looked up at me. Eyes like police sirens in the night.

'I'm Rebecca, by the way.'

'Nice to meet you, Rebecca.'

We laughed and shook hands.

'You're funny,' she said.

'Funny looking or ... ?'

'See, haha. Suppose you've got a bit more to you than that though.'

'I'm guessing gorgeous eyes, dazzling smile, great fashion, oh, and a shit-hot kisser.'

I leant casually against the towel rack like I didn't still smell of sick.

'You can add "a good mind-reader" to that list.'

Rebecca giggled and kissed me again. Somehow, in that mouldy, sick-smelling bathroom, something clicked, and we were happy with the thought we could never have to meet anyone ever again.

Finished, I look down at Reb-Rosie and imagine if she has a boyfriend or girlfriend. Who would be mourning her right now? I can't imagine Becca there on the bed. Some randomer filling her with fluid, applying her make-up. The thought makes me sick.

It will happen someday. I hope I'm not around to experience it. I'll be ash in the wind by then, hoovered up by the road sweepers on Ashton Old Road, wiped off someone's car windshield. I've never really thought deeply about Becca not being alive. It can happen to anyone. One step off the kerb, then *boom*. Hit by a bus.

I can't take that. I won't be able to live on. Becca's everything to me. The only reason why I care about my gambling and why I'm so desperate to get back on track. If I don't get out of debt or if she finds out, our relationship might as well be thrown in the machine with Rosie.

The two grand I won at the casino the other night is nowhere near enough. Amazingly, I haven't spent it all yet. Work has been too busy, not too busy to stop thinking about it, but too busy to spend it. As I prepared Rosie, talking about Rebecca and how much she meant to me, it only made me more desperate to win more. It reminded me how short life is.

I walk over and check my phone to see, within the space of an hour, I've lost every free bet Vince gave me. I not only need to up my game, I need to up my fuckin' stakes.

13

While I've been busy with Rosie, Janice has been busy in the casket showroom, using her witty charm to sell the most expensive coffins, the priciest urns. 'I know it's hard. She would have loved it. They only get one send-off,' she'd be saying. Slimy cow, but fuck me she has the gift of the gab. I can't imagine her not being in this place. I'll fight Eternal tooth and nail if shit goes any further with that buy-out. Openshaw just wouldn't be the same without this place, without Janice on hand to help everybody out.

With Janice busy, I nip home on my lunch-break and get what's left of my two grand. Within minutes I'm at Jim Ramsbottom's, filling out a football coupon. Five teams to win, a pretty standard bet. Until I get to the till.

'Are you serious?' says the young woman behind the counter. She's new, doesn't have a clue how much of a regular I am.

'Deadly,' I say. I smile through the Perspex glass. She thinks I'm fuckin' mental.

I slap the whole lot, a grand and a bit, on these five teams to win. I tell the cashier that I'm a VIP, that I know Vince Hannigan, so she gives me slightly better odds. Surely the main priority for bookies is to keep people like me walking through their door, so I'm not surprised the cashier doesn't think twice. If I win, I'll bag £500,000. Half a million fuckin' quid. Just imagine that. A few days ago, I had fuck all. Skint. Selling the valuables of dead people to get by. Tonight, I could be the richest man in Openshaw. All I need is for five teams to win. It's that simple.

The matches will finish around 9 p.m., so I have to go back to work. I nip out in the van to collect some bodies from the hospital, three to be specific. A homeless man pulled from Manchester canal this morning, a young, twenty-something man covered in tattoos who's overdosed, and a large woman in her seventies.

In the freezer, I put the old woman in the middle of the floor because the shelves are full. She lies there like a child's toy, ready to be gathered and boxed away. Because of the state of the homeless man, I have to deal with him first and get him in the furnace straight away. He's already in bad shape, and I mean proper bad. His skin has a luminous green tint from the sewage in the canal. He must have been floating, bobbing against the dockside for days.

The smell coming off him is like nothing I've smelt before. Ripe. Fermented. The type of smell that clings to the back of your throat and stays with you for days, weeks, years. If a jug of shite, dehydrated piss, curdled milk and white wine was left out in the sun for a week, it would be something close to this. He's already days into decomposition. Cheeks sliding off his face. Several layers of skin have already peeled from his arms and legs due to the water. Long scraggy hair and a full beard remain, still wet and festering like seaweed washed up on the beach.

The man has no family, no friends, and the coroner's fast-tracked his cremation, as the directory's full to the brim with bodies. I don't even know the fella's name, though Jan will have it somewhere on the paperwork. I take fingerprints and DNA swabs to be sent for analysis, but until we get the results and any family gets tracked down, his box of ashes will be chillin' on a shelf, unclaimed. This often happens with other bodies where we can't make the decision to embalm or cremate because we're waiting to hear back from the hospital or relatives, or waiting for someone else to pay us and give instructions. They lie for weeks, or sometimes months, in the freezer, waiting to be claimed and laid to rest. With limited burial spaces now and cremations costing a bomb, lots of family members choose to mourn in silence, refusing to pay or acknowledge their close one has died. For people like this homeless man, with no connections whatsoever, at least we have the freedom to make the decision and put him to rest.

As he lies on the cold conveyor, I notice a tattoo on his upper arm. The light-blue album cover of *Hatful of Hollow* by The Smiths – one of my absolute favourites. It makes me march back to the embalming room, unplug the stereo, and flick through a drawer full of uncased CDs until I find it.

I plug it in, playing 'Please Please Please Let Me Get What I Want', hoping this is a smidge of the send-off he would want. This man, who I've never met in my life, but suddenly feel a deep connection to. Our ears have shared the same riffs, the same vocals. Now here we are, enjoying it together for the first and last time.

The conveyer belt takes his green body into the mouth of the machine. It looks like a cucumber being shimmied along on a shopping checkout belt. I whir the flames into action, the lids of my eyes gathering tears as Morrissey sings the line about a good man turning bad.

Once I gather myself, I get to prepping Ben – the overdoser. On the bed in the embalming room, Ben looks timid and shy. Spots still sprout from his chin, fresh and unpopped. Tattoos of skulls, barbed wire and red roses curl around both arms up to the armpits. The lettering on his torso has been sliced and replaced by the 'Y' shaped stitching from the autopsy. On the counter by the sink is a blue plastic bag with his organs in. These are always removed during the autopsy and sent along with the body, ready to be dipped in formaldehyde and returned to the chest and cavity like a fucked game of *Operation*. This is exactly what I do, juggling and nearly dropping a slimy blackened lung on the floor.

Tube, drain, fill, wash, dry, then he's done. Ready for viewing tomorrow. A grieving mother who would later make a sound I have never heard come from a human before. A roaring, devastating cry of pain that only grief can bring out. Janice had to finally pull her away, still stroking his full head of black hair. The sound still lingered in the viewing room after she left.

Once I get the elderly woman out the way, I'm done for the day. I have to get Janice to give me a hand hauling her onto the gurney. The stretcher arches in the centre from her weight, thick arms dangling over the sides and catching on the strips of plastic as I try to push her through the corridor. The embalming is no easier either. I go to make the slits for the tubes but accidentally make an incision on the lower half of her body where the blood has gathered and settled due to gravity. This is called livor mortis and happens sometimes, dependent on the temperature and time of death. Blood starts spurting everywhere like a hole punctured in the bottom of a swimming pool. It projects onto the floor and walls like a murder scene. Thank fuck I have my safety goggles on.

My white coat is no longer white and my blue gloves are no longer blue. I force the tubes in, plugging her up as much as I can and directing the blood into the sink where it drains away. I slip on my arse twice because the floor is covered. She's starting to stink and ooze as well, which is often the case with larger bodies. Everything seems swollen, even her fingers, which I have to lather up with oil and Vaseline to yank her rings off. I end up sat on her chest, tugging away until they finally come loose. I fear Janice wandering in, catching me riding this dead woman, smothered in blood.

Like pushing a car up a hill, I manage to get her back in the freezer for whenever the viewing can be organised. I tell Janice to make it a priority and get her the fuck out of here. I can't be skipping over her body all week. Now finished, I bin my coat and clean off any excess blood in the sink, scrubbing away until my hands are raw with friction.

After mopping up the blood, I end up collapsing into a chair in the embalming room. Knackered and more drained than the big lass. I close my eyes, the back of my head resting against the cold wall. The lights hum above. The scalpels and scissors motionless on the tray. And then I remember. My bet. I look at the clock. It's nearly half ten. The games are finished. What am I doing sat here?

I leap up to get my phone by the sink and load up the Jim Ramsbottom's shoddy app, scanning the betting slip to my online account. A yellow wheel spins in the corner, loading how much money I have or haven't won. It's taking longer than usual. The time is killing me. Which teams have won? Which teams haven't? Just put me out of my fuckin' misery so I can start planning on what to bet on next.

The number appears. I drop to my knees. I try to make a sound but nothing is coming out.

14

I get in the van and absolutely tan it down Ashton Old Road. Vape shops and kebab shops blur either side. Beeping, swerving, missing pigeons by an inch. *Get the fuck out the way, I'm rich. I'm fuckin' rich!* I need a red light to calm me down and make me realise how fast my heart's racing. The steering wheel slick from sweat. Trainers twitchy on the pedals.

I park halfway onto the pavement and take three tries to get my seatbelt off. When I run in, Becca's got a mouthful of chocolate digestive watching *Say Yes to the Dress*.

'The fuck?' she spits, crumbs falling on the carpet. She thinks we're getting robbed.

I slap a fat kiss on her mush, getting her up and dancing round the living room. We hug, kiss some more. Me swinging her around like a puppet while she tries to process what the fuck's going on. The pack of digestives spills onto the floor. One rolls under the couch.

'Jamie, what the fuck you on?'

I laugh at the ceiling.

'Ha haaa, I did it. I won. We're fuckin' sorted, Becca. House. Dog. Whatever the fuck you want. You can have it!'

I run to the window and slam it open full whack.

'WE'RE FUCKIN' RICH BABY!!'

A granny pushing a trolley on the pavement tells me to piss off.

'Jamie, seriously. You're freakin' me out.'

Becca stands in the middle of the living room in a T-shirt and pyjama shorts. Arms crossed, thinking I'm on some psychedelic nonsense. I walk up to her and hold her shoulders, finding calm from somewhere, looking into her worried eyes. I'm so happy to see her face. She still has no idea our lives are changed for ever. She'll remember this moment for as long as we live. The worry. The fear. The digestives.

'Becca, I'm not kiddin' ya, I've won. I've won big.'

'Won what?'

'A bet. I put a daft bet on and it came in. I'm talking thousands. Thousands, Becca!'

She knows I bet now and again, it's part of being a man in my family and in Openshaw, but obviously no clue as to the extent. As long as it didn't interfere with bills, it was never worth talking about. None of that matters any more though. The past is the past. Any questions she has are irrelevant.

'Wh— How much?'

The numbers flash bright in my head.

'Quarter of a million.'

Becca sits down on the couch and stares at the cracked window-sill. I don't know why I didn't say half a million, the full amount. Don't ask. It just came out.

'What?' she says.

'Quarter of a million, Becca. We've won a quarter of a million quid.'

She looks into my eyes then. I can see it sinking in. The proof's in my face. My ugly, miserable mug can't stop smiling. She's never seen me this happy in all the years we've been together. It doesn't matter how I've won. It's the fact I have.

Becca looks at the mould on the ceiling, listens to the thunder of the washing machine drowning out the TV. The paint flaking from the skirting boards. The shelves bowed and layered in dust. The stacks of shoes, newspapers, towels and Christmas decorations teetering in every corner. The smell of chips wafting through the window. The screech of passing ambulances. The cry of the floorboards as she paces.

She manages a smile, then starts laughing, squealing, jumping at me with her legs wrapped around my ribs. We kiss again, clashing teeth. One of those desperate kisses where your emotions just pour out.

'You're a twat but I fuckin' love you, Jamie,' she says.

We laugh and spin until we're dizzy with happiness.

***

'What do you mean a week off?' says Janice.

I have the phone squeezed between my ear and shoulder, chucking clothes into a suitcase.

'I can't really explain Jan. I just need a break. A week, tops.'

I hear the flick of a lighter through the receiver.

'Well, can't you leave it a few weeks?' she says. 'We talked about this. I know you're fucked but we're overworked as it is here. There's a shit-ton of bodies coming in.'

'I know, I know. I'm sorry for the short notice Jan, I am. It's— I'll explain when I'm back. I promise. A week. That's all I need. Then I'll be back.'

'Have you cheated and you're doing a runner or summot?'

Becca's sat on her suitcase on the bed, trying to zip it closed from under her legs. Still laughing her tits off.

'Have I bollocks.'

'Who's that laughing then?'

'Look, I'll explain when I'm back, all right? And I'll make some calls about getting someone to come give you a hand. Okay? See you in a week.'

I hang up before she can try and talk me out of it.

Four hours later, me and Becca are on a plane to Santorini. We went online and booked the first place we'd seen which we could never dream of affording before. All inc, the full monty.

Booked it, packed it, fucked off. We're off to enjoy the start of our new lives.

We sit in the posh area of the plane, sipping on mojitos. I've never had so much fuckin' legroom in me life. A few hours ago, I was covered in some chubby woman's blood with not a penny in my bank account. Now, Becca's next to me, beaming, flustered every time an air hostess offers her a snack, a magazine to read, another cocktail.

With her eyes closed, head on the backrest, she runs her finger up and down the hairs on my forearm. Clouds hover below us outside the window. I can see her eyelids flickering, the possibilities building, realisation kicking in on how life-changing this is. I transferred half the money into my savings account and showed her in the Uber on the way to the airport. There it was on the screen. Six fuckin' digits. 250k. With no minus next to it. She brought the phone up to her eyes and stroked the screen as if the notes were there physically in her palm. Tears welled in her eyes. She kissed me long and hard. The absence of words enough to show how much this means for her, for us.

When we land, we do the British thing of commenting on how hot it is when walking off the plane. The tarmac of the runway wobbles in the distance. Big-bellied Greek men – golden and vacant in the eyes – usher us onward. Our hands clasped, sweating, not letting go.

Our hotel is paradise. After getting out the taxi, steep steps take us down to a platform jutting out from the rock face. The sun hovers above the sea opposite. The face of the hotel a balance of stark white and polished glass. Flutes of champagne greet us on arrival. A stumpy fella in a linen shirt carries each of our suitcases on his shoulders. We don't have to lift a finger. We keep looking at each other to check we aren't just dreaming this, ready to wake up to a siren outside, paint flaking from the ceiling.

Our room's more like an apartment. A top-floor balcony you can lounge on and watch the sunset. Facing us is nothing but crisp sea and the faint outlines of another island in the distance. Above it, the sun sears orange, peeking over the hills like a shy kid. Cruise ships sail on the water, leaving trails like slugs on a garden path.

The whole place oozes romance. I can tell why people cough up the big bucks to come here. Real postcard shit. I have to keep blinking. Maybe I'm in the embalming room, zoned out while waiting for the fluid to mix.

'Is this even real?' I say to Becca.

She's stood on the balcony with her champagne flute. A raspberry bobs in the middle. Her hair flicks in the wind like a shampoo advert.

I grab her by the waist and bring her in. I don't care about my belly squashing between us. I don't care my arms are heavy around her tiny body. We love each other. We're happy. She rakes back my hair with her nails. I feel her arse through the linen shorts and slap another kiss on her. Our faces hot and baking from the heat, the weather and the moment.

Before we know it, her legs are around my waist again and I carry her into the bedroom. Our bodies wriggle in the sheets, clothes flying at all angles and landing on lampshades. Legs akimbo, testing the headboard made of woven bamboo. It isn't the mindless sex we're used to lately. Silent bonks after late-night shifts, the scent of chemicals on my body. I haven't taken Trick's advice to spice things up in the bedroom. He's probably right. We need it. We're distant. Tired.

Already, this feels different. The sun sets through the open balcony door, drenching the room, the bed, in an amber glow. The light bounces off her freshly shaven legs. My arse, exposed to the world, moving with a rhythm I didn't know I had. Becca moans like we're the only ones on the island, not the type of sympathetic moan that's just trying to make me feel good either. I moan too, sweat beading on my forehead, slipping along the surface of her skin, drenching the cushions. We're lost in the moment, and a pretty long moment if I say so myself. We finish and crash out, panting, like they do in the movies. The sun is fully set now. A wind picks up and breezes against our wet bodies. The horn of a cruise ship honks in the distance.

Once our breathing settles, we look at one another.

'The fuck happened there?' we say.

***

What follows in the days after is pure magic. We eat tzatziki and sip cocktails on glass balconies, watching birds sail from island to island. We walk leisurely up and down the steps, admiring the blue domes of Fira. Every building pristine white and freshly painted. Stray cats meander along the pavements, a white patch on their arse from rubbing against the walls. Donkeys clop by, smelling of hay and hot shite.

As well as the fun holiday stuff – like slapping up my barnet with factor fifty or asking for the bill in the most Mancunian non-Greek accent ever – me and Becca finally have time to chat again. Becca tells me about her work lately and the latest clothing lines they've had in. Spring collections. The resurgence of sage green and baggy suits. I enjoy watching her speak enthusiastically, the freckles blossoming on her cheeks. She speaks with the freedom you only have on holiday. Where nothing else matters but you and your partner, making memories, enjoying the moment.

Becca's even cracking jokes again. We order Bolognese and she says:

'You know, the other day, my mate said I couldn't build a car out of spaghetti.'

'What?'

'Should have seen her face when I drove pasta.'

She laughs, being goofy, putting toothpicks in her mouth like a walrus as we eat olives. I don't even fuckin' like olives, but she makes me want to. She's ordering nearly every cocktail on the menu because we can and never get a chance to. Even though it's roasting, she's cosying into me, rubbing the back of my head affectionately as we look out at the sea after our meal. The best view, yet she chooses to look at me like she always does. Admiring, saying how my eyes match the waves, how the sunset matches my hair, how generous I am for taking us here.

For the first time since being here, I really feel like crying. The rays on my face, the cold lager down my throat, Becca smiling under my arm. Have I ever felt this happy before?

Days bleed into the next, our joy growing by the hour. I'm red with sunburn. Becca, radiant and bronze. We take photos on the peak of random rocks, the sea bashing away below. Becca wears colourful playsuits that flow with the direction of the wind. She belongs in a place like this. Beauty, elegance, calmness. Then there's me in my Bermuda shorts that still fit me from Malia five years ago, the faint stain of a Jägerbomb still noticeable on the thigh.

'You know who you look like?' says Becca. I have my top off doing a Superman pose on the peak. 'You know that starfish fella out of *SpongeBob*?'

'You cheeky cunt.'

I chase her and tackle her into a mound of grass. She laughs like I haven't heard her laugh in years. Later, she tells me Patrick is everyone's favourite.

That night, while Becca is wrapped in the white sheets after another session of romance, she asks me again how I won. Head resting on a bent arm.

'I told you, a bet,' I say, lighting a fag on the balcony.

'Football?'

'Yeh,' I reply, not too quick to show my annoyance. For once, I don't want to think about betting. I want to enjoy this.

'Must have been a hefty bet then if you won that much.'

I turn from the sea to look at her.

'Trick give me a tip. Borrowed me a few quid so I could have a go and I added on a few more matches. Easy as that. He'll just be happy he's getting his money back.'

I let out the smoke, not even bothered by how easy lying is now. I watch the white of the moon reflect the white of the buildings. Spotlights light the stairways of Santorini for miles along the cliff face. The faint trickle of vacant hot tubs and private pools can be heard from the apartments below.

Becca falls back into the pillows, a smile on her face. Satisfied.

'You lucky fucker,' she says, before breathing steadily into sleep.

I look out at the sea with no end, knowing I've reached mine. I'm done now. I've got what I wanted. Imagine how it could have went? How long could I have gone on for? This. Was this always meant to happen? Was I confident or just hopeful I could dig myself out? And did it even matter any more? I don't have to worry about the past. I don't have to think about how it happened or where things could have led me. They were dark, deadly corners I can finally avoid. I'm out now. I'm here, in the open, having a cig on a balcony in Santorini, watching the moon and listening to the waves as my girlfriend sleeps peacefully in our luxury apartment. In the morning, I'll wake and eat fresh fruit, have coffee from a coffee machine. I deserve this. I've earned this. Shit like this can happen to people like me. I've gone through enough for two people's lifetimes. Surely, I'm owed this cig, on this balcony. I get reminded enough in my job for Christ's sake: this shit doesn't last for ever.

We begin dying the day we're born, so why waste a day not living?

15

It's been three days since we returned from our week-long holiday of a lifetime. We can't stop talking about it. The Irish bar we didn't leave until 3 a.m. The Greek grandma who kept buying us ouzo shots. That catamaran we went on for the day, where we stopped off and dived into the crystal blue. The cuddles on the balcony. The chats. The sex. Our relationship has been revived by sun and cocktails. We've come back fresh, willing to leave those touchy conversations in the past. All those late nights in the club, coming home from the bookies broke and wankered, the casino night – it's like they never happened.

On the flight back home, I kept getting my online banking up and just staring at the number, remembering the days when Mam and Dad were together and worrying about money non-stop. Going day by day, scraping the backs of cupboards and the dark depths of the freezer to make sure tea was on the table for me. I'd tell them I was full so they could have more food, prepped to steal some lunch off the lads in school the next day. I'd give them a spontaneous tenner here and there that I won in the bookies, lying that I came first in a race at school or was rewarded for a good essay. It was meant to be the other way around. Them looking out for me, treating me, making sure I was okay. Whereas, really, I always felt like it was my job to keep an eye on them. They were vulnerable, had their own troubles. I do the same with Becca. Whatever I get, however I get it, I want to share it with the people that mean the most to me, the people who have made my life worth living, who would give every last penny to me if I asked. Seeing that money in my bank account, I finally can. I can finally give back.

Becca has to go back to work at Selfridges pretty much straight away. They have new lines to arrange and upselling targets to hit. I should've gone back to the directory too, but I'm on too much of a high to be around death. It's weird when you have that much in your account. You feel like you can spend your day doing anything you like. Why would I go to work? Janice can surely last a few more days while I get a plan in place. Am I going to even stay and keep my job? It's a lot of money, but it's not unlimited. I can't do that to Janice either. No matter how much money you win, it'll never change some aspects of your life, the aspects that matter most to you.

On the way to the club, I bump into Trick on Ashton Old Road. I suggest going for a cheeky pint and game of snooker at the club to avoid the fact I should be at work. We hadn't had a game in two weeks now, so we needed to make up for lost time.

'Fuck me,' he says as we sit down. 'You fall in that cremation machine or summot? You're burnt to fuck.'

Trick slaps me on the shoulders. The sting fizzes throughout my entire back.

'Where you been anyway? You didn't mention you had a holiday booked?'

'Spur of the moment thing,' I say.

'Skint, my arse,' he laughs.

'Becca paid,' I say. 'I didn't ask any questions. Just got on that plane and fucked off for some sun.'

Trick doesn't know I've won. I haven't told anyone else about it other than Becca. I'm not really planning to either. Not that Trick would treat me any different, but people get weird around money, especially in Openshaw where it's hard to come by.

'Where'd you go?' Trick's loading the red balls into the triangle. I like the normality of him hunched over the table, his purple head sweating like a cold glass of Vimto.

'Benidorm for a week.'

'Decent?'

'Much needed, mate. I was fucked.'

'I know you were. I can tell when you're stressed, your eyes get all glassy and worried. Janice all right with you going?'

'I'll let you know next week.'

We knock the balls around for a few hours. It's good to be sinkin' pockets and having a chat over a pint again. As nice as last week was, as buzzin' as I felt about my money now, you just can't beat a pint and a game of snooker with your closest pal.

While in Santorini, I phoned up Kevin, who worked in Longsight and was on the same embalming apprenticeship as me way back when. We weren't really mates, but I knew he'd take money for anything (I mean *anything*, but I won't go there). I got him to help Janice out at the directory while I was away and texted him to see whether he could do another week. I told him not to tell Janice and just work until I popped back in. I switched my phone off before he could text back. He was an annoying twat, I couldn't have my honeymoon period being disturbed. I've not turned my phone on since.

A game of snooker is nice and all. I need more if I'm to pass the time though, something to keep me occupied while I work out how I'm going to divvy up this money. That's why, the next day, I do something mad.

I go to the Dog's Trust in Ashton and come home with a Shih Tzu puppy called Mango. He has an unusual black and white coat and short button nose. Cute as fuck. Little fluffy legs that bounce around like a rabbit. He licked half me face off when the lady brought out the options. It was a no-brainer. Becca's gonna love him. She's always wanted a dog, a tiny teddy-bear thing. I was never keen. It's not about the pissing and shitting everywhere, I'm not arsed 'cause the flat's already a tip. It's the horror stories: the vet bills, the fifty dabs a month to get it trimmed, to get its nails cut. All that unnecessary faff you could do without when you're skint. I was scrambling for change to place a bet. How the fuck could I have looked after a little pup before the win? Now, every time I look at Mango, his tiny bottom teeth pointing up at me, I'll remember he kicked off the start of our new life.

I text Becca to let me know when she's on the way back from work so I can 'whack tea on'. I play it cool, sitting watching footy when I hear the keys in the door downstairs. I quickly hide Mango and return to the sofa.

'All right, babe.'

Becca throws her bag down and crashes on the couch next to me, fringe stuck to her damp forehead.

'Get me back on that fuckin' island,' she says.

I smirk, sipping on a beer.

'Rough day?' I ask.

'Rough as a bear's arse.'

Her head rests on my shoulder, eyes already flickering from exhaustion.

'Wouldn't mind getting me a pack of crisps, would ya?' I say.

I feel her eyes open.

'You're a lazy twat, you know that.'

Still, she gets up and wanders into the kitchen. I hear the cupboard door open, then a scream.

Mango's in the crisps box. Black tail wagging, knocking the fuck out of a pack of prawn cocktail. Becca picks him out with tears in her eyes, rubbing her face into his soft chest. Mango licks the tears that are falling down her cheeks. Eyes bulging, tail still doing a madness.

'Surprise,' I say, leaning on the fridge.

'You're mental.'

'Maybe. But you love me for it.'

Becca puts Mango down. He runs into the living room then comes back with a plastic pig in his gob.

'He's so cute. What's his name?'

'Mango.'

'Mango! Hello Mango, aren't you just the cutest?'

She speaks in one of them weird voices people do with dogs. It's nice seeing Becca sat on the kitchen floor, moving the pig back and forth. Mango boings about, going crazy when it oinks. Knocking into cupboards, bins, a big smile on his mush.

'Oi,' I say. Becca looks up, bemused. 'What about my crisps?'

***

Becca's in her element this week. Buying toys, blankets, bowls, a crate – everything you need and more. It's like having a fuckin' baby: there's a shit-ton that goes into it. Getting the bugger chipped, vaccines, insurance. Even more when they're only a couple of months old. Getting them used to sounds, interaction with other dogs, potty training. Luckily, Becca takes the lead, literally. She's taking him out to piss on lamp posts every two hours as they only have tiny bladders at that age. Not like she minds; I'm still in the good books. She's just happy I've cleaned up my own shit; I don't need to be doing Mango's too.

Still, I pull my weight, which is a fuckin' lot. I whip up meals Ramsay style for when she gets home from work. Tell her she can have the remote for the night. Do the washing and ironing. Massage her feet. Make her laugh. Even teach Mango to sit, stay and roll over to impress her.

Instead of spending all day thinking about what races are on and how I can win money, I'm thinking about Becca and how I can make her happy that day. Don't get me wrong, I still pick up my phone to have a scroll through the apps, keep an eye on the odds market, but amazingly I don't even turn it on, never mind place any bets. It would seem a bit pointless. I won't lie and say I spend a whole day without thinking of placing one, but soon as Becca walks through the door after work every day, I already feel like a winner.

I enjoy my time being at home. This one day though, fuck me. So, Becca brings these bags home from Selfridges full of clothes all the time. Shit that's good as new, clobber they can't sell any more because the stitching's a bit frayed or it's been tried on more than twice. Their collections are changing every two weeks so there's always bin bags lying around the flat, full to the brim with designer dresses, heels and even the odd shirt and pair of jeans for me. I might look like Yves Saint Le Wrong but you know me, I'll take any free shit I can get, especially when it costs a bomb. I often rock into the club with a pair of Levi's jeans or a Ralph Lauren T-shirt, everyone thinking that my embalming gig must pay a decent wedge.

Anyway, point is, I get home from the boozer after dipping out for a couple, and Mango has got to one of the bin bags. He's ripped a Michael Kors bag to shreds and nibbled on some Gucci heels. It's like a confetti cannon's gone off. It's teething time. He's already gone to town on the remote and chewed the fuck out the sofa cushions. I chuck the bin bag to the back of the wardrobe with the rest of them and hoover up the evidence while he looks at me from the couch, tilting his head from side to side, wondering what's going on.

The bastard shat in my shoes too. Putting on my new trainers and splat, a pair of white socks ruined. He sounds like a menace, 'cause he is, but fuck me he's cute. He makes me laugh every day. I'm surprised by how much I love him. I take him for walks down Ashton Old Road, making the old ladies laugh as he lunges for discarded chicken wings. We fight on the sofa while Becca's at work, tumbling and wrestling over a tennis ball. I end up throwing it too hard and smash a newly framed picture of us from Santorini. Another thing I have to bin and keep quiet about, hoping she won't notice. We have a pact, me and Mango, a lad's code. I even teach him 'paw' so we can shake on it.

It's a good time. The little bastard has changed the whole flat, making the shithole more enjoyable, more like a home, although it smells more like a shithole now. Becca's dropping the seed about looking for houses now we're back from hols. I knew it'd be a topic of discussion as soon as the plane wheels hit the tarmac. That's probably what pushed me to nip out and get Mango. Give her something else to focus on before I get my head together and decide on this big next step. I know it's coming, time's running out. I just need a little longer.

I've been off work for two weeks now. The boredom has had me reaching for my phone more and more. What harm would a cheeky bet do? Just something to kill the hours. I've still got all that money Becca doesn't know about. Even if I had a mad flurry of bets to pass the days, we would still be fine. We could get a *bigger* house. *Two* dogs. Fuck it, a snooker table for the garage.

Amazingly though, I've resisted. I haven't even turned my phone on still. I've kept it off mainly knowing Janice would be belling me up, begging me to come back and get rid of that weird fuck Kevin. Kevin would be on my case as well. I don't need it. I'm enjoying my new cushy life. Kevin's a wrongen but he's okay at his job, he can cope. He'll prep the bodies well and keep the conveyor belt running. I'm just not ready to go back yet. Not now I have the money cushion. I'm feeling better in myself too. I'm not knackered, I haven't placed one bet in over two weeks, even in the bookies. I feel new. I don't want that to change.

I'm cleaning up another one of Mango's accidents with a dustpan and brush when the front doorbell goes. It's midday, too early for it to be Becca. Fuck knows who it could be. Please not Janice. Please not Janice.

I wander down with Mango in my arms, chewing on my earlobes.

'Trick? The fuck you doing here?' I say, relieved.

'What the hell's that?' he says, pointing to Mango, who's panting, licking his own nose.

'Mango, Trick. Trick, Mango.'

'Mango? Fuckin' Mango? You tellin' me that's yours?'

'Becca's, technically.'

'What a soft arse. Anyway, you got a minute?'

I lead Trick upstairs and flick the kettle on. Trick sits, hugging the armrest, staring the fuck out of Mango so he won't come near him.

'He's friendly, ya mard arse.' I say.

'Don't give a toss. Shit dogs, waste of time.'

I laugh, walking in with the brews and passing him one.

'What do I owe the pleasure, anyway?' I say.

'You lost your phone or summot you?'

I sip the brew too quickly, burning my lips.

'Ay?'

'You. It's like getting hold of the bastard Pope.'

I lean to fetch my phone from the coffee table, wiping a film of dust off it, turning it on. It pings and pings and pings, whirring into life. Missed call after missed call. Janice, Kevin, Trick. But mostly Janice.

'Fuck me, who died?' I laugh. I throw the pig for Mango, who starts chewing it near the TV.

Trick sits silently, cupping his brew and staring into its reflection. My laugh peters out. My phone eventually stops beeping.

'Trick. There summot I don't know?'

He looks at me. Blank.

'You really haven't heard?'

I let the heat gather on my fingers around the mug until they start to sting. I keep them there, the pain building, trying to read Trick's face. Hairs stand on my neck, activating my sunburn.

'What is it?' I ask.

'It's Janice, mate. She's dead.'

16

We're sat in the directory waiting room in silence. Me, Trick and Kevin, twiddling our thumbs until the solicitor arrives. The room's deathly silent. A carafe of cold water sweats on the coffee table in front of us.

'What time they comin', Kev?' I say. 'I thought they said ten?'

'They did,' says Kevin, pacing up and down all jittery. 'I'll ring them again.' He disappears into the reception area, fumbling with his phone.

'Bit odd, int he?' says Trick, sat next to me on the sofa. He's itching the faded tattoo of St George on his arm.

I nod. Kevin's an oddball, but I owe him a lot for the last week or so. He's covered my arse and stepped in, holding the fort with all this shit going on. He told me Janice had passed around three days ago. Knowing we're pals, he must have chased Trick down at the club, informing him of the news before running everything on his own for the weekend: paperwork, embalming, viewings, cremations, the lot. Waiting until I came back like I promised. Fair play to the lad, he didn't have to do all that.

He said he knocked on Janice's office door after his Wednesday night shift, to say goodbye and all that. He heard no answer so poked his head in. Janice was slumped in her chair, mouth open and eyes wide. The lamp cast dark shadows on her face. Paperwork splayed across the desk as always. Ironically, a signed death certificate, a dried-out pen teetering on the edge.

She died of a heart attack. Seventy-three. The fags, the brandies at the end of every night, the takeaway pizzas she'd order into her office when she couldn't be arsed going home. I can do a list as long as Dave the Butcher's cock on what could have led to it. It doesn't make the shock ripple any less. You think a steely woman like that can go on for ever. That someone who works so closely with death can somehow avoid it. I thought death didn't have the balls to knock on her door this early. It works in weird ways. We're never too far from that freezer. She's lying there now, on her own fuckin' shelf, awaiting her fate.

'Sorry I'm late. Traffic's a bugger on that road.'

A tall woman with a blonde bob and light grey suit walks in. She has a narrow face, blue eyes, and gums too big for her mouth. Kevin tags behind like an obedient puppy, his white embalming coat smudged with ash.

'I'm Jane, by the way. So sorry for your loss.'

I nod. She shakes hands with us all.

'Now,' says Jane, taking a seat on the sofa opposite me and Trick, wanting to crack on with it. Kevin hovers near one of the plants behind me. 'I don't know how much you know about Janice's will or what was prepared.'

'I only found out about all this yesterday to be fair. And I didn't know she even had a will,' I reply.

'She submitted one to us about six months ago. Were you aware of her health issues at all?'

'Other than thirty fags a day and a shite diet, not really.'

Jane pours herself a glass of water then pulls some papers from her handbag.

'It's Jamie, isn't it? You work here at the directory?'

'Sorry, yeh. That's right.'

'And?' she asks, looking at Trick. I nearly interject to say his name's Barney.

'Oh, don't mind me, love,' says Trick. 'Just here for moral support and that. Stephen's the name though.'

'Nice to meet you, Stephen. Anyway, here's an overview of her specifications. I believe there's a coffin in the casket room. A blue and pink one, it says? Does that ring any bells?'

I snigger. The crafty sod, she did buy one for herself after all.

'That's right, yeh, I know the one. So that's what she wants, is it?'

'Not quite. That's what she's left in your name.'

I look at Trick, who's a bit flustered and awkward about the whole situation. He doesn't do well with death. Still, even he manages a smirk about the coffin. I showed it to him on the way in.

'Come again?' I say.

'The blue and pink coffin,' says Jane. 'That's yours. I remember her saying specifically she wanted you to have it.'

I stare into the carpet, chuckling to myself. That hideous fuckin' thing? That's what she's left me? After years of working my bollocks off here, I get a tacky bastard coffin?

Jane hands me the paperwork to prove she's not pulling my leg.

'Is that all she said?'

'Pretty much.'

'Anything else? I mean in the will or owt like that?' It feels cheeky asking but fuck it, that surely can't be it. She has no real close family, no nothing. She wouldn't just leave me a daft coffin. Maybe she clocked on that I was robbing from all them corpses, and this was her way of telling me to do one. Fuck knows.

'That's it under your name I'm afraid. She rented her place, so only left a few bits and bobs like jewellery to some friends and clothes to charity, but other than that—'

'What about the directory?' says Kevin, emerging from behind a pot-plant branch and sitting on the arm of the sofa. A whiff of smoke and formaldehyde comes off him.

'Yeh,' I say. 'Good point actually. What happens to this place?'

The image of the Eternal contract flashes in my memory. Did she sign it while I was off? Is that what could have tipped her over the edge, plucking up the courage to tell me she'd finally had enough of the struggle and wanted one final pay-off before she snuffed it? Maybe that's what all the missed calls were about. Not about getting my arse back to work but telling me what the crack was, that my job was on the line. Janice clearly knew she was on a timer. It rang out before she had the chance to tell me everything.

Jane flicks through more paperwork, a load of sophisticated jargon that goes right over my head.

'I can't see anything here that says it was left to anyone,' she says. 'When that's the case, it usually goes up for auction, or is offered on priority to any relevant buyers or local suitors within the death busi— sorry, funeral business. A community investor, someone like that.'

'You can say death.' I laugh. 'It's all right.'

Jane sips on her water sheepishly, tucking a strand of blonde behind her ear. You'd think solicitors would be comfortable with all this bollocks. You can tell the place is creeping her out. Maybe it's Kevin picking his nose, or the fact that Janice is only down the hall, chillin' on a shelf.

'And whoever takes it over,' I say, 'that all goes through you, does it?'

'I'm the middleman, really. But yes, I'll probably sort the logistics while overseeing the will.'

My knees crack as I stand and walk over to the mantelpiece. I look up at a big picture of a vase with pink roses sprouting from the top.

'And the funeral,' I say. 'Did she say anything about that?'

Another sheet of paper is pulled from Jane's handbag.

'No service. No burial. Just a cremation.'

She hands me the sheet. It's bare other than a couple of lines and ticked boxes. It doesn't seem fitting for such an important woman. Openshaw would want to celebrate her. She deserves more than this, a proper send-off. If it was up to me, I wouldn't have it that way at all. It's not right. But if this is what she wanted, I have no choice but to follow it.

'Fair enough,' I say.

Jane stands, flattening the crease in her trousers. She walks over to me and places a hand on my shoulder. Her voice drops into a smooth, consoling tone, one that's trained and saved for moments of grief.

'She loved you. I could tell.'

'I just ... it just doesn't seem enough, ya know? Thought she would have wanted more. I dunno why she didn't mention anything. I had no idea she was ill.'

'I know, it's hard. She was adamant in what she wanted. She was happy she was in a position where she could make these choices. Not many people get that privilege, you know that better than me. It may not seem much, but she didn't want it any other way.'

I'm frozen, looking up at the picture, concentrating to keep my emotions in.

'I unfortunately didn't know Janice too well personally,' says Jane, 'but I'm sure she just didn't want any fuss. People deal with illness in different ways. I'm sure things will become clearer with time.'

Jane leaves the paperwork on the coffee table, looping the handbag over her shoulder.

'It was nice to meet you, fellas,' she says, shaking Trick's then Kevin's hand. 'Sorry again for your loss, she seemed a lovely woman.'

'She was a cow really – a blue and pink coffin?!' I smirk, shaking Jane's hand. 'But thanks, ya know, for all this.'

'Just my job,' she says. 'It's nice to know she's in good hands.'

I see Jane through to the reception where she exits into the car park, using her handbag to shield her head from the downpour. I stand in the empty reception, the shelves behind the desk packed with labelled urns, ready to be picked up by family members. The door to the casket room is ajar. A flash of pink from the coffin edging through the gap. My shoddy inheritance. One of the few bits of her I have left. I look up at the cracked corners of the ceiling, kick at the dog-eared carpet tiles. I can smell the dust and musty walls. Everything is yellowed and worn. It's like being in the flat.

I find myself running outside into the rain, catching up to Jane's Mercedes as it starts pulling away from the bay. I tap on the driver-side window, rain dripping from my eyebrows and trainers squelching like fuck.

'Everything okay?' says Jane, lowering the window.

'What if I wanted it?' I shout, trying to be heard over the water rebounding on the car roof.

'What?'

'The directory. What if I wanted it? To buy it, I mean.'

Jane looks ahead, both hands on the steering wheel. The swish of car tyres sound like ocean waves on the road. I feel the heat from the car vents, smell the peppery leather on the seats.

'Can you?' she asks, seriously.

I give her the most assuring nod I can. I'm not pissing about here. I'm deadly serious. This place can't fall into the hands of those Eternal fucks or any other landlord cunt who would knock it down and turn it into ugly flats. The Openshaw Funeral Home has history, heart. It's one of the few staples in Openshaw that's left, that still serve a purpose to the community, even if it's about death and the ends of people's lives. We help people when they need it most. I can't let that stop. That's not what Janice would do. I could spruce it up. It's not as if I don't have the money. I could refurb every last bit of it, give it the makeover it's desperate for. Putting life back into death.

'Are you sure?' Jane asks. She knows people act weird in times of grief. Regretful decisions are most likely to be made after losing someone close. She also knows I know that, better than anyone. I'm more experienced in death than her. She knows I mean it.

'Positive. I want to do it. I need to do it,' I say.

'Here,' she says, handing her business card through the

window. 'Sleep on it and give me a call tomorrow if you want to go over details.'

Jane winds up her window and drives off into the rain, her car becoming a blurry mist in the distance.

I walk a wet trail back into the waiting room where Trick and Kevin are talking bollocks by the mantelpiece. I stand with the card in my hand, a puddle growing on the carpet around me.

'The fuck's happened here then?' says Trick, laughing.

'I think I just bought a funeral directory.'

***

'You bought WHAT?'

'Wait wait wait, hear me out here, Becca.'

It's a few days later. The paperwork has been signed. The schedule of payments has been arranged. There's no going back.

Me and Becca are at a posh restaurant in the centre of Manchester, munching on steaks over a bottle of wine which, for once, isn't the second cheapest on the menu. We're celebrating Becca's promotion to Senior Retail Manager at Selfridges.

'Jamie. Did you not think of sorting us out before buying a fuckin' funeral home?'

The old couple on the table next us give us a side-eye over their salmon.

'Just chill, will ya. It wasn't that expensive. Plus, it's more than that. It's my job. That place means a lot to me.'

'What, and *I* don't? How much we talking, anyway?' She chomps a bit of meat off her fork and chews viciously.

'Two hundred.'

'Sorry, can you speak up?'

'Two hundred.'

'GRAND?'

'No, chocolate fuckin' kisses. Yes, grand!'

Becca doesn't appreciate my sarcasm one bit. I envisage her

steak knife plunged into the side of my neck in approximately thirty seconds. Me trying to compress it with my napkin. She continues to chew, carving into her steak, grinding into the plate, possibly the table.

I look down at my bloody slab, charred around the edges. I poke it with my fork, playing with its spongey texture.

'Jamie, that's like nearly all of the money!'

Little does she know. Yes, I could just tell her the truth and end the argument now. But then what? Admit I'm a liar and encourage more questions? That would be insane.

'Do you get why I'm annoyed?' she says.

I don't look up. I poke and poke.

'Jamie, do you get why I'm annoyed?'

'Kinda, but—'

'Kinda? Kinda?! We finally get on track. We finally get money in our accounts where we can start building a life and move out of the shithole we're in, and you piss two hundred grand into the wind like that.' She clicks her fingers. 'I'm sick of living above a kebab shop, Jamie, and waking up to the smell of greasy fuckin' chips. I go into work smelling like doner meat and have to rinse the perfume section every morning. I'm sick of it. We finally got the chance to get away from that and you go and do this 'cause your fuckin' boss died.'

'Becca, don't do that.'

'No, look, I didn't mean that. I'm sorry that she died, I am, but you don't have to react like this. You have nothing to prove to her. You could get a job anywhere else, another directory, on a better wage probably. Wherever we get the house, we can prioritise the location on your job, I'll travel in, I'm really not arsed.'

'It's not about that. Have you considered that I might be doing this for me? That I actually love what I do and that that place means a lot to me? I've spent a big chunk of my life there. I look after people, I feel valued, and it makes me happy helping people who mean something to me. It won't be the same outside of Openshaw. It won't have the same connection. And yeh, Janice was a big part of buying it 'cause the place was her life and soul, but it's just a bonus that I can keep it going for her. Have you thought that it might be good for us in the long run? That we now own a business?'

'A business. You're going on like you've bought fuckin' Microsoft.'

'Am I bollocks. It's not as if we're not gonna make money from it. I'm gonna do it up, good and proper. Give it a lick of paint, bring in quality modern machines, extend our range of coffins and packages—'

'Great. Diamond coffins and machines that burn people quicker. We'll be rolling in it.'

'Becca, don't take the piss. I'm serious.'

'And so am I. That's life-changing money that, Jay. Life changing. And you didn't even think of running it by me or chatting to me first before doing it. I mean, what the actual fuck?'

'I knew you'd react like this, that's why.'

'Well, no fuckin' shit, Jamie. How else am I gonna react?'

'You don't understand.'

'You're right,' says Becca. 'I don't.'

We sit in silence. Our chips growing cold, our peppercorn sauce congealing on the plate. Our waiter appears beside the table in his bowtie, hands clasped behind his back.

'Is everything okay for you both?' he says.

'Oh, smashing, yeh,' I say.

'Lovely, thanks,' says Becca.

Our smiles disappear as he wanders away. Back to silence. Tension you could cut with a knife a lot blunter than the one I'm swirling, bored, in my fingers.

The restaurant's filled with a light hum of conversation. Tables radiate with candlelight, happy couples laughing so much their flames thrust from side to side. An elderly man twinkles keys on the piano. Corks pop, glasses clink. This should be a night of celebration, not confrontation.

'I was going to ask you a question,' I say. Becca looks at me and drinks her wine in big gulps. 'But I guess there's no real point now, with your promotion and all that.'

'What was it?'

'I was gonna ask, ya know, if you would work there with me. Doing what Janice used to do. The sales side of it all. I think you'd be really good at it.'

'You want me to be your receptionist?'

'Not a receptionist. It's more than that.'

'Where would I be sat?'

'Well, at reception, but—'

'Well then, I'd be a receptionist, wouldn't I?'

There's no point when Becca's like this. It's a long shot asking her if she'd come and help me out anyway. There's no chance now that she'll work at a place like the directory every day, being reminded of where our money has been 'pissed into the wind'. She's good at her job anyway, she loves it like I love mine. I don't want to take that away from her.

'Sorry, just thought I'd ask in case you wanted to.'

We've finished our food. I'm tempted to place my first bet in weeks on us not having a dessert. The odds would be very, very slim.

'Sorry. I'm just angry. Is there anyone else you can ask?' she says.

**

'Me?!'

Trick has a pint in his hand, foam on his top lip.

'Yeh. Why not?'

'Me? A fuckin' receptionist?'

'It's not a receptionist!'

I slide the cue along my bridge hand and power the ball into a group of reds.

'You're having me on,' says Trick.

'I'm serious. It'd be a laugh. Plus, I know you've been struggling for work recently. You're in here pretty much every day. I thought I'd help you out a bit and give us the chance to work together.'

Trick chalks his cue, embarrassed. It's obvious he's hunting for painting jobs. Word spreads quickly. It's nothing to be ashamed about – you're lucky to go months without a dry period. Blokes in the boozer get worked up about that shit. Providing is all some of them have to go off; it's how they're judged as men. It's not even about the money, it's about having a purpose, maintaining your pride by being able to get a round in and not leech off your mates for weeks. It's not nice everyone knowing you're a bit skint and a bit desperate. It takes a mate to notice it and help out if he can. Trick would do it for me.

'So,' says Trick, getting the bridge rest from the bottom rack, 'what would I be doing then? I can't be dealing with bodies and shit Jay, there's no fuckin' chance.'

'Nahh, there'll be none of that. I'll do all the prep work and the cremations. We can even do it so you don't see a body for as long as you're there, though I can't guarantee it.'

Trick's hunched shoulders shiver as he hits a shot.

'It would mainly be dealing with families and people to do with the funeral arrangements, all that jazz,' I continue. 'Ya know, certificates, paperwork, payments – it's a piece of piss, honest. I'll talk you through it all. Of course, there'll be a bit of upselling too, but you won't have a problem with that with your gob.'

'Upselling?'

'Yeh, selling caskets, urns, funeral packages. It's a business at the end of the day.'

Trick takes a seat on the flat bench and drinks.

'I'm not sure mate. Just seems a bit wrong, dunnit?'

'I can give you about two and a half grand a month.'

I long-pot a red then smash the black into the middle pocket.

I go on a run, manoeuvring round the table, stretching over the felt and resting a knee on the table, knocking balls in left, right and centre.

Trick deliberates over his pint. A group of lads play dominoes under the TV showing horse racing. Sinatra plays from the radio behind the bar.

'When would you need me?' says Trick, peering under the hot table light.

17

Janice's nails are still painted pink, the varnish chipped. Her freezing fingers laced within mine. It's the first time I've seen her since I went away. The frown below her perm looks cemented in a rage that was ready to unleash whenever I got back. Her eyes are still open. Two cloudy voids looking up at the ceiling lamps. I sit on the swivel stool, holding her grey hand, my head bowed and muttering the same sentence over and over again. *I'm sorry. I'm sorry. I'm sorry.*

What am I sorry for? I'm not entirely sure. For having my first holiday in years after winning a bit of money and wanting to get my life back on track? For getting carried away with my happiness and ignoring her, forgetting her when she needed me? It's probably that, the guilt of not being here, whether her heart attack would've still happened or not. It's the unknown I'm sorry for. Sorry for not being here for her when she needed me most, when she'd always been there for me.

As the forms said, Janice isn't to be buried or presented for viewing. Still, I wheel her into the silent embalming room. I've already been sat here for an hour, holding her hand, looking at her. After my apologies, I'm comfortable enough to start telling her about Santorini, almost to justify to her why I wasn't around. I tell her about the money, how I planned on treating her to that cruise she always wanted to go on, that new hickory collection of caskets, that new plush sofa from DFS she said would look lovely in the waiting room. Although I'm tempted, I don't stroke her hair or thumb the veins on her hands. Holding hands seemed as far as we could go, alive or dead. I can't help but cry though. I hear the tears fall from my chin onto my white coat. By the time I stop talking, I have a big damp patch on my chest.

Janice has the white sheet pulled up to her collarbones. Her jowls and cheeks have lost flesh and definition from being in the freezer for days. I make a start with the make-up. Why not? Even if she's to be thrown straight in the burner, she didn't leave any instructions about not looking the part for it.

I powder up the brush and gently dab at her cheeks and forehead. The grey transparency of her skin starts to liven with colour. I apply the purple eyeshadow she liked to wear whenever we had a visitation from a wealthy family who were here to choose a coffin. A faint lilac lippy to go with it, applying it onto her mouth like the arc of a rainbow.

I brush her hair, then use a pencil to twirl strands into curls. They spring and bounce over her forehead like they always used to, whenever she was animated and bitching about someone. I take extra caution and go at the pace of a brain surgeon. If a hair falls onto her shoulder, I immediately get the tweezers and dispose of it into the bin. If I smudge the new lick of nail varnish while leaning over her, I give it an extra coat straight away.

Janice needs to look perfect when I roll her into that cremation machine. I want to press that button, confident I've done all I can to make up for not being here when she died, and to send her off to heaven with the best chance of nabbing a fella. She would have relied on me for that, knowing full well it would probably be me who'd spruce her up.

While I apply some mascara, I think how funny it would be to burn her in that blue and pink coffin she left me. Maybe that's how she thought I'd react? That would explain it. I'm not sure how I would feel walking into that casket room though and not seeing the coffin there, looking garish and dominating the whole room. It's a reminder of her every time I walk in. She's with me still somehow, under this moulding roof. It's got me through these last few days, that coffin. I can't get rid of it now.

I step back from the table, looking at her from a distance, then from a bird's eye view. I think I'm finished. She looks like she used to do going to the bingo, or Saturday nights when there was an act on at the club. Halves of lager, glasses stamped with her purple lippy. Her eyeshadow becoming bluer as the night went on, the sweat from dancing making it blotch and sparkle.

I'm happy with how she looks. She looks like Janice again.

Before I came in this morning, I had a root around the back of the wardrobes on my hands and knees, Mango licking at my ankles. I pulled out two bin bags that Becca had recently brought home from the shop and threw them into the back of the Transit. They were on the countertop near the sink now, bulging with all sorts.

I start having a rummage through. An acid-green DKNY blazer – too garish. A Louis Vuitton foil skirt – too much. A silk Burberry nightie – just no. I dig through Valentino handbags and shoes with heels thinner than a chopstick. Nothing seems right for Janice. I want her to have something proper. She could never afford these clothes. She could never dream of even wanting them. Still, Janice was always a woman who cared about her appearance. Her business started with the way she looked. If she looked presentable, or at least attempted to look presentable, she always thought people would understand she'd got her head screwed on, that she worked hard, and she would look after her loved ones as she looked after herself. It was never a question of brand, it was about principle. I mean, look at this place – shithole. But me and Janice worked fucking hard to give every single family the service they deserved and were entitled to.

Near the bottom of the second bin bag, I find a black silk blouse and a black Gucci suit that is double-breasted and frilled at the sleeves. Janice always wore black. It made her look both professional and respectful. It only seems right.

I try the blouse and suit on her, keeping her modesty and keeping my eyes up on the ceiling. It fits perfectly, almost tailored for her. I find a pair of black tights to match too. To finish off, I can't resist using some ballet flats with a bow on the toe, exactly the same shade as her pink nails. A pop of colour she was always accustomed to.

I feed her wedding ring back on and clasp the small, gold-link bracelet around her wrist. I tie it twice around because they're so thin. I find a pearl necklace with matching earrings too which make her look elegant, dangling from her lobes and neck. Janice deserves to go looking like a million quid. An exception I will only ever make for her.

My final time with her lasts four hours. It's a mix of not wanting to rush and needing to make the most of my last moments with her. I could have taken longer, but too much time outside the freezer would only make my work pointless.

Janice lies under the lights, suited and booted, dolled up to the rafters. She's ready for whatever comes next now. In a way, so am I.

I wheel her along the corridor, making sure she can take in the sights of the walls, the smells of the place, the business she built for herself. We journey to the cremation room for the last time together, nice and slowly, like we've done so many times in the past. The room is warm and spotless when we enter. I haven't burnt a body since I've been back. I'm almost nervous. I'm a lot of things, but I'm never nervous in this place.

I fire up the machine and manage to lift Janice onto the conveyor belt from the gurney, first by the head, then the feet. I smooth out the creases on her blazer. Licking my finger and dabbing mascara from her eyelid. As the flames grow thicker with light, sound and heat, I bow my head, hold my hands behind my back, and say the last words I will ever say to Janice:

Fuck, I don't have a clue how to start. You were always the yapper, not me. I'll try me best though, for you.

My feet shuffle.

I really wish you could have had more than this. More time obviously, but more of a send-off too, with the whole of Openshaw here to show how much they appreciated you. But I understand you didn't want that. For me, that only reflects why you were so great and why you were so loved around here. You cracked on, without any fuss, and didn't want any attention for it. You've helped the majority of families in this community at a time when they needed you most. Whenever anyone was grieving, or ever needed a natter, you were the one they came to. You were the one I came to. And I'm going to miss that. I can't even begin to explain or thank you for what you've done for me, Jan. Fuck knows where I would have ended up if you didn't give me the chance to learn the ropes here.

Remember that first time you give me a tour of the directory and told me to lie in that fuckin' coffin? I thought, What the hell am I doing here? This woman's off her barnet. I can't work with her. And I wasn't wrong, you were off your barnet, but you didn't half teach me a bit about life, what to appreciate, and how to crack on with a smile on your face every day. We had some laughs, didn't we? And I definitely wouldn't have a career or start in life without you. I may never have been able to move in with Becca or start building a life with her. Oh, and by the way, I have a dog now. He's called Mango. Yappy little thing. 'Shitting machines,' you called them, and you're right, but I think you would have took to him. He likes his meat too. Anyway, I know you've got fellas to be cracking on with up there so I won't leave you waiting, but I just wanted to say thank you again, for everything, Jan. I mean it. I'm going to keep this place going for you. I'm going to do it up, like proper nice, with new modern bits of furniture and equipment that you never had the chance to do. I'll make you proud, Jan, and you'll be with us here along the way. I promise to take care of it, and keep that coffin you left me pride and place in the casket room. Until I give in and burn the fucker.

I step around the belt and hover my finger over the green button. The heat from the fire doesn't stop my eyes from filling with water. I look down on her. It's as peaceful as I think I've ever seen her. I pull a cigarette from the pack in my chest pocket and wedge it between her fingers. There, now she's ready.

I press the button, sending Janice slowly into the flames. Once the hatch door's shut, I turn away and make for the door before I turn to take one last look.

Sleep tight, Jan, I'll miss ya.

18

From the club and pubs along Ashton Old Road, I gather every builder, painter, joiner I can find – fuckin' anyone who can hold a drill. I get them in reception, with Trick behind the counter barking orders, telling them what the crack is. He's roped in most of the lads he's worked with on jobs in the past. Grafters he can trust. Lads who will understand the task and put their sweat and blood into it. Oh, and Spud, because he needs the cash and felt left out.

'That,' says Trick, pointing to a framed picture of Janice on the shelf next to the urn of her ashes, 'that's why you're gonna do this, lads. And trust me, it's a decent wedge you'll be getting. So call whatever contractors, whatever jobs you have coming up, and fuck 'em off. Because you won't need them for at least a month. If they want to speak to me they can do, I don't give two shits, pass on my number.'

Butch lads with tanned biceps and pencils behind their ears look at each other, nodding. It's like the Village People have walked in wearing hi-vis vests. Good lads though, I could tell by the way they shook my hand and looked me in the eye. They knew what this meant.

We need energy. There's shitloads to be done if we're gonna make this worthwhile. Even the bald, pot-bellied ones are true grafters. They're here at 7 a.m. on the dot every day, and make their brew and fag breaks quick and snappy. All because of that woman on the shelf there. They don't need telling twice. All these lads must have known her or had her deal with relatives that had died in the past. Everyone in Openshaw owed Janice for something.

Financially, I figured out I could be closed for two or three weeks without bringing any bodies or income in. That way, we can hit it hard, get as much done as we can, then get business rolling again. Trick's definitely on board now, waddling from room to room with his tool belt knocking about on his balls, giving young-ens a bollocking if their pointing isn't up to scratch. It didn't matter if it was a crematorium he was in, if he's within four walls ordering a load of workmen around, he's in his element. Deadlines and quality decorating is what makes Trick tick. He's good at what he does, which is why I knew he would be perfect for this first step. Then, after, when he's behind that desk doing the salesman shit he doesn't fancy, at least he can look around and see what he and his boys have built to get him through the day. Once it's all finished, Trick will be connected to the place, just like me and Janice are.

It's been a couple of weeks and the jobs are taking longer than we thought. Mould was found in a wall, so we had to knock it through to extend the casket room. We built an extra storage area for the boxes of paperwork stacked in Janice's office. Skirting boards were crowbarred off and replaced. Ceilings plastered. Walls repainted in calm, neutral tones. Embalming room ripped out, retiled and refloored. The cremation room took the longest – it needed all the guys to make the modifications to the machines. State-of-the-art upgrades that can fry a body in half the time, the swanky addition of gutters for any fat and excess fluid to drain into compartments that are easier to dispose of. We ripped up the carpet in the reception area and added a faux marble floor. The desk was replaced by a varnished mahogany one to reflect the style of casket we wanted customers to cough up for. The urn shelves were replaced and modernised. Outside the main entrance, fresh flowers were planted, and an accessible path laid to create a more welcoming arrival, getting rid of the wonky disabled ramp.

It's cost tens of thousands. I dipped heavily into the pot Becca has no idea about. I have nightmares of her popping by the directory to have a look at what's going on and asking how the fuck I'm managing to do it all. I've told her we're too busy at the moment, that she'll see it eventually, secretly hoping time will pass and she'll forget the place has even changed.

It's costing way more than I thought. I have to keep remembering why I'm doing it. This isn't just for me, or even Janice really. I mean, the money I gathered to pay for that fuckin' bet came from the items of the dead. The necklaces, the watches, the rings. The least I can do is give something back. Repent for my sins.

With the money dwindling, and my time no longer occupied with preparing bodies, I start to bet again. I have to. I'm a waste of space around the directory, a too-many-cooks situation. Wires hang from the ceiling and paint rollers crisp up on the dust sheets. Trick advises me to leave it to the lads; they know what they're doing. I'll only get in the way. He tells me to take the time off while I can. It'll be full-on as soon as it opens. I mean, look at Janice – she didn't have a holiday for forty years. Trick's right, I need to stay away. Whether that's good for me or not is another thing.

I go into Jim Ramsbottom's for the first time in a month. The smell of body odour and inky paper make me feel reenergised. Fuck, I've missed it. I've missed seeing the same old people by the slot machines, leaning on the counter scanning over the newspaper listings, chewing on blue pens looking up at the TVs. I want the feeling of that small pen in my hand again, scribbling away on a betting slip, the adrenalin of not knowing whether my bet will come in or not.

I have a couple of small dog bets, limbering up, finding my feet again. Outside, rain comes and goes, the sun dipping in and out of clouds. As time passes, I get more and more brave with my bets. I have money to play with now. None of this really matters. I'm in here for fun, for the entertainment. I start slapping on bigger stakes.

My regular £2 bets become £200. I've never had this freedom. Not caring whether a £200 bet wins is different. It's a win-win. I'll still have money if I lose, a kind of insurance. The dynamic has changed but the fun remains. Whether you have £1 in your bank account, or £100,000 – betting is never really about winning.

I leave thousands of pounds lighter. I still have plenty in the bank. I go to get a kebab from Sol's and eat it on a nearby bench on Ashton Old Road, watching the world go by. Drunken men sway at cash machines. The local preacher babbles nothings on the corner where the Royal Bank of Scotland used to be before it got petrol-bombed. Buses chug to and from the city centre, groups of rowdy teens on the top decks banging on the windows and squashing bare arses against the glass.

Not many people would love this place. I can't imagine not doing. Becca wants to move and start a life in one of those gentrified villages with driveways and signs like NO BALL GAMES. She's from Levenshulme, down the road from Openshaw. She's not connected like I am. I'm providing a service for these people, I feel like they'll need me like they needed Janice. Yes, I can move away and still work here, but I'll feel like a fraud. It's about knowing them, having a pint with them, buying a loaf of bread off them, bumping into them in the street and asking how their kid is doing. It's a job you have to live. I've watched Janice do it for years, wondering whether she'd get fed up and fly the nest. Now, I realise why she stayed. She lived it and loved it. That's what I have to do too.

I have a thought when my teeth sink into the last bite of doner and mayo. I not only want to make the directory successful and do Janice proud, I more importantly want to make sure I make up for all the dodgy shit I've done to get here. I won't forget selling Umar's jewellery, Dave the Butcher's signed United shirt, stealing from the club till. It's wrong, of course it's wrong. Should I have done it? I don't know. It got me here now. It's what I needed. A few quid in the bank is all I wanted to get back on track and do right, with both the directory and Becca. The ones I stole from are piles of ash now; I can't fix that. I have to make things right some other way. I have to give back, somehow.

I get home to Mango jumping up and licking my nostrils. Becca's at work, so he's on the sofa, knee-deep into a rawhide treat. Once he gets bored, I go to our wardrobe and gather every bin bag Becca's brought back from Selfridges over the last couple of years. I throw them all in a pile on the bed. Mounds and mounds of the stuff. A fuckin' fortune within these bags. I'm not gonna sell it for betting money; I don't need that any more. I'm gonna make every dead body that gets wheeled into that directory look the dog's bollocks for whatever they choose to happen next.

It'll be a free part of the service, a complimentary gift that separates us from other funeral homes. Expensive, designer dressing service. The best clothes for the best people. Hopefully mourners will understand how much I care, how much I want them to have the best of the best. Every body will leave this earth looking like a million quid, whether that's dolled up in a fancy casket, or burnt into a tub of designer ash.

I've robbed from the dead. I'm not proud of it. Now it's time to give them what they couldn't experience when they were alive – feeling and looking the most important person in the world.

**

A month and a half has passed since we started renovating. It's taken even longer than we thought, which I'm not too arsed about. It needs to look right. There's no point in all this if it doesn't look right.

Trick phones me one Tuesday, asking me to come in. I'm nervous, hands fidgety, tapping on the steering wheel at a red light. When I pull into the car park, I'm struck by a burst of colour. Splashes of red, yellow and green from the planters. Flowers fresh and blooming, tickling the bottoms of newly fitted windows. A sand-bricked path leads to an entrance that's almost unrecognisable. The entrance doors are floor-to-ceiling glass and automatic, opening into a marble-floored reception. The place oozes class and professionalism. Janice would love it.

I'm alone when I walk in. The front desk shimmers from the wax. Shelves of urns behind, polished and glinting in the light. Bushy plants in either corner make the place feel comforting, like a hotel reception at a luxurious resort. The tone is mellowed. The walls spruced up with the colour of skin tones – beige, browns, mushroom and cream. It looks bangin' alongside the dark wood of the desk and the side tables along the wall, layered with brochures and funeral packages.

A wide opening in the reception links to the new waiting room. The old, grandma pictures of vases are replaced by calming landscapes. The beige carpet plush underfoot. A larger, plump sofa sits in the middle of the room along with a coffee table big enough to lie a body on. The walls have a patterned wallpaper and a chandelier hangs from the ceiling like a hovering crown. I honestly can't believe this is the same place. The lads have worked a miracle.

I have to take a breath before walking into the extended casket room. I haven't yet seen the new deliveries of walnut caskets or the wider range we now have available. I've only circled coffins in a catalogue and sent the orders to Trick. They've been delivered and arranged based on a diagram I drew. I want the space to be as welcoming as a casket room could. Wide walkways to lead families through. Spaces for the family to breathe and take their time. A cramped, dark casket room is the worst. Families want to feel soothed and not rushed in any way. And this is exactly how the room feels.

Strips of LEDs spotlight the coffins like a halo. Every casket is arranged perfectly along either wall, separated by vases of white roses. Our biggest sellers lie in the centre, surrounded by a wide, spacious walkway. The floor is soft, stopping the loud clip-clopping of heels which can distract from trying to explain a type of wood, or the design of a handle. Much easier to wheel coffins in and out too. It's both practical and beautiful – I can't do the place justice with words.

It's at the back of the room though, under a specially designed arch, where I stand with tears streaming down my cheeks. Within the arch, illuminated by two cosy lamps, is the blue and pink coffin. The front half is open, exposing the blue silk lining. Light bounces off the polished pink wood, creating a beacon in the room that your attention is immediately drawn to.

There she is, in all her glory. A polite sign of 'Do Not Touch – For Display Purposes Only' on the wall. I stroke the wood, tap it, and look around the room. The coffin has a full panoramic view of everything, as if we're presenting to Janice what we've built. I'm so incredibly proud standing in this room. I'm desperate to get started now, to get business back on the road and make this place the best funeral directory in Manchester.

'Not bad, is it?'

Trick's leaning by the entrance with his arms crossed. Dolled up in a grey suit and tie. I can see the sparkle of his gold tooth from the other side of the room as he smiles.

I walk over and bat away his attempt of a handshake.

'I love it, mate. Thank you.' I hug his broad shoulders, squeezing tightly.

'You deserve it, pal.'

Trick leads me into Janice's office, where she spent so many nights underneath that lamp. He opens the door and I almost expect to see Janice in the chair. The entire room is different apart from the same lamp on the desk. The walls are a cool blue and a window has been knocked in to invite diagonal rays that bathe the desk in light.

'Is it okay?' Trick asks.

I take a second to catch my breath.

'Perfect, mate. Fuckin' perfect,' I say, clutching his shoulder.

'All the building paperwork, invoices and stuff are on the desk there. Just needs to be signed then we're ready to go.'

I'm still looking round like a deer in headlights, amazed by every detail.

'Anyway,' says Trick, 'I'll leave you to it. I'll be out front if you need anything.'

Trick closes the door and I sit, creaking into the leather armchair. Sheets of stapled paper layered neatly in a pile on the desk. I flick through. Building regulation certificates, gas testing certificates, hygiene test certificates – everything but death certificates. There are invoices for the builder's wages and proof of payment for all the resources. Paint, plaster, flooring, tools, delivery costs, pipework, electricity rigging, plumbing, flowers, artwork, furniture, windows, doors, coffins. The list is fuckin' endless. I turn page after page of payments. Big bold numbers staring back at me.

I get the calculator up on my phone and get to work. The tip of my finger numbing from pounding the buttons. I scribble sums onto stray envelopes. I do my best to section everything into labour, appliances, hardware, flooring, lighting, but it's all too much. It comes from the same pot at the end of the day, a pot that's looking a lot smaller the more numbers I punch in.

Even Trick's not asked any questions yet, which I'm grateful for. He's probably a little suspicious of how much this is all costing, and where all the money's coming from, but I hope my passive lies about Janice's loans, my mates' rates with the builders and Becca's savings will do the trick.

It was always going to be tough at the start; we haven't had business for nearly two months. I have to tell myself, before I press that equals button, that whatever number pops up we can earn back with business. I check my bank account before I do. It's a fuckin' decent sum that, why am I worried?

I press the button and stare at the number. I look at the speckles of dust floating through the air. I listen to my breathing, the cracks in the leather as I grip the arm rests.

I explode, launching all the paper at the wall and sending my fist crashing down on the lamp. Shards of glass sprinkle over the desk and onto the carpet, my knuckles dripping with blood.

Last month I had half a million quid, thoughts of travelling the world with Becca and buying a nice house. Now, I have a funeral directory, a pissed-off girlfriend and a bank account that's back in debt.

Debt. That fuckin' word, back to chew me on the arse. I feel like I've bet on the directory and lost. My horse fell, or worse, I've backed a non-runner. Becca was right. This was a terrible, terrible idea. She can't know that. I have to somehow make this work. Prove to her that this was a profitable investment. I just have no idea how.

19

As a thank you for betting big with him and helping him get in his boss's good books, Vince offers me two free tickets to Man U v West Ham off the bat. No strings, no contracts or any faff like that, just a friend rewarding a friend.

To be honest, we've barely spoken about what being a VIP actually involves. He's discreet. Glossing over by focusing on the amazing odds he can get hold of, the free bets he can offer. The exclusive, direct contact I'll have at the bookies through him. He still always mentions how he's in with Jim Ramsbottom's, which is even better. If I can snazz a couple of free tickets along the way, I'm not gonna grumble. As long as I'm getting all that, we'll get along fine. Fuck the small print.

'Spotted your funds are running a little low on your betting account so I've put a few bob in so you can have a dabble on the match too,' says Vince over the phone. 'Enjoy, mate. Go cop a winner.'

Times are hard at the directory. Business is coming in but I have so much to claw back, there doesn't seem an end in sight. Vince has been a saviour, offering me great bets, at least opening a door for me. My luck is lower than a grannie's tits though. I can't hit a barn door at the moment. Everything I touch is losing. My bank account is hitting crisis mode again. An empty fuckin' casket. The only upside is that I'm lucky Becca's busy with work and not on my back about the house or whatever shite we can blow our winnings on again. Santorini gave her the taste for a lush lifestyle. I have to try and nip that in the bud now we have no money left.

At snooker night, I ask Trick if he'd like to come to the match with me. A thank you for all the work he's done on doing up the directory and for helping me out taking over Janice's jobs.

'How'd you get hold of them, ya jammy get?' He's wiping the stem of his cue with his T-shirt.

'Friend of a friend. He's busy that weekend so offered me on a discount. Belting seats as well apparently.'

'Fuckin' too right I wanna go,' says Trick, all giddy. 'Should be a good game that as well. Hammers are on fire.'

I sup on my pint. Trick racks up and wastes no time pinging the balls about the felt. I'm feeling so grateful for his graft, I consider letting him win.

'Let me offer you summot for them though, pal,' says Trick.

'Ahh bollocks, man. It's fine. Not after all the work you've done for me.'

'Nah nah, honest. Happy to chip in.'

Regardless of my mood and excitement for Saturday, my bank account is weeping big time. Deep into the overdraft again. Any hope of a little dosh that doesn't need to go back into the directory bills is bound to tickle my interest.

'Fletch, let me pay, come on.'

'You sure?' I say. 'It's fine if you're—'

'Fletch, shut up man. I'm giving you my half. Just let me know how much whenever you need it. Or take it off my wages – I'm easy.'

Trick pots a couple of reds and colours, sweat beading on his bald head like oil in a puddle.

'Forty, mate,' I say. 'but no rush.'

'Sweet.'

We carry on playing snooker, talking about all sorts of shite and making our predictions for the match. I wonder if Trick will hand over the cash tonight as I'm leaving so I can have a dabble in the bookies on the way home. Maybe I'll ring Vince up and ask for some tips, see what meetings are worth a tickle this weekend. I have better options now. I'm ahead of the game.

I still win, even though my snooker's well off. Trick was sniffing round the pockets, failing to find the sweet spot between the cushions. The face on him after missing a couple of bankers made me worry I wasn't getting my money tonight.

I feed him more pints and let him vent about Rachel. She's annoyed with all the time he's spending at the directory lately. I offer advice, as if I of all people am in the fuckin' position to, and make him see the light in the situation. How her going out for a bit of me-time with the office girls is important for their relationship, to make her realise the good fella she's missing at home. Or that her barmy spending on overpriced clothes is only her putting effort in for him. They were in a marriage for fuck's sake, it's not meant to be a doddle. I tell him that's what I'm here for, to get things off his chest. That's what mates are for. I tell him to nick a few designer clothes from the bin bags we have lying around the directory. Treat her, keep her sweet and all that.

Trick thanks me and hands over the forty quid quicker than a cheetah with a rocket up its arse. My gabbing worked a treat.

'Cheers mate,' I say, slapping hands. 'Meet you at half twelve in here on Saturday, yeh?'

'Look forward to it, pal. See you then.'

I wander out into the night, rain on my cheeks, heading in the direction of Jim Ramsbottom's. I'm not in there for long. I don't wanna push it, especially with not seeing Becca much lately. My early dart means I leave with about two hundred dabs in my pocket. Perfect for a cheeky bet at the match. I go home all smiles and talk to Becca about how Trick is and how we have to work 'overtime' on Saturday so I can't be home to walk Mango. She's fine with it. She's just happy to see me.

Becca has her hair down and those skimpy silk PJs on, so we end up nailing on the couch. We haven't had sex since Santorini and you can tell. Animals we are, like we have the sun beaming through the balcony door again. Sol's chip pans are probably rattling downstairs. Becca's legs on my shoulders, vibrating like a drug dealer's burner phone.

Afterwards, lying on the couch sweating, staring at the cracked roof, I say we'll do it. We'll save for a house. I'm that confident I can get money back soon. I have a plan with the directory. A way to get money in quick and fast. I look into Becca's eyes and say it again. Loud and clear.

'We're doing it. We're getting that house.'

She gets on top and we do it again.

The things you say after a session.

***

Trick arrives in the club in his '99 United shirt, belly bulging like a clown's nose. Three-quarter-length shorts exposing white shiny shins and a pair of red Adidas trainers on. Looks like a fuckin' post box he does. I make an awful joke about how if his wife tried to walk out the house like that, he wouldn't letter. His belly jigs under his shirt from laughter.

'I'll give your head a first-class stamp, ya bastard,' he replies.

I call Kevin to look after the directory for the day so we can have a few scoops before heading to Old Trafford. The taxi has TalkSport on, discussing the line-up and whether Rashford will start on the wing or up top. Between programmes, Ray Winstone's voice booms the latest odds from Bet365, reminding me to have a tinkle on the ol' betting apps while we wait in traffic. Nearer to the stadium, billboards and posters all loud and vibrant let me in on more odds. 'When the Fun Stops, Stop' is pasted small at the bottom of 'em. All those ads ever do is remind me of how fun it is.

We have time for a few scoops on Busby Way, soaking in the atmosphere and chatting to some season ticket holders. This geezer called Kenny with a grey ponytail and specs corners us. Babbling on about how we won't finish in the top four this year, the miserable old sod. The whites of his eyes are yellow with sadness. I ditch Trick with him for as long as I can while I have a spin on the fruit machine in the corner. When I return, Kenny has a moustache from his pint, grilling Trick about his name. They both sit at a rickety wooden table, sticky from beer rings and littered with dog-eared coasters.

'So why they call you Trick then?' says Kenny, tail resting on his shoulder.

Trick sees me approaching and gives a nod.

'Here. I'll show ya,' says Trick. 'Any deck of cards in 'ere?'

Kenny points to the shelf above his head where there are two packs of cards and a faded box of Scrabble. I pass Trick the cards and take a seat next to him.

Trick lays out nine cards in three rows of three, suits face-up.

'Right,' says Trick, 'I want you to point to one of these cards while I look away and I guarantee, every time, I'll guess the right one.'

'You having me on?' Kenny switches his gaze between me and Trick.

'Swear down, mate. I'll get it every time. That's why they call me Trick.'

'Fuck off.'

'Point to one then.'

Trick hides his face in his hands and stuffs his head behind the curtain for good measure.

'Ayy dickhead, let me see your face so you're not cheating. I know them curtains are thin.'

Trick laughs, putting his head under the table instead.

While I sip on my Guinness, Kenny looks at me all confused before pointing to the nine of diamonds, the centre card. He watches the back of Trick's head like a hawk and anything I'm doing or showing on my face. I sit there chuckling, putting my pint down on a mat to show him I'm not doing anything with my hands under the table as an accomplice.

'Right. I've picked,' says Kenny.

Trick pops up, rubs his tattoos in concentration and within about two seconds points to the nine of diamonds. Kenny's jaw drops, revealing a bottom row of wonky piano teeth.

'Fuck off,' he says. 'Fuck off.'

'See.'

I watch Trick's beer travel down his throat into that red gullet. The cheeky look on his mush is a picture.

'Right,' says Kenny, shuffling in his seat, determined to crack it. 'Go for a slash and I'll pick one. See how fuckin' good you are then.'

Without even hesitating, Trick gets up and necks the dregs of his lager.

'Sweet. I need a piss anyway.'

He's gone. Kenny studies the cards, checking either side of them as if they have some mechanism that communicates to Trick which card he's picking. He starts twirling his ponytail in concentration. Can't lie, it makes me feel a bit sick. I imagine him dressing up as a little girl while he asks his wife to feed him, or me having to comb the nits out of his hair after he dies. Maybe I'm being harsh, but I still shiver in my chair, washing down my bile.

'This one.' He points to the jack of clubs in the bottom right. 'No wait. This one.' Ace of hearts, bottom left. 'No, fuck that.' He looks behind him towards the gents to check Trick isn't spying. 'Yeh actually, this one.'

Kenny sticks with the first. Jack of clubs, bottom right. I'm finishing off my dregs when Trick emerges from the bathroom, letting out a burp that vibrates along the floorboards to my toes. I place down my glass and cross my arms, just like I did the first time so Kenny isn't suspicious.

Trick's cheeks don't even reach the seat before he points to the jack of clubs.

'Easy,' says Trick.

Kenny looks like punching a window in. His wiry eyebrows curling, jowls wobbling in disbelief.

'You mad cunt. How d'ya do it?'

'It's magic.'

'Magic my arse. Tell me.'

'Just living up to the name, pal.'

Kenny's frustration gets to him, he has a right cob on then. A couple of lads start sniggering behind him. He thinks he looks stupid for not being able to crack it. My and Trick's smiles burrow into his ego. He bursts, swiping the cards off the table. Trudging through the falling cards and out of the door, his tail bounces on his back like a horse's arse.

'All right, keep ya hair on,' someone shouts from the bar.

Me and Trick bump fists and get up, leaving our empty glasses. Mine is placed on the bottom right corner of the coaster, where the jack of clubs is positioned.

***

Out of the musky pub and into the daylight, swarms of red shirts filter down Busby Way. Scarves windmill through the air. The scent of pies and open-air urinals. The tickets that arrived in the post are folded crisp in my pocket, alongside my recent winnings. While Trick's in the bog, I head to the concourse betting shop and pile it all on first goalscorers, correct scores, number of corners, number of yellow cards, number of red cards, half-time-full-time predictions, anything. If there were odds for the ref shitting himself mid-game, I would chuck on a cheeky quid.

With all bets placed, Trick arrives at my shoulder. I'm looking over the odds again. He's intrigued, trying not to look interested. I know he hasn't put many bets on in his life, not even when we went to the casino. His missus snuffs her nose at that sort of stuff.

'Having a go?' I ask.

'Nah, I'm good mate.'

'Go on ... just first goalscorer, or correct result.'

Trick hesitates, gazing at the odds, not knowing where to look.

'Go on,' I say. 'Might as well while you're here.'

Trick gets his wallet out. I spot a couple of crumpled twennies peaking from the slot. The leather looks heavy with change.

'Bang us a fiver on Rashford, 3–1,' he says, handing me a tenner.

No matter how small the sum, there's just something about physical money in your hands. I let my hand hover, eyes scanning the coupon. I pat my pockets as if I've lost my keys. A grimace of the lips. A look at the floor.

'Put one on for yourself as well, pal,' says Trick.

I give him a wink and scribble our bets into the scorecast quicker than I can write my own name.

'Cheers bud. Appreciate that.'

On the way to finding our seats, I get our tickets out to check, sending an avalanche of betting slips falling out of my pocket.

'Fuckin' receipts,' I mumble, picking them off the floor as quick as I can.

We shuffle along our row and gaze out at the stands. Squares of red seats fill up. Our view's mega, right on the halfway line. The pitch like a carpet, a luscious green. The stage for so many great moments over the years. Goals, legends, trophies. I nudge Trick where his ribs should be and tell him to drink it in. The plastic creaks happily under the weight of our arses. Being a VIP isn't half bad.

After tannoy announcements and some last-minute bets on my phone, the players emerge from the tunnel to a deafening roar. Grown men screaming 'UNITED, UNITED, UNITED' as loud as they can. I imagine Kenny with his bobble out, shouting his musty breath onto the poor fucker in front. Smudged United badge tattoo on his forearm, fist clenched, punching the air. 'UNITED, UNITED, UNITED.' Songs boom from the Stretford End. Vintage shirts of the glory years, green and yellow scarfs with 'Glazers Out' pasted across. Trick's tooth winks as he sings songs about Ryan Giggs, Cantona, Park Ji-sung. A smile on his face. A smile on mine.

The players shake hands and jog into their positions. West Ham in their sky-blue away kit, massive Betway sponsor across their chests. It reminds me to check my bets one last time before kick-off. I take cheeky glances while Trick is balls deep into his hot dog, ketchup disguised on his shirt. The hoardings around the pitch flicker with bright betting adverts. Even mid-game, watching the ball get passed along the back, I can find out the latest odds without turning my head or moving a muscle. It's everywhere: the hoardings, the shirts, the bookies by the snack bars, the billboards, the radio adverts, the street up to the stadium, the matchday programme, the newspapers, social media. I'm surrounded by gambling, wherever I go. Sucked into the dream of winning. I love it. So much I don't really give a fuck whether my boyhood team wins or loses, as long as it's in my favour.

***

United win, and so does my bank account. It was a dirty game. The referee waving cards like the Statue of Liberty. High-intensity stuff, a shitload of corners and goals, ending in a victory for the boys. All of it worked exactly in my favour. The slips in my pocket aren't just hopeful pieces of paper any more, they're loaded with cash. Thirty-pound, fifty-pound wins. Trick lost. I don't even think he remembered putting a bet on. He thinks the grin on my face is down to the spectacle, to United nabbing the three points.

It's a scorcher for Feb too. Sun raging and beating down on our sweaty scalps as we shimmy out of the stadium. Red shirts wobble at the end of Busby Way. Matchday programmes used for fans, scarves for towels. We analyse performances on the way back to Openshaw in the taxi. Air con on full blast. Pasty thighs clinging to the leather seats.

'Really appreciated that, pal,' says Trick. 'Top day out.'

'Ahh, no bother mate. Just glad it was a decent game.'

Trick looks out the window at the packed drive thru at Maccie Doodles. Sweaty mums with a car full of kids, passing Fruit Shoots and nuggets to the back seat.

'How's all the paperwork and that?' he asks. 'All the payments looking okay and everything?'

It takes me back a bit. Who thought Trick would ever care about the directory? His wages depend on it now. It's a project he's proud of. It'll be a problem if he gets *too* connected, *too* involved. Sooner or later questions will be asked about anything that looks dodgy. I fear I've been walking round the corridors with a worried look on ma mug. Was I making it obvious? All solemn and depressed like I usually am when money's on my mind? He's good at clocking these things. Another one of his tricks.

'Ermm.' I look out the car window. An ice cream melts into a white pool on the pavement.

'Fletch?'

I contemplate it. Telling him. How I'm in much more trouble than the directory. I hate abusing Trick's generosity. Neglecting our friendship, using him to fuel the addiction he doesn't have a clue about. Because this must be addiction, if I'm still in this mess? The guilt I'm feeling is too much for it to be anything else. I could probably talk to him about it. I would if the shame wasn't too much. What the fuck would he think of me? I could lose my closest friend. He'd try to understand but he never could. The best way he can help me is not to know, keep his distance, and pass over a few quid now and again. I want him to help out at the directory and keep his mouth shut. That's all. He can't find the answers. That's for me to find out.

'Here,' he says.

Trick rustles around in the back pocket of his three quarters as if he's scratching his crack. A wad of notes appears miraculously like some prison smuggler. Is he still doing painting jobs on the side, the jammy get?

'Trick, ya don't have to. Honestly.'

'Here, mate. Take it. Until you get on your feet. I know the directory's been a lot for you lately. Doesn't take an accountant to know it must have cost a few quid.'

I look at the notes curled between his sausage fingers. Nibbled nails and a scratched gold ring. The possibilities in those fleshy palms. I wonder what he's thinking of me splashing money on United tickets when I'm on my arse. I hope he believes it's an honest gesture to reward him for being such a good mate, for keeping an eye on my sorry life.

I want to tell him so much. How long can the lies go on for?

He drops the money in my lap, continuing to look out the window. The sum looks chunky. Two hundred? Three hundred maybe? It's enough to make me feel guilty. He has no idea I have more than that in winnings in my pocket. That, two months back, I was halfway to becoming a millionaire.

One of the things about being a gambler is you don't really care where the money comes from. If it's dropped from the fuckin' heavens into your brew, you don't bat an eyelid. Shrug and go 'nice one'. Our lives are built on luck. Just like Dad – he felt everything that came his way or went against him was solely based on luck, on odds, on outcomes out of his control. He never held accountability. It was never the fault of him, the gambler. If money was there, it was there to be spent. Fuck wherever it came from.

I take the money. Of course I do. I take the money and squeeze Trick's shoulder. It feels like a cooked leg of lamb, juicy and riddled with sinew. He winks at me; it's no bother to him. I've always admired how Trick gets his kicks from kindness as much as I do from the gambling. Giving money to his closest pals is him feeding coins into the machines. The decision to help me out is him spinning the roulette, taking a chance. He thinks it's a safe game, a win-win. The odds are so small, he's winning anyway because he knows he's helping out a pal.

'I hate to see you so glum mate,' he says, the taxi stopping at a red light.

'I cremate people, Trick. I'm not gonna be moonwalking down the corridors.'

'You know what I mean. I can see you've been a bit off all day, and over the last couple of weeks or so. I get all the stuff with Janice is still fresh, but I don't even think it's that. I knew it wasn't the footy so thought it must be the pennies. Checking your phone, looking bare agitated and all that. I know how stressful it can be. You can't enjoy the things you're meant to enjoy when bills and all that are fuckin' you up the arse. It's mingin'. Can spot it from a mile off.'

I don't deserve a mate like Trick. He's one of a kind.

'I dunno what to say, mate. Cheers for looking out for me.'

'Don't mention it. It's a struggle, it always is. Just don't let it grind you down into a miserable old fuck. I seen it with me old fella. His life revolved around money, fuckin' obsessed with the stuff. I told him "it's only paper", when it actually was paper, but would he bollocks listen? Turned him into a grumpy sod, arguments left right and centre. He died a miserable man, Fletch. Turned him fuckin' evil. Don't let that happen to you. Life's too short for all that toss. Look at Janice, she lived the right way. Make sure you do too.'

Trick's words sink in. They stain, like ink. The hot, stuffy car seems to fill with his wisdom. In life, he seems to be in control of everything other than a snooker cue. He has a mortgage. A working marriage. A general respect from anyone he meets.

I let his advice marinate. How do I achieve all that? He's right, it'll be ugly if I carry on like this. Continuing to hide money from

Becca in my dying years, chasing that next bet, dreaming of having that quarter of a million in my account again. Dying with guilt, a sorry, evil man. Drowning in debt, leaving Becca capsized.

I pocket the money and thank him again. I make a silent vow to repay Trick tenfold whenever I get the house and directory sorted. It's time to stop pissing about and dreaming the dream. I need to throw myself at this head-on. I need to focus. I've done it once, why can't I do it again?

As the taxi turns onto Ashton Old Road, a giant billboard lights my eyes with green and gold. This baking sun, this tease of spring means only one thing. The best horses. The toughest courses. The ultimate meeting. Christmas is on the horizon, only weeks away. Those big letters peer down at me, the weight of excitement leaving me short of breath.

Cheltenham Festival. Where dreams come true.

20

Handlebar moustache. White combover. Dennis was a strapping fella, aged like a fine wine. His skin has an ambient hue, a physique that suggests he shouldn't be in this room for another twenty years yet. I pick him up from the hospital on an overcast Thursday morning. He suffered from organ failure the previous day at seventy-eight, leaving behind a family of grandkids that could fill the top deck of the 201.

I'm making the incision below his collar bone and feeding in the tubes when I think of meeting Becca's parents for the first time. Dennis reminds me of her dad. That fresh, youthful look you find in some old people. There are few people you meet in life who make you feel instantly relaxed. Dennis has that energy about him. Even now, still on the bed. I'm relaxed. He waits patiently for me, telling me he has all the time in the world. He's ready to start whenever I'm ready to start.

Becca's dad was like that. I prepare Dennis, letting him in on the first time I met Frank:

It was 2007, Den. I'd just started my apprenticeship and I'd been at Tesco a few months, stacking shelves and nicking meal deals, when Rebecca asked me if I wanted to meet her parents. I can't lie, I couldn't really give two shits about all that. Never phased me that bollocks, having some sort of interview to confirm if I was good enough for whoever's daughter. If we liked each other, and we're both happy, that should be enough, shouldn't it? Everyone else's opinions were irrelevant, family or not. We'd already been fiddling for over a year, opting for my house so Becca could get away from her mam and all that. I thought I'd never meet her parents at one point. I guess she didn't expect us to last that long. Eventually, it reached an unavoidable stage where I kinda had to meet them. It started to feel weird having not.

Anyway, Becca seemed pretty nervous about it now, asking me over a Subway in Arndale food court. She said it would mean a lot to her. I didn't know what the fuck had brought it on but I said 'All right' through a mouthful of meatball marinara. I didn't know we'd be heading there as soon as I wiped the sauce off me bumfluff.

It was at the colder end of Autumn, where the leaves are crispy underfoot and the supermarket aisles are lined with pumpkins and giant bags of Haribos. Pissing down it was, rain peppering the bus windows. She lived in Levenshulme, opposite St Mary's Church where her mam apparently went whenever she was running low on candles for around the bath. Pat was on the dole and didn't work. Becca didn't shy away from calling her a lazy bitch who only smoked fags and itched her fanny while watching CSI all day. Her dad, the one who's a spitting image of you, was more of a soft fella by the sounds of things. Did all the cooking for her, worked mad hours at the McVitie's biscuit factory on Stockport Road. Came home smelling of digestives, packets of them in his arms for her mam to sit and scoff on all day.

Becca liked her dad, had a good relationship with him. He was always giving her a few quid here and there to treat herself to a nice lunch, new eyeshadow or a brand-spanking pair of Converse. Probably bit after your time them, Den, but they're cool and not necessarily cheap.

She made it clear he wasn't minted though. She said he had a part in him that despised her mam, that the money he treated Becca with was meant for their heating, their weekly food shop. It was only her mam freezing and starving at home so he didn't mind. As long as he saw his daughter happy.

I start washing Dennis, scared his tan might rub off. His grey chest hairs sit on his pecs like a winter rug. I feel his muscles under the towel, amazed how this lad kept himself in such good nick.

I'll paint the picture for you, Den. The wheels of the bus sent a puddle flying through the air. It coughed to a stop. The pavement was a river crashing against our trainers. Hoodies drenched through. We had a smooch in a seedy doorway until the downpour settled to a spit. Luckily, her house was only a few streets away. A road cracked and uneven, with lines of cream terraced houses on either side. Wheelie bins were on their backs, spilling out their insides. The rain drowned the gutters. One or two kids dressed as witches and werewolves bounced past us, sweet buckets filling with water as they kicked puddles down the street.

The bicep there. Jesus.

One doorway glowed halfway down. Pat stood in the arch with a curled fag between her fingers. Her tired face looked like it had fish hooks drawing her skin towards the pavement. She had hair curlers in, as if she was getting ready for a night on the town. The teddy bear nightie said otherwise.

'Hey, Mam, this is Jamie. My boyfriend.'

We stood in the light rain opposite her. It clinked loudly off the roof tiles. She didn't move an inch to let us in and get dry. Her faded blue eyes looked at my extended hand as if it had its middle finger stuck up at her.

'Hi Pat. Nice to meet ya.'

'A bit on the porky side, int he love?'

I lowered my hand and looked at Becca's face, glazed with water. She smiled. This wasn't a woman to meet if I was the sensitive type. Becca knew I could take it.

'It keeps me warm,' I said, laughing it off.

'You must be fuckin' boiling then.'

Pat turned and trudged down the hall lined with striped wallpaper. A claw curled round to scratch her arse, making her nightie ride up to show a map of varicose veins on her legs. A cupboard clunked. The rustle of a packet. We stepped in beside the mobility scooter at the bottom of the stairs and were hit by the smell of digestives.

I get down to the groin, where the Hollywood stardom starts to fade. Poor fella. Still tanned though. Must have liked his French beaches, our Den.

Becca made the brews, Pat's with three and a half sugars. We cupped our mugs on the couch while Pat rocked in her chair, scanning over the evidence on the telly to try and guess the killer. The lined wallpaper led into the living room where school photos of Becca and portraits of grandparents hung wonkily on the walls. Shelves were littered with old people things like gold plates, ballerina ornaments, a brass horse and carriage. The carpet had pockets of stains, mainly in a halo around Pat's chair where her bare toes wiggled into the fibres.

'So what you do then?' said Pat through a mouthful of biscuit when the adverts came on.

'Erm, I work at the big Tesco in Openshaw. Ya know, the one opposite the Salvation Army?'

'Course I fuckin' know which one it is. Ya can't miss it.'

Becca sighed, wiping her wet fringe.

'And it pays well, does it?'

'Not bad. Enough to get by for now.'

'Not showering her with pointless shite, are ya? She's always been a needy one, her. Never happy. I'd run now if I were you son.'

'Mum!'

'I'm only joking, love, fuckin' hell. Loosen up, will ya?' Pat's fingers wriggled in the biscuit packet like a rat in a bin bag. 'She's a sensitive one, Jim. Careful of that.'

'It's Jamie, Mum.'

'Tomayto, tomarto.'

I listened to Pat's chewing drown out the rain splattering against the window. The street was black behind the mesh curtains. It felt like only this room existed. Anywhere on the outside was a murky abyss.

'So you live around there then, do ya? Openshaw?'

'Yeh, me mam and dad grew up there. Still in the same house me mam was born in.'

Pat's face scrunched at this. I couldn't tell you why. The room felt cold and uncomfortably hot at the same time.

'Don't mind Openshaw to be fair,' she said. 'Nice food market there, do a cracking rack of ribs. Met a fella round there yonks ago. What was his name now? Daniel? Dave? Ah fuck knows. Anyway, hung like a horse he was. Think he's locked up now for child abuse or summot, I don't know. Inmates will have some fun with him, that's summot I do know. Wait, your dad's not locked up, is he?'

I didn't think Pat had the capability of laughing but she let out this loud cackle which made me flinch. The chocolate in her teeth looked like she'd gone to town on a turd. I half expected her gnashers to fall out and bounce around on the carpet like that novelty toy you wind up.

Becca had her head in her hands, regret written in her eyes. Then the front door went. Someone shaking rain off their clothes in the hall.

'Oh here he is,' said Pat. 'King of the castle.'

She stuffed the remaining biscuits down the side of her chair and laced her talons on her lap.

Frank was a hunched, fragile man. He moved very slowly into the living room as if he was intruding in his own home. His chocolate-brown hair was wet and slicked into a comb-over. Belting moustache, like yours Den. A smart chequered shirt and green cardigan. He was a man who took care of himself, who prized himself on how he was viewed by others. What struck me most was his face. He was fuckin' gorgeous. Like a fifties movie star.

'Oh, sorry love. I didn't realise we were expecting guests.'

Frank patted his hair down and straightened his back.

'Hi Dad. This is Jamie, the boyfriend I told you about.'

Boyfriend. It still sounded weird. That's what I was now. I stood and offered my hand. Frank gripped it firmly with a soft palm, strange for a factory working man.

'Jamie. Of course. Nice to meet you son, how are you?'

'Good thanks. I've heard lots about you.'

'Oh Christ, really?' said Frank, raising his eyebrows at Becca. The way they looked at each other was something special. Something I never had with my own dad. 'All good I hope.'

'Mostly,' I winked.

'Come, let me get you a beer. Less of that.'

Frank pointed at my steaming mug on the coffee table and guided me into the adjoining kitchen. Pat didn't acknowledge him, pleased now that the adverts had finished. Becca followed, happy to leave her mam alone, how she wanted to be.

Dennis's face doesn't need much. He could get away with just having his eyes capped, jaw wired and lips glued. I powder him up anyway. Death transforms the face by the hour. I can't take the risk, having him look all pasty and Ray Fletcher-like when his poor widow comes to visit.

Two cans of Boddingtons were fizzed open and placed on the kitchen side. Frank washed the black muck off his hands and dabbed them dry with the grace of a butler.

'So, how's it going with you two?' he asked.

Becca cupped her mug in the doorway, shocked at how direct he was.

'Err, really good Dad. I think. Aren't we?'

'Course we are,' I said. 'Well, depends on how your parents are first.'

Frank chuckled then took a swig of beer.

'Looks like you're doomed then,' he said.

We waffled for a bit. An hour or two actually. How we met at *that party. The places we've gone to in town. Films we've seen at the cinema. How it was weird that me and Frank hadn't met yet and how Becca must be embarrassed about one of us for it to take this long.*

Me and Frank got on like a house on fire. I could see Becca's eyes were lit up as she smiled and observed in the doorway. We laughed, took digs at each other as if we were friends in the bookies.

Frank was a City fan so we talked about footy and had some banter about that. Like my dad, he liked his films, things like Westerns and the Bonds. He also liked jazz music, the first time I heard it when he put the radio on quietly in the background and tapped his slippers on the linoleum. His eyes looked like caramel. Cheekbones sharp in the white kitchen light.

The thought reminds me to flick the radio on so Dennis has some music to listen to. Soft beats of a song I don't know, making me apply the make-up with rhythmic strokes.

Becca buttered us all some crumpets, leaving yellow blobs on our plates. Mugs with messages like, 'It's Gin o'Clock' and 'Keep Calm and Fuck Off' dried by the sink. It was a small kitchen, but one that was organised, well looked after. You could tell this was Frank's space. I guessed the cupboard with the wonky handle was where they kept the biscuits.

'Sorry if she's been a bit cold,' said Frank, before washing down his crumpet. 'She's had a rough few months.'

'Oh, behave, Dad, she's always been a moody cow.'

Frank gave her a look which I couldn't read. Maybe he understood Becca's frustrations about Pat. Maybe he had sympathies for her that only a husband and wife could understand. Maybe he truly hated Pat but had the decency not to reveal it to his daughter. A failed family is a personal failure for some men. I'd seen it in Dad.

'She has her reasons,' said Frank. 'All I'm saying is don't take it personally, Jamie. She's not the best with people.'

Becca chuckled sarcastically and dropped our plates into the sink. She squeezed Fairy liquid into the basin and flicked on the tap.

'I don't know why you're so nice to her, Dad. She treats you like shit.'

'Rebecca, that's enough now.'

'What? You know she does. I don't get it.'

'I said enough!'

The thundering of the tap broke the silence. Becca stared into the water, the whirlpool of suds. She started to scrub the plates with a wire sponge, grinding them down like Frank's patience.

'Sorry,' Frank said to me. He had his hand on the kitchen side, face bowed like he'd been nutted in the lip. 'Becca and Pat don't have the best relationship.'

'I wouldn't call it a relationship,' said Becca. She had her back up. We'd been together long enough for me to be on the bad end of it a couple of times. I was still learning about her. She spoke her mind. It was the best and worst part of her personality.

'It's okay, honest,' I said. 'You don't need to explain anything.'

Frank's beer can perspired in the muggy heat. He raised it to me in a strange gesture that only men seem to do. You know how it is, Den. A look, a connection that says no words are needed. It feels rude, as if we're superior to anyone in the room when we're not. A battle with Becca is a battle none of us wanted, that's what we understood. That understanding alone proves we're not the superior ones. The men I know hide from anything they can. Frank looked like a man who hid more than most. It wasn't worth the bother to him.

He rinsed the dregs of his beer and kissed Becca on the cheek.

'I like you, Jamie,' he said, offering me a second handshake. 'Sorry to dart off so early but I reek and need a bath. Pleasure to meet you though.'

Wet from the can, his hand still felt soft.

'Pleasure was mine, Frank. Hopefully see you soon.'

Those hazel eyes burrowed into mine. It was the first time his celebrity glamour looked tired. He looked more like an actor on the back end of his career, living off his classic movies and accepting any pay cheque for shite films to stay relevant. The charm was still there, but slowly, slowly fading. He leant his head close to mine, so only I could hear him while Becca continued with the pots.

'Make sure you take care of her, bud. She's getting harder to keep an eye on.'

He didn't need my words as a reply. He needed my actions. Without another word spoken, Frank sauntered through the living room, past the ghost of his wife, and upstairs to run a hot, soapy bath. I imagined the tub surrounded by Pat's church candles like some fucked-up vigil.

Rain showered heavily against the window opposite the sink. With Becca's back to me, I snuck behind her and hugged her waist like the romantic I was becoming. I hadn't said it yet but I loved this girl. I didn't even care how my belly rested ugly against her back. Lost in my happiness at how the night had gone, it took me a minute to realise Becca was crying.

'Woah woah, what's up?'

Droplets fell from her chin and rippled the water as if the tap was still on.

'Becca.'

I spun her round and parted the wet fringe away from her eyes. Her face was red and puffy.

'It's nothing.'

'My arse it's nothing. Talk to me.'

We joined hands. Joined heads.

'I'm just sick of this fuckin' house. Dad's great, I love him, but sometimes – sometimes he just doesn't understand me. I hate to see him getting walked all over by that fuckin' witch.'

I watched the rain over her shoulder. I wasn't good at the caring boyfriend stuff yet. Maybe I never would be. Becca made me willing to try though. The girl was changing me in ways I could never have imagined.

'He just cares for you,' I said. 'You can tell he loves ya. And he seems a smart enough fella to look after himself.'

'I know he does. That's not the point. I'm just done. I can't be arsed being around it. I'd leave this house tomorrow if I could.'

The suds in the sink popped one by one. The water looked cold. Becca shuffled in tighter to my chest and, for the first time, I felt she needed me. It was strange, the thought of another person caring for me or relying on me for any bit of happiness. That day, in her kitchen, her crying on my shoulder, my role changed. I had to be a proper boyfriend. I had to look after Becca, like Frank said. I had responsibilities for people other than myself now.

'It's okay,' I said, rubbing her back. 'It's okay.'

Becca looked at me with glossy eyes, a slight smile on her face. Very rarely was she serious, very rarely did she show emotion. But right then, she had more walls down than Berlin.

'Why don't we move in together?' I said.

'What?'

'Why don't we? We can rent somewhere, get you out of here. Try it.'

'Jamie, you're seventeen. Are you mad? That'd be impossible.'

'Why? The least we can do is try. I'll get my mum to sign everything, be a guarantor or whatever it's called when young people try and rent. If I say I'm leaving, she won't even bother looking and sign that shit twice over. We'll be fine.'

'What if it's not that straightforward, though?'

'It will be, trust me.'

Becca shook her head at how ridiculous I sounded.

'Oh yeh, and how do you know that?' she said.

'Whatever you want, I won't stop until I get it, because you deserve it all. You can trust me, Becca, you stick with me and you'll be happy. I promise.'

The rain seemed to be coming to a stop outside. Every tap seemed *to shut off, with the water in the sink, in the gutters, on her cheeks, all becoming still. A month later I found the flat above Solomon's kebab shop. We needed nothing more than a few signatures from my mum and Becca's dad. Even then, I was madly in debt but madly in love. A part of me hoped living with Becca would make me feel like a winner every day and steer me away from the urge to win elsewhere. I was wrong. Once you win once, you never wanna stop winning. And as much as you can be addicted to someone, by loving them, by wanting to spend every day with them, it doesn't change the fact that some addictions are stronger than others.*

No matter what decisions I made to change the course of my life, the odds always seemed to be against me. It's mad, Dennis, how far we've come. She was over the moon to be moving into that flat. Fuck knows what buying a house would feel like for her, for us. I'll make it happen, I guarantee it. We'll have that house soon, and as soon as we do, I'll get my head sorted out. We won't last if I carry on, I know that. I'm sick of it all. I just want to be happy.

I comb Dennis's moustache and hair then bring the sheet up to his chin.

Right, Den, enough of me, let's get you set up for viewing.

We've installed a new room, accessed through a door in the embalming room. Almost like a walk-in wardrobe. Only small, with railings that span the length of each of the four walls, loaded with clothes. I took every bin bag from the wardrobes at home and put everything on hangers, ready to be used on the bodies. Cashmere sweaters, designer suits, overhead shelving that holds heels and polished brogues. We've created a mini-Selfridges for the dead.

Lucky for me, Becca says she has now taken on the job of getting rid of all the old stock at her work, as the girl who used to do it apparently got sacked for taking all the security guards to the changing rooms on her lunch break. Ever since, Becca's been bringing home more bag loads and filling up the wardrobe, ready to sell on eBay when she gets round to it. Fuck knows if it's even legal the way she's handling old stock, but surely they must all be at it to get some extra dosh? Anyway, who am I to ask questions? It's not like she ever looks in them, but I bulk them out with old bags for life and stuff them behind everything just in case, hoping she won't finally go rooting.

I take a Hugo Boss suit off the rack which looks like it would fit Dennis's frame. I dress him carefully, using a lint roller to get rid of any dust or loose strands of cotton. He looks like James Bond with that tan and crisp white shirt. It makes me happy seeing them looking a million quid. It makes me feel better for the shit I've done. At the end of the day, it's only clothes. Pointless bits of material. Positioning him in that viewing room, knowing friends and family are going to walk through that door and be proud to see Dennis there looking spick and span. It feels good. It's exactly what I didn't get with my dad. I'm committed to remembering why I got into this job in the first place. To make these final memories memorable for the right reasons.

I tie the laces on Dennis's black shoes and pull up his socks.

Looking dapper, mate. I say, patting him on the toe. *Looking dapper.*

As I'm cleaning up, an advert comes on the radio for Cheltenham. *'The greatest horse racing meeting of the year is finally here!'* I stand in the middle of the room with my eyes shut, hearing the thud of the hooves, the cheer of the crowd come through the speakers. A tingle rushes from head to toe. The possibilities. The fuckin' possibilities. I listen to the crackling commentary of historic wins, can practically smell the tufts of grass being kicked up in the embalming room. The only thing is the betting money. How do I get it? You've got to bet some to win some. I've done it before, so I intend to do it again.

'Cheltenham Festival . . . will you be a winner?'

I open my eyes and take a deep breath. This time it really feels this will either be the start of everything or the end of everything.

21

As good as I am at my job, I still need to make more money. Following Dad's mantra, I have to play dirty again. I own a business now. Rather than rinse the dead, I've decided to turn my attention to the customers. And I've got two weeks to do it until Cheltenham is upon us.

I sit in the office on the computer, modifying the price lists. I near enough double the price of gold- and silver-plated urns, making cardboard boxes not an option any more. I include flowers on every package available, justifying the extra two hundred quid thrown on top. I paint our lowest quality coffins in a cheap varnish, charging them for a lacquered, walnut casket when it's only pine. I even bring in a postage and packaging, hand-delivery service where people can have ashes delivered to their doorsteps. I'm gonna have Trick zipping round like a fuckin' Deliveroo driver, dropping off your nan like a chow mein.

It's funny how little people know about the funeral industry, the ins and outs of when someone dies. Most of the time, people want it done quickly, listening and trusting every word you say because they believe every funeral director is compassionate and actually sorry for their loss. Do they forget it's a business? We need to pay the bills. Dealing with grief every day makes me kinda numb to it. I know Janice didn't give a toss either. I have no choice but to play on that false trust if I've got any chance of getting out of this mess.

An old hag comes in, mid-eighties. This one's alive, visiting with her son to pick out a coffin.

'May I ask who the coffin's for?' says Trick, all polite in his white shirt. He looks like a blackcurrant lollipop.

'Me, you daft bugger,' the woman says.

I've just finished off an embalming so I tell Trick I'll take care of this one. I remove my white coat and usher them through to the calmly lit casket room. The woman's in a red blazer, a golden brooch pinned to the collar. The son, probably forties, in a pin-striped shirt and brown shit-flicker shoes, looks like he's got a bit of spare cash to spend on his dying mother.

I dwell around the expensive walnut options, giving them a catalogue of coffin handles or the option for bespoke engravings. The son's rolling his eyes, edging towards the cheap shoeboxes. Little does he know I have this biddy in the palm of me hand.

'I'm sorry to hear you're having to think about this so soon,' I say.

'Oh, you sweetheart. I'm eighty-six, love, I can't go on for ever.'

'Never! Well, you're looking good, madam. You know, I always respect people who plan ahead. I think it's really important knowing everything's going to be okay when you go.'

I place a hand on her quivering arm. Her blazer's made of cheap nylon.

'You're right,' she says. 'I want a proper send-off. That one would throw me in Manchester canal if I didn't plan it myself.' She points at her son.

'Ahh we can't have that, can we? I've got just the thing if you want to do it properly. Make it that special day you deserve.'

I get out several leaflets of our most expensive packages, freshly printed. They include luxury colour-schemed flowers, horses and carriages, gold-plated urns with engraved designs, and the complimentary service to be dressed in designer clothes, of course. Her eyes light up, the thought of having a funeral fit for a royal.

The son peers over her shoulder, scanning the revised prices, which I still plan to upsell.

'Bit steep, int it?' he says.

'It's our luxury service. We only get one send-off, don't we? I know I'll be choosing this when I go.'

'I'm not sure, Mam, how about these coffins down here?'

'Also,' I say, before he has the chance to scoot her off, 'you can get added extras, like the printing of the order of service, and planning the route of the hearse. All these added extras are a second thought for most funerals. How many have you been to that seem thrown together? With this, every step is just the way you've always wanted it.'

'Ooh, I've been to plenty of dodgy funerals, love,' she says. 'Andy, remember our Maureen's? Got stuck at Bredbury roundabout for half an hour. Thought *I* was gonna be dead by the time we got to the church. Sad affairs, too, the lot of 'em. I want mine to be a celebration. People laughing about the good memories we had together.'

'Exactly,' I say, catching the son's eye. 'We'll make sure this is so put-together, it will be remembered for as long as you are. And definitely no roundabouts. It's only what you deserve. Plus, not many people have the privilege to plan their own funeral. You're in a very lucky position.'

Soon, we're walking through to the waiting room to sign the papers for the most expensive package we have. She even enquires about the blue and pink coffin, wanting to go out in spectacular style. I say it isn't available, unfortunately, but thank her for the interest.

The son shakes my hand, hard enough for me to show how he really feels about swizzing his mam out of thousands. The old lady hugs me, thanking me for being so accommodating and honest about it all.

She leaves looking forward to her own fuckin' funeral. That's how good I was.

'You're bent as fuck, you know that,' says Trick, after I walk back in from waving them off.

'Pays our wages, dunt it?' I say, a big grin on my face.

I realise, then, I sound just like Janice.

***

Families come and go. Crying ones, stubborn ones, sad ones, happy ones. I learn how to deal with each type of mourner, when to push the upselling and when to tone it down a bit and not go too far, to the point where they walk out disgusted. Trick still does the day-to-day average Joe walk-ins, whereas I step in when I smell money. A reservation booked in for months, or if they look like a wealthy businessman or local bigwig. I become a chameleon, a proper salesman. Moulding to the shape of every buyer, working my charm, promising them the world.

If I get sent information direct from the hospital after someone's died – which we get all the time if they have a pre-planned package with our directory – I make some subtle changes before the family arrive to sign off the paperwork. I add imaginary tax, hike the price listings, lie over verbal agreements about large sums of cash being left to charities in the local area. Local charities and churches that are really linked to the directory's bank account. I've had family members crying in front of me, amazed by how generous their parents were, or even gutted that valuables they were promised weren't left to them. I only do this now and again, when something is worth taking the risk on, or I'm feeling particularly devilish. It's not something I'm proud of but some things in life are worth being a dick for.

I'm slowly getting back the money, enough to bet with and have a go at getting out of this rut. As much as I don't want to, I've started keeping the jewellery of each corpse I throw into the burner, hiding the collection in a spare urn I nicked from the shelf. I keep it in the top cupboard in the embalming room, where Trick isn't allowed because he isn't medically qualified. That's true, but I play on the bullshit to make sure I'm the only person to step in and out of there.

The urn is currently filled with rings, watches, necklaces, bracelets, even the odd piercing and golden filling I've found raking through the ash. Once it's full, I'll visit the different Cash Converters or sell them on eBay under different names to raise no suspicion. I tend to keep them in the urn for a bit, in case any of the family members have a random thought as to where their mam's necklace ended up. I've not had any questions yet but you can never be too careful.

I tell the mourners that during the cremation process, all the jewellery melts down and will be mixed in with the ashes, which isn't true. Truth doesn't really matter any more. When you lie so much, you end up forgetting you're lying. I've established a new routine that's working, and working well. I reckon in a year or so, that one bet will come in and I can be out of the pit I've buried myself in. I can finally focus on building the thriving, profitable business I promised Becca after buying it. I can run it properly then. I don't want to treat people like this. I know it's wrong. But what other choice do I have?

At the back of my head, I know a year is too long to wait. Too long for Becca anyway. She's more onto me about the house. I've even had to give in to a joint bank account specifically for the mortgage. I transfer money into it from the directory now and again to prove I'm not on thin ice and actually want to move. And that's not even the serious shit. She's been wanting me to get Trick to mind the directory one weekend so we can go to a mortgage advisor and make an actual application. Imagine that? Sat opposite some young, spotty twat in a suit behind his desk, listening to him tell my girlfriend of nine years that I'm severely in debt and miles away from getting a mortgage accepted.

For weeks, I'm deluded. I need to be if I'm going to find a way out. Trick's been asking if I'm okay, telling me my eyes are bloodshot, that I'm looking a bit jittery and jumping to the sounds of closed caskets. Becca's saying maybe I should take some time off again. We could go to different areas and scout the properties, try the local pubs. No. No, no, no. I don't have time to act like I'm okay. I'm not. I try to blank her texts as much as I can, playing on the workload now I'm overseeing everything and dipping my toe as a salesman. I just don't know how if I can stay silent for much longer. I say the bare minimum and save my energy for what matters. Studying and winning.

I'm coming home late often, mainly from the bookies, where I'm still trying to reel in a few wins to tide me over. I'm managing to bet in the hundreds nearly every night. The jewellery in the urn slowly dwindling down. I jump and fist the air when a corpse comes in blinged-up to fuck, big bobby-dazzler rings on every finger and chains that could anchor down the *Titanic*. The clang of them falling inside the urn gives me the same thrill as hearing the bloops of the slot machines. It's my money jar, my piggy bank. My life's in that urn, the remains of what's left of me, what's left of my life and what I can make of it.

In all honesty, the betting isn't getting me anywhere and it's only two weeks until Cheltenham. I'm losing more and more. Desperation is getting the better of me, moving me like a puppet. I'm handing money over the counter like I'm having an out-of-body experience, watching on from a distance. I need all the money I can summon up so I can hit Cheltenham hard and win some major, life-changing crumpet.

I start spending an hour or two in the bookies every day without putting a penny down. I study and study and study. Head in the *Racing Post*, dissecting form, trainers, jockeys. I watch telly with Becca in the evenings, with odds dancing on the TV stand, on the mantelpiece. My eyes are on the screen but I can't get Cheltenham out of my head. The House Fund jar stares at me, crying to be filled up. Away from Becca, I start kissing it before I go to bed every night, speaking to it like the bodies. I promise it'll soon be full to the brim with notes, manifesting my way out of trouble.

I lie in bed, visualising the races on the ceiling. Horses jump over the lampshade and romp to a 33/1 win by the wardrobe. My dreams are dominated by winning. I jab at the organs of the dead, thinking of the money in my bank account rising as the fluid crackles through the tubes. I'm having hour-long shits on the bog, or I get the *Racing Post* laid out on a body while the fluid transfers through the veins. Massaging with one hand, scribbling notes with the other. I spend every waking minute narrowing down my options, coming up with a list to give me the best chance. I honestly feel I've never been more prepared for anything in my life.

I'm set to focus on getting more money for the big day when I have a slight hiccup. I run into Tommy Murphy in the off-licence on Ashton Old Road one weekend. We both have that morning's *Racing Post* under our arm, holding a pack of fags, ready to pay.

'Any tips for Cheltenham then, Tom?'

He's fingering his grubby palms, searching for the right coins to pay Raj, the young cashier. A bright background of scratch cards and chewing gum boxes highlight how grey his complexion is. Stubble covers his cheeks like burnt grass. Nose hairs poking out.

'Plenty Fletch, plenty,' he says.

I pay for my paper and fags while Tommy dilly-dallies with his coin pouch.

'Well then?'

'In the Gold Cup, bet you've gone for Diamant, haven't you?' he says.

Of course I've gone for Diamant, every seasoned punter fancies Diamant.

'It was an option,' I say.

'They're all a fuckin' option, Fletch.' Tommy scatters the coins on the counter, leaving some spinning. 'Trust me, it won't win. Diamant won't win.'

I'm stumped. Tommy knows his shit, I'll give him that, but this tip is ridiculous. Diamant has won her last five races, over difficult ground and with a field of decent horses. The trainer's tipped to win the most races throughout the festival. It's been odds-on favourite for a year, ever since last season's festival finished. You're never too confident in the Gold Cup, I get that, but Diamant has a cracking chance. No one can deny that.

'And why's that then?' I ask.

Tommy takes a raggedy tissue out of his trench coat and blows out a bucketful of goz from his nostril. The man never looks well, always seems to be grinding through the days one by one. He's outlived a good bunch of the old codgers round here. And always has money to gamble with somehow. Always. Whenever I see him, I think how I might end up like Tommy Murphy one day. Whether that's bad or not, fuck knows. He looks miserable but I know he's happy. This is his life. What's the use in seeking more? It's all he's ever known or all he needs to know.

'Just trust me, Fletch. Diamant won't win.'

Tommy Murphy is a grotty, stinking wizard sometimes. He makes predictions when he doesn't have a reason. Occasionally, they come true. Don't get me wrong, a lot of his ridiculous tips never come off as well. What's niggling me is a good few do, no matter how crazy they sound. I should have learnt by now the worst thing to do is ask Tommy Murphy's opinion. No matter what he says, you never know whether to go with it. Tommy studies more than me, longer and harder. He lives for studying. There's only so much you can do. It comes down to the horse on the day, and for me, Diamant never has an off-day. She's born for days like the Gold Cup.

Tommy pockets his fags and rolls up his *Racing Post* like a baton. His boots shuffle out into the morning haze, towards the club where he'll ruminate over more bold predictions. On leaving the offy, I go to work with my paper and study, leaning on the blue and pink coffin. It's quiet, with Trick talking through packages with a family in the visitor's room.

My notepad and paper look like a mental patient has gone on a doodle session. I've settled on a good few races, knowing I've done all I can. I leave no stone unturned. Now is the hard bit. Being clever with my money, finding it first and spending it with me noggin rather than my heart.

I tap my pen on the coffin. Maybe I can sneak in a few more snooker games with Trick, up the stakes and talk a few more pennies out of him? Too risky though, he knows I'm skint and will only blame blowing it on the directory. I can sell some of the clothes from the recent bin bags Becca brought back from work? Would take too long though, and who's going to buy a Gucci bag in Openshaw? I need to be smarter. It needs to be quick money.

I go to the club to think it over with a pint. It's midday, empty, until Spud walks in, all squinty-eyed and chirpy. He looks like an Egyptian king with all them gold chains round his neck. Bulky Argos watch to match, dirty with sawdust and paint where you can barely see the time. What I'd do to get my hands on them. Every little helps in desperate times.

'Fletchy boy!'

'All right Spud, not working today?'

He leans on the bar with both elbows, close enough for me to smell the smoke on his breath.

'Pulled a sicky, dint I. Said I got the shits after a dodgy madras. Off to the boxing tonight so didn't wanna be too knackered, know what I mean?'

I get him a lager, which he looks at like a chalice of golden wonder.

'Oh right. Who's fighting? Is it on pay-per-view?'

'Nah, nowt like that. Couple of lads on site had a scuffle last week and wanted to settle it. Tesco car park at nine if you fancy it?'

'Barmy fucker.' I laugh.

'Mate, I got Two Tools Timmy at 8/1 from the lads on our tea break. Couldn't cut a sandwich, never mind a plank of wood, but he's got one juicy right hook on him.'

I snigger and think of Spud's life as a belting film. I slap twenty dabs on Timmy there and then.

Spud goes to sit with Big Mike and Tony in the corner, jibing them to get in on tonight's brawl. Linda rakes the coins I left on the bar and springs open the till. Rows of red and purple notes stare up at her, lying in their beds, ready to be woken up. Even the coin sections are brimming. More queen's heads than Henry VIII had on his pillow. Must've been a busy week. A couple of bands on, a few wakes, bingo on Tuesdays and Thursdays. Why didn't I buy a working men's club instead?

I return to my *Racing Post* on the bar. A smoky haze eases across the room as if it were back in the 1980s where fags were lit, ash being tapped into glass trays. Regardless of the laughs, there's a sad silence to the room. It's a time when the regulars can enjoy their peace before the stragglers, the pimple-cheeked youths fancying a tipple.

In the midst of chesty coughs and clinking glass, I question the thought of dipping into the till again. I've done it once before. The last time was blamed on Coley because he's always hovering by the bar, filling up his own pints when no one is looking. Barred for two weeks he was. Not a sniff about me.

Linda's out of sight, Shaky Derek's upstairs tugging one out or watching *Only Fools*. Spud's deep into one of his Magaluf stories by the jukebox. It's the perfect opportunity. I look from my *Racing Post* to the till. My mind manifesting. The winning slips cosy in my pocket, me kissing the TV screen, me crying, punching the carpet after Diamant wins the Gold Cup.

One more time. That's all. I have to make it worthwhile this time: no pissing about. I can't do it while the lads are still in, though. I have an idea to make some extra change before I go for it.

'Right, lads,' I say, walking over to Spud, Big Mike and Tony.

Their ears perk up as if I'm coming over with free pints. I have an empty glass in my hand with a few pound coins in. 'We're doing a collection for Derek, if you wanted to chip in. He has an appointment at the hospital next week about those legs, finally. Said they can sort him out sweet but that the operation'll cost a few hundred. I know, robbing bastards. Said it was a rare gig and can only go private or summot. Anyway, he's proper down about it, been drinking away his sorrows up there all week, the poor sod.'

The lads all take a swig of their pints, listening.

'Anyway, I know shit's always tight, but if you can spare a few quid I'd appreciate it lads. Trying to help him out as much as we can, will perk him up a bit. You know how down he gets. He doesn't know we're doing it though, so don't go babbling. Be a nice surprise and all that.'

The lads don't need asking twice. They rummage around in the depths of their pockets, where the crumbs and bits of fluff haven't been touched in years. Wallets are emptied. Tony even runs out to the cash machine to throw a couple of twenties into the glass.

'You're goodens, you lads. Appreciate it!'

'No worries,' says Spud. 'Do owt for Derek. As long as he sings us an Elvis number on the jukebox after it – gonna miss those shaky bastards.'

I get them all a round in and look at the pint glass brimming with notes and coins. When they leave to go to another boozer, the club's empty. I quickly bolt the door while Linda's down in the cellar changing a barrel. I pocket the money from the glass. I turn over a few of the wooden tables slowly so Derek doesn't hear upstairs. I snap a stool leg, smash a few pint glasses softly in a tea towel and sprinkle them on the floor. I manage to jab the till open, shocked to feel the lack of guilt in my actions. I rinse the entire thing dry, stuffing my pockets until I can't get any more in. I'm a walking bank account. If you shook me upside down, it'd be raining more cash than a strip club.

Now the hard bit. I stand at the bar, looking at my reflection behind the optics. I ready myself. Take a deep breath in. A deep breath out. Three ... two ... one ... boom! I punch myself in the face as hard as I can. Not even a mark, so I do it again, again and again. I headbutt the bar, right on the edge. Blood gushes from a cut on my eyebrow. The socket starts to balloon instantly, the lids slightly closing after a few more hits. Smearing the blood across my cheek and dropping specks onto my white T-shirt, I look again, dazed, at my reflection and the battered mess I've caused. I rip the collar of my top and ruffle my hair for good measure. I'm that determined for this to work, I even contemplate ripping a tooth out. I'm an ugly fucker as it is, I can buy a whole new mouth when this is all done.

I zip up my jacket pockets, even put the notes in my socks and unbolt the door. Before sitting on the glass-sprinkled floor, I throw a bar stool and make as much noise as I can. I time my actions with the road works drilling outside so Derek and Linda won't hear. A few seconds pass. The chugging outside continues. Okay ... time to win that Oscar.

'DEREK ... LINDA ... GET IN HERE!!!'

***

'You get a good look at him or what?' says Derek, sweating from running down the stairs.

I'm sat on one of the unbroken bar stools, a bag of frozen peas on my cheek Linda fetched from the freezer.

'Not really. Had a hood on, and one of those balaclava things. Couldn't see a thing.'

'Fucking twat,' says Linda.

Derek's pacing in circles around the pile of broken glass he's swept up. The broken stools are discarded to the corner near the jukebox, ready for the bin man. The tables return to their upright position, pushed to the side to give me room to stretch my 'sore leg'.

'So he just stormed in here with, what was it? A baseball bat?'
I nod.

'Stormed through the tables and all that, lamped you with it, then got off with the money?'

'Pretty much,' I say. 'I chucked a pint glass at him to try and scare him off but didn't even flinch. On his own as well so must have been a tough fella. Tried to fend him off but he gripped me, beat the shit outta me, then sent me flying into one of those tables there.'

'And the till. How the fuck did he even get into it?' says Linda.

I rustle the peas and wince a little. One side of my face is throbbing like fuck.

'Just fuckin' hammered it with the bat.'

Derek's legs are going crazy. Put him in the sea and I bet those legs could motor off across the Atlantic and back again. His soup-stained vest is sopping wet. Sideburns glued to his chops. It's shit to see him so panicked. This bit I didn't really consider. I think I feel okay knowing I'll be able to return it all. The grass is greener on the other side of Cheltenham. Shaky, Linda, the lads, Trick... they never have to know. I can keep them as mates and live the life I want to live. This is playing dirty. This is necessary.

'I knew I should have got them bastard cameras fixed,' says Derek.

Swear to god I nearly poo right there on the floor. Cameras? Fuckin' cameras? Since when does the club have cameras? I look at where Derek's mumbling to himself. In a dusty, spider-webbed corner above the ladies' bogs is a tiny square camera. It has a black wire feeding into the wall but looks older than Tommy Murphy's trench coat. Even a cut-throat razor couldn't make a closer shave than that. I guess, for once, luck's on my side.

Linda goes to call the police while Shaky paces a little more. He smacks the bar as hard as he can. His back slides down the wooden panel until his arse hits the floorboards. I look down on him from the stool, at the greasy black barnet lolling between his knees. The man looks more broken than the stools.

I get up, 'limp' over, and sit next to him, our backs resting against the wood.

'It's all right, Derek,' I say, putting an arm around his hairy shoulders. 'We'll find the fucker.'

22

A week before Cheltenham. Vince, who's still been supplying me with offers, calls asking to meet up for a bevvie in town. There's only gonna be one topic of conversation. He's a businessman at the end of the day. How successful I'll be at Cheltenham has an impact on him. If I win, he wins. I mean, why else would he be giving me all these free bets? His commission's probably higher than anyone else in Manchester. Next weekend is a biggy for the both of us. We're there to help each other, to win together.

We met at the Pev off Bridgewater Street, or the Peveril of the Peak to tourists. A lime-green tiled pub dating back to the nineteenth century. A relic of Manchester, serving the locals for over two hundred years.

Vince proper looks out of place sat in the corner under a blurred photograph of Nancy Swanick, the owner, now in her nineties. The wood-panelled musk of the place clashes with his pink ironed shirt. The space feels too small for his money. An old bloke scratches at his yellow beard two tables down, gawping through his John Smith's at the flashy cunt in the pink shirt.

'Fletch. How we doing buddy?' He stands to greet me. Arms outstretched, that happy pink face I'd last seen grimacing over the roulette wheel.

'Good, mate. Good. Listen, thanks again for those United tickets. Had a top day out.'

'Ahh no bother. Like I said, that was only a little sumfing. Glad to hear you had a top time. Not a bad game too, was it?'

'Fuckin' right there. Fancy another pint?'

I point to the falling foam in his glass.

'Don't be silly. Today's on me. Sit your arse down there.'

Vince doesn't move an arse cheek and gestures to the young barmaid, clicking his chunky fingers. That's a definite no-no in places like the Pev. Them lasses aren't waitresses, they're one of the lads. That gesture alone says a lot about his lifestyle. Where he drinks, the people he's used to being around. Having not sat down yet, I save Vince the grief and order our drinks at the bar.

'Cheeky cunt, int he?' says the barmaid, hammering down the pump as if she has Vince's bollocks in a vice. I roll my eyes in agreement and return to his table.

'So, how's things with you?' I say, plonking two frothy beauties down.

'Ah same old, same old. Just all eyes on next weekend. Feelin' confident?'

'Confident as I can be. As long as there's no banana skins I should be sweet.'

I look at the pink floral design of Vince's upturned sleeves. He lifts the pint to his lips and sinks the ale as if it fuels him. Blotchy cheeks, puffed eyes. He looks like he's gone through a full tank of tissue builder.

The overpowering aftershave stinks out the pub. He's a man who you can tell lives the good life. How many people like me does he have under his wing? If this guy wants me to win, then surely I should be feeling confident? He's used to winning. I'm certain next weekend we'll both be phoning each other, waffling down the phone like lovers, reminiscing about that fateful night in the casino.

'Right, listen here,' says Vince. A seriousness that cuts the small talk in half. 'I got some beautiful odds for you in the Gold Cup but we'll get to that. What you fancying for the one o'clocker?'

'Err, can't see past Pied Piper if I'm honest.'

'Good lad. 8/1 I can get for ya. You'll get shorter odds for that nosy geezer getting a leg over tonight.' He points to the bearded man still giving us the side-eye.

Vince punches me in the shoulder and lets out a rumble of a laugh. Eights for Pied Piper is obscene. This lad is like the Gandalf of gambling, plucking odds from thin air and helping a fat little hobbit like me on his journey to glory.

'I know,' he says. 'You won't get that anywhere. So, Gold Cup, what you thinking?'

I go through my options, five in all, including Diamant. I explain the pros and cons of both: weather, ground, jockey, trainer. Why each one is still floating round my head a week before the big day. The Gold Cup is always tricky; it's the best of the best all in one race. Usually, you have a couple of fiddles and a banker that you fancy more than Margot Robbie. I don't give much away. He seems happy. The most I get out of him is a nod and a sniffle. His biggest reactions only ever come from his own voice, his own jokes.

'Well, let me know nearer the time and I'll fire over some last-minute odds for ya. But they won't be mega. Think you might have to pile it on to make it worthwhile. Fuckin' Cheltenham though, innit son? If you're not betting big there then you might as well pack it in.'

His salesmanship sounds like me in the casket room. We know each other's game, not like it's relevant. If we get money at the end of it, it doesn't matter how we get there.

A few stragglers filter in from the street, talking racing too. One lad is bigger than me with his underbelly on show, wheezing lungs that say he's got ten years max left in him. Even his mate looks like he's eaten more chips than a casino. I imagine the fat leaking from him in the cremation machine, clogging up the gutters.

'Now Fletch, I know you've been having a stinker lately.' Vince leans in, risking those shirt sleeves on the sticky table. 'But I'll throw in a few quid for you next weekend, all right? I know you'll get a few winners in.'

Part of the VIP status is having my betting apps linked up to Vince's account. It was explained in one of the surveys I had to fill out in exchange for fifty quid in free bets when I joined, as well as other questions like my favourite sports, my hobbies, even my favourite colour, which was odd, but whatever helps me win more money, I guess. I can't receive these exclusive perks without Vince keeping an eye on how I'm dishing it out on the horses, which is fair enough. I could be drawing it out and spending it on Manchester's street corners for all he knew. The scheme means Vince can follow my form, study it as much as I do with the *Racing Post*. There's no hiding with betting apps. Even when I bet in-person, I always scan the slip to my online account so I can track the bet live. Vince has eyes on my every move, my every penny. He knows my habits, my urges. He also knows I can't hit a barn door lately.

'Study though,' he says, 'Be clever with it. You don't need me to tell you there's a shitload of quality horses running next week. I'm asking around all the bookmakers and trainers for any insight this week so I should have some more guidance, but just warning you if you were wanting to have a dabble before then.'

It's the first time since I started all this that I feel responsible or monitored for my betting. Gambling has always been about the freedom of it. A private world. If I won, or if I lost, it was always my decision and the only person it impacted was me. I was the one to live with it so none of it ever mattered. I could always handle it, hide it, dig myself out. As soon as Vince came into play, everything seems a little different. I know on Cheltenham weekend I'll be betting with him on my shoulder, knowing wherever he is, he'll see my bets feeding through the app. Judgements are being made. My betting is no longer secret. It scares the life out of me knowing someone knows. I feel exposed. Comparing it to the perks I'm getting though, the added opportunities to win big, surely this is the smallest gamble? I need him. I need these odds if I'm to live a happy life.

As soon as that day comes, I'll pack it all in and run with Becca. Run to that new house with all our cash, leaving my problems in Openshaw. I won't need to bet any more. I won't want to bet any more. I won't blow it like I did last time. What would be the point in gambling when I have everything I need?

'I appreciate that, Vince. Honest. We'll win big next week, I guarantee it.'

I think of Becca, Trick, Shaky Derek crying on the club floor. Vince smiles, cheeks turning into two red snooker balls. I've won big once. I can win big again. This time next week, it will all be over.

We clink glasses and cheers to our big break.

23

The radio's bellowing Cheltenham adverts every half an hour now. *One week to go. Get your bets on. Will you make history?* I wash my hands thoroughly with soap, the image of horses leaping fences on the white walls, projected by my imagination. I'm smiling to myself, manifesting the elation, the phone call to Becca. *I've done it*, I'll say, *I've done it. Everything's going to be okay.*

Andrea is laid out on the table, looking like one of those mummies you seen in the museum as a kid on a school trip. Shrivelled, curled up, skin tight against the outline of her skull. Her hair is frayed, the colour of cigarette ash. Black freckles dot what's left of her cheeks, raining down in clusters on her thin body. She's so small on the table, like Dad was. I have to lean right over to wash her with the towel. I imagine her being motherly, whipping up a nice stew or watching daytime game shows with her husband. A cup of tea steaming between her mitts. It makes me think of my own mam. Every thought of Mam inevitably comes with the thought of Dad. Like light and dark, one doesn't exist without the other.

There's a loud slap as I ping on my blue gloves. I wheel the trolley by Andrea's head and start arranging the scalpels, checking I have all the right tools so I don't have to go back and forth to the cupboards. I'm missing the forceps, which I go and grab, switching on the tissue-builder machine while I'm over there.

I arrange the towels, make-up and tubes on the trolley and sit down to prepare.

You'll like this, Andrea.

Me mam said to me dad once during an argument: 'The only way you become a millionaire through gambling is starting off as a billionaire, and you, Ray Fletcher, started off on your fuckin arse.' She had a good sense of humour back then, me mam. I was under my United duvet with my hands cupped over my ears. I'd only heard Miss Doyle shout that loud when Reece lit this girl's bag on fire with a Bunsen burner in science. She was a genius at that, me mam, throwing puns and wordplay into a heated argument to throw Dad off guard.

'You bet on a horse at ten to one and it doesn't come in till fuckin' half past three. Why don't you use that money to put food in the fridge?'

'Poker with the lads? You fold more than a pissin' map.'

'I know I can walk out that door right now Ray. Ya know why? Cause a gambler like you would do anything to win me back.'

Even though I knew Mam was always gonna win, it didn't make it any easier to sit there and listen to it. Their voices boomed through the floorboards and made my superhero figures rattle on the shelf. Doors slammed. Cutlery clattered. It was a part of my youth that became normal. I can't say I ever knew what they were arguing over. I always thought Dad wanted fish and chips instead for tea, or wanted to watch United while Coronation Street was on. It never seemed that deep to me.

One of the nights – I can't remember which one because they arrived more regularly than the 201 bus – I finally got a bit of kip, drooling a lake into my pillow. Was probably dreaming about the new United kit I'd get for Christmas or some spicy lass I fancied at school. Anyway, I was snoozing, and heard the distinctive creak of my door go. The hinges moaned in a way that could never fool me. I knew it was Dad. The clumsy footsteps, the raspy breathing. Like

Christmas morning when Mam used to put one or two prezzies in the sack at the end of my bed, I pretended be asleep with my mouth wide open, catching flies. Bit like how you look now, Andrea.

I thought Dad was creeping in to look at his son, sit in silence after his argument and look at me as a reminder for why he gambles how he does. I kinda understood it, even at that age, but could never try and explain it to Mam. Growing up, I just knew never to mention anything like that to her. Her knowing Dad was influencing me would have had him out the door years before he finally went. We had this bond, me and Dad. That's why I stayed there, pretending to be asleep. He didn't want me to wake up. I knew that. I knew what he was in my room for.

My bedside drawer creaked open. A rustling. Searching fingers. They settled on my piggy bank, the one I was using to save up for a new pair of football boots, like the ones Beckham played in to win us the Treble. The coins rattled into his palms. Clinking metal. Falling into his empty pockets. He returned the piggy bank to the drawer, me knowing where the money had gone and knowing I wouldn't speak a word. The hinges creaked to a close. His hefty boots thudding down the stairs and out the front door to the bookies. I slept soundly that night. Knowing I was making Dad happy and being the son he'd always wanted.

I get lost in my babbling and start preparing Andrea. Tubes. Machine. Fluid. Blood.

'Work' by Rihanna starts playing on the radio. I nearly start twerking, remembering how rich I'm gonna be next week. The blood hoovers out of Andrea, spurting into the tray like filling up a tiny paddling pool.

Andrea's daughter mentioned to Janice she was a fan of classical music and chose some Mozart number for her funeral song. I think she'd like something a bit more mellow, so I switch the radio over to Classic FM. The vibration of violin strings and the delicate twinkle of piano keys drown out the fluid machine.

I upturn the corners of Andrea's mouth slightly as if she can hear every note, feeling the music move through her with the formaldehyde.

I look at her for a little while. She looks so at peace. The music starts to make me feel warm. I have one of those moments where I realise I love my job. I'm doing my best to make Andrea's last moments joyful. Wherever she is, I like to think she's dancing right now, swaying with the pitch of the music, feeling more alive than she ever has been.

As I start to massage the fluid around her body, I lower my voice to nearly a whisper, carrying on my story.

I started to nick money for myself when I first moved into our flat above Solomon's. Now that I was paying rent, I was short on gambling money. The lifestyle I'd made for myself meant rent was always gonna be an uphill task. It would always come second. I used to rob the odd cig from Mam's purse or the occasional Yorkshire pud from her plate, nothing to get me in too much trouble. The first time I nicked something was a Lucozade from Abdul's, the corner shop near school, which couldn't afford cameras and had a dim shopkeeper that gave you back a tenner in change when you paid with a quid. I was always coming out of there with more money. Probably made robbing shit easier to settle with. If anything, I was giving back to the poor bastard, taking things to compensate for all the random pennies he handed over.

Never getting caught made me more confident than I should have been. I tried the big guns like Tesco, or B&M on the retail park. I had to do a runner from security and avoid it for a couple of weeks to be safe. A couple of close shaves that would have had Mam spanking me arse like I was three again.

Don't get me wrong, Andrea, I never had it in me to be Openshaw's Al Capone. Geezers like Coley and Tommy Murphy took care of that, having their coats lined with whisky miniatures and discount boxes of washing-up powder. Coley even offered me a hundred toilet rolls once. A fuckin' hundred! If doughnuts like them could do it, I didn't really have to worry about pocketing the odd item.

I used to go for random shit like a five pack of doughnuts, a pack of Wagon Wheels, a family bag of Walkers Sensations. Ya know, the easy shit, to work my way up. I always said to myself I'd stop when I got caught, but I never did get caught. I worked my way up to beer cans, then them cheap litre bottles of cider, or six tins of Spam. Even got away with a full turkey crown for Mam one Christmas, pulled a blinder at the till saying I had a hernia in my side. Stupid lass on the counter referred me to her GP, writing the number down on a receipt and all that, sending me on my way. Couldn't believe it. I felt like Tiny Tim.

The gambling started to hit harder when me and Rebecca moved into the flat. I was getting more pissed off with my losses. This was a couple of months after we moved in and we were paying for all new shit like plates, cutlery, bog roll (ironically). Rebecca wanted new everything, like chopping boards, coasters, candles. All that bollocks you didn't need but she wanted to make it feel 'homely' and 'cosy'. She was on a high from finally getting away from her mum, who had decided to stop speaking to her full stop. That only made Becca happier. She worshipped the flat and had me spending a fuckin' fortune every weekend in Wilko and B&M. She even dragged me to IKEA, knowing full well that place is hell on earth to me. Floors and floors of random wooden shit, fooling idiots like Becca into buying pointless crap like a tea light holder. Drives me mad. Anyway, the pennies were wasting away on stuff I hadn't planned for. My overdraft was creeping into crisis territory, towards no overdraft at all. I ditched Reece and Pinky to work more hours, sneaked in the odd job with Trick and helped my Mam out with stuff like her wallpapering and a paint job to get in any cash I could.

It was dire times. A period where I should have been revelling *in the enjoyment of a new flat and sharing every day with Becca. I always knew it was gonna be a stress those first few weeks. I just needed to get in and settled, buy all the essentials and then get back on my feet. It wasn't that simple, though. It kept coming. Rent, gas bills, water bills, council tax, insurance. I was on my fuckin' arse.*

The sound is wet when I remove the tubes. I stitch the incision hole, slot in the eye caps, wire the jaw, glue the lips and brush her hair. It's wiry, like the strings of the violin still playing from the radio. Even her hands look like those made for piano playing. Long and slender fingers. Everything about Andrea screams classical.

I often wonder what it would be like to be talented. Becca says what I do is a talent, how my attitude towards my work and how much I care about the dead is something rare and special. I don't know about that. Surely that's just having morals? Taking pride in your community? Becca can play the penny whistle and do the splits, but whenever is there a time to whip any of those out at a party? I think I'd rather be talentless than having one and never being able to show it.

Unless gambling's my talent? Or losing money? I suppose there's not many people in the world who can do that like me.

I was in the club one night, Andrea, sat on a bar stool with empty pint glasses round me. Trick was being a good mate as always, getting the rounds in, knowing I was struggling. He got talking to this pretty bird from Longsight, nice brunette fringe and a tattoo of a rose on her neck. She was proper into him, his tattoos especially, twirling her hair and feeling his arm whenever he made one of his shit jokes. I was left to drink on my own, which I didn't mind too much. She was getting sloshed on the vodka Cokes, which probably made me do it. Even Trick knew she was frazzled but we were all having a good time. The handbag she had draped across her shoulder was unzipped, a bright twenty wiggling out the top of it. Trick didn't notice. Neither did she. I nicked it during one of her fits of laughter. I pocketed it on the way to the bogs, looking at it in wonder as I gushed onto the urinal cakes. Even then, in my hands, it didn't feel mine. The ease of it though. She didn't have a clue, and that excited me in ways I knew it shouldn't. I blagged a sicky, blaming the flat ale, and bonked off to Jim Ramsbottom's across the road, feeling naughty.

Then it started getting ugly. I manipulated Trick into upping the stakes on snooker night. I persuaded Becca to dip into her savings because we deserved a big TV in our brand-new flat. We deserved that swanky kettle even though all of them just boil water. We deserved a microwave even though we never microwave anything. The loans were more than the actual items, but Becca was never to know that. I won the money back to repay the loans, eventually. That only changed my psychology to think all risks pay off, that I can always dig myself out and be the good guy no matter what.

Potential holidays to Majorca became holidays to Skegness because the money vanished into 'house stuff'. Meals out became a Maccie D's on the sofa. Bottles of Baileys became bottles of Irish Cream from Aldi. The little wealth we had seemed to be falling all the time. I made it happen in a way that seemed natural to Becca. It was just the cost of living. The credit crunch. We had a flat, it was the reality we had now. Grinding by, surviving.

I never nicked directly from Becca, not from her purse or money jars. It seemed too upfront to me, too heartless. I had a line. When all our bank stuff turned digital, like when we used one account to pay bills from, it removed some of the emotion from it. You could convince yourself you weren't being a thief when it's just numbers on a screen. When you've got a twenty quid you didn't earn in your pocket though, that felt different. You had to think of the bigger picture. Keep asking yourself why you're doing it, no doubt like Dad did when he rinsed my piggy bank.

That's why, after coming home yesterday from meeting Vince

at the Pev, I didn't feel as guilty as I thought I would. Standing opposite the mantelpiece, the House Fund jar sitting there, a film of dust on the lid. Becca's twenties and tens curled up inside, pound coins sprinkled down the side like a cup of pick 'n' mix. Becca was still at work. I'd say I'd transferred it into a bank account so we could keep an eye on it, see how much we'd accumulated. I'd say it was full, it needed emptying anyway. And empty it I did. I was crossing the line, but I felt I needed to.

I've finished brushing Andrea's hair and applied her make-up. She's done. A complete composition. An artist ready for her encore.

I wasn't telling Andrea fibs either. It's true. I got one of my old rucksacks from the back of the wardrobe and shook all the House Fund money into it, along with the wad I'd robbed from the club. I cashed in all the jewellery left in the urn and added a few hundred more to the bag. The weight of it gave me shivers. I sat on the living room floor and brushed my hand through it all for a few minutes. Mango hovered around wanting to dip his head in and see what was in the bag. He looked at me all confused. What was I so interested in? Why was I on the edge of tears?

I sat there thinking, this time next week, after Cheltenham, I could fill ten bags full. Twenty. Who knew how the odds would go in my favour? Not for one second did I question whether I was doing the right thing. It was practically impossible to go into Cheltenham with this much money and not come out at least even.

I ended up laughing. Just sat there like a loon laughing at this bag of money I'd managed to get, laughing at Mango who started barking in response. Wasn't it mad how I still found ways? My eye was still swollen blue, half-closed from punching myself. A shooting pain zipped from my jaw to my plastered eyebrow. Becca took the bait that the club was robbed and I got lamped by the geezer on the way out. My head was off on one. I was crazy. I knew that. I also knew this was worth the risk. I knew it would all be fine.

I calmed Mango down and stuffed the bag of cash to the back of the wardrobe under a load of old coats. I was tempted to get it back out and count it all when my phone started ringing.

'Vince?' I answered.

'Hiya pal, sorry to bother. I forgot to mention yesterday, I've got a few tickets going spare for Cheltenham next week. Coach, travel and hotel included and all that. You fancy 'em?'

'Does a bear shit in the woods?' I said.

I still can't believe it. I'm going to Cheltenham.

24

Becca texts me, telling me to be home for seven tonight. My heart drops. I think the worst. She's found the fuckin' money, she must have. Why else would she send a blunt text? No explanation. Not even a kiss or anything. It's always about something I've done wrong, something I'm going to have to grovel over. Maybe she finally knows about the bets, the wasted money, robbing from the dead, everything. I want to go to the club and get pissed. Hide away from it. Have one last bet as a free man. Why hold it off though? It's going to come eventually. I have to face it and move on.

I lock up the directory and drive home at a snail's pace in the Transit. My pits are leaking with nerves. I take the deepest breath before putting my key in the lock and turn it. The living room smells of vanilla. The curtains are drawn. A makeshift dinner table is made out of a towel draped over the coffee table, two cushions for chairs on either side.

'What's this?' I say, trying to keep my voice settled. Killing me with kindness before ripping me to shreds?

Becca walks in from the kitchen with a corked bottle of wine, placing it next to the tea light flickering on the table.

'I've cooked,' she says.

Becca hardly cooks. Something is way off. Has she found out how bad the directory is in debt? Is she reproducing our argument at the meal to prove a point? I notice a scent of garlic mixing with the vanilla candle. I'm so fuckin' confused.

'Fuck me, at least try not to look worried,' she says. 'Go on, sit down. It's ready.'

I sit on the cushion Mango is chewing the corner of. I ruffle his fluffy head and ask him if he knows anything about what's going on.

'Voila!'

Becca waltzes in with her crusty oven mitts. She plonks down a tray of Lasagne which looks like it's been run over.

'Looks ... yummy,' I say.

'From scratch.'

Her face is a deep red, sweaty fringe plastered to her forehead. You know when people come out of the gym, looking all sticky and reeking?

She sits on the cushion opposite and starts pouring the wine. Lasagne bubbling between us.

'It looks shit, doesn't it?' she says.

'That doesn't matter,' I say, leaning over to kiss her damp head. 'What's all this for anyway?'

Sounds of the radio trickle in from the kitchen. Mango continues gnawing on my cushion.

'I have news,' she says, offering me a glass.

This is good. This is really good. Pay rise? Another promotion maybe? Unless it's actually good news for her and not me, like she's found our dream house and has already slapped a deposit on it without speaking to me about it. Sort of a payback for me buying the directory without running it by her. I'd even settle for that. Anything other than the betting.

I attempt a grin, trying to read the excitement on her face. I can't lie, I'm shitting myself. All I can think of is if it'll cost me any money. I don't need any curveballs right now.

'I'm pregnant,' she says.

Ahh shit.

***

I eat the lasagne, drink the wine, get through it. We smile and laugh, celebrating us and our next step. I think I'm convincing. I'm happy, I actually am. It's amazing. I'm going to be a dad. It's just the timing. I can't raise a child now. We aren't ready. Becca probably thinks we have enough to get started, that we can give our kid the best start to life possible. She has no idea I'm back in the red, praying that bag of cash in the wardrobe will get us both out of the shit. Or us *three* now.

While Becca clears up the plates, I go to the bathroom and dunk my head in a sink of freezing water. I look at my dripping face in the mirror. Ginger beard wet and glossy. The stakes are suddenly a lot higher. At least before, if I lost the lot at Cheltenham, it was only me and Becca to deal with it. Adults, we always find a way. I literally can't lose now. That wasn't an option before, but it definitely isn't a fuckin' option now. She will leave me. Becca will leave me. She'll need to. I wouldn't be able to provide. I wouldn't be able to be the dad and boyfriend she deserves.

Staring into the mirror, I imagine my worst nightmare. Being a vacant dad, just like mine was. Becca keeping our child out of my life because I'm a drunken gambling addict, forever trying to get out of my own mess. The endless cycle would reach a point where our son or daughter would be looking over me, dead in that coffin, wondering where I've been all these years, wondering why I died so young and why I was never there for them. They'd cry over my absence, not for the fact I was actually dead.

I can't let them go through what I went through. I either need to come clean to Becca, now, tonight, or ride my fate at Cheltenham next week.

I dry my face and, like everything in my life, I leave it to luck. I get a coin from my pocket and toss it into the air. I pick heads as it spins, until it lands in my palm. I look down and close my eyes.

25

Full from lasagne, we both crash out on the couch and watch some wank police drama. Within minutes Becca is asleep, twitching, my head on her lap. I swivel round, looking at her belly, amazed a tiny little foetus is growing in there. A year from now, it'll be out, chasing Mango around the flat or wherever we'll be living.

I stare at Becca's belly and start whispering, careful not to wake her.

Hey little one. Your, er, future dad here. Well, not your future dad, but your real dad. I'm your real dad, like – ah fuck. Sorry. Let me start again. I just wanted to say I'm looking forward to meeting you. I'm gonna look after you, I promise. You won't have to know any of the shi— I mean stuff I went through because I'll be out of it. It will just be me, you and Mum. We'll have money to buy you toys, take you to the beach to have an ice cream, go on holidays to the arcades, just like your Gran and Grandad used to take me.

And you're gonna be really lucky, having a mum like yours. I remember the first time she even mentioned kids. It was after a night at the dogs. Dogs are these four-legged hairy things that race round a track which your Dad bets on and hopes he wins. Mango's a dog who you'll meet eventually. You'll love him; he's very cute. So, this night at the dogs. I'll set the scene for ya.

It was a windy night, a tad damp. The sandy track started to spot with rain, darkening the harder it fell. Me and your Uncle Trick were in the stands, surrounded by the hustle and bustle of late-night punters. A man in a beige trench coat and bushy moustache bellowed odds from a stepladder. He pointed to a long board, the odds shining red, the names and trap numbers moving up and down as people threw fivers, tenners, twenties into his palms. I piled a few quid on trap six; Uncle Trick had a few dabs on trap two. The rain pattered our coats. Heavy and loud on the stand's tin roof. We'd never skipped snooker night before, we didn't think anything else was worth our time for them few hours of freedom and chatter. Uncle Trick took some persuading, but you'll soon find out your dad always finds a way.

Thursdays at Belle Vue weren't half a decent night out. The track sat on the edge of Gorton and Levenshulme, about a five-minute drive from Openshaw, where we live. It had a history of punters that went back yonks. Even then it attracted the age-old grandpas as well as the fresh-blooded polo-necks on stag dos. It was a good laugh, always was.

Uncle Trick had never been before, which made me more determined to drag him there. He sipped the lager from his plastic cup over the balcony, watched the dogs get walked up to the traps.

'That the thing that goes round then? What is it, a cat or summot?' said Uncle Trick.

'Daft get, it's a hare.'

'Could do with some of that maself.'

Trick rubbed his bald head, spreading the rain about.

All night, we carried on getting merry. Losing. Winning. Losing. Winning. One of my dogs didn't get released and Uncle Trick started singing Elvis. Everyone turned and laughed as he shook his legs like Shaky Derek, singing, 'you're caught in a trap'. His belly jigged along with his flailing arms. Didn't half crack me up.

Anyway, I'm getting off track here. It seemed a pretty standard night when we left. We weren't too late compared to the time we usually swan out the boozer, after Uncle Trick throws down his cue. We embraced in a strong bear hug on the gravel car park, only a tad less money in our pockets than what we walked in with. Uncle Trick went home to his missus. I went home to your mum.

I was drunk. Not steaming, but drunk. I scranned some chicken wings from Uncle Sol's, who I was just getting to know at the time, and managed to slot my key into our front door on the second try. Your mum was in the front room, crying her mince pies out. It was the first time I'd seen her properly upset because of me. The curtains were half-drawn. Just sat there on the couch under tepid moonlight. Wailing.

'Woah, what's up?'

'Don't you come near me, you pig!' There were a few swear words in there but I'll leave those out.

'Woah woah, what's all this? Calm down.'

'Get your hands off me, stay there. Don't even start.'

'Start what?'

Her pyjama top was damp. Tears teetering on her chin.

'I know,' she said, pacing.

'Know what?'

'You know.'

'I don't have a clue what you're on about.'

I was stone-cold sober by this point. I wish I wasn't. Did I leave betting slips lying about where I shouldn't have? Did one of her mates see me leave the bookies and grass on me?

'Can't help being a flirt, can ya? It makes sense now. All those nights sat up in bed on your phone. All those late nights out. All them spontaneous night shifts that you have to work. You don't fool me, Jamie. Honestly, you don't. I've always wondered why you're dead protective with your phone. I'm your girlfriend and I don't even know your passcode, for god's sake. You don't let me anywhere near it.'

I leant on the mantelpiece with my elbow. It's the closest she'd ever come to finding out.

'Babe, come on. Sit down.'

I try taking a step towards her.

'Away. Honestly, go away. Don't come near me.'

'Becca, I don't even know where this has come from? I'm not

protective with my phone at all. Look, you can go through my messages if you want.'

I unlocked it and tapped quickly onto my messages, scrolling them in full view for her to see.

'See.'

I pocketed the phone with the hope that'd be enough. There was no way I was handing it over. Having ten-plus betting apps staring back at her, all with a mix of sums in their accounts. I never realised how it looked. Me up in bed, tapping away at the screen. Staying out until the bookies shut, trying to win as much as I could. Working mad nights at the directory to pay back the gambling debt. I'd always been deliberately vague with your mum, never talking about my days at work and, it's true, never letting her near my phone just to be safe. It wasn't worth the risk.

'What more do you want?' I asked, 'What do you wanna know? I'll call Janice right now if you want, she'll tell you about the shifts I've been working. Or Trick, talk to him if you want? We have one night a week where we have a game of snooker and a pint, is that a crime?'

Your mum's face scrunched into disgust. It wasn't the best play to try and turn it on her.

'You're a right one you are,' she said.

'I'm being honest with you. Why would I mess this up Becca? Why?'

I looked around the living room, around the flat – the one you're in now, hearing this story – as if it was a palace. As if we'd worked flat-out our whole lives and this was the result. We weren't minted, we were never gonna be at this rate. But we were lucky to have what we had.

'Listen,' I said, taking her hands in mine now that she would allow me, 'you think I'm gonna do anything like that when I have you? Look at me, Becca, I'm a lump. A pudding. I couldn't get a girl like you in a million years. I'm the last guy to go fiddling about.'

Your mum looked down at the floorboards, shaking her head. The tears hovered, threatening to drop.

'I love ya,' I said. 'I know I don't say it enough but I do. Please, believe me. I'd never do owt like that to you.'

I thought maybe I was wasted after all. Confessing my love like that. It was all true though, I meant every word. It just always sounded sarcastic and mad coming from my mouth. I looked down at myself. My expanding waistline, the belt that's missed a loop. The T-shirt that's too tight for me, making me look like a vacuum-packed roast chicken. The receding ginger hairline and gobstopper cheeks reflecting in the TV. I looked back to your mum, a much prettier sight. The side I hope you'll inherit.

'It . . . It just seems a bit weird,' she said.

She started to respond, playing with my chunky fingers, swinging our arms lightly.

'I get it,' I said. 'I do. I understand I've been a bit off lately, but I've got nothing to hide. Honest.'

Lying to your mum was hard. I never intended to do it. Even though my whole life, our entire relationship had a lie running through it, it was still hard to say out loud. I had a lot to hide. A problem too big to share with anyone, even your mum.

She eased into my arms, her head on my collar. Hair smelling of coconut, fresh from the shower. Your mum deserved better. I knew that the day we met at that party. She'd always deserved better, but she picked me for some reason. A fat gambling addict. If she knew, if she knew everything, a tiny voice in the back of my head said she might be fine with it. It wouldn't surprise me if she would have been. She's that supportive. Still. Some odds aren't even worth betting on. The stakes are too high, the consequences too drastic. I wasn't prepared to risk our relationship on pot luck.

'Where are we going though?' she said.

'What you mean?'

'Like, us. I don't know what you want. Whether you even see a future.'

I shook my head.

'Becca, of course I see a future, what you on about?'

'Like kids. Do you even want kids?'

'I'd love to have kids.'

'How many?'

'However many you want. As long as you're their mum.'

She smiled then, looking down at her wet top.

I held her shoulders and pulled her into a hug so her head was on my chest.

'You'd be a great mum, you know that?'

'You think?'

'Hundred per cent.'

'And what about a dog? Do you want a dog too?'

I leant back to catch her eyeline.

'No chance. We're never getting a dog.'

'Who you talking to?' says Becca, stirring awake, shielding her sleepy eyes from the flash of the telly.

'No one,' I say, lifting her up to her feet. 'Come on. Let's get you to bed.'

26

The coin I tossed in the bathroom landed on heads. The day has arrived. The day everything is gonna change. I counted horses instead of sheep and still didn't get to sleep last night. I didn't even place a bet before bed, or the whole of yesterday. This means that much. I needed every penny for today. I remember staring at the ceiling last night, looking at Becca lying beside me asleep, dreaming about our future family. How in nine months, I'll have that little baby cradled in my arms and I can tell them: *You can have anything you want.*

Throwing coffee down me in the morning to get the brain switched on, I get suited up, pockets full of the tender I hid at the back of the wardrobe. I board that coach from Manchester Piccadilly without saying a word. This morning's *Racing Post* tucked snug under my armpit, ready to be blitzed to fuck and scribbled with all sorts of analytical shite. Becca thinks I'm picking up a priority body from Bury and have a day-full schedule of corpses to embalm. Regardless of what happens, the next time we see each other, our lives will be changed for ever.

Vince gave me four tickets in the end so Trick's come along. We cancel all appointments and close the directory for the day, even giving Kevin the day off. I thought Spud and Bog-Eyed Si would be a good laugh so they meet us at Piccadilly too. I make a point not to tell Tommy Murphy, who I'm pretty sure would slash necks for a ticket to Cheltenham. The guy has the personality of a lamp post and can't be stinking the coach out with dehydrated piss.

Spud supplies tinnies on the coach in return for his ticket. Knocking them back for two and a half hours, not needing a piss once. Bog-eyed Si's catching looks from the stag do that have boarded with us. A group of eight to ten lads, clobbered up to the rafters in Ralph Lauren shirts and shoes you can style your hair in. We get chatting and absolutely wipe the floor with 'em. Si brags that he could enjoy two of their mams at once with the gift of his peepers. Trick's brought a pack of cards along and shows off his magic act, me using the *Racing Post* instead of a coaster, moving my can about to show which card they've picked. Had 'em all baffled, slapping the windows and wobbling their quiffs in disbelief.

We have a good time ripping the piss out of each other to kill the time. Punters are always up for a giggle. It's like it's in our nature to take risks, to push the barriers, and that always makes for good banter. It settles my nerves a bit. This is Cheltenham for fuck's sake, the cream of the crop, the meeting of all meetings. I feel horny with excitement, imagining that roaring crowd as I try to get a bit of kip. All the years watching it in Gran's living room. Dad, Uncle Mark, Uncle Lee and Grandad jumping about like the stained carpet was a bed of hot coals. I imagine what it's gonna be like in the thick of the crowd, hearing the thud of the horse's hooves, bookmakers shouting odds through a megaphone. I can't fuckin' wait. I'm happy *now*, imagine how I'm gonna feel on the way back?!

The coach pulls into a Premier Inn where only us lot get off. The poncy lads are in the Hilton or some other swanky boudoir that charges you for each sugar in ya brew. We let them crack on and throw middle fingers up to the windows. As the coach edges away, I pray we don't see those quiffs bobbing in the crowd later on.

We don't waste no time. Bags in, a quick spray of the pits. Trick's moaning about the toenails on the pillow and floating turd in the bog. The pints are calling, who gives a shite about the hotel room? I convince him we'll be in the Hilton with them lot tonight. All you have to do is pick the right horses.

I tell Trick to cop us a taxi and loosen up a bit.

'Relax,' I say to him. 'Just enjoy yourself. Imagine Belle Vue dogs on steroids.'

Trick's been quiet on and off since the card trick on the coach. He looks on edge, probably wondering how I suddenly got tickets to the biggest race meeting of the year when I'm still on my arse. How can I afford shutting the directory for a day? Suspicious eyes, as if I've been saving the money he lent me to pay for this rather than keep my light bulbs on.

Fuck this. The mood's too high to worry about Trick today. He'll get into the swing of it, just like at the casino, the dogs. I don't have time to babysit anyone. Today's between me, my money, and the horses out on that track.

On the journey, Vince texts through some decent odds I like the taste off. An outsider in the three o'clocker. He's managed to get offers that pay four places instead of three. The guy is slashing odds left, right and centre. Prices you wouldn't even get six months ago, never mind on race day. I don't ask questions, just pile on the money. The numbers rattle down across all my accounts. Divvying out evenly on each app to show Vince I'm being clever with it.

Good lad, he texts me, *get them winners in! ;)*

We get out of the taxi and, sweet Mary and baby Jesus, I'm in heaven. I'm hit with the humdrum of a meaty crowd. Waves and waves of heads. Balding ones, wavy ones, hatted ones. Pretty birds in dresses, lippied up. Swanky lads in suits and crisp shirts. We even made an effort ourselves. Digging out our funeral suits, looking like the Rat Pack. Spud's trousers look like flares, shirt untucked and a blazer smeared with bacon grease. Trick looks smart to be fair, sporting a red rose on his breast like Don Corleone from *The Godfather*. I'm hoping a few of these bookmakers are gonna make me some offers I can't refuse. Si just looks like Si, lucky to have his shoes on the correct feet.

Beyond the sea of heads, far as the eye (wonky or not) can see, is the lush green track in all its glory, parted with fences ready to be ploughed. We get a few down us in the Guinness Village, a big sector reserved for nothing but the black stuff. Barmen pump relentlessly, lining up cup after cup to let them settle, ready to be topped up. Six quid a pint though! I'll be lucky to have any left to place a bet at this rate.

Over the paddocks and glorious white stands is a clean sheet of blue sky. There isn't even a wind to send the betting slips walkabout on the path. The conditions are bang on. The booze bang on. The company bang on.

The four of us meet our plastic cups in the air, arms raised above the moving crowd. The lads scan over the programme and the morning papers, giving me time to swan about, eyeing up the grass over the railings and the beautiful beasts trotting past. Buckets full of water rainbow to keep their bodies cool. I finger the money in my blazer pockets. Weeks of hard graft and necessary lies. I transfer some to my apps but keep the majority in bulk, ready to hand over to the bookies on sight. There's just summot about handing the money over and getting a fat wad handed back after the race. Also means I'm away from Vince's prying eyes. A freedom's returned to my gambling, like the old punting days.

I want the first race to start now. I don't give two fucks about anything else. I'm ready to go. I know my choices. I can relax. When I find the lads again, Trick gives me a nudge, asking me to decide between two horses he's stuck with. He's the only one who knows I have a bit of brains about all this. I keep my expertise quiet, pointing a finger on the paper listings to give Trick some swaying. He knows the crack, winking and tapping his nose to thank me. Spud's busy supping, eyeing up the birds in purple dresses and those weird mesh things they stick on their heads.

'Fascinators,' says Si, pointing. We all turn to frown at him glugging his Guinness. 'Those things on their heads. Fascinators. That's what they're called. Honest.'

'I'm too shocked to even rip the piss out of ya,' says Spud.

The first race sets off at one o'clock. It feels like a fuckin' lifetime. This wait at Cheltenham is like the gambler's equivalent of being in labour. We kill the time boozing, nosing around the place, getting a burger down us, or trying to get in the background of the ITV cameras.

At 12.50, the tannoy rings through the crowd, listing the horse's names and numbers. No more waiting. The mild sun beats on our faces, making us sweat under our blazers. I spare a thought for Dad and Jan looking over me. For Tommy in the club, staring up at the TV screen, bets in hand, wishing Diamant would break its leg when it comes round to the Gold Cup at five.

A few minutes earlier, I jogged round two or three bookmakers, weighing up the last-minute odds. I hedged a couple of bets with it being the first race and all. That meant whatever bets I put on in person, I bet on alternative likely outcomes on my apps, increasing my chances of winning or hitting even.

A bookmaker with one squinty eye and skin like a ball sack barked odds at me. We exchanged money, his assistant fanning notes into her pouch, brimming with the stuff. It felt like getting a drink in a busy nightclub, barging back to the lads with betting slips clutched to my chest, trying not to spill them.

Our view is golden. Elevated above a sea of hats, of balding heads, of 'fascinators'. Jockey strips gleam in the paddock. Reds. Yellows. Blues. Greens. Pinks. Checks. Stripes. Hoops. You name it. Silky jackets reflect in the distance, trotting leisurely to the start line. It feels like the world is checking their bets at this point. *Who've you got then? Which colour's yours then? Which jockey? Who trained it?* As the orange tape wobbles across the track – the horses sweating white, lined up, eager – it seems the whole crowd holds their breath. The tape pings. The horses lunge. The crowd roars to the start of Cheltenham.

Everyone clutches each other's shoulders, craning their necks.

An Irish voice booms from the speakers, monitoring every switch of position, every outstretched nose. The fences burst, strong legs tanning through them. Legs, shoulders, bulging with sinew, thudding along the track at mental speed. It's beautiful. More beautiful than I could have imagined. I zone out for a second. Watching the limbs in slow motion. The scathing heat. Bottling this moment that will stay with me for the rest of my life.

I've backed Pied Piper in this one. Relentless form, experienced trainer. It's holding steady in second about a length from the front runner, I Like to Move It, which Spud and Si have gone for. Uncle Mark had a superstition. If the horse's ears are pricked, it's running well and in for a fast finish. Pied Piper's ears are daggered upright. Black plaits running down its jutting neck. Blinkers on, focused on nothing but that finish line.

The track stretches. Trot after trot. Lengths weighing on the legs. Horses tiring, panting big bursts out of big nostrils. In front, I Like to Move It begins to faulter, just like I expected. It drops like a kipper into third, fourth, fifth. Mine engines on, gliding over the fences without its toes even touching the tops. Pied Piper stretches further from the field with each gallop, the jockey not even bothering to whack its arse. It's a stylish horse. Watching it in real life makes it look even more special. It crosses the line with the rest of the pack furlongs behind. I'm celebrating and consider getting a pint in before the others finish. I Like to Move It comes in second last. I mark a big juicy tick on my *Racing Post*. What a fuckin' start!

We make a pact: whoever gets a winner, gets the beers in. Even though I'll be getting a lot of rounds in, I don't mind. It's pennies compared to what I'm gonna be walking away with. The lads are more determined after the first race, studying the programme harder as I leaf through my winnings. Vince texts me with a thumbs up and some odds for the next race to keep the ball rolling. I oblige, supping on my cold Guinness in the hot sun.

The next two races continue as expected. I've been watching

Colonel Mustard for months and am not surprised to see it win by a few lengths. Hillcrest in the 14.30 is a bit more of an arse-twitcher, nicking it over the line by a nostril. Si's horse comes in second, making him kick a bin over in frustration and get a warning from security. I give him an earful myself. There's no way I'm getting booted out on this sort of run, there's no way I'm having a repeat of casino night. I'll wring his neck, make both those eyes useless. The lads look at me to cool it. I'm letting the stakes show, a tiny glimpse of what is on the line. I apologise.

'Just the drink,' I say.

About halfway through the day, the booze kicks in for real, the Guinness forming a fuzz around my head. I'm throwing on an extra tenner here and there, nothing major. I'm able to with the winners I'm churning out. Life's merry, the buzz is hitting new levels. We float around, from lads to lads, revelling in the crack and pulling ties into a peanut knot, like we're in school again. It's all shits and giggles. A big piss-up really. But as the day goes on, I need to give myself a talking to while having a slash or a smoke in the open. I'm not here for a piss-up. I'm here to get straight. I need to do my business and get home. Repay the club and Trick in time. Sort the bills at the directory. Explain to Becca and start our next step, start our family. That's what I'm here for. Nothing else. My life depends on it, my relationships with the people closest to me. Fuck it up and I have nothing left; I might as well end it all.

The problem is – when you're with Trick, Spud and Si, in the baking heat next to a Guinness Village – you've got more chance of shagging Miss America than skipping a round. The black stuff keeps on coming. My stomach bloats with it, top lip sopping. I somehow find room. The horse names on my betting slips become blurry. They continue to cross the line first or finish in positions where I get some sort of money back. My pockets start to plump out like the bodies. A maze of notes. Enough to fill the House

Fund jar over and over. Cash. Zipped up and secured. Stacking up by the hour.

Everything is going to plan. Everything. I already have enough money to reload the till in the club two-fold and repay Trick for all he's given me. Half of my problems are solved. It's a nice feeling, finally a light at the end of the tunnel. I haven't counted, but I'm pretty certain there's a sizeable amount to get the ball proper rolling on a house too. The studying has paid off. Those hours and hours scanning the papers, going from bookies to bookies for tips. Scrolling through betting apps all day, cross-referencing odds, keeping an eye on trainers' form, jockeys' form, even injuries and weather reports on what the ground might be like. Every single minute has contributed to this moment, to get me back on my feet. The Guinness starts to taste sweeter. The sun gets hotter. I finally get to start enjoying my day.

It gets close to five o'clock and the lads know I'm having a blinder. Even by my standards, I'm on fire. Vince is texting emojis left, right and centre, pound signs littering my inbox. I can tell he's feeling the cash, monitoring my apps to fuck and seeing win after win come in. He encourages me to carry on, saying streaks like this don't come around often. There are two races left, but the next one is hardly a race. It's too much of an event to be labelled that. This is the biggy. The finest, the best, the greatest race in the horse racing calendar. If you come in the first three, you remember the year and name of your horse for years. Engrained into Fletcher folklore – everyone knows Uncle Mark has the most wins, that Dad got the first winner in 1989, that Grandad never backed the winner. Ten minutes. In ten minutes' time, I'm going to witness greatness. The horses trot round the paddock in the direction of the start line. It's all on this. The Cheltenham Gold Cup.

Standing there, in that crowd, I feel something I've never felt before. It isn't happiness. It isn't excitement. I've been on that high all day. Something else is locked in my throat, knotting my stomach and making my hands tremble. My pockets are lined with money. Was it enough though? If all this is for the house, our family, surely it's nowhere near enough. I'll have a child soon. An extra mouth to feed. If I walk away with this amount, all of the risks would have been for fuck all.

If I'm to fully repay the debts at the directory, I have to back the winner. If I'm to pay Trick back for the years of generosity, for the countless tenners here and there, I have to back the winner. If I'm to give Becca what she wants, to put a deposit down on that house, regain her trust in our relationship, build the family we've always dreamt of, I have to do it, I have to claim my spot in Fletcher folklore. I have to pick the winner in the Gold Cup.

Do I sound dramatic? Could I skip the Gold Cup and go home with a tepid amount and say, *Here Becca, this is what I've come back with after rinsing the House Fund jar. This is the risk I took to come back with pennies that make no difference at all?* No. I'm not here for pennies. All them punters, lined with tweed suits and chequered trousers crammed with crazy bets, they aren't here to come back with pennies. Yeh, of course it's a belting day out, but Stanley Street on a Saturday is a belting day out. Cheltenham is different. This is a place of dreams. Where lives are changed. Where men and women come to solve their problems.

I spend no more time dawdling. I make way for the bookmaker in the green flat cap. A square pair of glasses sit on his red nose. The man screams high cholesterol, late nights on the town and seedy strip clubs. A wad of twenties sit crisp in his hand, a bright green and yellow tie shining bright on his shirt. He can see me approaching. We've been doing business all day. Hand-in-hand, back and forth. He knows my ambition, my type. He can see the hunger in my eyes. Ignoring the young punters waving pound coins at him, the man asks me what I want.

'Diamant!' I yell. 'Throw it all on Diamant.'

I empty the cash in my pockets, throwing it into his palms in three or four fistfuls. Money falls around my feet. I give it all to him. Everything I've won today. Every fuckin' penny I owned was in his hands.

The people around me look on in amazement, the bookie included. His assistant counts like a lunatic, notes whipping through his palms at mad speed to get the bet on before the race starts.

'Diamant,' I repeat. 'All on Diamant!'

A cheer roars around me. The lads are nowhere in sight. I make sure of it. There's no doubt they would pull me out and back to the hotel. One punter flags the ITV cameras down and points to the presenter jogging through the crowd to get a bit of the action.

'What's the bet here then?' the presenter shouts to the bookmaker, cameraman riding the crowd behind him.

'This lad's put it all on Diamant.' He fans the money through his fingers. 'Over three grand on Diamant for the win.'

The presenter stuffs the microphone under my gob. I'm too pissed, too dazed to give a sensible response. I don't care that Diamant's dropped to 9/1 throughout the day. The ground is too perfect for her not to win. The new favourites prefer it softer, with cooler weather. They're just being backed because of the trainer getting a few winners today, nothing else. Diamant's basically free money at those odds.

'COME ON DIAMANT!!!' I shout into the camera lens.

I'm in another world. Another galaxy. Like Vince said, it's Cheltenham, you need to up the stakes and bet big. It needs to be done. I know it does. The crowd roars again, the presenter swings an arm around me, cutting back to the studio. Going back to the lads – with random geezers ruffling my hair and the presenter calling me a crazy bastard off-air – I imagine Tommy Murphy sat in the club looking at the TV screen, my ugly mug shouting into the camera. He'll be shaking his head, taking a sip of tepid cider.

'I told him Diamant wouldn't win, I fuckin' told him,' he'll say under his breath.

Linda would be leaning on the bar, overhearing Tommy's muttering. There I am, throwing three grand on a horse, on live TV. It will all make sense then. Of course. When was the last time anyone robbed a club round here with a baseball bat? Jamie Fletcher. The sneaky robbin' bastard!

***

The swarming crowd are around me. The horses set off.

Diamant starts well, riding steady in third. There's a long way to go. She's happy to fend off the favourite, Moonlight Cassidy, over this distance. A 150/1 shot rides ahead, getting excited and guaranteed to die off halfway round. The tension is high in the stands. Even the pissed-up groups are silent, whispering their horses along in a moment that makes men and women act in ways they never thought they would.

Sweat rings off my forehead, my neck, my back. I'm strangling the betting slip. I blank out the lads cheering on nothing bets. My whole fuckin' life is on this race. I ignore my pinging phone. Vince asking what I've gone for, that no bets have come through my accounts for the biggest race of the year. I've rinsed every penny from my accounts, draining my apps and withdrawing any cash I can from the ATM under the grandstand. I've chucked it all on Diamant too, doubling my stake to six grand. Not like those numbers will matter soon. I'll have ten times that amount and Vince won't have a sniff of what happened or which horse I backed. 'Cause this isn't about Vince. This is my life and my money. I can run away from all that as long as Diamant gets over that finish line first. My life will be defined by the next two minutes, here at Cheltenham, with the sun beating down, the crowd muttering on, and the horses roaring to the finish line.

The home stretch. The end of the line. Diamant is in second

and running well. Ears pricked. Moonlight Cassidy is in first and clinging on. It's clearly between the two. Coming up to the last fence, I bark with the back of my throat for Diamant to make it. The crowd barks with me. *Jump the fucker, just get over the bastard.* And my god does she fuckin' jump it. Like a fuckin' plane at Heathrow she is. I was worried she wasn't gonna come back down. The jump makes her nose stretch far in front of Moonlight Cassidy, who nicked the fence. The favourite is tanking, failing, running out of fuel. Diamant stretches away with furlongs to go. The crowd cheers on. Half are Diamant, half are Moonlight Cassidy. It's a race for the history books. The battle of the two giants. One of the greatest rivalries ever seen.

Five furlongs to go, five and she's cruising. My eyes go itchy. The jockey is beating her arse. I've swatted a fly harder. 'Hit the fucker!' I shout. Diamant – with her luscious grey coat, fluffy white nose band and spotted black legs – romps and romps further and further to the finish line. I'm smacking Trick's bald head with my betting slip. I snog Spud on the lips. I find the strength to pick Si up and parade him round in circles on my shoulder. Diamant is going as I expected Diamant to go. She's going to win the Gold Cup. Have that, Tommy Murphy, you daft smelly bastard!

And then it happens.

How it does, I don't know. But it happens.

Diamant's front leg goes.

I mean, properly *goes*.

It snaps.

Snaps to a right angle.

I can see it from here.

Tumbling to the turf.

Jockey unseated.

Rolling.

Buried.

Done.

Moonlight Cassidy engines past Diamant's falling body. There're metres left. The young jockey in front is already waving his whip. Those blue and white checks flap across the line with the rest of the pack in their wake. Diamant wriggles uncomfortably on the turf, an orange tent being erected around her. The jockey is starfished on the turf, whacking the grass in anger.

I can't hear anything. All I can feel is the mud on my knees, seeping through my trousers. Hands are on my shoulders. Words are being spoken. I can't move my limbs. I can't move my mouth to speak. I watch my life break and tumble right before my eyes. Just like when Dad died, I want to cry but I can't. The scale of it hasn't hit me yet. All I want to do is run, even though I have nowhere to go. I bury my head in the grass and feel the emptiness in my pockets, nothing other than the lining and Vince's crumpled card. I can feel the ITV cameras on my back. The burning eyes of the crowd, the world. I imagine Tommy again, sipping happily on his pint, using the winning bet as a coaster. *I told you, Fletch, I told you.* I don't even wanna contemplate what Dad is thinking. How Janice would react if she was still here.

I would have stayed there for hours, days, the world closing in around me. An arm appears under my armpit to lift me up. I lose it. Good and proper. Nothing can pick me up, not now. Nothing else matters. It's all over. I get up, turn, and punch the fucker in the face as hard as I can. Trick's gold tooth goes flying into the grass. I hit him again, his mouth pouring with blood and dripping onto his red rose. I leap at him, rugby tackling him into the grass, arms windmilling, spit firing out of my mouth as I scream and scream and scream. I let everything out. Screaming. Punching. Screaming. Punching. His face feels like beating a chicken breast flat. It doesn't matter who it is. I would have hit anyone to get this feeling out of me. Then, so many arms on my back. Fistfuls of blazer, pulling me off him. I kick my legs, wriggling like a lunatic. I yell at them to let me go. Anyone who wants it can have it. I think I see Spud and Si go over to Trick to pick him up but I can't be sure. Everything is misty. Only a glimpse of their shirts spotted with blood. He isn't moving.

I manage to kick free and connect with a couple more jaws before sprinting off. I have one shoe, my sock damp in the grass as I charge through the crowd. Running with nowhere to go. Disgusted faces part to let me through. I sprint, not knowing if anyone is following or who else I'm gonna hurt on the way out. I run until I reach the car park, where I cry onto the gravel. Wet dots in the dust. I starfish in the dirt like my fallen jockey, watching the clouds pass overhead, wishing the world to end.

There's silence. A weight has been lifted. I have nothing to chase any more. It can't get any lower than this moment. It's over. It's all finally over.

***

I get the train home after lying in Cheltenham station for three hours. My suit is ripped, dusted, hanging off my body. I've finished crying. On the whole journey back to Manchester, I gawp out the window without a straightforward thought passing through my head. Not even worried if the ticket conductor finds out I've jibbed on for free. Nothing seems worth thinking about, worth crying about any more. I'm entirely numb. My brain is somehow getting me home on autopilot mode. All I really want to do is find a hole or a big ocean to climb to the bottom of. I welcome the hole now; I'm tired of wanting to dig out. As long as I have Becca at the bottom with me, drying my wet cheeks, telling me everything's gonna be okay.

I walk, one shoe, all the way from Piccadilly station to home. My foot is bloody, seeping through the sock. I realise my face is too when I catch myself in a shop window. I must have taken a few punches in the scuffle. The cut above my eyebrow is open again. It reminds me of Sally's wounds after her tumble off the Glossop hills. Scratches and cuts etched into my forehead. Bottom lip busted and bubbled blue.

I stand looking at myself for a few minutes, long enough to not recognise the lad looking back. The look of him scares me. A brawler, a nutcase, a soon-to-be dad. No one wants to know a guy like that.

I get to our front door. On the doorstep are two holdalls zipped open with my clothes pouring out. A letter stuffed into the side pocket without needing to label who it's addressed to. I can't read that. I just can't bring myself to read what's on that paper. This whole time, I really thought I could do it. Build us the life we wanted without her finding out. I drop to my knees again. The pain of the concrete. I thought it couldn't get any lower.

I scratch at the bottom of the front door. I wail and beat against the wood.

'BECCA. BECCA. COME ON, JUST LET ME TALK TO YOU. I'LL EXPLAIN. BECCA. PLEASE!'

Nothing. I beat that door for a good fifteen, twenty minutes before sliding my back against it in defeat. It's late. The street lamps hum above. Even Sol's is closed with the shutters down. I can't even crawl there for help.

The letter is heavy in my hands. What my life has come to. One piece of paper to confirm what I've always feared deep down this whole time, what I risked with every bet I placed. How she's found out, I don't think I even care. I open the envelope and take a rattled breath.

Don't ever try speaking to me again. I can't even begin to start with how angry and upset I am with you. I loved you, I thought I knew you. How could you go behind my back and do this? That was our money, our future. It all makes sense now, those late nights out, never letting me near your phone, staying up in bed. You convinced me years ago you never had anything to hide and

I was stupid to believe you. You're a fucking disgrace Jamie, you need help. We're over and you'll need to find somewhere else to live. Go fuck yourself and don't ever try to contact me. I can raise our child without you.

Becca

I leave my bags where they are and walk to Tesco car park. My shitty Transit is parked there, a snake of trolleys behind it blowing along in the wind. I get in and start it up. Trolleys crash into the boot and tumble over as I reverse through them. Fingers tingling around the wheel. Bloody foot aching on the accelerator. I speed round to the entrance, run in the shop with the engine still chugging, and return with half the booze shelf in a bag for life. It takes me to the end of my overdraft limit. I speed off without thinking what I'm doing. Maybe I should try contacting Becca? Maybe I should check if Trick is okay, or reason with Shaky and Linda about why I robbed the club? I should do a lot of things. But if I really gave a fuck I would have done them by now.

The decisions are done. I'm relieved I have no more to make. I've made my final one. And the odds of it happening, for once, are pretty much certain.

27

I'm pelting it at about ninety down the M62. The sun's setting, making the clouds bare hazy and purple. An empty bottle of JD slides back and forth in the passenger footwell. I need a piss so I have a piss. A puddle seeping through my trousers, gathering by my groin on the seat, streaming down my leg towards the pedals. Bloodied sock on the accelerator.

I'm disgusting. I'm a monster. A fat, ugly, stinking cunt. The sour, mingin' smell fills the car, overwhelming the whisky. It means nothing to me now. Everything's irrelevant. All that matters is me, weaving between the lanes, cracking open another bottle, going nowhere.

The blue overhead signs get blurry. Trees blending into a smudge on the side of the road. The whisky starts to taste like water. I continue to tan it, expecting the bonnet to start smoking any second, for the wheels to come off. There's a coffin with my name on it. That blue and pink one. What I'd do to be lying in that now with the lid closed, shut off from the world.

The purple bleeds into blue. A set of headlights pass on the opposite side. The world winds down. People going home from night shifts, jetting back for a hot meal before getting some kip. To their happy families, their child running into their arms as they step through the door. I'm done dreaming any more of that shite. The good life, all rosy, hunky-dory bollocks. I had my chance at that. A normal life.

I watch the speed dial move clockwise. The accelerator pedal is to the floor. I'm hitting a hundred, one ten. I wonder what happens when there's no road left? Would I keep on driving or would some random instinct kick in? Would I feel anything that I collide with?

In the rear view, my eyes are puffy and teary. My right socket bruised yellow and green. I taste blood on my gums, the whisky stinging my split lip. I could be concussed, or wankered, or just psychotic. It doesn't really matter. Gone are the days when all I was arsed about was my receding ginger barnet, or my swelling beer gut. Years of self-punishment. Midnight doners and after work bevvies. I have no one left to impress now Becca doesn't want me. I have no one to trim my beard for, to shower for, to try and be a decent fella for. I'm sat here in my own piss, for fuck's sake. I'm already a ghost, floating in and out of the lanes. Invisible. Haunted.

It's only when I get out of Manchester that I start to feel it. Not the booze, but something... I don't even know. Cosiness? Clarity? I throw the half-drunk bottle onto the betting slips and beer cans piled on the passenger seat. I light up a cig and feel the nicotine tickle my limbs. My body relaxes into the seat. It feels nice. I even manage a smirk. The tip of the filter fizzes. Sunlight peaks through sheepskin clouds onto the tarmac. Tightening my hands on the wheel, I let the smoke puff. The motorway eases into a bend ahead. I think of all the decisions I've made recently. Becca, Trick, Janice, Vince, the betting, the booze. I think of what I've become and what I'll leave behind. I think of when I whizzed home to tell Becca we were rich. I start to laugh, building to a hysterical scream. I laugh uncontrollably at the windscreen, at the many times I had enough money and blew it away.

As the car veers left towards a ditch and thicket of dense trees, I lean back into the seat, taking a deep drag of smoke. I let go of the wheel and close my eyes. I stop laughing. The gurney seems to stop rattling in the back. Everything falls silent. The sliding bottle. The rattle of the unhinged glove box. The thrum of the tyres. It all vanishes. I open my eyes to see the trees getting closer, to see the road disappear as the tyres spin onto the hard shoulder. This is the time when fear's meant to kick in, but all I feel is relief. The car will finally stop. It'll all finally stop. And that's okay. No more mistakes. Nothing else to lose.

I close my eyes and wait for the impact.

28

There's a beep. Steady, like the start of *Casualty*. It's black. Nothing but total darkness. I hear a shallow breath now and again which I think is mine. Irregular. In and out. There are other voices that I can't make out. Is heaven this dull? If it even is heaven, not like I've ever believed in any of that bollocks, but it must be something if I have thoughts? Heaven is peace, happiness, and if this is it, where are the hunnies? Anyone could be up here with me. Michael Jackson? Marilyn Monroe? I could tell Elvis all about our jokes with Shaky. The voices start to fade out again. The beeps sound like they're underwater. I start to feel sleepy when I'm already asleep. Bursts of pain come and go. Whether it's real or not, I can't tell. Whatever this is, I'm scared. Really fuckin' scared.

This happens for days. Or I think it's days. Hearing muffled sounds. Always the same voices, varying in pitch. One day, the darkness gets a little brighter. An opening. It burns like you won't believe. I can hear the beeps distinctly now, one after the other like a reversing lorry. There are shapes either side of me. Blurry outlines of people. I look for a diamond glove, a blowing white dress, a pair of sideburns. As my view sharpens up, I realise it's Becca on one side, and some man on the other. It's then I realise I'm not dead. That I can't even do that right.

The two of them are asked to leave for a minute as a blonde woman in a white coat comes in with a clipboard. Am I about to be embalmed? The smell of chemicals and rubber gloves suggests I am. My mouth won't move. She speaks to me but I can't reply.

The woman prods me lightly in places, sending unimaginable pain through my body. My convulsing makes me notice I'm on some sort of bed, wired up to shit. The beep I've been hearing is my heart. If she is about to get a damp towel out to wash me or start fiddling with some tissue-builder tubes, I'm gonna do everything in my power to go apeshit and get out of here.

The woman leaves, Becca and the man come back in. I can only see through the small window of my eyelids, but I'm sure the man looks messed-up. It's like a thousand wasps have gone at his face. Ballooning cheeks, bloodshot eyes and a nose, busted and skew-whiff. He's in a suit with a red rose pinned to his chest. His shirt is darkened with blood. Then it clicks. I wonder why he's here. Is he here to get me back? To bury a pillow over my face? If so, he can crack on. He'll do a better job of topping me off than I did.

'Jamie? Jamie, can you hear me?'

Becca's voice. She's here. Here beside me, looking after me, like always. I want to tell her how much I love her, how I won't do anything to hurt her ever again, how sorry I am for all of it, for everything. How much I'm looking forward to seeing the baby we made. All of this I want to say and I can't get a word out. I have to watch her talk at me while I lie here like a cabbage, not even the wriggle of a toe to give a sign.

After an hour or so, they leave the room to get a coffee, if I heard right. They flick the telly on that's mounted to the wall, leaving me to watch *Bargain Hunt*. Pure torture. I would be tempted to turn my machines off if I could reach them.

I watch that posh bloke with the moustache give advice on a seventeenth-century potty. It gives me time to think, to try and piece together how I got in this bed. As mangled as my body probably is, I can remember the whole thing. From losing the Gold Cup bet, to getting the train home, to the letter, to getting in the van and driving. The last thing I remember is that big tree trunk getting bigger and bigger as I hurtled towards it. And that sound.

Thinking of Becca before it all went white. Nothing else was meant to follow. She was meant to be free from me, free to live the life she's always wanted.

***

I can speak after two weeks. There's bleeding on the brain, blocking my speech like a brick wall. They knock me out and drain it from my skull. A big bag of red hanging there on the drip stand, showing it off to me like a pissin' trophy.

'Ffffckin ell,' I manage. I see blood every day. It's weird when it's your own. You can't help but think, *That's meant to be inside me, why's it there in a bag, why is it not inside me?*

I start to move my arms too, using them to wave to Becca as she comes in to visit me every day. Her cheeks are always soaked with tears. She looks knackered. I can't begin to imagine how worried she is, how many shoulders she's cried on. That's how Becca would react to the old me anyway, the one she trusted and loved. I don't deserve her tears. It's amazing to see her. Of course it is. I never thought I would again.

She can't hug me but she kisses my forehead and squeezes my hand gently, just like she did on the plane to Santorini. No words are needed. We hold tight to whatever we have left. She doesn't let go the whole time she's there. Funny that when I get my speech back, I don't know what to say. We sit there, looking at each other, listening to the beep of my heart rate. Her brown eyes shine in the fluorescent light. Hair greased from sleepless nights, beauty still radiating from her.

'Jamie, what were you thinking?'

I don't have an explanation. Not yet. When I tell her I want to tell her everything.

Her thumb strokes mine. I never thought I would find enjoyment in wiping her tears away. Having her face here, beside my bed, and having the strength to touch her, to feel her. It's incredible.

'I'm so sorry, Becca. I'm so sorry.'

We haven't cried together this much since I told her we won big. There are many words to say, now just isn't the time. We're happy to be in the same room again. Alive, together. I have serious explaining to do. I have work to do. I need to get myself right to be the man I always should have been for Becca. I'm still here. I still have a chance to make her happy, to end the tears. I'm fuckin' sick of it. I need to give her everything, all that's left of my fat, useless body.

With two more weeks of steady tests and regular speech under my belt, the doctor comes in to deliver the next steps. Becca takes a seat, clutching my hand again, ready to combat whatever she's gonna throw at us.

'So,' the doctor says, taking a seat by the drip stand, 'I don't think you need me to tell you you're a lucky man, Jamie.'

'Not as lucky as you think,' I say.

The doctor's not one for jokes. Her dull expression hints that the news isn't good. I haven't felt my legs since I woke up. The doctor confirms they're semi-paralysed due to crushed nerve endings in my spine. There's a chance I could walk again but it would need rigorous training and months of rehabilitation. I soak in the information as best I can.

'What else?'

'You sustained five cracked ribs, a broken tibia, whiplash, and severe concussion that could have put you in a deep coma. If it wasn't for the airbag or the ambulance's quick response time, I'm afraid you wouldn't be here.'

We all know that. Hearing it out loud hits different though.

'Do we know what's next then?' says Becca.

The doctor pauses, leafing through some papers in her file. She gets out a wad of coloured pamphlets, all with bold letters and images of people wincing in pain.

'Here. We'll need to put you on a rehabilitation programme, a few times a day to strengthen up your legs and get you walking again. It'll be hard. Really hard. But I've seen patients come back from worse in the space of a couple of months. If you're up for the challenge, we can get you on it as soon as you feel ready.'

I look at Becca, the warmth in her eyes. I'm not alone in this. I don't need to fight my problems on my own any more. I nod at the doctor, at Becca. I feel a flicker of guilt water up my eyes. I should never have let it come to this. I need to erase everything that happened before the crash. I deserve the punishment. I need to take it on the chin. Overcome it. Pay for playing dirty.

'I'll give you these as well.' The doctor hands over a separate pair of pamphlets. 'Before we turn our attention to the physical recovery, we need to make sure you're okay first. No matter how long it takes, okay? It's important to remember that this isn't a race.'

I think it's a gambling joke at first but realise there's nothing funny about any of this. One pamphlet is about mental wellbeing and key steps to recovery. The other is specific to gambling addiction, with information on support groups, how to avoid relapsing and making sure victims share their battles. That's always the hardest thing for me. I was, I am, an addict, not knowing how severe the addiction was or where it could take me, all while hiding it from the person I loved most. I couldn't share the biggest part of my life with her. Like her letter said, she thought she knew me, but she didn't. If I'm to get over it, if we're to get over it, I have to tell her everything. That's gonna be the hardest part about this whole thing.

***

After a month in the rehabilitation ward, I'm back at home with Becca. A long set of parallel bars stretch from the TV to the kitchen for me to practise walking. I do an hour or so each day, sweat licking off my forehead and my arms wobbling like a shit gymnast. Mango runs around my feet, urging me on. He's grown so much since I last saw him. Becca helps me, on standby to catch my arm if I get too cocky. She's my cheerleader, even putting a cold can of Guinness on the finish line to give me something to aim for. Cheeky cow.

It happens after one of my successful sessions, a whopping two metres, when Becca turns *The Chase* off and settles two brews down on the coffee table. The pile of leaflets sit next to them, staring me in the face, reminding me what a long journey I have ahead of me.

'Shall we talk about it?' she asks, pulling the hoodie sleeves over her hands.

'Okay,' I say.

I place pillows carefully behind my back to get comfy. I take a good breath in. I tell her everything. Everything I should have told her before it could ever get this far. I start at the very beginning: the arcades, wagging school, Saturdays at Gran's, Dad, Uncle Mark, Uncle Lee, Grandad and our Cheltenham traditions; then onto Jim Ramsbottom's, the pull of the slots, the horses, the dogs, the casinos. Even Vince and all that VIP shite, how in hindsight he probably wanted me to sit at that roulette table in the casino with him and rigged it so I won, knowing my value as Jim Ramsbottom's prime punter, and how he abused my trust to fuel my betting, the feelings it boiled in me, the buzz, the excitement, the risk of it all, the late nights sat up betting on Romanian football, how losses could easily become wins and wins became losses. I tell her about the directory, the urn of dead people's jewellery, travelling between Cash Converters, swindling families into overpriced funeral packages to fuel my addiction. I tell her I won more than I said, but still blew the lot, on refurbishing the directory and more bets. Then Shaky crying, that awful decision to rob the club, the one thing he worked his whole life to build and keep going, robbing the till, faking the robbery, faking everything for a few quid. Then, most important of all, Becca. What a shit boyfriend I've been, the lies, the deceit, the constant secrecy, the House Fund jar, the squabbles after coming in drunk when it was all the result of failed sessions at the bookies, drinking away the hurt to make me feel better, make me forget, make me live with myself. Even robbing the clothes she brought home so I could dress up the bodies and make myself feel better, convince myself I'm actually a good person. I can never apologise enough, still I apologise anyway. I tell her how much she means to me, how much I still love her even if she doesn't love me. I would understand, I would agree. Finally, I make it clear how my decision to get in the van that day, going ballistic down the motorway absolutely sloshed, was in no way her fault. It was all me and the guilt I caused myself. I couldn't cope with hurting her any more. I couldn't cope with raising a child that hates me, being a vacant dad and a failure. She deserved better, our child deserved better. They still do. I wanted to do her a favour. Allow her to live her life with no more hurt, no more lies, no more me.

Becca sits there on the edge of the couch, staring into the carpet. Tears spot on her grey hoodie, sweat patches form in her pits like little puddles. Her eyes have been puffed since I managed to open mine. Lids like marshmallows, filled with pain.

'That's a lot to take in,' she says.

'I know. You don't need to say anything.'

She sets her eyes on mine. We're both blubbering wrecks. It took every bit of strength, from deep within my chest, to wretch all that out. Hearing it out loud is so fucked up. It's like telling another Openshaw fable about some dickhead fuckin' up his life for no reason at all. The truth scares the shit out of me, it always has. Even though I don't wanna hear it – wishing the car had put me in a coma, given me memory loss, or done its job and sent me six feet under – something about saying it out loud is comforting, knowing Becca knows everything now and can make her decision on what sort of person I really am.

'I think I do need to say something, just to get it off my chest,' she says. 'Throughout all this, years of hiding it from me, you never once thought about how it could affect me. The nights you were out getting pissed playing snooker with Trick or throwing away your money in the bookies, I was at home after a fucking long shift, waiting for you to get home. I'd cry, where you're sitting now. I'd cry, with the telly off 'cause I couldn't concentrate on anything but you and where you were. I'd sit in the dark and just cry, wondering where you were or why you'd rather spend a night with the ale, or other women, than me. I couldn't give a fuck about you robbing my clothes, what's more important is that I've never felt good enough being with you. You always go on like you're the one that's punching, the overweight one, the "heifer", that I'm the beautiful one and you're the lucky one. It's not as simple as that, Jamie. Especially, these last few months, I've felt so unloved, so unappreciated, it's ridiculous. I moved out of my mam's to get away from being treated like shit. It just hurts more coming from you, the person I thought loved me more than anything in the world. Even fuckin' gambling. I mean, do you even remember what you said to me in my mum and dad's kitchen the night you first met them?'

I shake my head even though I do know.

'You said, "*You can trust me Becca, you stick with me and you'll be happy. I promise.*" You promised me, Jamie, you promised.'

Becca's right. She was always a secondary thought to the betting. The whole time, I had my own blinkers on, on a mission to try and win us both enough money to start a good life for ourselves and get out of this shithole flat. The same flat that made her mum stop speaking to her, and who she hasn't spoken to since. All because of me and making her that promise. I always thought the finish line was in sight when I never even got out the traps. I was kidding myself more than anyone. Thinking I was the good guy. Making up an excuse to justify the money I was putting on the line. That's what gambling addicts do. They make excuses to try and convince themselves what they're doing is right. And if that doesn't work, win enough so you don't have to think about it any more. I took it too far. I know that now. I was gambling with our relationship, our child's future. Money didn't matter. I'd already won the woman of my dreams and didn't realise it. I already had everything; she was sat at home crying on the sofa.

'And what I wrote in the letter,' she continues, 'I know now, but when you're staying up in bed on your phone all night thinking I'm asleep, how do you think that makes me feel? Of course I'm gonna get suspicious, especially with how secretive you are with your phone. You never let me near the fuckin' thing. You get a text through and are off to the bathroom for half an hour, or we're trying to watch telly and you're side-eyeing your phone, checking the screen every five minutes. It took me ages to clock on that you might be fiddling. Ya know, seeing some slag from the club or summot. It explained the late nights out, the extra shifts that came out the blue, the drunken slurs trying to explain yourself. I always knew you were lying. I just thought it was about a girl. Someone you actually wanted to spend time with, someone you actually loved. I just didn't wanna believe it. I loved you too much to say anything. I didn't want to ruin all we had been through together.'

Becca takes a sip of her brew and hands me mine. My fingers ache as they feed through the handle. The brush of her skin reminds me of how lucky I am to feel her. My legs are still numb to fuck. As long as I can feel her near me again, that will always be enough.

'I can't explain how sorry I am, Becca. There was never anyone else. I promise you it was all gambling. Everything was the gambling. It took over me. It was all I could ever think about. I hid my phone to not give me away, to feed my addiction for as long as I could. The amount of betting apps on there were insane, the money in the accounts was mind-boggling. You would have finished with me on the spot, I know you would. I couldn't take that chance. I tried my best to hide it from you, not knowing how much damage that could cause . . . '

I sip the tea and wash down the knot in my throat.

'. . . and the texts. That was all Vince. Ever since that day at the casino. Sending me tips, odds, tickets to the match or the races. We were in contact every day. I was probably one of his best customers, throwing thousands at him every week. He lured me in and I bit every time. I wanted to bet as much as he wanted me to. I was making him insane amounts of money. Even my losses were plumping up his pockets, never mind my wins. It's what being a VIP's all about. Mental jail. All them texts were him dangling it in my face, teasing me, giving me the shovel to dig my own grave.'

Just from the first few GA meetings I've been to, I've learnt all about the VIP scheme and can't understand how stupid I was to fall for it. Betting companies like Jim Ramsbottom's hire VIP managers to head-hunt gamblers who're tanning large amounts of money on a regular basis. The most vulnerable, the most desperate. People like me. We're walking cash machines to them, a guaranteed revenue they can keep feeding with free bets and tickets to the match or the races. Addicts like me are their safe bet, their odds-on favourite.

Vince would have been paid commission and bonuses every time I lost large amounts, when I thought he won whenever I did. The more I lost, the more he would feed me with free bets to keep me active. He was charming, patient, and shit-hot with the numbers – everything a good VIP Manager needs to be. I filled in that survey when I joined without a clue I was telling him everything about me and offering him ways to keep me trapped. He knew my weaknesses and didn't care one bit how it was ruining my life, as long as he and the betting companies were making their money. For so long, I believed he was rewarding my loyalty, when this whole time he was manipulating me and risking my life for profit.

The truth. It's what she wants to hear. It doesn't mean it makes the situation any better. I take full responsibility for her pain. I let it get to this stage. My intentions were to win for us, every bet I placed had her in mind. I knew that wasn't enough. It should never have been about the money. It should have always been about Becca. I thought it was, but it's never that simple.

I think she's done now. Exhausted. Mentally drained. It took a lot out of me too, spilling my guts on the table like that after so long. I need a fat nap; some heavy drugs wouldn't go amiss either. It'll be a process. Too much damage has been done to patch it up in one night.

'I know that's a lot,' I say. 'We can leave it there for now if ya want? But anything you wanna know or are unsure about, I'm here. The main thing is that I'm here.'

I reach for her hand, my arm quivering, struggling to reach. She nudges closer and clasps both her hands around mine.

'I'm happy to be here, with you,' I say.

'You mean that?'

'I do. It was a stupid decision getting in that van. I never should've done it.'

'Good,' she says. 'Don't fuckin' do it again.'

Becca takes our half-drunk mugs to go and heat them up in the microwave. I can see the sink piled with sticky dishes. A Jenga tower of pots and pans, ready to tumble. I follow my eyes along the skin of dust on the mantelpiece, along the TV cabinet, along the bookshelves, the windowsill with the white light blinding through. Below the windowsill, I can see a holdall. The one I left on the doorstep. The one that has the letter peeking out of the side pocket.

I ease back into the cushions, wiggling my toes like I've been asked to do for training. I let my mind wander. Thinking about that day, that letter.

'Babe?' I shout into the kitchen. Becca peaks her head around the door frame.

'Yeh?'

'How did you know?'

'Know what?'

'You said you were angry and upset with me. That I went behind your back and blew our money. I know the jar was empty, but how did you know it was for that, or even know I was at the races? Someone must have told you something to make you throw my bags on the street?'

Becca picks at her nails, her fringe moving as she blinks and blinks.

'Trick,' she says.

29

It feels weird being nervous for snooker night. I get there early and wheel myself into the smoky back room. Becca had picked a wheelchair up from our local clinic, saying I still needed to get out and about while my rehab was ongoing. I don't care much for what the lads in the club might have to say, that's if they've even joined the dots or had suspicions about my antics. I'm past caring about any of that. I need to focus on myself. All I care about is getting better for Becca.

I'm only meeting Trick, even though I haven't spoken to any of the lads since Cheltenham. Fuck knows where I'm gonna start. I'm hoping it'll just come to me. In an ideal world, we'd crack on and forget about the whole thing like the old mates we were. I'm smart enough to know there's fat chance of that, not with how I exploded on him for no reason. I don't think I deserve to try and explain myself anyway. Trick simply agreeing to a pint is a start. That alone shows the integrity of the man.

Like I've seen countless times before, his shiny head bobs through the double doors. Under his eyes, a greenish tint shows the next stage of bruising. A big plaster arches over the bridge of his nose. Chin stamped with hashtags from the stitching. The fact he still has wounds shows how much I didn't hold back. We clock eyes. He doesn't react to me sitting here, wheels glinting in the snooker table light, sipping sorrowfully on my Guinness. He gets a pint from Linda, who reluctantly let me in, and makes his way over. It's eerily quiet. Totally opposite to the raucous laughter and slurred tales we're used to hearing ping from wall to wall.

'Fletch,' he says, sitting down across the table.

'Thanks for coming, Trick. I appreciate it.'

If I could stand, I would. The snooker table is opposite us, two cues lifeless on the felt. Balls settled in their racks. I can't even walk around the table if I want to. Believe me. I'm desperate to get up and have a game. To feel that cue sliding away, powering through the balls, spinning off cushions and watching them sink. The joy of these Thursday nights. I'll let Trick win every Thursday for the rest of my life if it means being pals again. Sat here, I can't even look the guy in the eye. My best fuckin' mate.

'Got some dig on you, haven't ya?' says Trick, breaking the ice. 'Where you been hiding that?'

He offers a faint smirk, showing the gap where his gold tooth should be.

'I don't even know where to start. I can't explain how sorry I am, mate. I don't know what came over me.'

'You do. And I do as well.'

'You mean?'

'Come on, Fletch, I'm not as dim as you think I am. All that borrowed money. Bills and paperwork lying around the directory. The way you'd been acting all shifty, like at the match, checking your phone every five minutes. I knew something was up. That's why I was a bit off at the races. I knew it wouldn't be good for you. I could sense it. The reason I went really was to keep an eye on you.'

'How? Not good for me how?'

'You were an addict, mate, plain and simple. Even Spud and Si said so after the casino night. Spud even mentioned you might be getting lured on by one of those dodgy VIP guys. Just 'cause you hide your money and all that doesn't mean you're invisible. We walk past gamblers every day on the street, for fuck's sake. Openshaw's full of 'em. You forget I grew up round here as well, ya know? It's in the eyes, I can't explain it but I can spot 'em a mile off. It took me a while, don't get me wrong, but it made sense when it clicked. Buying a bloody funeral directory. Getting tickets to all these random things out the blue. Summot wasn't adding up.'

I huff loud, mopping up the condensation on the glass with my finger. This whole time, with Becca and now Trick, I could have just talked about it. I could have said, *Look, I'm struggling, I need help*. Was that so hard? Wasn't that worth the chance if it meant being dead or alive right now?

'How long had you known?' I ask.

'Months. Before I started working with you anyway. One of the main reasons I took the job was to keep tabs on you. I didn't know it was this bad, know what I mean? But still.'

I stare ahead at the plastered wall, where fists have knocked chunks off, where flying ale has splashed and dried to leave brown stains. I think back to all the times I've seen shit boil over in here. The bar fights, old geezers going off their rocker after all day on the sauce. Gripping their best mates by the collar, ruining years of friendship with one swing of the knuckle. Dickheads, man. Avoided for months on the streets. Barred in every boozer. I've never spared a thought for what ran deeper. Why some men react like they do.

'And you still gave me the time of day?' I say. 'Still gave me money when I wanted it?'

Trick rubs his tattoos anxiously. Those meaty hands that could have pawed me off easily when I was on top of him giving it large. He understood enough not to react, that it wasn't the real me who was swinging digs at him.

'You're right,' says Trick, 'I probably should have drawn the line with the money, maybe not given you any. You were struggling though, pal, maybe not so much money-wise, but I could see it in ya. You were sad, worried about summot. I tried to pretend it was stuff with Becca, ya know, saving for a house and all that you mentioned. Or getting over Janice being gone. Deep down I knew it would all probably be blown in the bookies, I'm not an idiot. It brightened you up, though. I thought it was harmless. Well, not harmless, but not as fucked as it was, and I'd rather you were getting cash off me than someone who didn't give a shit, ya know? I just wanted to be a good mate, raise your spirits a bit.'

'You *were* a good mate. A top mate. I can't even begin to—'

'Ah leave it out, ya soppy get. Don't need any of that. Anyway, like I said, I never knew it was this bad. For ages I thought it was a few bets a week here and there. Even when I knew it was worse than that, I didn't think it was drowning-in-debt territory or throwing-all-the-money-you-have-on-the-fuckin'-Gold-Cup territory. I wouldn't have done it otherwise. I should have kept a closer eye on you. Never should have let you place that bet.'

Looking at Trick, the morbid look on his chops implies he's the one feeling guilty, as if he holds some responsibility for all of this. I can't believe him. There he is, face bruised and cut like a rare sirloin, worrying about how he could've done better when it was all me. All of this is my fault, not his.

'You know, the worst thing is,' I say, 'it probably wasn't even about the money. It could have been the thrill of it. I could have kept going and kept going for as long as it would let me. I don't think I could have stopped. I was an addict, Trick, like you say.'

As if forgiving me wasn't enough, Trick's been running the directory for the last couple of months while I've been working on my rehab. He roped Kevin back in to look after the bodies and sent bits and bobs over email if I needed to sign any paperwork. After how I treated him, he continued to run the business and help me out while I got better. I don't have any words left to describe how much I respect this man.

'Get that sad look off ya mush,' I say. 'None of this was your fault. You're a wanker if you put any of this on yourself. It was my problem, my money that got out of hand. Not yours. Honestly, I can't have you thinking that, after all the shit you've done for me. I won't have it.'

'Come on, Fletch, if I didn't give you that money in the taxi . . .'

Trick looks down at the wheelchair I'm sat in. The pint glass resting on my frail legs.

'Trick. Shut up, mate. I'm telling you now, you did nothing wrong. Look at the state of your face for fuck's sake, you think you did that? No. No, mate. And if you don't get that in your head I'll open up that nose again.'

'Steady on. We're not there yet,' he says. 'I'm still pissed you turned on me like that. No matter how bad the gambling was.'

I have nothing to say for the violence. Sorry won't cut it. I look at his face and make myself – like, really make myself – realise what I've done.

'I've never seen you like that, Fletch,' says Trick. 'Never, in all the years I've known you. It scared the lads shitless, me included. It was like summot took over you. You were out of control.'

I drain my pint and return it to the coaster.

'I can't remember much of it,' I say.

'Probably for the best.'

The light outside the front windows is fading. A cosy musk drifts round the club. The dim bulbs flicker on and fill the back room in an orange warmth. Smoke floats in from outside as people come and go for fags. Halves before the bingo. Footy-chat pints and bitchy G&Ts. A buzz returns to the place. The hum of a working men's club, making me wanna close my eyes, listen, and cry. I never thought I'd hear it again.

'I had to tell Becca, mate,' says Trick. 'After seeing you that way, I had to, quick. I was worried.'

He turns to me dead on, his hairy forearms on the table. Running his hands over his faded blue tattoos.

'I'm glad you did, pal. I might not have been here if you didn't.'

'I phoned her straight away. As soon as you pelted off. I knew you might be going there first, to try and explain to her what you'd done. Well, that's what I hoped anyway. I didn't wanna think the worst, where else you might be going. I had to phone her.'

'What did she say?' I ask.

'I've never heard a woman so angry, lad. And you know what my missus is like.'

That doesn't surprise me. As soon as Becca gets the facts she runs with 'em. She doesn't need any context, any explanations or opinions. She heard how much I'd lost and flipped. Why wouldn't she?

'I tried to reason with her,' says Trick. 'To calm her down and that, but she hung up.'

'I appreciate it, pal. You didn't have to do any of that after what I did.'

Trick, spotting my empty pint glass, guzzles the rest of his and flags to Linda for two more. The amount of times both of us have done that simple gesture. Not clicking like Vince, but a gentle wave, thumbs up and a nod. *One more round. Just one more. Ahh fuck it, let's have another. Ahh we might as well. Go on then.* But after all this shite, Trick waving in two more pints makes me a bit emotional. I manage to keep it in. Dicing with death has made me a sentimental, soppy get. The fact he still wants to sit, drink and natter with a mess like me. I'm running out of words.

'Of course, I had to help,' says Trick, getting up to go for a slash. 'You're me best mate for fuck's sake.'

***

The doctor's a bit knocked back when I start walking after another month. It's slow, laboured, but I'm walking with the support of crutches. It's taken intense sessions on the living-room bars. Buckets of sweat and hours of grit. As I improve, I practise going to the offy with Mango for me morning papers and having a chat with Raj, or downstairs to have a chat with Sol. I glance at Jim

Ramsbottom's across the road, its bright red sign below the glum clouds. It'd take me about an hour to cross the road if I wanted to. My mind a few months ago would have done it. As long as a bet was at the end of it, anything was worth the strain. I would have found a way.

***

The crash was four months ago, and I haven't had a bet since. As recommended by the doctor, I've been going to these Gamblers Anonymous meetings at the local community centre. They aren't my cup of tea at all. I still go, to let Becca know I'm trying, which I am, but fuck me it bores the piss out of me. One thing it does help me with is opening up about it all, getting everything off my chest, not being judged. I feel like I do when I was talking to the bodies, like no one is going to talk back and tell me what an arse I am. Everyone just listens. That's all I ever needed.

I vent off about this bet or that bet, and they continue to listen. It's strange speaking to people about it who've been in the same boat. People who actually have the choice to talk back and who aren't dead, lying there, listening to me waffle on. This one geezer in the meeting – ex-bouncer, neck like the tree trunk I went head first into – threw his entire mortgage on Liverpool to win this game and they drew. This other lad, a VIP gambler when he was still a student at Manchester Uni, used to go days without sleeping, playing poker in his room and tanning his student loan. The rest of the group are made up of people like me, your seasoned gamblers who took it a step too far, who'd rather see their own lives ended than ruin that of their loved ones. The odd grandma who fills the slot machines up with her pension makes up the group. It's amazing to see how many people are suffering in silence and being sucked in by the lights. All ages, all walks of life. I never knew it was this much of a problem for so many people. I've felt alone all along.

I get a badge for each week I go, which I stick on the fridge like a primary school kid coming home with their crayon drawing to show mummy. Becca makes efforts to reward me, ordering in a Domino's or stacking the fridge up with an ice-cold six-pack whenever I come home with one. Mango even gives me extra licks. All the training and toing-and-froing to the hospital means I've shed a few pounds for once in my life too. My ribs have said hello for the first time in twenty years. I've gone down two extra belt holes and had to chalk up for some new jeans that fit snug. I've even shaved my wiry ginger beard off to see if my jawline is still there. And it fuckin' is!

I'm feeling good about myself. I'm not just back on track, I'm on a completely different one. Apart from the beer and the odd takeaway, I'm making fewer trips to Sol's and eating less junk in general. I'll just go in for a chat with him and update him on my progress. I make efforts to exercise regularly, every day. Not just my legs, with my strength and distance improving by the week, but my body, my arms, my stamina. Becca was pleasantly surprised when I flung her about during a bonking session for the first time in a long while. We're back at it again. I'm less flexible, obviously, but still find my angles. I feel more confident in myself. I want to make myself a man she can love and trust again. I want to be better than I ever was. I just want to feel like myself. I want to be happy, and not feel I like I need to earn anything or win anything to improve my life.

As for Spud and Si, I meet up with them for a couple of pints to explain myself. I tell Trick not to come along, that I need to be up front with them about it all and tackle it by myself. As expected, they're less understanding.

'You're lucky I'm sat here having a pint with you, you know that?' says Spud. 'You're a cunt for what you did. You touch Trick like that again and I swear to god, gambling will be the least of your worries pal.'

He aggressively chugs his pint. Si sits beside him, shaking his head, refusing to look at me with *both* eyes.

'It was fucked, Jamie, man,' he says. 'I know it might sound harsh, but I can't look at you the same. Like, ever.'

This isn't the time to laugh or take the piss with eye jokes. I've let them down. I've done damage I can never patch up. The way Spud and Si are looking beyond me, rushing their pints so they don't have to waste their breath on me. It hurts. I can't even blame them for leaving me in the past.

'I know, lads, I know,' I say. 'That's why I wanted a pint, a chat. Is there anything I can do? I don't want shit to change. You're cracking pals, always have been.'

'Well,' Spud drains the rest of his pint, nods for Si to hurry up, 'should have thought of that before belting your best mate. Come on, Si, fuck this.'

They both walk out without another word and there's nothing I could say to bring them back. I have to consider myself lucky. That Becca and Trick haven't fucked me off too. I mean, what did I expect? Laughs about the fight? About that ridiculous final bet? Talk openly about the crash and why I wanted to end my life? Everyone knows that by getting in that car, I reached a point where I didn't wanna live any more. Even if they did understand, men in the boozers never get to a stage of conversation where our emotions are being discussed, or whether our problems might boil over into something dangerous. Even now, after going through it, other lads just ask how I'm holding up, and I say *yeh, not bad*. That's all they need to know. We all have our problems, some more difficult than others. As long as I'm truthful, that I say I'm okay when I'm okay, and say I'm not okay when I'm not, then that's all they ask.

It might be pointless to think about, but it makes me question what might have happened if I did have the space to talk openly about my addiction. Gush out all my worries to the lads over a pint. Allowing their advice, welcoming their concern, their desire to help me out. What is it about having a cock and balls where you feel like you can't talk about your feelings or explain to each other what is obviously, slowly ruining your life? How much was it being an addict and how much was it simply being a man in Openshaw that got me to this stage? It's so stupid. It might all have been different and I might still have Spud and Si as mates if I did talk.

Still, I was never gonna cry on Spud and Si's shoulder. That's not how we deal with things. I get it out with Becca or in the GA meetings. They're the lads, to pick me up in other ways like blowing the foam off their lager into each other's faces or telling me stories about their threesomes in Malia, and how they got kicked out of the hotel for Si having a shit in the footbath. They cheer me up. I'm grateful for how, in times past, they could forget about the daft shit I did and laugh about it. It could be annoying sometimes, how they treated everything as banter, though it paid off in tough times. Everything has a limit, though, and they've reached theirs for now.

I come clean to Shaky and Linda about robbing the club, too. I promise to pay it back, with regular payments each month. They hesitantly accept, but like Spud and Si, let it be known that nothing will be the same. They still let me in and serve me, but make it clear it's only because of Trick and his faith in my recovery. They don't speak to me any more than they need to. They see people struggling every day, they know the lengths people go to to get money, to survive. But what I did was inexcusable. I didn't just rob them, I robbed the whole community, the people that trusted me. What bigger crime is there than that?

***

It's a Monday lunchtime when I get up from the sofa with only the assistance of the armrest, and get my coat. It's pissing it down. The clouds are dark, rain pouring sideways. I walk as fast as I can manage on the wet pavement towards the directory. My head down, rain lashing off my hood.

When I get to the door, I breathe in the faint whiff of lacquered wax. I've worked here, with the dead, for years now. I'm experienced in death. I've seen all sorts of shit get wheeled in through that door. Knowing I was close to being on that gurney and hauled onto a shelf in the freezer is hard to swallow. Just like seeing Dad there in that coffin. The aspects of your life that are so familiar can easily become the strangest, scariest things.

I limp into the reception and am met with the image of Janice on the shelf next to the urn. I nearly lost everything, yet the directory is still here for me, just as it has been most of my life. I thought briefly about remortgaging it to clear some of my debts, soon realising how impossible that would be with my credit rating. I wouldn't want to anyway. This place is too special. And looking at that picture of Janice, I don't think she would want me to either.

'Good to have you back, pal.'

Trick emerges from the corridor with a white lab coat in his hand. When I put it on, I feel safe, happy, alive.

30

'What about this one?'

Becca has her legs up on the couch, laptop resting on her belly. Eight months in, she's really showing now, ready to pop. She waddles around the flat, massaging her belly, breathing out in short spurts as if she's already in labour. Our due date is the middle of next month. We have only weeks left of normality, until our worlds are turned upside down. For the better this time.

I'm scranning a bag of cheesy Doritos next to her, United on the telly, watching Pogba spread balls about the pitch like butter.

'Not bad. Kitchen's a bit small though,' I say.

'Like you fuckin' cook anyway.'

'Got to walk in there for a beer, haven't I? I'd have to walk in sideways through that pissin' gap.'

Becca's on Zoopla, searching houses in Beswick or nearer the city centre. A few nice houses have been built recently, all that up-and-coming, two-up-two-down malark. Even a driveway for the new Transit that Trick has bought for the directory. Me and Becca prefer the terraces near Matthews Lane ourselves. It's our first house, it isn't gonna be the fuckin' White House. Still, we want something decent. Somewhere we can call home and raise our family.

'What about that one?' I say, pointing at the screen.

Becca clicks on it, images appearing of the street lined with your average terraces. Big windows and varnished doors with them fancy gold knockers the Amazon guy could use. I picture a new plasma in the corner of the living room, right next to the mantelpiece, and maybe a sofa under the window where we can cosy up on Friday nights with some tinnies. I could whip up a Sunday roast in that kitchen, spreading everything out and filling up the sink with all sorts of shit 'cause we could, 'cause it was ours.

I'd wash the pots, looking out of the window at the patio garden. Little birds chirping away, sat on the washing line. There'd be a tiny paddling pool in the corner filled with murky water and dead leaves, which Becca only gets out every two summers to dip her toes, or for Mango to swim in and keep cool. And the bedroom: I won't go into detail what would happen in there but blimey, we'd have a king-size that wouldn't half get some use. Maybe we'd have another kid, expand the family. We'd line the hallway and stairs with pictures of us, young ones of us hugging in the park, in Santorini, or more recent ones outside restaurants, or on long walks with Mango around the reservoirs. We'd do things like put the bins out, invite neighbours over for a games night. I could invite Trick round for the match. Becca could have the girls round from work for a Kardashians night or whatever the fuck they watch. We'd pay bills, a mortgage, save for other things like holidays and a bigger telly for World Cup year. We'd have our new life, our new beginning. But, this time, I have to make sure we get it first before I start enjoying it.

'I like it,' says Becca.

I look at her.

'I love it actually,' she says.

'You serious?'

'Yeh, look, it's got everything we wanted. And the price is more than decent.'

'You're right,' I said. 'It is.'

Becca flicks through the images again, then about another twenty times. She's right. It is perfect. Stupidly close to a nursery and we both could easily travel into work. Becca sits up. We both know there's still a long way to go. We're still clawing back enough for a deposit. My credit rating is gradually improving, and we still need to get approved for a mortgage. But we're on track, we're so nearly there, and we'll let the sellers know we are desperate to make this home the start of our new lives. We beat the odds getting this flat and we'll beat the odds getting the house too.

This time is different. I don't think she can believe we've reached this point. Here, living it, and so close to our new home.

'Ouch.'

'You okay?' I ask.

'Yeh. Just a kick.'

'I think she likes it too.'

I place my palm on the mound of her stomach and feel movement, like the beat through a speaker. My baby girl, kicking harder than any horse I ever backed.

'Shall we go for it? Chase up on that mortgage approval?' I ask.

'You sure?' she asks, smile waiting to burst onto her cheeks.

'I wasn't asking you,' I say, putting my ear on her belly. I wait a few seconds then nod.

'Never been more sure about anything,' I say.

Becca rolls onto me and crushes the bag of Doritos with her belly. She kisses the orange dust off my lips and doesn't stop for a good five minutes. Mango jumps out of nowhere and starts licking our nostrils, ending our kiss with laughter.

***

Six months. Six months without a bet. The furthest it's gone is Becca putting the lottery on for me now and again. As boring as those GA meetings are, they've taught me that the gateway bets are the worst, the little dabbles that relight that flare. It'll always end up in bastard flames. Even Jim Ramsbottom's – I haven't set foot in it once. Rumours are that it's on the brink of shutting down and being replaced by a hipster cafe that sells IPAs and those disposable vapes.

My head feels clear. My attention is on other stuff now. I'm more bothered about where me and Becca can take the dog at the weekend, or how me and Trick can improve the directory and offer people the good, honest service we promise. I love it. I'm happy and free for once. My home, my job, my lifestyle – everything has finally aligned and clicked into place.

My biggest attention is on saving for the house. For real this time. We've filled up the jar once already, cashing it and transferring into Becca's account to be safe. We both trust the steps I've made, I just want to use it as a sign of my commitment to us. I've been trying to restore her faith as much as I can. I'm opening up more, talking more. If I think about gambling that day, I tell her. I get it off my chest, then we watch *Love Island* or some bollocks to take my mind of it. She understands me, she reassures me and praises me for how far I've come. I try to remove my guilt, which settles and sticks in my stomach like fat in a pan. It's going to need time and work scrubbing it off, a long time until it feels clean again. The main thing is we're heading in the right direction. Soon we'll have our home, then life will be new. The old life, along with the guilt, will be tossed and forgotten. Stamped out like a lit cig.

Leaving the past in the past doesn't sit well with me. I know I have a lot of ground to cover, a lot of graft to repay for some of the shit I did. After the directory started turning over profits due to other local directories shutting down, I gathered up a couple of hundred and dropped it off at the club as a one-off payment. An apology, and then some. Shaky got the jukebox fixed so we can listen to some new tunes. Not like he enjoyed me using it. I didn't want thanks, I just wanted them to accept it.

Me and Trick still meet every Thursday for snooker night. I'm still unbeaten, even though my back twinges and my legs lock, or I take a stumble now and again. I have a limp, which the lads threaten to create a nickname out of before realising there's only ever one man with shaky legs round Openshaw. A limp is nothing in the grand scheme of things. I'm lucky enough to be walking again. For that I'm mad grateful. It's been the biggest threat to my unbeaten snooker streak since I pulled my arm having a wank in Year Eleven.

Trick has put Cheltenham behind him and has his plump, fleshy purple face back. A new gold tooth as well, which I delivered to him in a little ring box for his birthday, getting down on one knee in the club, which made everyone giggle. Spud mentioned to Trick about going to Cheltenham next March, hoping to replace bad memories with better ones, forgetting what it could trigger in him. He's still a daft bastard. I might get to the point of returning one day, if I build up enough willpower. I can't see it myself. That place makes me feel things I can't fight against. The memories. The history. It means too much. I'm not about to risk that again.

Help from Becca and the directory's steady profits have also given me the chance to pay Trick back, something I was desperate to do even though there's other debts still to take care of. One snooker night, I hand it over in a seedy brown envelope like the gangsters do in the films.

'What's this?' he asks.

'My debt.'

I raise a hand before he has time to question it. He understands and pockets the envelope. It's what I need, all part of me putting things right. Trick knows that. If it helps me, he's on board. It feels good being on the other side, getting that off my mind and knowing I have my old pal back.

'Not gonna get you into trouble this, is it?' he says.

'There'll only be trouble if you don't accept it. It's the least I can do, Trick. I'm straight now, the directory's doing well. I owe a lot of it to you.'

'Cheers, pal,' says Trick. 'Just don't tell me missus. She'll have the catalogues out.'

***

Me and Becca send an email enquiring about the property. We get an email back straight away to arrange a viewing the following day. Becca goes for a shower to cool off before we go out to celebrate. She tries not to leave me on my own now, in case my thoughts get the better of me and I do a random bet to get the ball rolling again. This is an exception, though. She's too excited for our next step to worry about leaving me alone for ten minutes. Hearing her sing through the walls, I sit on the couch, watching the football, not believing how far we've come. We nearly never had any of this.

The clock ticks to half-time in the match, with me sat there grinning. I ease into the sofa, feeling the rock-hard cushion under my arse knowing I'm gonna be on a bigger, plusher one soon. I look around at the mouldy corner of the room, the packed-up parallel bars gathering dust behind the TV. The stained carpet. The reeking kitchen fridge. The rattling washing machine that threatens to plough through the floor into Sol's chip fryer with every spin. It will all be in the past soon.

The pundits waffle on before it cuts to the adverts. Bright green and yellow banners flash on the TV. A familiar voice shouts the half-time odds, the limited offers that *won't last for ever*. The song 'Sweet Caroline' in the background, bringing positive happy vibes as it shows lads laughing in the pub, betting on their apps while holding an ice-cold pint. Cheering. Winning. Dancing about, money rattling into their accounts. *When the Fun Stops, Stop. Be Gamble Aware.*

I can't explain what I'm feeling. Words won't cover it. Memories flash through my head, good and bad. It's like meeting an old school mate out the blue and you're unsure if you're gonna like them now that so much time has passed. Another two betting ads run back to back within the same break.

I look at my phone sitting there on the cushion. I'm a different man now. I'm mentally stronger. I'm not as vulnerable as I used to be. Me and Becca, we're good, we have savings now, we're getting a house. All my debts are on the way to being cleared. I'm in the best position of my life. The odds are finally in my favour. So why do I feel this way?

The last betting ad ends on the TV. It's so much more difficult to watch a football match now and not be tempted. It'll be so easy to pick up my phone and download an app. I could have a bet on in seconds. The second half would be much more exciting. I reach for my phone. Unlock it, hesitating.

31

I'm back at the directory, washing bodies and filling them with formaldehyde. It's weird to say I missed the smell, missed whisking people into the cremation machines and pressing the button that ignites the flames, but I did. It's what I know; it's the comfort and normality in life that I've been craving during rehab.

Now I'm in a better headspace, I can truly appreciate the new directory we've built. The chemical smell of paint in the air, the earthy textures of varnished wood. After everything, I'm proud to still have this, proud to still have Trick by my side keeping things ticking over. He can sell underwear to a nudist now, that fella. It's like how Janice brought me through the ranks, teaching me the tricks of the trade, the meaning of death.

I've been thinking about Janice a lot lately. I miss her. She'd love to sit me down and call me every name under the sun for what I did to Becca, what I did to myself. Gambling with her business, gambling with my own life. That's not what she taught me. I'm better than that. Part of me wonders whether I would have got to that stage if she was still around. Whether she would have put me back on the right track. She already gave me a lifeline offering me a job at the directory. I could really have done with another one.

Maybe it's the GA meetings, or talking it all through with Becca, I dunno. Opening up has hit me with an overwhelming sense of grief. I feel okay to be exposed now. My emotions are on the surface. I have to be honest and truthful. I have to share and not keep everything locked away.

I've never really grieved Janice. All of it happened so fast. Maybe that's why I find myself stood in front of the blue and pink coffin, thinking about whether the best option is to get rid of it and move on. She's made her joke, she's had her fun. I don't really need reminders of that turbulent time of my life.

Thinking of the time Janice gave me the tour and told me to get into the coffin, I find myself climbing in and resting my head on the blue silk cushion. Don't ask me why, it just feels right. It's even uglier on the inside. I hate that it fits my body size perfectly. Mad to think I actually could have been in one of these six months ago. Singed to a crisp or under a mound of soil.

I start to cry again. Thinking of Janice, thinking of nearly dying, nearly losing Becca and our little daughter. I don't know what exactly I'm crying over; it's all just overwhelming. Locked in for years, going through an ordeal I was never able to share. I grip the blue lining and bawl my eyes out, tears flowing down my face and dampening the silk.

I cry and pull with anguish. Bellowing like a wounded animal. Pain pouring out. I tug at the lining, that fuckin' ugly baby blue lining, wanting to wrap it around myself and hide from everything. I tug and tug until I feel something within the silk. Something falling and hitting the base with a thud. A hard shape. Beside it there's another one. Then another one. Then it clicks. I feel the shape in my hands. Wads of cash line the walls of the coffin on both sides.

I lie there, still, as the tears dry on my cheeks. Imagining her looking down, cackling with delight.

The End

Acknowledgements

This book wouldn't have been possible without the support, guidance and laughs I've been lucky to have throughout my life. First of all, thank you to my teachers: Miss Doyle, who first told me I had a knack for writing; Miss Jarvis, who bought me a notebook to encourage my creativity; and Miss Hinchliffe, who steered me towards the path of academia. I'm grateful to Claudia Stein, whose words of positivity kept me in university. And a special thank you to Lisa O'Donnell, who helped me find my voice and gave me the confidence to write about what mattered most to me. This book would never have existed without their kindness.

I'm indebted to many writers who've been invaluable in my research, particularly the works of Gordon Burn, Walter Tevis, James Kelman, Rob Davies, Caitlin Doughty, Patrick Foster, Paul Merson and Roddy Doyle.

I owe the stories, humour and joy of this book to the people of Openshaw – the most positive, generous, hilarious people I've ever met. I hope their stories from the Rag and Stanley Street Working Men's Club are immortalised in these pages long after I'm in a cheap urn of my own.

Thank you to my Nana Margaret and Grandad Jack – you're a true inspiration and I'm incredibly privileged to have you both in my life, supporting my every step.

To my wonderful in-laws, Bruce and Jain – I'll always be grateful for the support and platform you've offered for me and

Mel to pursue what we love. Your enthusiasm spurs us on more than you know.

I owe a huge thanks to the Hutchys. Without my family's stories, I would never have dreamt of being a writer or have had the material to complete a novel. Words can't describe how happy it makes me to share their jokes, their tales, and their generosity with readers. They are the reason I write. And to those this book is dedicated to – Grandad Alan, Auntie Jane and Uncle Simon – I hope this would make you proud.

To my incredible agent, Philippa Sitters, I can't thank you enough for your enthusiasm, patience and genius ideas with not just this book, but everything I've written. I'll forever be grateful to you for taking a chance on me, building my confidence and making me believe my work is worth reading. This book would definitely not exist without your continued belief.

To my amazing editor, Olivia Hutchings, it's hard to emphasise how much your connection with this novel meant to me. I'll always remember your faith, excitement and understanding of what I was trying to achieve. And thank you to the rest of the Corsair team for making a random lad from Manchester very happy.

Thank you to my dad, Pete – my best friend, rival and inspiration in so many ways; my mum, Gaynor – whose love, chats and support throughout my life could never be repaid; and my sister, Megan – whose love for books, art and shit jokes has always been inspiring. I couldn't have achieved my dream of being published without you all. I'll never forget everything you've done for me and how you helped me get to this stage. I love you all.

And, above all, I owe everything to my fiancée, Mel. Your love, advice and belief from the very beginning has spurred me on in ways that'll be impossible to explain. You've been my number one cheerleader and there would be no point in any of this happiness if I couldn't share it with you.